OMNIBUS

HeartsBlood

SELINA A. FENECH WRITING AS

LENA FOX

unLife

HeartsBlood
BOOK ONE

As an out of work actor, I often find myself in shady situations.

Like sharing a three-bedroom condo with ten people I barely knew.

Or trying to sneak into said housing by climbing in through the balcony to avoid my live-in landlord from hell.

It was only one floor up, and an easy climb, thanks to conveniently placed brickwork. I'd first realized it could be a good way in and out when I watched one of my house mate's boyfriends doing a dash down there when her *other* boyfriend showed up unexpectedly.

That she had the time and energy for not one, but two—or possibly more—relationships, left me a little jealous. But I didn't know much about her or how her life really was. Same with all my house mates. Our living conditions may have been close, but nothing else about our relationships were.

The sun was high, spreading yellow light over the scrubby, rocky hills. The sky-high palm tree casting a shadow over me had little cooling affect and sweat beaded over my pale skin.

With a final grunt, I rolled myself over the railing and came face to face with Lisa, squatting on the dusty sun lounge having a smoke.

She choked. "The fuck? Kitty?"

I cursed internally as well. So much for avoiding my landlord.

"Sorry, I left my keys in my room." I pointed through the dirty glass sliding door toward the tiny converted walk-in cupboard that I was lucky enough to not share with half a dozen others like the larger bedrooms. I kept moving, heading in that direction, hoping to pass by without incident.

Lisa shot to her feet and blocked my path. She was a tall thin redhead, with adorable freckles, and a tongue like a viper. She was also one hell of a guitarist and got an occasional big gig with whatever band she hadn't yet been kicked out of. The condo we all lived in had belonged to her grandparents, and she rented rooms out to struggling wannabes to make the rest of her ends meet. She really was undeniably a bitch though. I think she enjoyed lording the fact she'd made something of a name for herself over those of us who hadn't.

I forced out an awkward chuckle and tried to side-step her, as though she wasn't obviously getting in my way on purpose.

She took a long drag, and her words came out smokey in my face. "You owe rent."

That, I knew. I was just hoping to avoid having to pay up for a little longer. I was overdue on a bunch of bills, and my bank account was like Mother Hubbard's cupboards. Bare. Pilot season had been a bust, and I was eking out the last of my pay from a shoddy car dealership commercial.

I sidled a little closer to the door. "Oh, sorry, slipped my mind! I'll get it to you soon."

"Today. And it'll be an extra fifty on top."

My mouth dropped and I froze with my fingers on the door handle. "What? Why?"

She flicked her cigarette butt over the balcony. Her eyes were narrowed by a sly smile. "Rent's gone up."

A million arguments and furies rattled around in my brain. I was already paying way too much for a space I could barely lay a sleeping bag down in. Lisa helped herself to my belongings as though anything in the building were hers. She even charged an "admin fee" on top of utilities share. The whole thing was a rort.

Her eyes narrowed further. "What's up, Kitty? You don't like it, you can leave. Can't say I've heard good things about the housing market at the moment though. And for someone with a credit rating like yours …" She tilted her head and pouted, as though there was any sympathy in her venomous blood.

My shoulders sagged. My voice came out scratchy and too high. "I'll get the rent to you."

Somehow. If I could only pull magic money out of my ass.

I tugged the door open and skittered through, across the jumble of living room and three house mates lounging in there, then shut myself into my tiny, private space.

The screen on my phone had a nasty crack, but it still connected well enough to the neighbors Wi-Fi to avoid data charges. I sat on my sleeping bag, leaned against my suitcase-slash-wardrobe, and checked my emails, hoping for a miracle.

Scrolling through the spam, a subject line caught my eye.

Re: Casting for Downtime Dirtbags

Eyes wide, I held my breath and opened the email.

Thanks for auditioning, yadda yadda, great technical skills, missing the right emotional oomph, appreciate your time, not for us.

I groaned and thumped my head back against my suitcase. No miracle for me today.

Unlife

It always seemed to be the excuse. I had put so much work and time into my acting skills, but I was always missing *something*.

I had blamed my agent, Harvey, at first, for the lack of roles coming my way. But lately I'd been trying to get out on my own to make things happen, and still, nothing. Maybe it was just me. *Maybe I don't have what it takes.*

I flicked through all the open tabs in my browser for casting calls and extra work, getting to the tab at the end. The Jenny Kurtz agency. My dream agent. That tab had been open since before I left home. Before I signed with Harvey instead, telling myself he was just my way to get started, until I'd proven myself in the industry enough to shoot for bigger goals.

If I had been brave enough to try for the Jenny Kurtz agency right away, would things have been different now? Could I still turn things around if I went to her? Would she even consider me?

I wouldn't ever know. I didn't have time to dream about becoming a star right now. I had to earn some quick cash so I didn't end up homeless.

There was only one thing for it.

I was going to have to go to Harvey and beg him for any job he had going, then beg even harder for an advance. I could already imagine the leer on his greasy mouth while he told me he had a hemorrhoid

cream commercial or 'useless infomercial woman' role for me. *Ugh. I hate him so much.*

Harvey Hall was a second-rate agent to struggling actors. His one claim to fame was that he'd signed a few of the bigger names when they were still broke enough to hope that his representation would lead to a big role. I had no illusions about good old Harvey, and I'm sure he harbored no illusions about me either. As soon as I built a resume, I'd be leaving his ass in the dust without a single look back. Since he'd been too busy to answer my calls after signing on a whole new stable of girls fresh off the bus—girls willing to work naked or be billed as *Hooker Number Three*—me dreaming about better agents didn't feel unfair.

Harvey had been giving me the cold shoulder for a while now, so I stormed out to go to his office in person. The LA lunchtime crowd was hectic, sidewalks filled with people networking over food that I eyed jealously. I'd never afford half those meals.

If I ever do get rich and famous, I swear I'm going to be one of those stars that the paparazzi always catches coming out of some trendy restaurant. I love food in all of its forms, and I read menus like some people read travel brochures, making lists of the places I want to eat at when I have enough money to afford them. Good food for me was better than sex. Or at least was more easily available and with less attached baggage, which was far more preferable.

I moved fast, hoping to get to Harvey's while his secretary was on her lunch break. I arrived just as she was trotting out.

I lurked out of sight, waiting for her to leave, then dashed in. I felt a little ashamed that I let the cold, glasses wearing matron that guarded my agent's door scare me off, but the woman was truly frightening. I'd rather brave a dragon than her.

I appeared in a burst in front of Harvey's desk, wide-eyed as though I'd even startled myself at my daring appearance.

"Ah, Kitty, how nice of you to drop in." He managed to sound happy to see me even though his mouth twisted like he'd licked a lemon. Something of an actor himself. "What can I do for you?"

Deep breath. Ask for what you want. I stuttered, "I was hoping you could get me a job. My rent is due, my car actually needs gas to run, and while I could stand to lose a little weight, starvation is not a good thing." I bit my tongue on that last bit. I was giving him more ammunition to use against me. He'd been on my back to lose weight ever since I'd signed with him. I wasn't overweight, but I enjoyed my food, and sometimes I didn't make it to the gym as often as I could. "I just, really need something right away. Anything."

"Calm down, little lady. You're a keen one, aren't

you?" He steepled his sausage fat fingers together and said, "Actually, this is great timing. I may have something for you."

The smugness in his voice made my relief tentative. "What is it?"

"It's a Live Action Role Playing event," he said, "Not an on-screen acting job, but it's still acting, and it pays well."

I frowned. "Role playing?"

"I'm not talking about some kids fighting orcs in their backyard, this is real prestige stuff. A club downtown runs these vampire nights now and then. A bunch of guys who like to pretend they're bloodsuckers and chase pretty girls around. The club brings in a few willing victims, actresses hired to take part in the game. The girl who was supposed to do it got a lucky break and landed a nice role on a new series. Great for her, but she can't make it to the gig tonight and has left me high and dry. How about it, you want to play the victim?"

Are you kidding me? "You want me to play a game?" I stared at him. His greasy moon face was filmed with sweat despite the air conditioner's steady cooling blow. He stank of cheap cologne and cigar smoke, just like some slime ball out of a noir flick. I had to wonder how much of the shine was from sweat and how much of it was from the pomade trickling out of his thinning, slicked back hair.

I could see my own reflection in the gleaming surfaces of the awards hanging on his walls—a pale, oval face, dark hair, and a mouth that is perhaps a trifle too thin by some standards. I can't count the number of times I've been told I should get collagen injections. There was a little too much white showing around my eyes and a slight tremble in my chin. I looked scared, and I didn't like that at all. If I could see that fear so could Harvey, and Harvey is like a dog. Let him smell fear and he will move in for the kill. I could tell from the way he was watching me that he knew he had me.

He locked me in his gaze. "High end LARP events like this are easy money. Isn't that what you're after? You get these rich bastards willing to spend good money to play out their fantasies. Sometimes we get warlords from alternate universes who want to enslave a buxom wench, or wannabe Lords of Crazyshit Manor who want to duel at dawn and win the fair maiden, and so on. Lots of actors do it, not that they'll ever admit it. There's a non-disclosure agreement you have to sign, and you can't tell anyone because discretion matters to these folks. Are we clear?"

The mention of rich bastards and NDAs threw up red flags in my head. Wasn't there some rumor about some of Harvey's girls going on weird jobs and never coming back? Whether it was snuff films or some event that turned them off the industry for good, no one knew. It was just conspiratorial gossip mostly. But I couldn't shake the shiver of doubt.

"Come on, Harvey. I've been in seven movies already, two of them as the lead. I know they were B-movies, but still … Surely you can find me something better than some weird game." I was pleading now. I doubted any real actors did this kind of gig. It sounded strictly amateur to me, and I was getting tired of being an amateur. But what other option did I have?

"Listen, Kitty, it isn't my fault." Harvey went all serious, leaning across his desk so far his puffy belly melted into the edges of it and rolled over the top. "Every casting director with a movie on their desk is looking for a cute blonde with a huge rack and a nice ass. Blonde is back in style, and you and your bookish goth chick look is played out. Not that I'm saying your rack isn't nice."

I wanted to smack the sleazy grin off his face, but just balled my fists at my sides where he couldn't see them past the edge of the desk. As much as I hated him, I needed Harvey right now.

"It isn't just the hair color either, sweetheart. Saying your last films were B-rated is like saying root canal surgery is a pleasant way to spend an afternoon. Three of them were so bad they died untimely deaths in the cutting room, never even made it past editing before they were canned. Those included the two you had the lead role in. That's hardly a selling point in Hollywood, kiddo."

Ouch. I dropped back in the hard chair that sat across from his desk, and tried to decide whether to punch him in the face or ask for a loan to get a boob job and dye my hair. Maybe I should just take what he was offering me. But it somehow sounded shady. "I'm not doing porn, Harvey."

He guffawed. "With a name like Kitty French, you could."

The urge to slap him returned, but his chuckle faded and he waved the air as though to clear my concerns. "There's no sex. This is all high-class stuff, I swear!" Harvey swiped an X across his heart with a finger. Or at least where his heart would be if he had one. "Okay, okay, you're going to get guys nibbling on you a bit. That's a given, it's vampires for crissakes. But nothing more serious than that."

I should hold my ground. I should demand a real acting job, in a real production, but the words wouldn't come out. Only excuses flew through my mind. I wasn't good enough. I needed any money I could get.

"How much does it pay?"

"Two grand. Are you in?"

My eyes popped. That was more than I was expecting, especially for a late notice gig.

I said yes, what else could I say? The money

Harvey offered would be enough to cover rent and ensure I could eat something besides ramen noodles cooked by soaking them in cold water on a hot patio. If it were as tame and easy as Harvey promised, maybe I could even turn it into a regular gig. I could get my own place, cover my living costs while trying to get real acting work. Maybe it would all turn out fine.

A girl had to hold onto hope.

2

The venue for the LARP event, a club called *Dark Raine*, surprised me. It was all class, with shining black marble floors, and sparkling crystal chandeliers, cozy nooks for couples sharing cocktails, and businessmen unwinding after work. A young man in a tailored black uniform that matched the décor greeted me at the door. After my bewildered explanation of why I was there, he directed me to the third floor.

Stepping off the elevator, it felt as though I'd walked onto the set of a classic Hammer horror film, with billowing, tattered curtains, black leather furniture, and huge candelabras with candles guttering in their grips. They looked like diseased trees, and I felt a tingle of unease run down my back. A woman claiming to be the event liaison directed me to the dressing room and handed me my costume. The flowing, medieval style chemise was of a fabric that was just transparent enough to make you question what you were seeing through it, and torn strategically to show off legs all the way to the hip. An ivory corset went over that, and the woman helped lace me up, leaving the top few eyelets at the front undone so the spill of cleavage was accentuated.

It was too late for second thoughts, but I was having them anyway. Maybe it was the scantiness of the costume, or the fact that I was beginning to wonder if there really was a porn movie in the making here, despite what Harvey promised me.

Thankfully, the event liaison confirmed that participants weren't allowed to take off clothes—mine or theirs. Though they were allowed to touch and bite a little.

Two other girls were there waiting, looking bored, as though they'd done this a million times already. One gave me a nod and little wink, then chuckled at her own joke about me being new blood. I grinned politely in return. Seeing I wasn't the only victim for the event calmed me a little, until the paranoia that this was really a porn shoot came back. The winky woman was already in her costume and went to take up her starting spot in another room. Her ass was entirely visible through the sheer fabric of her gown. I looked again at the fabric of my chemise and hoped it wasn't the same.

Adding to my discomfort was my overfull belly, squeezed into the corset. That was entirely my own fault. Harvey had given me a rather tidy advance on the two thousand I would be making. I made for the nearest steakhouse so fast I'm surprised I didn't run down a few diners trying to get into the place. Oysters on the half shell for starters, then a perfectly rare filet mignon with roasted asparagus. I managed to refrain from dessert, thanks somewhat to common sense kicking in, reminding me not to blow my new windfall too fast. But mostly, it was on account of being entirely too full. Totally worth it though.

I was given my directions and starting position. *It's just like any other acting job*, I tried to comfort myself, *with a lot more improv.*

At least it would bring in some money and wasn't quite porn. I'm not sure if that would make my mom feel any prouder if she found out about this little escapade. *She will never know about it,* I promised myself.

I lay on a vintage chaise lounge, awaiting the vampire hordes. Above me, the red lights flickered, and a soundtrack of distant thunder played through hidden speakers nearby. A whisper of a shiver ran up my spine. I was doing my best to get into my role while I waited for the players to appear, and the effects they had set up for the event did a decent job of building the mood. The décor was a little over the top and cliché, from the smoke machine mist drifting across the floor, to the lights flashing behind fake windows, to simulate lightening. The expense put into the event startled me, and that wasn't even counting my wage for the night, or that of the other victims.

The lights flickered again and I stared upward, my body going rigid as the first rustles sounded in the distance. They were coming. Despite being told what to expect, I was nervous. A deep animal instinct welled up in me, and it was all I could do not to run. But I'd committed to this crazy job, and I was going to be professional about it. I would run, but not until the players were ready to chase me. I swallowed hard and focused on the prize, the cute little one-bedroom place I had checked out that afternoon. It was in West Hollywood, not far from where I currently lived, but it would be just mine. Not sharing with nine other people would also make it easier to date again, or even just hook up more often. I hadn't been laid in forever. My living conditions weren't entirely at fault though. I worked too hard on getting my career off the ground, and seemed to have the worst taste in guys.

unLife

My last boyfriend had been a down and out loser by anyone's standards. Seth, with his leather jacket, motorcycle, and nasty habit of borrowing money. By the time I kicked him out of my life, he owed me over five thou. That wasn't the only reason our relationship had ended though. He was a poet, and had always insisted that he needed certain things to feel inspired. Alcohol and sex, primarily. Apparently, that's how he ended up in the woman's restroom at open mic night with a woman named Irene.

I should know by now that bad boys are just that—bad.

The air conditioning chilled the room, making goosebumps spread across my bulging cleavage and bare thigh. My cheeks flushed at the thought that I was about to be set upon by a stranger, lying here so exposed. Not that I hadn't done physical contact and sex scenes before, but the lack of cameras, crew, and director made it feel off. You'd think having an audience would make it feel weirder, but the lack of one was worse.

The rustling grew louder, and I threw an arm dramatically over my forehead and feigned sleep. From beneath the shadow of my arm, I cracked open my eyelids to watch what was going on. The dark deepened, and a tall figure came at me from the shadows. I shrieked, and it wasn't fake. Adrenaline spurted into my bloodstream. I hurled myself off the lounge, running for the double doors to the right. It was just a game, but between the suddenness of it all and the darkness that seemed more sinister than it had a moment ago, I felt real fear. My logical brain reminded me that the club had security watching in case someone went too far, but terror made me panic as the man chased me around the room. Curtains swirled about me like caressing ghosts, disorienting me as I spun around and came face-to-face with the vampire.

I almost laughed. Okay, yeah, I did laugh. So much for staying professional. A guy that looked like a friendly accountant peered at me. He had a little bit of a paunch that spilled over his burgundy cummerbund. Contact lenses made his eyes a rich red, and he wore gothic clothing with a long cape and stiff high collar. He bared his fangs, waggling his eyebrows at me from under a heavy coating of glitter. *Oh, THAT kind of vampire.* I wasn't so scared anymore.

He hissed and drew his ridiculously long cape over his face like a wannabe Bela Lugosi. I faked a swoon, letting my eyelashes flutter dramatically against my cheeks. My knees bent as though about to give way. He reached out to grab me, but I ran into the next room with a girly shriek. I swear I heard him chuckle as I fled. He followed slowly, enjoying the chase. I wouldn't admit it aloud, but I was almost starting to enjoy myself. Acting was my passion, and even something as nonsensical as this stirred my blood. I let myself get into it. I tapped into the hundreds of horror movies I'd watched, calling on that archetypal, innocent, Victorian maiden stereotype that seemed so omnipresent.

I dodged between tattered curtains, the smell of dust and rain swirling through the air. *Did someone open a window?* Maybe my imagination was running away with me. I could hear the sounds of the club downstairs over the fake thunder and noise of a downpour. I nearly crashed into a candelabra and paused to catch my breath, looking around wide-eyed and panting. A slight shift in a shadow caught my attention, and another dark figure appeared. This one had a bit more going for him in terms of being tall, dark, and deadly serious. He extended a hand toward me, each finger tipped with a long, sharp nail. I hoped they were fake. I watched his hand for a moment as though mesmerized.

Then I shook my head and bolted, going for the first set of doors I could see. I sure was getting my cardio today. My pulse roared in my ears, my heart pounding in my chest.

The next room was set up like a Victorian banquet hall, complete with a long dining table and roaring fireplace. As I ran in, two more men appeared out of the shadows, swooping at me. I was seized on both sides and lifted off my feet as I screamed. I

struggled, but the men kept a strong grip on me as they laid me on the dining table. I was supine, pinned down, at the mercy of three vampires. *It's okay. They aren't real. Just men playing a game.*

That didn't stop my gut reaction. I tugged my arm, and one of the vampires had a hard time holding me down. I relaxed slightly. Those hours at the gym have helped, but I was being paid to play a victim. Knowing I could probably break free if things got out of hand did make me feel better. I just had to be careful not to make them feel less powerful. They wanted to feel like they were in control. I continued to squirm and struggle weakly, still panting from my adrenaline driven sprint. My torn gown crept up as I kicked, leaving my legs bare.

A tongue licked across the lowest point of my neck, right where my pulse beat. A frisson of desire ran through my body, startling me. I reminded myself this was just a job. *Stay professional.*

The vampire-men crowded around the table, crawling onto it to get better access to me. I was dinner for them tonight. A hot mouth met my cleavage. I gasped at the sensation, then screamed. I wanted to strike the man off me but stayed in character. It wasn't the first time I'd put up with being kissed or fondled for a scene. Hell, my first big part had been a high school student making out with her boyfriend in a car. I died in the first five minutes of the movie. Standard old slasher pic. That had been one of the ones that had gotten all the way through production. And straight to DVD.

My mind wandered as I tried to relax into the role and let the men play their vampire game with my body.

Then one of them bit me.

He didn't bite hard, but he wasn't exactly gentle either. *That's going to leave a mark.* I was sprawled on the table, teeth nipping at me in three places. Their plaything. I let myself go limp with a quiet moan like a victim finally overcome. I silently congratulated myself on how realistic it sounded. Hot hands tangled into my hair, and warm tongues slid across my skin. Someone tugged my hair a little harder and I gasped, arching my back. I suddenly realized there was a reason for the highly sexual reaction to vampires as portrayed in so many movies. This was surprisingly, undeniably, *hot.* Fake fangs pulled at the bared flesh of my cleavage, arms and neck. Little shivers stole up and down my spine, making me whimper, and a delicious ache built inside me. It was so unexpectedly provocative I hardly realized I'd almost entirely lost my composure. I was legitimately beginning to enjoy myself, and not just because I loved acting. I had just about decided that I really needed to get laid soon, when an icy finger ran up my thigh, yanking me out of the delectable stupor I had tumbled into.

I felt a cold nose press against my neck and breathe deeply. I heard a small grunt of desire.

"Stop. This one is mine." The smooth, cultured voice seemed to spear through my body, deep and commanding.

My eyelids, gone heavy during the biting, flew open to see my vampires backing away. Their faces had gone blank. It looked like someone had reached in and erased them from within. Lights on, nobody home.

A new man stood above me at the side of the table, silhouetted by the dim scarlet glow of the lamp behind him.

Just another player? Something seemed different, and a primal instinct to escape invaded me again. I tried to scramble away across the table, but icy cold hands dragged me back and up into his arms. *I'm hallucinating*, I insisted to the panicking, animal instinct in my brain. He was probably wearing cooling gloves, or something to give the illusion of being corpselike. A hardcore player, more so than the other vampires who had fallen back. Except that even in the dim light, I knew he wasn't wearing gloves. His lips whispered against the side of my neck. I shivered at the coolness of his breath. He was stronger too. No matter how much I struggled against him, I couldn't get his fingers to budge. It was like he was made of stone.

I heard him inhale deeply, his mouth just below

my ear.

Then his teeth sunk deep into my neck.

This was no small bite. Pain went from searing hot to icy cold, both sides of it so intense I screamed in agony. I closed my eyes as the pain made my vision swim, threatening my consciousness with the sudden fierce agony. I thrashed and kicked, but his arms locked my upper body in place. I flailed my hands ineffectually, trying to push him off. I could feel the blood leaving my body in the strangest sort of internal suction. Gradually, my struggle lessened, no strength left. My throat grew hoarse from screaming. Dizziness overwhelmed me.

The silent players stood there, watching vacantly. I stared at their emptied out faces over the attacker's shoulder, wondering where the help I had been promised was, how this could be happening. Was I going to die?

My fingers curled weakly in the fabric of my attacker's shirt, still feebly trying to pull him off me, or maybe just trying to steady myself as the world spun away. It was getting hard to think, like my brain was filling with fog and cobwebs.

Fake lightning. Fake mist. Real blood.

Darkness rushed up from the floor.

I saw one last candle, spitting its fire in the grotesque candelabra, then everything went black.

3

*D*eath ... *death is* ... *Death tastes like coconut. Wetness, on my lips, on my chin.*

I opened my eyes as coconut water dribbled from my slackly open mouth. It was being fed to me by a blank-eyed creature with a nest of black hair, the grey face of an English schoolmarm, and a wide, wicked grin. Her lips were coated in blood red lipstick, so badly applied it smeared up her cheeks and on her teeth. At least, I hoped it was lipstick.

What is going on? Am I dreaming?

The last thing I remembered ... I had been bitten. Bitten by what, a real vampire? All reality and reason had fled my world. Vampires didn't exist. I, Kitty French, did not believe in hocus pocus like that. I was a thoroughly modern woman. I was simply in

the grasp of some lunatic who believed himself to be a blood drinker.

Thirst raged in me. I didn't know what was happening, but if I was thirsty, I couldn't be dead. I tried to focus on the room I was in, but pain sank like talons into my throat, wrists, and shoulders.

"Hrrrgggh," I got out before the woman doused me again, the juice spilling from the spoon and onto my chin. My tongue instinctively shot out, lapping at the liquid trickling down my face. It wasn't enough to soothe my parched throat. My vision was fuzzy but gradually starting to clear. If I didn't struggle and didn't move my head much, the pain faded to a throb that I could handle. Barely.

I hung from my wrists against a wall. My arms restrained above my head. I stared upwards at the complicated contraption of heavy black chains connected to a pulley system. Looking up made my neck ache and stab with pain, so I let my chin drop and stared ahead, trying to see what else I could find out. My toes curled against cold tiles, and I realized I was able to touch the floor and that my ankles weren't shackled. I had been hanging limply, all my weight on my wrists, but now I was coming back to my senses I set the balls of my feet on the ground. My legs wobbled weakly but took my weight. I almost cried in relief as the strain lessened.

I looked wildly around, trying to work out where

I was. I was surrounded by kitchen appliances I would have envied if I had not been scared shitless. The granite countertops were immaculate, and the chefs' knives displayed along a magnetic strip on the wall looked expensive. The irony was that I was in, without a doubt, my dream kitchen. Except that I was strung up from the wall instead of the fine hunk of cured Spanish pork that should have been there.

The woman who looked like Halloween warmed over, spoon feeding me coconut juice, was also out of place. She belonged in a haunted library, or a rundown, creepy sideshow. Not what appeared to be a fairly modern high-end home. The rich colors in the cherry cabinets, and slate tiled floor, seemed to wash her out further. Her blank look jarred my memory. The fake vampires had worn that same look when the one with the cold hands, and really sharp teeth, had appeared …

Movement. My gaze whipped to the left and there he was.

I'd half expected to see a grotesque monster. The media had shown so many types of vampires over the years, that when presented with what could potentially be the real thing, I didn't know what to expect. *Not that there is such a thing as the real thing,* I tried to tell myself, not sure what my foggy brain believed at this point, but it seemed sensible to try and hold onto logic a little longer. Regardless of whether he was monster or man, he was surprising.

Only the white, lifeless skin made him seem anything but human. It was pristine, like alabaster or fresh, unyellowed ivory. The kind of skin Victorian women and goths would have killed for. He had deep brown, swept back hair. The color was too rich to be mistaken for black. It was like really good, really dark chocolate. His eyes were fringed with lashes so thick it looked like he was wearing mascara and so long that when he blinked, they seemed to brush his cheeks. His face was built of sharp angles and high cheekbones.

His long body was clothed in all black: silk shirt clinging to his broad shoulders and accentuating his narrow waist, and black jeans that outlined his lean legs and hips. He couldn't be anything but human. When I met his eyes though, there was nothing there. No humanity, not even curiosity. No soul.

This man's eyes were a true void-like black. Deep and endless, they drew me in, inhuman and so cold I felt goose bumps shiver up my skin.

Under normal circumstances I would have found him desperately handsome. But not now. Not this inhuman thing that all parts of my being wanted to run from. When I looked at him, my body screamed *PREDATOR*, sending off alerts through all my internal systems.

He stared hungrily at me, like a chef preparing

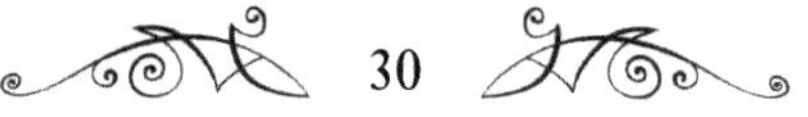

a particularly expensive cut of meat. At least it appeared to me that the sensual way he ran his eyes over my body was akin to the way I eyed rich ice cream.

"You need to stay hydrated. The coconut water will help. Drink," he said.

The spoon actually made it between my lips. I swallowed greedily. I needed to get rid of the burning in my throat. One spoonful wasn't enough, but it did help.

He nodded. "Good girl." His condescending voice prickled the hairs on the back of my neck and made my face twist into a snarl.

Not doing it for you, monster.

I glared at him, hating that he ordered me to do the thing I wanted and needed. Hating that I couldn't refuse him. Anger rose in me. I despised this creature thoroughly, and I was already planning what would happen when I escaped. I was going to report his kidnapping ass to the police and enjoy it when they dragged him off to rot in jail.

The kitchen was lit by weak, early morning sunlight, but he stood in a small pool of shadows, his face turned away from the windows. The cedar shades allowed dusty bars of lemony yellow light in. I stared at it, trying to think past the immediate situation and to my future survival.

I managed to look down at the condition of my

body. My corset was stained where dried blood pooled on one of my breasts. I didn't feel pain or signs of violation anywhere except my neck, and was glad that all my clothing was still on. That was a start. The amount of dried blood worried me though, and the dizziness I was fighting made a little more sense. How much blood had I lost?

More juice hit my cheek. "Sstaaa...." My throat was so sore I couldn't speak. My hand automatically tried to go there, to comfort the wound. The chains made a musical rattle of protest at the motion, and the reality of my situation struck me hard.

I'm someone's prisoner. Some monster's prisoner.

Terror exploded inside me. Black, blinding terror that sent me into a writhing, kicking, scratching, frenzy that was short-lived due to the fact that I could not scream nor move in any real direction, and the only thing the thrashing accomplished was to make my arms and shoulders ache even more. My wrists felt the strain as I scrambled to find my footing again and ease the pain. Exhaustion and despair poured through me in waves.

Tears seeped from my eyes, but I blinked them back. I wouldn't let that monster see me weak. I managed to scrape out a raspy, "Why?"

It was a damn good question. I mean, all I had done was try to earn a living. No way did I deserve to be chained up in a vampire's kitchen.

unLife

No, just a vampire poser, I reminded my blurring brain. I was thinking of him as a real monster because I hated the idea a human would do this to me. But I knew the world was full of human monsters who would do this and worse. My eyes went back to his ghastly pallor and the way he stood so far back in the shadows. Maybe he was just a whack job who had taken the whole thing too seriously. Looking at the woman who was haphazardly feeding me, I thought she could be a junkie. Then again, the players at the LARP scene had definitely not been junkies. There hadn't been time to slip them something. Hypnotism maybe?

If I could accept hypnotism as an excuse, I might as well believe it was real vampiric compulsion, just like I've seen in so many movies. Could he be a real vampire and the woman his human thrall? My mind was going back and forth like a ping-pong ball.

I didn't know. I couldn't know. I wanted some other explanation, so I asked again, "Why?"

"What's your favorite food?"

I stared at him, bewildered by the response. And what a question to ask a die-hard foodie. What was my favorite food? Lobster tail drowning in fresh drawn butter, couscous plump and rich with leeks and the mildest of cheeses? Maybe simple freshly baked bread still warm from the oven, its outside brown and crisp and its middle delightfully chewy, slathered in the best French butter? The strangeness of the question sent my mind into a tailspin.

He didn't seem to take my not answering as an offense. "Mine is strawberries. Or, it was, back when I could still partake in food."

I was confused. Why would I care what his favorite food was? I could understand why he was asking about mine. Perhaps this was like death row, and I was going to get a first-class meal before he punched my exit ticket to the next world, but why was he telling me about his? If he really was a vampire, then I already knew what his current favorite food was.

He tilted his head, examining me with dark eyes. "If you found a strawberry plant that grew the most exquisite berries in the world, so ripe, so plump, so perfectly sweet with just a hint of tartness lurking in their firm red flesh, would you strip it bare? Would you tear it up from the roots to gorge yourself on the fruit? No, you would tend it, care for it, so it would stay alive, and continue to grow and bear fruit so you could savor the taste of its berries until the end of its short season."

I didn't like where this was going. My head shook side to side, denying him. I refused to draw the parallels he was trying to make.

His eyes met mine, their black so deep, gaze so empty of soul or emotion that my whole body shuddered in fear and revulsion. "You are my strawberry. I will keep you alive as long as possible, and you will be my only food until you finally die. There is something about your blood, something so delicious I can't bear to part with you or consume you all in one meal. I aim to have you as long as possible."

I couldn't speak. I could do nothing but stare at him. Was this really going to be my fate? Run away from my family to a place I had no friends, to work for a few years in meaningless roles, and then die to some crazy? Some monster who thought I *tasted* good?

I didn't have to respond, because he turned away, then said over his shoulder, "It is too late in the morning for me to have any strength left. I will see you this evening." Then he disappeared, as though he had never been there at all.

See me for what? Dinner? My neck ached, and the thrall dipped the spoon into the juice again, splattering it against the side of my nose. With the vampire gone, she stood there confused for a moment then walked away, her arms and legs jerking like a possessed marionette that had been let off its strings. I stared at the remains of the coconut water, lying just out of reach. It was all I could do not to whine like an abandoned dog.

I watched as the woman started to clean the kitchen, and it became clear she wasn't going to come back to feed me. I called to her, begged her for help, for freedom, for my life, scratching my tender throat bare. She made no sign she even knew I was there as she mechanically scrubbed the counters. Then she left the room with a vacuum cleaner tucked under her arm, carrying it like a load of groceries.

Alone in the kitchen, I let myself cry. Tears trickled down my cheeks, stinging the wound on my throat as the moisture loosened the dried, caked blood. I could only imagine how I looked, mascara running down my face, one side of my body drizzled in blood. I forced myself to settle, blinking rapidly and sniffing hard to stop my nose from running. Hanging around indulging in a big tear-fest was only wasting time. Tears wouldn't help me now. What would help was to get out of these chains and out of this crazy house. My eyes went to the rack of kitchen knives on the wall nearby. I glanced up at the pulley system, trying to judge how far it would let me move. If I could reach a thin fillet knife, I could try to open the cuffs that were against my wrists. And if that didn't work, maybe I could defend myself against the vampire when he came back to eat me.

The chains had some give, and when I pulled hard, they ran through the pulley system and let me bring my arms down, but it took a lot of effort. When I didn't pull hard enough, the pulley started reeling me back in. My muscles shook and strained from the effort. The metal made a harsh whispering sound as I tried to creep along the floor to the counter. I was brought up abruptly by the bonds though, just inches from the counter and the knives. I strained against the shackles with everything I had, bracing against the wall with my feet, hoping they would break or come undone, but that only exhausted me. The chains reeled me back in and left me hanging with my face pressed into the cold tiles of the wall.

There was blood there. Dried and flaked, much older than anything I might have left behind. *I'm not the first victim.* Is this where the other girls ended up? The ones Harvey had sent out that never came back?

My head buzzed and there was a distant roaring in my ears. Something warm and thick dripped down the side of my neck, soaking the top of my chemise and corset. I'd torn my abused neck open again and it bled freely. The light faded out around the edges of my sight and I groaned, too weak to keep on fighting although every part of me wanted to. The last thing I saw was the thrall, with her clown-from-planet-crazy smile, coming closer. Strange, I hadn't even heard her come back. Had she been watching me this whole time?

Don't bite me, you bitch.

Then I was gone.

4

There was a sound, a slow, soft sound that made me raise my head. Darkness surrounded me, and I hung limp from my bonds. All my senses were numbed, but I could tell I was dehydrated, starving, and nearly bled out. I fought death with every fragment of strength left in me but felt it creeping into my core. More than anything I felt cold. My muscles ached with the intensity of the shivers that rattled my body. The movement beat the chains against each other in a discordant cacophony.

My eyelids drooped and I dragged them back up, seeing only short blinks of the last moments of my life.

The thrall stood beside me, wiping a spot on the counter over and over, her face caught in that

same wicked expression. As I drifted in and out of consciousness, I swear I caught her shooting looks at me, sly little glances. The kitchen was eerily dark, and not just around the edges of my vision. It was lit by slivers of silver moonlight trickling through the blinds, sapping the color out of the world.

A light came on. The vampire appeared.

He looked at the scene before him, and his expression changed to something fierce and dangerous. His entire body seemed to thrum like a taut bowstring. I could almost feel the carefully restrained violence. Except that I couldn't really *feel* anything. Even that realization seemed distant and dreamlike.

He shouted at the thrall. His words, and all other sounds around me, were muffled, and I couldn't make them out. But the vampire's words seemed to affect her like a wave of force. She turned and ran, frantically and madly, colliding face first with the wall.

She twisted and crumpled. Blood broke from her nose but she never made a sound. I shuddered helplessly. She rolled over to the counter then got to her feet, still smiling her ghastly ghoulish grin, a trickle of blood running down the side of her mouth. She skulked away, looking back over her shoulder until he roared at her again and she left at a ragged trot.

unLife

He was beside me faster than I knew how. His fingers pressed against my pulse and he cursed. I tried to speak, to ask for mercy but there was nothing left in me. My breath simply wheezed out, wordless. He broke the cuffs with one movement and I fell into his arms. *How could he be so fast, so strong? How could I ever hope to escape if he was strong enough to break steel?*

That was when I knew for sure. I knew, no matter what this man was, he was not human.

He lifted me in a swift, gentle movement. I rolled weakly into his chest, feeling the strength of his muscles as he carried me through the huge house. His body was cold, so cold it sent shivers down my spine.

The world blurred around me, then I found myself being carefully laid down on a bed. I sank into a soft mattress covered with silky sheets. A cool night breeze came from somewhere, and my teeth chattered violently.

The vampire left me like that, vanishing again. I wasn't restrained. I tried to move my feet, my hands, but could not muster the energy. I lay there weak and senseless. *This is my only chance at escape and I'm blowing it!* The anger that surged into me at that thought gave me a second wind and I rolled onto my side.

Before I could even attempt to put a foot on the floor, he was back.

He held a tray filled with gauze padding, bandages, and a handcuff. I wanted to fight him, but it was all I could do to stay conscious. My fingers fluttered in weak protests against his hands, trying to fend off the new cuff. My wrists were chafed from my struggles and hanging in the unforgiving manacles. Welts had formed where they had been abraded the worst. He caught my hands in an iron grip. He placed the thin cuff of gleaming steel around one of my wrists and ran a very long, thin chain through it. He locked it to the bed neatly. I stared up at the shifting shadows on the ceiling and began to weep softly, unable to hold it in any longer. I was completely at the mercy of this monster. I was just so tired. I wanted to be home in my bed with a pillow crammed over my head, wishing my rock-star wannabe roommates would shut up so the rest of us could get some sleep.

But I wasn't at home. The world swam around me, even my mind was lost for a moment in the agony.

The vampire dipped his head toward me. *This is it,* I thought wildly, my foggy brain not even pausing to wonder why he would chain up someone he intended to kill now. Any doubts I'd had about his status as inhuman fled my mind under the cold touch of his fingers. The touch of his tongue against my neck startled me, but I couldn't do anything but twitch and shake. With long, sure strokes, he lapped the blood from my throat and collarbone. His soft murmur of pleasure left me feeling sick.

After he pulled his face away, lips red with my blood, his long and elegant fingers stroked my neck, pressing some stinking ointment into the wound. Pain sizzled along my nerve endings. I passed out momentarily but came back to find him bandaging my neck with the same gentleness he had used to carry me to the room.

But there was no gentleness in his eyes. They were still empty, calculating. It was the gaze of a predator making sure its food supply remained viable. He'd told me he would tend to me like a strawberry plant, and here he was, trying to repot me after I'd been ripped out of the ground.

More coconut water appeared, and the vampire spooned it slowly through my cracked lips. Unlike the thrall, not a drop spilled on me, and I sipped it slowly, letting it replenish me. I needed my strength because I intended to do everything I could to stay alive. I didn't know how much time I would have, but I wanted every minute of it. The longer I could stay alive, the longer I had to figure out how to escape. I still felt so weak though, wavering in and out of consciousness.

He sat beside me, feeding me silently for what felt like hours. I may have slept at some point, but couldn't tell, because whenever I was awake, he was there, tenderly caring for my wound or rehydrating me spoon by spoon.

A small glow of light warmed the room. It came from wide double doors, open and leading to a balcony from the huge bedroom. I had some strength back, and when the vampire tried to feed me again, I pushed him away, took the cup from the table, and drank it myself.

He brushed tangled hair away from my face. His hand was soft but cold, and he murmured words that were hardly reassuring. "I thought I'd lost you, my Strawberry. I was careless for not giving my maid stricter instructions on how to look after you. But you are revived, and I will see you stay healthy. I intend to feed from your delicious blood many more times before you die."

How thoughtful, I wanted to snark at him, but fear held my tongue. *There have been times I've had some deep and intimate feelings for chocolate, but I still ate it all up till it was gone.*

"How can you treat me like this?" My throat throbbed, and I wasn't sure if it was from all the screaming or the bite in the side of it.

His gaze held mine, empty and cold. "You're nothing but food to me."

I searched for something in his expression that said otherwise, but only saw the monster, only that inhuman, unfeeling stare. But he seemed at least logical, ethical even, in the treatment of his 'food'. Maybe I could convince him to see me as something more than a meal. If he could see me as a living, feeling person, surely he would let me go free.

I grasped at that, desperate words spilling from my lips. "My name is Kitty. Kitty French. I'm an actress, I live in West Hollywood. And since you asked, my idea of a damn fine meal is rare steak with shavings of black truffle and triple cooked potato." My throat ached with each word, but I couldn't seem to stop them. And I knew I shouldn't speak, I should save my strength, but I had to try to make myself seem more human and less vampire cuisine.

A strange fury filled the vampire's eyes, and he stood up from the side of the bed. He stormed to the door. My plan to appeal to him had failed. At least him leaving might give me the chance to escape.

At the doorway he hesitated. He spoke over his shoulder. "Owen Raine. That's my name, Strawberry."

"That's not *my* name, Vampire."

The corner of his lips twitched. *A smile?* He glanced at the balcony and the brightening sky beyond, then left without another word. I latched on to that fleeting smirk, hoping I hadn't imagined it. If he had a sense of humor, maybe he wasn't completely out of reach. The ability to laugh, to feel at all, was something so human that it had to mean he wasn't completely monstrous.

"Owen." I rolled the name off my tongue like a promise. That I would not call him by his name until he called me by mine. I was not his strawberry. I would make him know me, see me. It might be the only chance I had to survive.

5

 watched the open door he'd gone through while the sunrise brought thin beams of warmth into the room. The smell chlorine and the sea floated in on the breeze. *He has a pool and we're near the ocean?* He had to be loaded. Or maybe, the house belonged to the thrall or some other victim of his. It was hard to say. The world had gone crazy, or I had. Vampires were real and I was at the mercy of one. I thought through all the tales of crosses, stakes to the heart, garlic, transforming into bats, and sleeping in coffins, creating a mental file of stuff pop culture had told me about vampires. There must be some weakness I could exploit that applied to the real thing. Daylight hurting them seemed true enough. Owen obviously avoided it, but he seemed able to deal with indirect sunlight, hiding in the shadows. Other than that, I had little idea what kind of creature I was *really* dealing with. But logic said he was going to be sleeping all day, which meant I might actually be able to get away from him. This was my chance, not to be wasted as the earlier one had been.

My wrist was still caught in the silver loop of the cuff, and when I sat up a slight dizziness washed over me. I was still weak, but who knows how weak I would be tomorrow, or the next day, slowly being drunk dry. I did feel stronger than a few hours ago. I tried not to dwell on the way I shook every time I moved, and the way the world swam when I sat up.

My first move was to find the bathroom. The need to escape getting trumped momentarily by the need to pee.

Swinging my legs off the side of the bed and trying to stand showed me just how weak I was. I prided myself on my working out. After all, I loved a good dessert, and if I was going to make it big as an actress, I had to work off that slice—or three—of cheesecake after dinner. *Oh, cheesecake.* Thinking about it made my stomach rumble. Now that my thirst was mostly quenched, I suddenly became aware of how horribly hungry I was. If the night before last had been the night after the LARP, then it was going on thirty-six hours since my decadent meal. It seemed far longer than that though, as though the steakhouse existed in a different lifetime. I was starving. Anything to eat would have been good, even if it was just a packet of instant ramen.

My legs were shaky and I had to sit back down, take a few breaths, then stand again. Three false starts later I staggered across the room, the chain dragging behind me. It was clearly long enough to let me move freely within the confines of my cell, but I doubted I'd make it much farther. The chain was thin but the sheer length of it made it heavy. I barely felt like I had the strength to lift my arm. The loop of metal that closed around my wrist was smooth and polished, pressing into my skin with surprisingly little discomfort.

"I feel like a damn dog," I muttered as I stepped into the bathroom. Out of some sense of privacy I tried to close the door, but it wouldn't quite shut with the chain in the way. I left it ajar, too tired to bother with it.

I immediately forgot my anger at the sight of the exquisite marble tiling, floor to ceiling mirrors, thick Turkish towels, and a huge tub that looked like it could hold a party of four. I bet the tub was real marble too. The stone was cold under my feet and made me shake, remembering the deadly cold that had crept through my body earlier. I wanted to soak in that tub, immersed in hot water to chase the chill away.

The toilet was hidden behind a tiny partition and I stumbled to it, pulled down my panties, plopped onto the seat and sighed with relief, until I looked up and caught my reflection in the mirror.

My face was streaked with dried tears. My hair was a rat's nest, the blue-black waves sticking up in dry hunks and tangles around my paler than usual face. My lips were normally rosy, but they were a bleached-out gash. My eyes had dark shadows below them, and my neck had a huge purple-yellow bruise around the carefully wrapped bandage. Dried blood crusted the front of my costume, and sweat stains showed under my arms. The mascara that had been thickly applied for the game had migrated below my eyes, enhancing how sunken they were. All my other makeup seemed to have smeared off at some point during my ordeal.

I looked like hell.

And I stank.

The smell hit me all at once and I gagged. I stared at the tub, a deep longing for a good soak sinking into me. I could imagine how it would feel in there, up to my neck in hot water made fragrant and silky by the jars of bath oils that lined the tub's edge. This time though, the longing wasn't for the warmth but for cleanliness. I fantasized for a moment how it would feel to scrub myself off in the gently perfumed water and then step out, snuggling into one of those plush

white towels. Every part of me longed for comfort.

But there was no time to clean up now. I had to push my thoughts forward, toward escape. Until then, maybe my offensive odor would make me less of a tasty treat.

I set my jaw hard in resolve, imagining a future where I survived, where I would have the comfort I yearned for. *When I'm free again. When I'm free I'll have the most perfect bath ever.* I ignored the fact that the tiny bathroom I shared with a bunch of other people wasn't anything like this. It didn't even have a tub. It had a grimy shower stall full of other peoples' stuff.

Cleaning up wasn't in the plan, but I considered that getting more clothing would be useful. The long, flowy chemise and corset were not practical for escape attempts at all. A pair of pants would have been just my cup of tea right then, or at least a shirt. Anything to get the blood crusted thing off me and make me feel a little less exposed.

I limped back out to the bedroom. In the daylight the furnishings made me stare. The bed was a huge four poster, the carpet plush and soft. My toes sank into the pile, welcome warmth after the coolness of the bathroom tile. A leather sofa sat in one corner below deep windows, and one wall was lined with bookshelves. From the placement of the window in the bathroom and on two walls in here, I had to be

in a corner room of the building.

Testing the boundaries of my leash, I found I could reach all parts of the bathroom, and bedroom but not the balcony. I could make it through the bedroom door to the top of a large staircase made of teak and surrounded by a black wrought iron railing. A hallway below seemed to go on forever, and I could see an immense modern living area down the stairs. It looked like something out of a magazine or hotel, dark leather couches with glass and black metal tables. The floor was hardwood to match the staircase with what looked like a real Persian rug laid under the coffee table. I couldn't quite reach the railing to look over it, but I could see broad double doors of solid wood—the entrance, or rather, exit? There were also several windows, giving me a glimpse of a driveway and a well-groomed front yard. I couldn't work out where the kitchen was. Reluctantly, I pulled my eyes away from the sunlight filtering in the front windows.

I searched for a tool or weapon I could use. The dresser drawers yielded nothing but a stray puff of dust and blank spaces. The armoire was also empty, so I was stuck in the vintage costume. Even the heavy side table was bare, not even a lamp. The room had the feel of one that was rarely, if ever, used, like a forgotten guest room. Only the bookshelf held anything at all, a dozen or so volumes. I tried wrenching the dresser apart, hitting it with a heavy book to smash free a sliver of wood to use as a stake, but I only succeeded in destroying the book. Looking down at the tattered pages, I sighed. It really was a shame, it looked like a fine old book. I tried not to feel bad about it. I wouldn't be destroying things if I hadn't been taken prisoner.

The chain was locked around a post of the bed with a huge and heavy padlock, and no matter what I tried it would not come loose of its mooring. In desperation, I planted my feet in a straddle-legged pose and tried to yank it free. *Fucking rich people, they never buy the flimsy pressed wood stuff.* While normally I would have approved, it certainly made my attempts to escape harder.

After a few minutes of straining, I gave up. The bed was solid and it wouldn't budge.

Or would it? If I could move it enough to get to the balcony, I could scream and wave for help. Surely a woman in a blood-soaked gown would attract some kind of attention. Even if I was at the back of the house, they might hear me. I was on the second story, so my voice should carry.

The bed was heavy as hell. I had to get behind it and push it inch by inch across the floor. It felt like it weighed more than a car. Frequently I had to stop and rest, leaning against it. I was grateful that the pitcher of coconut water had been left on the dresser so I could continue to drink, otherwise I wouldn't have made any progress at all. The going was slow, but desperation is a great motivator. A few times, there were tearing sounds, and I grinned. *Screw that monster and his expensive carpet.*

The clock on the wall showed noon before I got the bed a few feet across the room, far enough that I could reach the French doors. I was shaking and covered in a fine sheen of sweat. Dots danced before my eyes, and my throat was sore again. I checked it gingerly. No blood was spurting out, that had to be a plus.

The balcony beckoned. I pushed the doors then stumbled out, only to stare in disbelief. I leaned on the railing, teeth gritted in frustration. The high hilltop was barren and isolated. The dun-colored slopes were covered in scrubby little bushes and stunted trees. The hills stretched away on either side without a single other building in sight. A thin gray ribbon of what had to be a private drive stretched for about a mile to a small highway below. The view was stark and beautiful. And we were completely alone.

I scanned the immediate area. A pool directly below was made to look like a river complete with waterfall, and not far past the property's boundary walls, a cliff dropped away to the sea. Around the other side was a tennis court, though the leaves gathered in the corners made me think it hadn't been used in years. I hadn't been quite right when

Unlife

I thought I was in a corner room. The house was nestled into the hill, the levels distributed over the varying ground. The part of the house I was in was practically a tower that rose high above the surrounding, uninhabited landscape.

I screamed anyway, bellowing my cries for help into the wind. They blew back, uselessly. The caws of gulls in the distance seemed to mock me.

When I turned back to the bedroom, a tray of food sat on the bedside table. A shiver chilled me, wondering when it arrived, whether Owen could move about during the day, or if the creepy thrall had slunk in while I cried at the empty sky.

The serving tray held a still warm teapot that gave off the delicious odor of jasmine and vanilla, a plate on which rested a single slice of toast, neatly cut in triangular quarters, a tiny dish of jam, and a peeled and sectioned orange. The teapot, cup, plate, and dish were all made of safe, smooth edged metal. No cutlery, no ceramic or glass I could smash and use as a weapon, like I was some patient on suicide watch. If my captor was already thinking it, I wondered gloomily how long it would take me before I tried to kill myself as a form of escape. Not for a while. I wanted to live. And to live, I needed strength, and food.

I poured a cup of tea and tipped it back. I'd gone through all the coconut water and I was desperate for a drink. It was heavenly on my tongue and soothed my throat. I would have liked some sugar, but there was none, so I dipped a finger into the jam and tasted it.

My eyes closed involuntarily in delight. Choke-cherries are almost inedible by themselves but they make an incredibly velvety jam. I dipped the toast into the jam pot, and gobbled down the orange, wiping my sticky fingers and mouth on the soft bedsheets as a small act of rebellion. I relished every bite. The bread was artisan, clearly fresh despite being toasted. It had been buttered lightly, and the faint hint of salt enhanced the sweetness of the grain and the jam that I dipped it in. The orange was succulent and perfectly ripe. Rarely did I get to eat this well. It was a welcome change from a diet heavy on beans, rice, and pasta.

Renewed, I considered my situation. I couldn't break the chain. I could find no weapon to defend myself with. I knew I was valued as food, but food doesn't get freedom. I needed to be seen as a human who deserved to be free. This morning I had received the vampire's name for my efforts. Maybe, if I kept playing on his sympathy, what little he had, I could achieve more. I was meant to be an actress after all.

This might be the role of a lifetime. Rather, it might be the role that saved my life.

6

The sun eventually dropped behind a bank of clouds. I watched it set, tears standing in my eyes at the beauty of it. Carnelian, pink, gold, and indigo blue lit the dome of the sky. Clouds, white and puffy, turned a brilliant orange and then a deep shade of lavender. *Would this be my final sunset?*

It reminded me in a lot of ways of the last sunset I'd seen back home. I'd watched it from the roof of my family's house. In the rural area where I had grown up, the sunsets were beautiful and pure. In the city, the sunset was spectacular for different reasons—pollution fogging the clouds and creating wild colors in the sky. It was a different kind of beauty; one I didn't appreciate nearly as much as the ones I'd grown up with. The breeze grew cold but I was reluctant to leave the fresh air that was as close to freedom as I could get.

The last ray of sunlight faded, and Owen appeared on cue. He eyed the room, the scraped carpet, the bed out of place. I stood defiant before him. The hell was I going to the effort of pushing that monster bed back to hide my escape efforts.

He tossed me onto the bed, and with one quick flick of his wrist the bed shot backwards, flying across the floor like an out-of-control rocket ship until it crashed against the wall. A startled scream escaped me, and I huddled next to the headboard, a white knuckled grip on one of the posts.

Before I knew it, the vampire was on top of me. He gripped my jaw in one hand, pressing my head back to inspect my neck. He tsked softly. "Strawberry, escape is not possible for you. I am not going to let you go, do you understand? All you will gain by attempting to escape is to cause yourself unnecessary pain."

The chill coming off his body was palpable. I put my best, most vulnerable, expression on, opening my mouth to begin a plea for my life, but it went still and silent on my tongue. He was looking directly at me, and his dark eyes were decidedly not human eyes, no mercy, no compassion lay in them. Nothing of that moment of hesitation and indecision I'd seen that morning. Nothing but a monster.

I squashed the shiver of fear in my gut. I was an

actor. I could transmute emotions the way alchemists were supposed to transmute lead into gold. I dug deep to find the rebellious teenager in me, channeling all my fear and desperation into bravado and anger.

I could strangle Owen with the chain, but I wasn't sure if he even needed to breathe. I stared daggers at him instead. "I will *never* stop trying to escape from you, monster."

His pale face didn't change expression, and I shuddered.

Owen moved off me casually, leaving in a blur and returning with a silver domed tray which he placed on the bedside table without ceremony. The mouthwatering aromas coming from the tray made my belly growl angrily. I didn't want the vampire to see me slobbering like one of Pavlov's dogs, so I focused my eyes elsewhere. That didn't do one ounce of good. I could smell truffle, butter and rare meat, and my stomach let out another loud and feral yelp.

Owen removed the dome to reveal the exact meal I had described myself as enjoying. An incredible slab of steak with an amount of fresh truffle shaved over the top that would cost me a few month's rent. The roast potatoes on the side looked fluffy and crunchy and golden through. For some reason, the meal choice infuriated me. I turned my back on it, and him, like a spoiled child. It also made me think. *He'd remembered.* Did that mean I was getting through to him? Or maybe he thought it was the most likely way to get me to eat something. Not that it would have taken much at this point with my stomach howling to be filled. Make no mistake, I was starving, and yet here I was being contrary. I never could be sensible.

"You must eat."

"So *you* can eat me?" I scoffed bitterly.

"Yes." His voice was crisp, with no hesitation as he answered me.

He was honest, I had to give him that.

"I'm not your food or your slave, Vampire. Think you can just put a nice meal in front of me and I'll be you're willing victim? Go fuck yourself." I knew I was goading him. It was a side of myself I was rarely brave enough to show, my sarcasm and snark normally hidden under fear of confrontation. But this monster had *imprisoned* me, and I had no desire to be polite to him.

Part of me almost hoped he would snap and kill me. I didn't want to die, but I wanted even less to be held prisoner so he could feed off me at his leisure. Another part of me was hoping to tease a reaction out of him. Any reaction that would show me there was still a man beneath the frigid, casually cruel exterior.

My words had no effect. He merely began to carve the hunk of Kobe beef into bite-sized bits. Juices ran across the plate, pooling nicely against the baked potato. The meat practically fell apart at the touch of the knife. I was certain it would melt like butter on my tongue.

"You must replenish your iron."

He tapped the fork against my lips. My traitorous mouth opened to accept the steak. My lips closed around it, and my eyelids fluttered as I savored the delicately seasoned morsel. I was such a sucker for good food. *If Owen doesn't kill me, I will likely die from over consumption.* It tasted as good as I imagined. Truffle was something I got so rarely that the taste always surprised me in the most delightful way. Earthy and rich, it mingled with the juicy steak.

The taste of the food made me realize how little I wanted to die. My life was precious. The thought startled me as I swallowed the first bite. I'd had so much to complain about lately. Failing career, absent relationships, infuriating housemates. I had worked my ass off to get where I wanted to be in life and hadn't gotten there. I felt like I wasn't getting anywhere. Faced with the possibility of dying, all of that seemed irrelevant. Sure, there were issues, my life was still a work in progress, but I loved being alive, experiencing every tiny, beautiful moment.

I opened my eyes and stared at Owen, my eyes tracing the curve of his cheek, the soft fan of his eyelashes as he looked down at the plate. How could a monster be so beautiful?

I rebelled with words only. "I'm not eating for you. Despite you being the devil for tempting me with this fucking incredible meal. I'm eating *for me*." I didn't have anything left to fight with but words at this point. I couldn't turn down the food. It was too good, and I was too hungry. At least with him feeding me, I could savor each bite. If I had control of the cutlery, I'd be stuffing my face in the least glamorous way. Owen's slow delivery of each bite was an exquisite kind of agony that nearly made me weep.

Still, I couldn't get any reaction from him. He was like an animated corpse, only caring about keeping his food supply viable. He placed another bite of the meat in my mouth, and I decided to try a different tactic. Time to switch acting roles.

I clutched at my stomach and buckled over onto the mattress in fake pain, crying out and writhing. Far from my best performance, it was still good enough to make Owen put down the steak knife to come to my aid.

"Strawberry, what's wrong?" His voice held no worry, more a clinical curiosity one might show a houseplant that wasn't growing well. He just didn't want his strawberry plant to stop fruiting so soon.

I rolled to the side. The knife was within reach. It was large and looked wickedly sharp.

While I still had the element of surprise, I grabbed it and stabbed it straight into his chest.

I worried that his body would somehow deflect the blade, like he was made of stone, but it didn't. The blade went in. At least, it went in a little way. His skin was cold, dense, and the blade lodged hard into it, blocked by muscle or ribcage below.

The knife may have stopped but my hand didn't. It kept going and my palm streaked along the razor-sharp edge. Blood swelled from the wound, dripping down his shirt front.

For a moment I just stared stupidly at my hand wrapped around the knife blade and the blood flooding out. More blood I didn't want to lose. Then the pain hit me.

I pulled my hand back, screaming, unable to bear the sight of my body losing more of the precious liquid that kept me alive. I'd seen enough of my own blood in the past two days that I never wanted to see it again.

"Troublesome food." His anger was not white-hot, as it had been with his thrall, it was arctic cold. It was subzero. His face had frozen into an expression of such rage I was sure he was going to reach over and snap my neck right off of my shoulders. Instead, he pulled the blade out. The tip of it, the part that had been lodged in his chest, was clean, but my blood lay on the length, thin and red and beading up slowly, like tears on the steel.

His tongue came out and licked the blade with a

slow sensual motion that made my belly flop loosely. His eyes never left me, his expression suddenly back to that deadly neutral look. As though he felt nothing. I knew that wasn't true, but it unsettled me all the same.

"You obviously don't want to eat," he said in a low but lethal tone. "I do, however, and see no reason why both of us should go hungry."

I screamed and thrashed, but his cold hands shoved me into the mattress. Hot, salty tears fell down my cheeks, and my feet kicked and flailed. One of his hands pinned me down between my breasts, and the other grabbed my bleeding hand by the wrist. I bucked my hips to try to throw him off, but he was too heavy. His face rippled and changed, becoming more monstrous. Fangs appeared, needle sharp over his lips.

Those fangs plunged roughly into my wrist, drawing deep from the large artery there.

Dizziness spun through me. I was so weak and tired that my body could not decipher at first what was happening. I could only feel the ice of his lips, and the hot flush of my blood rushing out of me. His jaw clenched around my flesh, and I could do nothing but stare in horror at the monster on top of me. My mouth opened in a silent cry. Darkness washed over me. I felt like I was drowning in fire. Nothing made sense as my mind spun, and I hardly felt his lips leave my skin except that my body jerked in an automatic reaction, a whimper of relief torn involuntarily from my throat. I fell back onto the pillows, wilted, and drifted into black nothingness.

7

I woke up the next morning to the sight of my bandaged hand and wrist on the pillow beside me, the curtains tightly closed, and Owen in a chair near my bed.

He looked tired and drawn. He rubbed his forehead with his long fingers, and his eyebrows were low over his eyes. It was so different to his normal, cold composure that I watched him, stunned, feeling like I was looking at an entirely different person. Not the monster I still wanted to plunge a knife into the heart of, but someone more human.

He caught sight of me staring at him and shifted awkwardly. Reaching out, he lifted my head slightly to put a glass of sweet milk to my lips. I swallowed it, then he laid my head back down with a tenderness

I would never have believed him capable of. It felt different this time. Not just being careful not to damage something prized. It was actual caring, or maybe even guilt. I could see it in the wrinkle of his brow and softness in his gaze. Somehow, something had changed. Like that flicker of hesitation I saw once before.

There was a vulnerability in his voice when he said, "I'm sorry if I hurt you. I don't usually react so violently."

Who the hell is he kidding? He's a vampire. He lives off violence.

I bit down my retort. I didn't really want to make him angry again.

I lifted my bandaged hand, holding it up in front of him as evidence. "You did hurt me. Look what you've done to me in just two days. How do you expect me to survive this?"

He shifted in his chair, turning away from my wounds on display. "I'm sorry. I will be more careful."

"I don't want you to be careful. I want you to let me go! Keeping me here like this, it's inhuman." *Of course it is, you idiot. He's not human.* But he did seem more human now than any other time we'd interacted. There was an almost palpable guilt coming from him. Maybe there was something of a man inside him after all. Maybe I could reach that, make him see me as more than just food. That was my only hope.

I stretched out, taking his hands into my fingers. He turned troubled eyes to meet mine, and I spoke as pleadingly and sincerely as I could. "I don't want to die."

He shook his head, releasing his fingers from my grasp. "All humans die."

"Okay, let me rephrase that. I don't want to die *imminently*." I couldn't keep the bitter tightness out of my voice.

"I will keep you alive as long as possible." The words were like a tender promise and he shook his head again, this time as though trying to clear it. He rubbed his fingers down his temples and schooled his expression back to neutral. He was clamming up, shutting down. The opportunity to connect with him was slipping through my fingers before I'd had the chance to do anything useful with it.

I decided to push harder. "Gee, thanks. That's not what I mean, and you know it. I want to go home. Being kept here, like this, is as good as death. Do you not see how cruel this is? Keeping me here, so you can nibble at me until I'm all dried up?"

"Do you enjoy crab legs?" He was looking down at his hands, laced tightly together in his lap.

The question caught me off guard. "Yes, I love them. Why?"

"Do you consider it fair to yank a crab from its

home, tear off one leg and toss it back?"

"I've never—"

"They harvest stone crabs one leg at a time. The leg grows back, but each time that crab is caught again its leg is taken. Is that humane behavior?" He finally glanced up at me, and his face was cold. Something moved in his eyes, as though the darkness there had lightened unperceptively.

Was he using this comparison to convince me, or himself?

Either way, I'll never eat crabs again, I swear it. I needed to change tack. "You used to be a human. Can't you remember what it's like?"

"It was a very long time ago." He settled back in his chair and tugged at the cuffs of his shirt.

"How old are you?" I asked, looking from his lean and elegant fingers to the wrinkle-free skin around his eyes. He didn't look like he'd hit thirty. I wasn't even sure why I was asking. Grasping at straws I suppose, keeping him talking in the hope I could find something to use, some leverage for my freedom. A way to show some kind of connection between us. Anything to make us equals. You don't feed on equals. Right?

"I have not been human for four hundred and thirty-one years."

I choked. Four hundred and thirty-one years? That was older than ... well, older than the Constitution.

My grasp on history had never been very good, and I left the comparison at that. I struggled for another question to keep the conversation going. He wasn't much of a talker, though he seemed to be answering my questions easily enough. "Why did you become a vampire? Were you afraid of dying?"

"I do not fear death." He looked at me, strangely defiant, as though I were challenging him. "Nor have I ever feared it."

"But I do. Can you not understand that? Can't you just let me go?"

Something flashed across his eyes. "No. If you were anyone else, if you had any other blood, you would be home already. Normally I feed, then make the human forget before releasing them. I have never kept anyone this long before. It's far too risky, the chance of being discovered. But your blood is too delicious. I cannot let you go." He ran a hand over his hair, no longer perfectly slicked back but falling in a tousled mess. "I don't even understand it. It is as though I am mad for the taste of you."

"Please!" I begged. Even now, when we could almost have a conversation like real people, I wasn't getting anywhere, and desperation broke over me like a cold sweat. "Do that, please. Brain wipe me and drop me off on some corner. There are probably people out looking for me. Lots of people." *No one. No one would be looking for me, except for debt collectors.*

I didn't need to force tears for this scene.

"I'm sorry." As soon as the words left his mouth a confused expression crossed his face, then the anger slammed back over his features like a lid. "This is wrong. There's something about you, having you here … Stop speaking to me. I will not apologize to my food. I should not have to."

"I'm not food." I threw myself at him, grasping at his shirt. "I'm a person! Please! I'm a person! My name is Kitty French. I'm an actress who lives in West Hollywood. I live with ten people and I can barely pay—"

He wrapped his hands around my forearms, halting my assault. The grip was almost bruising and it made me stumble on my words, interrupting myself as I hissed at the sudden, dull pain. A dark and troubled expression traveled his chiseled face.

With a grunt, he set me free, his expression pained as he paced the side of the bed. He ran his hands up over his hair, mussing it, and seemed to be fighting a battle in his own mind. He was a completely different person to the cold monster from the day before. What had changed?

He'd fed.

Between the undead monster who'd tended to his strawberry with detached precision, to the man before me now, struggling with his emotions, he'd fed.

Maybe having a good drink of human blood left

him warmer, more human himself. A little less monstrous, but definitely more troubled. Maybe my blood really was sending him mad. That didn't sound like a fun result.

"This isn't good for you, keeping me here," I said. "It can't end well, for either of us."

His eyes met mine, and there almost seemed to be a slight shimmer of color in them before they turned dark again. There was something in his expression that ignited a shiver of undeniable attraction within me.

Ugh. No! I refused the feeling. I didn't care how beautiful he was, he was a *monster*. But looking at him right now, the monster barely seemed present.

"Please," I said.

"I ... can't." With a confused and angry look, he vanished.

Screw this shit. I was quickly going to go insane trying to judge the emotions and motives of my captor. I had to get out of here with no one's help but my own. The chain rattled and shook as I strained against it. I was sitting on the floor with my feet against the wall and pushing as hard as I could. My back ached and sweat rolled down my body, drenching my costume, but the bed posts held and the chain was still in place.

The door opened and the thrall came in, the same madhouse stare and smile on her face. I waved at her but she didn't seem to notice me. Instead, she set the tray that held my breakfast on the dressing table then stripped the sheets off the bed.

I couldn't help but wonder if she would have made the bed with me in it. The way she tossed the sheets on and tucked them in made me think of the Stepford wives, only she was a hell of a lot less well-kept. I cringed a little at the sight of her handling the sheets. Her nails were long and cracked, black with grime.

Her eyes were vacant when I looked into them, the wheel was still turning but the hamster was dead. I waved a hand in front of her face and she didn't even blink. Pity welled up inside me. Had she once also been his meal plan? Blueberry, maybe?

Owen said he'd never kept food as long as he's kept me, so this woman was different somehow.

I shuddered all over. I would rather be dead than be a senseless … thing.

That thought made me remember just how much I did *not* want to be dead, and how little I trusted the vampire to keep me alive.

Despondent, I sat on the bed and looked over at the breakfast tray. Tea slopped out of a pot, and there was a small saucer but no food on it. Maybe the maid was feeling the same strain I was in captivity and rebelling in small ways. Too bad it meant going hungry for me. I wondered if I should say something next time Owen came. I wanted to, to make sure I

didn't go hungry, but at the same time, I didn't want the woman to be punished.

I followed her path out to the banister, peering down the stairs until she vanished through a door that gave me a glimpse of the kitchen. I yearned to follow her, partly for the freedom it offered and partly because of the food I dreamed was there. A few bits of steak and a glass of milk wasn't enough to keep me from starvation. With a sigh, I headed to the bathroom. I stared gloomily at myself in the mirror for a while, denied the bathtub's lure again, then decided to go back to bed. In the bedroom, a glint of silver caught my eye. There on the nightstand was the silver domed tray from last night. I swore I didn't remember it there before I walked out of the room. *Did crazy-clown lady bring this in? What is going on?*

I approached it as if it were a trap, checking on all sides before I slowly lifted the lid. Inside was the partly eaten meal, the steak already cut into tiny bites. The only silverware was a spoon, but I didn't care. With careful discipline, I devoured every bite and savored each flavor. I decided in that moment that I would never turn down a meal from Owen again. I'd relish every meal like it was my last. I might never know when it would be.

8

Two nights passed. Owen didn't return. I hung there in that bedroom in a suspended state. My body gradually began to heal. The thrall brought me nearly endless pots of tea, but food was random and sporadic, only enough to nibble on. I hadn't had a proper meal since the truffle steak. I tried to talk to her, get her attention, but she just skulked in and out, creepy as all hell. The one time she actually looked at me, even briefly, I thought she was going to beat me to death rather than help me escape. There was something wild in her eyes, underneath the glassiness of Owen's hypnotism, that disturbed me to my core. I came to believe that she really had gone mad under his control. Pure human insanity scared me, maybe even more than Owen himself did.

I had nothing for company but the books on the shelves. They were a mixed bag of archaic philosophy, history texts, and long dead poets, but they were better than nothing. On and off I kept trying to plan an escape, but no new weapons miraculously emerged and the chain remained strong. So, I spent my days with Neitzsche, Descartes, Poe, and Shakespeare, and the nights standing at the full length of my leash, staring out over the ocean through the French doors.

At dusk on the third night, Owen finally came back. Tired of being alone, I was almost happy to see him. I set the book of old poetry on the bedside table, briefly considering trying to brain him with it. I figured the book wasn't that heavy and would probably be less effective than my attempt with the steak knife.

Then he approached. His face was cold and still, remote as the moon that hung in the corner of the open doors of the balcony. Any hint of humanity that was there when I'd seen him last was gone. This was all monster.

My body reacted to him again like he was the predator and I was prey, filling me with warning cries of, *Oh shit. He's going to kill me.* A cool trickle of fear ran through my belly.

Owen gave me a distasteful look, then disappeared briefly into the bathroom before returning. The closer he got to me, the more his face twisted with disgust.

I remembered the way he had softened when he drank from me last, and was almost desperate to get him to bite me again. I didn't know why that was, but it made some kind of sense. Even the best of us gets grouchy when hungry. And it had been two days since he last fed. I wanted him to change from this dead monster into the almost human man I could talk to, that I had a chance of reaching. *I have to keep him on my side, try to get in control of him or his emotions.*

"Been a while," I said. "You must be hungry." *Oh, gee, that was really subtle.* I should have just tilted my head and said, *here vampire, have a suck.*

He didn't seem to notice my slip up. "I am. But you are filthy. Why have you not bathed?"

I wouldn't. Not until I was free. It was the small pact I'd made with myself. There was too much temptation here, luring me to give in and stay, live in luxury and be fed exquisite food—when that food actually arrived—at the not-so-small price of giving up my personhood and being food myself.

I deflected. "Why haven't you been around? Your nutty maid has been all but starving me." I hadn't meant to bring her into this, but hunger and fear made me careless. I didn't want her punished, or for him to put her under more scrutiny if she was managing to break free.

Owen frowned, but there was no caring in the

expression, just more distaste. "She has been strangely disobedient lately. I don't know why. I will see that you receive adequate food from now on. Now, I require *my* food to be clean."

In a swift movement, he uncuffed me and hauled me to my feet.

Instinct kicked in. I flailed my arms, hitting him in his sharp and straight nose. He seemed shocked by the blow and dropped me. There was a small bit of satisfaction in that, but even more satisfying was my run across the floor. My fingers reached for the doorknob, but before I could turn it his muscular arms wound around my waist, and he lifted me from the floor. My legs kept going, feet running nowhere as I was hauled backwards.

I screamed every curse word I had ever heard and even made a few up. I beat at his hands and arms, kicked his shins, and head butted him, which made me see stars but didn't seem to faze him at all.

I was too busy screaming and fighting to notice where we were going, until he dropped me in the middle of the bathtub. Water splashed up around me and slammed, wave-like, across the floor. My screams stopped, cutting off as abruptly as an air siren.

The tub was so deep my chest was submerged. I rubbed my aching ass cheeks, shooting Owen a nasty glare. The sodden gown billowed out around me, and the clotted and crusted blood on the front

came loose in tiny, dark burgundy threads. Owen grabbed the corset and tore it from my body easily, as though it were wet tissue. I gasped and slipped in the water, managing to dunk myself again.

When I sat up, my drenched hair shedding water across my face, I screamed, "Are you trying to drown me?"

"Bathe." His voice held command.

The chemise remained on me, covering me a little, but it swirled and floated, the thin fabric's transparency accentuated by being wet. I still had a strapless bra and panties on underneath, but they were also thin and lacey. I curled forward, pulling my knees up to cover myself. "What if I don't want to?"

"Then I will make you."

The fuck you will. I'm normally an easygoing person. Hell, I've never really had much of a stomach for confrontation. When I told my folks I wanted to move to LA to become an actress, the uproar was so great I simply waited until they were asleep one night, then packed my stuff and left town. I wrote them a note. It wasn't like I ran away. I was twenty-one when I drove off from home. I didn't talk to them for a few weeks, until they had calmed down, just because I couldn't stand to fight with them. Even now, years later, we didn't talk much. I don't think Dad ever forgave me.

That's been my pattern my whole life. I hate to

fight and usually run from one. The only thing I had ever *really* fought for was my career. Or was it? I could see now how that wasn't true. I had been a coward, settling for parts I knew were no good. I had chosen a low-rent agent, who had trotted me out to a game that had landed me here, in the house of a vampire, because I was afraid to try for a better one.

I looked back at my career and wanted to laugh and cry. I had come to LA with such high hopes. I wanted to be rich and famous in a career I loved. I had found acting through a summer camp my parents had sent me on. There were always openings for the plays they put on every year, and I was in almost every single one of them. In acting I could be the person I always wanted to be, could be anyone else but myself. It was my escape route.

I had thought it would take me right out of my mundane little life, and it seemed like that dream would come true, at least. I had been taken out of my life in a way I'd never expected, with a high chance of losing it on a more permanent basis.

Rebellion surged inside me. Rebellion and a reserve of courage I had never known I had. I was going to fight him, and I was going to get out of here alive, period. I was not willing to die politely for him, or anyone else. I had dreams and plans and a life to live.

"I'd prefer to remain a stinking, filth-covered animal than wash for a fucking monster like *you*."

"Bathe," he said again. His eyes dilated, his fangs grew, and a shiver of force washed over me. My mind clouded, and terror iced my veins. Then it cleared just as quickly, replaced with anger.

"Fuuuck. Youuu," I replied, dragging out the words.

He seemed taken aback. Had he tried to compel me? Control me with his vampire will? If so, it hadn't worked. *Take that, one point to Kitty!*

His eyes narrowed. "Fine. Then I will bathe you." Owen's cold hands shot toward me. I gawped at him, all my thoughts of fighting him gone as he dipped a soft washcloth into the water, lathered a bar of sweet-smelling soap into it, and began to wash me.

Foamy circles bloomed on my shoulders and arms. I tried to squirm away from him, but his grip was tight and the tub too slippery. He unwrapped the sodden bandages on my hand and neck. He wiped tenderly around my wounds, clearing away more dried blood before washing my back with a strong, massaging motion.

I continued swearing at him, trying to argue with him, but he was completely non-responsive.

He washed my hair and I stared at him, trying to force him to look me in the eyes and really see me, as he gently wiped my chin, cheeks and lips. He just continued about his work, like a kitchen hand thoroughly rinsing every speck of dust from the corrugations of a lettuce leaf. I huddled over,

my cleaned hair hanging like dark threads in the water, trembling with anger. I felt so powerless.

I could have taken over and at least washed myself, taken that control, but it felt too much like being obedient. Making myself be clean food for him. At least this way he had to work for it.

Once I was washed, he hauled me out of the tub effortlessly. The loose-fitting chemise hung wet and heavy, clinging to me in a way that left nothing to the imagination. He approached me with a towel, and I pushed him away, snatching the towel off him. It was done. I was all washed up. I didn't need to have him drying me, too. I held the towel up between us and shimmied my shoulders until the saturated gown slipped off and squelched on the floor. Then I wrapped myself, wet underwear and all, in the warm, fluffy fabric, taking a second offered towel for my hair. I didn't have the energy or will to dry it, so I just wrapped it loosely.

I felt wilted as Owen led me back to bed and returned the shackle to my wrist. Drowsy and flooded with emotions. I had lost that round. It was clear the futility of fighting him when he was like this. I would gain no ground until he fed.

The satin sheets were slick and chilled, and I curled up into them, wanting only to cry myself to sleep, but he rolled me onto my back.

The mattress sagged beneath his weight as he

bent down on top of me. I tilted my head, revealing the undamaged side of my neck, and whispered, "Do it. Take my blood, Vampire."

His teeth grazed my neck then went lower, hovering below my collar bone.

When his teeth sunk deep into me, I barely felt the pain, but I couldn't stop the soft and involuntary cry that came from my mouth.

His weight hovered over me then came down. I shivered at the cold radiating from his skin, and my fingers curled into fists. I knew he had to bite me because it made him more human, but self-preservation, instinct, and hatred won over. I raised fists to hit him, but my hands fell to the mattress as he gripped them tightly in his own, holding them captive. His body pressed along the length of mine, and while I knew it was to hold me still, I couldn't help but writhe, feeling the heat rising in me to drive off the chill that came from him.

I could feel my blood flowing into him, strengthening him. I looked down. His dark head was just above my breast, and his powerful mouth brought tiny trails of blood welling up.

His body warmed, and one of his hands moved, tracing gently up my arm. My breath caught sharply in my throat.

Then it was over.

His teeth withdrew but his firm and heavy body

was still on top of mine. Owen looked at me with a deep frown, then traced the bruises on my neck with a finger. I already knew that my newest bite would not bruise the same way. It had felt different, gentler, if that was possible. Was I getting used to it, or was he being more careful?

Owen was so close I felt his cold, lifeless breath against my skin when he spoke. "I was too hasty. I thought you were merely a sweet meal when I first bit you, and once I started, once I truly tasted you, it was almost impossible to stop. I hurt you more than I should have, and for that, I'm sorry."

His voice was so achingly low, creeping into the deepest parts of my body. There was almost a tremble in it, the same confused, troubled tone he'd had after the last time he'd fed. Feeding really was what changed him. The man here with me now wasn't the same monster that had just bathed me like a damned vegetable.

I sought out his gaze and held it. The black of his eyes had also lightened slightly again, and there was the tint of some other undiscernible color. *Please, let me reach him.* "You hurt me more every minute you keep me captive."

A small growl emerged from his throat and he moved until his heartbreaker of a face was inches above mine. "This pleading has to end. There will be no more conversations between us, no more heart-to-heart talks. I do not have to keep you from feeling fear or treat you kindly. I will not apologize to you, and I will treat you as I see fit. You are food, nothing more."

His voice caught, and he seemed to force the words out. His eyes were filled with an uncertainty that didn't match what he was saying. As though he was trying to win a debate on a topic he didn't believe in.

And I want to win this round. I reached up, trailing my hand down his cold cheek, hoping for him to feel the warmth of my touch, to feel me as human.

I whispered, "Nothing more?"

His gaze flicked over my face, and his mouth parted, then he turned away, looking deeply confused.

I bit my lip, my eyelids lowering as I tried to determine what that confusion meant. Had I finally gotten through to him? No. That was different. That look had almost seemed lustful, and not just for blood.

My chest tightened beneath the fluffy towel, and my mind raced.

Maybe he is seeing me as something more.

I could use that. If he was feeling something, anything for me, I had to keep trying. It's not like I hadn't acted my way through sex scenes before. I'd do anything in order to get out of there.

He shifted, lifting his weight off me, and I was worried he was simply going to up and leave. There

seemed to be no other way around it. I had to get his attention, and fast.

I propped myself up on one elbow and pressed my lips to his. There was a risk that I'd read him wrong, that he'd simply rebuff me. But he didn't.

He paused for a moment, then kissed me back.

Our mouths pressed against each other; hot meeting cold. His tongue slid against mine, tasting of blood. There was desperation in his touch, his chilled fingertips running over my arms, leaving burning trails behind them. A soft growl came from his throat.

He wants me. Not just my blood, not just as food. He wants me.

The idea thrilled me more than it should have. It was power. It was opportunity. It was also disturbing, the way my body responded in return.

I'm acting, I told myself firmly, ignoring the low ache of desire that built within me.

I tugged at his shirt, releasing buttons as his shoulders rolled above me. The firm waves of his chest muscles delighted my fingers. He was sculpted, but only his temperature reminded me of stone. His skin gave under the press of my fingers. His muscles twitched and rippled under my touch like a true human lover.

Owen's hand drifted down my body, loosening the towel around me, and coming to rest in a strong grip

on my thigh. I moaned and shuddered with need.

I thrust a hand to the fly of his black jeans. The handcuff scraped against his abs and rattled loudly. We both paused. I jerked my hand again, making a show of how the restraints kept my hand from reaching that bit farther, even though the chain was simply tangled beneath us. *Release me*, I begged with my eyes.

Owen's gaze went from heavy to wide-eyed. His body went rigid and he got off me.

He was two feet away in a flash, his brows knitted and lips twitching. "You ... you were seducing me in an attempt to escape?"

You couldn't blame a girl for trying, could you? It seemed he could though, so I said nothing. His hands clenched and unclenched, and he paced, shooting me wild glares. He was furious and it showed.

"I do not know why you make me feel as you do, Strawberry, how you leave me so ... confused. I've half a mind to kill you now and be done with it."

Scared shitless doesn't begin to describe how I was feeling. Then I remembered something, he was just as much a foodie as I was, but in a different way. He would savor my succulent blood until he could not get any more flavor or enjoyment from me, whether he liked it or not. Or whether I did either. A gourmand wouldn't light their favorite restaurant on

fire just because the veal got a bit frisky with them.

"Go on, then. Kill me now, Vampire. Do it," I challenged.

He left, slamming the door so hard that books tumbled off the bookshelf. Making him angry was a bad mistake. If he ignored me for a day or two, he might come back all undead and unemotional, and kill me for the hell of it. He might decide I was like that trendy restaurant with the great food but the bad wait times and sloppy service. He might not think me worth it anymore.

I might have to rethink my strategy. Or rethink whether it was still a strategy, or just an excuse to let my body have its way. Was I really attracted to him? That monster? No. That was a hard no.

But when he was different, more human … I had to admit, there was something there. He was still the man who had kidnapped and hurt me, who would probably kill me. *Is this what Stockholm syndrome feels like?* I didn't know, but I did know it was taking the hot bad boy attraction thing to a whole new level. I pulled my towel up and rolled over to try to sleep. There was nothing more I could do now.

A quiet cackle at the balcony jerked my head up. The thrall met my stare with her normal grin, but her eyes were bloodshot and dangerous. They weren't vacant as usual. Instead, a sinister glee lingered in them. How long had she been standing there watching me? Watching me and Owen? I jerked the satin sheet up over my exposed body.

"Prrretty girrrl." The thrall's voice scraped from her throat in a long, slow whisper.

I clung to the sheet, scared out of my wits.

The maid backed away into the unlit hall, the glint from her teeth the last thing visible in the dark.

I collapsed onto the pillow, curling up on my side. I had to get out of this madhouse.

9

I woke up the next morning, tangled in the towel with only my underwear on. A quick visit to the bathroom confirmed the corset was ruined, and the chemise remained in a puddle on the floor. I hung it to dry for later, but for now I had access to no other clothes. The room was always a pleasant temperature, so I probably could have wandered around mostly nude, but I had some modesty left in me.

I considered tearing and tying a sheet together into an elaborate toga, but resorted to simply wrapping a new big fluffy bath towel around myself.

I was happy to have something on when the maid came in again.

She surprised me, showing up at a time outside of her regular routine, her eyes lit with something not there before. She held a giant meat cleaver in one hand, and a raw whole chicken in the other. She was wearing the same ratty, dirty clothes. *Did she ever change?* Even from across the room the smell made me gag so I doubted it. The only upkeep she seemed to do on herself was to smear that bright red lipstick around her mouth in a horrific clown smile.

I don't think she saw me standing at the bathroom door, but I watched her like a petrified deer.

"Pretty girl," she crooned as she set the chicken down on the nightstand and began to cut it into bits and pieces. I kept still, hoping she wouldn't notice me and decide she wanted to chop me up as well. Terror rose in me, greater than the panic I'd felt when Owen had first sunk his fangs into me and left me fighting for my life.

The thrall kept chopping. Pieces of raw chicken flicked onto the wall. The mangled corpse minced smaller and smaller. Bones cracked. The cleaver dripped thin pink blood onto the carpet. The woman hummed a quiet song through whistling teeth. It was so bizarre, so surreal that hysteria bubbled up in my chest and I laughed silently. I covered my face with my hands to try to muffle the gasping breath I couldn't seem to control that was halfway between a sob and a giggle.

Tears welled up and I battled them back. I could not afford to cry. Tears were a luxury, and right then what I needed was a stronger, harder emotion, one that would shake me to the core and help me survive. I just couldn't seem to find it.

The chopping sound ceased. *Was she coming for me next?* If she killed me now, all it meant was Owen couldn't have me for supper.

No. At least with Owen, I still had time and the hope of escape.

I uncovered my eyes, preparing to defend myself, but the thrall stood vacant and eerie in the center of the room, staring at the ceiling. The sun picked out the grey streaks in her hair, and I realized how old she was. How many of her years had been lost in this twisted servitude? Terror of a new sort hit me. Was I going to wake up one morning, old and bent over and used up? Just how long would he keep me alive as his food? I had been thinking in terms of weeks, months, but what if it was years, or *decades*?

I suddenly felt an overwhelming surge of pity for the woman before me. Against the instincts clamoring in my head to stay quiet and hide, I edged into the bedroom.

I kept my voice soft and gentle. "Hey. What's your name?"

I don't know why I asked. I didn't really expect her to answer.

Time ticked by. I counted the seconds in the beats

of my heart.

A grotesque smile stretched its way across her painted lips, and she batted her eyelashes before saying, "Loretta." Her voice was lilting and sweet when she replied, girlish even.

Sorrow filled me. She still had a name. Perhaps she was a lot more like me than I cared to recognize. She was a prisoner here, too. Maybe more so, since her mind clearly wasn't as free as mine.

I moved closer, in slow, careful movements, circling around beside the bed. "I'm Kitty."

"Kitty …"

"Yeah, that's right. Kitty."

She crooned, "Kitty, kitty, kitty. Meeeow."

I blinked at her. The reply was crazy talk, but at least I was getting replies. My mind raced with the possibilities. I could conceivably reach her, enlist her help in escaping. Both of us could escape.

"Loretta," I said softly, as she began to clean my room in her jerky autopilot manner. Except instead of a duster or cloth, she was using a chunk of chicken, smearing the severed neck across the top of the dresser and over the bookshelves. "Loretta, do you want to get out of here?"

"Get out. Out of heeere." The word was a drawn-out hiss of air. Green rot had set in along the upper edges of her teeth, turning her gums a speckled black. My stomach churned, but I couldn't let her see my disgust. I was reaching her. I knew it.

"Yes, wouldn't you like to go home, Loretta? Where are you from?"

"Get out, kitty kitty." Her eyes became cunning and her mouth twisted into the upside-down smile of an insane clown. "Kitty, kitty, meeeeeeeeow!"

"Yes, I'm Kitty." My optimism faded with every passing second. "You're Loretta. We're prisoners but we could both get free if you would help me." I could tell I was losing whatever ground I had won. Her eyes were glassy, but something wicked sparked inside them.

She barked like a dog, lunging at me and yipping loudly. I recoiled, her body odor hitting my nose like a stone wall. She slunk closer, her mouth opening and closing in huffing pants, her tongue hanging out almost to her chin. Drool dripped in silver strands down her chest.

I backed away and hit the bed, falling onto it. "Loretta, please, listen—"

She lunged at me. The crazy-assed creature thought I was a cat, and she was a dog! She pounced on the bed and I rolled off just in time. Her jaw snapped on the air where my nose had been a moment before.

I ran around the side of the bed. Loretta went straight over and caught up with me. Her teeth closed around my arm. "Get off!" I howled, beating at her head with my free hand. When she fell back,

I saw to my horror that she'd broken the skin. The impressions of her teeth on my arm welled with blood.

Loretta stumbled backward, her tongue lolling out and her eyes rolling madly like marbles in their sockets. She barked again and I ran for the bathroom. I got there just in time, slamming the door shut as far as it could go given the chain stuck in it. She howled and barked and giggled and shrieked. I could hear her feet pattering up and down in front of the door. The chain pulled taut as I strained to break free, wanting to put some solid wood between the two of us.

Her feet quit moving, but I could see her through the crack in the door. I pressed my back to it, bracing my feet on the toilet partition wall to keep her out. The door shuddered as she kicked and punched it.

"Stop it!" I screamed. "Stop!"

My cries seemed to enrage her. The blows landed harder, jarring my spine and sending bolts of pain through my legs and feet. It felt like she was throwing her whole body against it, and I could hear her long, cracked nails scraping at the wood. I grabbed towels and wedged them like doorstops under the door.

The bathroom window was the only other way out, but I wasn't going to get far while still cuffed, so it didn't seem worth it. Until Loretta began to hit the door so hard the wood split open under her blows. I ran for the window and attempted to open it. It was stuck, but after a few frantic moments of shoving at it the frame gave with a rusty screech, and the window flung outwards.

Cool air slapped me in the face. It was raining.

I hoisted myself up, balancing my stomach on the sill to look out. The drop was sheer and long, at least two stories, if not three. When Loretta burst through the door behind me, I didn't think about it, I just tumbled out. I tried to cling to the sill, to dangle from it out of reach until she left me alone, but it was slick with rain and my fingertips slipped.

For a split second, I was in free fall.

I reached the end of the chain and my body snapped in the air, sending pain shooting into every part of me. The chain swung me like a pendulum, and I grabbed it with my other hand, clinging for dear life. The towel I wore slipped loose and fluttered to the ground far below. The cold and the sharp jerk that nearly dislocated my shoulder left me gasping and blinking to try to clear the stars out of my vision.

Icy rain hit my nearly bare body, but terror chilled me more when I looked up at the maniac's face hanging out of the window, her hands hauling at the chain.

Part of me hoped the yanking would somehow sever my restraints. If only I could survive the fall … I glanced down again. It was so far up.

"Let me go, you psycho!" I yelled, digging my feet

into the side of the stucco walls. Blood bloomed against the rough side of the house as my toes scraped and found purchase then lost it again.

She let go. I dropped a few sickening feet and screamed like a banshee. Loretta opened her mouth and howled as well. She leaned out, her ratty hair creating a stinking nimbus around her slack face. She grinned wildly, gnashing her teeth as she continued to grunt and growl like some wild animal.

She angled farther and farther out, perching like a gargoyle in the window, her eyes searching for a way to grab me and bring me back in. Little trickles of pebble-filled sand fell past me, but I didn't comprehend the danger until there was a low groaning creak.

The windowsill gave under her weight. It shot past me, a chunk of it hitting me in the side of my head. Loretta never even screamed, she just went down, her witch-like hair standing up in a nearly comical peak, and her tongue still hanging from her chapped, raw lips.

She hit the fence with an explosive crack, then smacked onto the concrete of the tennis courts. Shards of thick wood lay scattered about her bloodied and broken body. The green of the court was marred by a spreading maroon pool. She didn't move.

I buried my face into the wall. The rain could not wash away the tears that fell from my eyes. There was no way to survive that fall.

My wrist ached. I was sure it would break, or my hand would just tear free from my arm. My other hand grew slick with blood, trying to haul myself up time and again, slipping away from the chain and causing me to drop sharply each time, my weight causing fresh agony in my bound arm and wrist. The rain chilled my skin, and the wind blew into my eyes, forcing me to close them. I couldn't stop shaking.

10

Twilight hovered over the world.

Owen's face appeared out the broken window. He quickly surveyed the scene, and I thought he would reel me in like a fish on a line. Instead, he jumped out of the window as well.

He held what remained of the sill with one hand, and brought me in to him with his other, tucking me against his shoulder. He was cold, but for once, I was colder, and clung to his dry clothes desperately for warmth.

With the ease of something like flight, he lifted us both back inside.

When my feet touched firm ground again, my legs gave away underneath me, but Owen kept me upright. All of my limbs were shaking, and my head felt like it was about to detach from my body. The arm I'd hung from had no feeling left in it at all.

Owen scooped my legs up and cradled me as he stepped into the shower and ran the hot water. He wore a fine silk shirt, suit pants, and leather shoes, but didn't seem to care. He stood with me under the water, letting it drip warmth back into my body.

He undid the manacle from my tortured wrist, and I wasn't surprised when he simply moved it to my ankle. He started gently massaging the life back into my fingers.

Even though he hadn't fed since the night before, there was still some hint of humanity in him. His face had gone the color of milk—deathly pale, but with a slightly cream cast, rather than the purer white it had been. Water beaded and dripped from his long lashes, making them cling together, star-like.

"Tell me what happened," he said in a soft voice.

My teeth chattered around my words. "Your nuthouse slave attacked a chicken."

"I saw."

"Then tried to eat me."

Owen glanced at my arm, where her round, blunt teeth had left a semi-circular mark

"I'm sorry. I had no idea she'd become so free from my control." That concept seemed to trouble him deeply.

It troubled me more.

"It was probably your control that sent her insane. Keeping her brain numb, making her serve you. It was worse than being a prisoner."

Owen gave me a level look. "You would not pity her if you knew who she really was. She was one of my employees until I first realized the psychopath she was. She had killed at least three husbands and two of my waitresses before I turned her into my thrall."

In death her face had been calm and still, wiped clean. She looked like an aged woman at peace. Was she really a murderer? I recalled the gleeful way she had chopped up the chicken's carcass, the way she'd hunted me, and looked back at him. "Why didn't you let her just stand trial?"

"Do you really think that is the only justice in this world?" He snorted, and I saw his lips curl in disgust. "Do you think I didn't try that first?"

I didn't have an answer to that one.

"Things are rarely that simple, Strawberry. She was a dangerous woman, her mind lost to violent illness before I took her in. There is no need to pity her in life or death. When the justice of your kind failed, I decided I could not allow her to roam free."

Tears gathered in my eyes, then fell and splattered his chest. "But it was my fault. I tried to talk to her, tried to run away. I made her snap. I killed Loretta."

"Loretta killed herself." The words were mild. His

arms tightened almost imperceptibly around me.

I squeezed my eyes shut, but tears pushed out insistently anyway. "She didn't have to. Why didn't you just let her go?" I yelled, angry with him for no reason at all, or maybe for every reason.

"Would you rather her be free to torment innocents?"

"Why didn't you just kill her then?" I was hysterical, but I couldn't seem to stop the angry, bitter words.

He paused for a long moment. "It gets lonely."

The words opened my soul, cut me to the already raw core of my being. It got lonely in this isolated, windswept little spot of earth. In the long years that made up the centuries. In the dark hours of night without seeing the day.

He was lonely.

I whispered, barely audible over the sound of the shower running around us, "That still gives you no right to hold people against their will."

Owen set me down on my feet.

"Do you hate me so much, Strawberry?"

My feelings for him were incredibly conflicted. On one hand, I had begun to care about this side of him in ways that would have seemed unimaginable to me a few days ago, but on the other, I longed to be free of his teeth inside my flesh, and to be able to walk in the sunlight unencumbered by fear.

I dropped my head. "I hate the monster you can be."

Owen turned the shower off and carefully dried

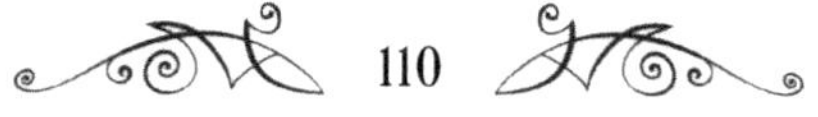

me. He wrapped me in a warm towel, then left the bathroom without a word. I didn't move, except to sit on the edge of the bathtub. I wasn't sure my legs would support me yet, and my abraded toes stung. I felt so incredibly tired.

It was some time before he came back. He returned in dry pants, bare feet, and still buttoning up a new shirt. The moonlight filtered through the windows, outlining his incredible body and handsome face. The bloodsucking thing had kidnapped, me but he was undeniably gorgeous. He picked me up and carried me out to the bedroom. I didn't try to resist.

The bedroom was spotless, cleared of any chicken remains and mess from my struggle. I looked around, amazed at how fast Owen could be when he wanted to.

I caught him staring lustfully at the pulse in my neck.

He must have noticed. "I won't feed on you after all you've been through. You need to recover."

"No. You should drink. I want you to. I like you better after you've eaten." I didn't bother anymore with games or tricks. My cards were on the table.

I sat on the edge of the bed.

Owen stood close in front of me, and I almost reached up to feel the lines of his stomach muscles I'd just seen under his shirt.

Then he knelt between my knees. His fingers traced my neck, where he'd bit below my collar bone,

and then the bite on my wrist. I held my breath, and the uncontrollable shivering I'd just recovered from struck again.

He took both of my hands in his, staring again at the damage the handcuff had done, then gently lifted my other hand to his mouth. His lips touched softly against my palm before moving to my wrist, just below the other bite mark.

I barely felt his teeth go in, just the hot rush of blood flowing between us. I swooned, and he caught me around the waist, pulling me tight against his chest, my legs wrapped either side of where he still knelt at the edge of the bed.

With my legs wrapped around him, and his arm wrapped around me, he stood up, lifting us, still clutching my wrist to his mouth and drinking. A confused rush of desire blazed through me, and I leaned into him, pressing my cheek to his neck.

He bent forward, laying me on the bed with him on top of me. His chest pressed down over mine gently. I felt a sudden, strong yearning for him to be closer. The pounding of blood rushing through me, and a blur of emotions, left me panting. My body moved of its own instinct, my hips pressing up toward his.

Owen pulled his teeth from my wrist, kissing away the blood.

When he rolled off me and sat up, I tried to hide my disappointment.

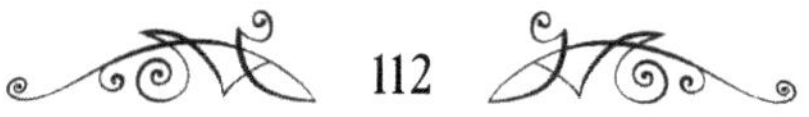

"I hope I didn't take too much. I worry about your health," he said.

I probably looked more feverish than ever. "Nah, I'm fine. I hope you, you know, had enough to eat."

He smiled. It didn't reach his worried eyes, but it was still a smile. I didn't realize that was possible. I gaped up at him in surprise. He looked … normal. Like a person instead of an undead killer. His face had color, and his eyes had expression. His skin had gone a beautiful warm ivory, but when I reached for his arm his flesh still felt cool beneath my fingers.

His hand stroked my hair tenderly, and I turned my cheek into his palm, seeking comfort even though he was the reason I needed it.

Too many complex emotions struggled to unleash themselves from inside me. Abruptly, I remembered writhing against him in a stupor of passion and blushed so hard my face felt like someone had held a blowtorch to it.

"Soooo," I finally said, making the awkward silence more awkward.

"This is so odd."

I blinked then said, "Yeah, being held against my will by a vampire who is trying to kill me slowly is certainly not anything I would've put in my yearbook as a future plan. But calling it 'odd' feels a bit understated, to be honest."

He chuckled and shook his head, his still damp

hair falling over his eyes. "You are doing something to me, Strawberry. I am feeling things I have not felt in centuries. I've never had blood like yours before. I've never been so … warm. I'm not sure I like it. It's as though when I drink from you, I become weakened somehow."

"Maybe you should let me go then," I suggested. "Keep us both happy."

My attempt at humor fell flat. His lips thinned to a line, and his shoulders sagged.

"Look, my blood probably just tastes good because I like eating nice things. Bring in any old vampire groupie and feed them that fancy food you've been giving me, and you'd probably get the same result. You don't need me."

"No, there is something uniquely special about you." It almost sounded like an apology.

His fingers weren't as cool as usual as they reached out and touched mine. I shivered at the disconcerting sensation of him feeling so human. Dawn brightened the windows, rosy little hints of light barely cracking across the uppermost edges.

Owen noticed too and stood up from the bed. How had the night passed so quickly? I remembered the stories of *Arabian Nights*, how Scheherazade stayed alive by telling the bloodthirsty sultan stories he couldn't resist. I wasn't sure what I could tell Owen that would keep me on his good side longer, so I asked him a question instead.

"Do you miss daylight?"

"I can still see sunlight, from a safe distance. I will sometimes brave it, for the right sunrise. It makes me weak though."

"Is it worth it?"

"Most things that make us weak are." His lips twitched.

A confusing realization settled heavily over me. I hated that he took my blood, battened on me like a leech, but I liked the person he became afterwards. Genuinely *liked* him.

I tried to swallow that feeling away and focus on the monster side of him. "How did you turn into a vampire? Is it like on TV? How does it happen?"

He eyed me seriously. "I won't make you a vampire, if that is what you are angling for."

"Oh darn," I retorted in as sarcastic a voice as I could muster. "What a shame, I would love to give up eating crème brulee in favor of a little O neg."

Owen smiled almost wistfully, then tucked me into the warm covers of the bed. The fluffed-up pillows and thick comforter were like heaven compared to the rough side of the building lashed with rain. I nestled into them, my eyelids growing heavy. Owen sat down above the covers. As he settled in next to me, I couldn't help but wonder what he had been like when he was alive.

That was dangerous thinking. I knew that it was. He was a vampire, purely and simply, and even though he looked human at times, he was not.

I probed again, regardless. "You didn't answer my question."

Owen looked at me. "Strawberry, you should not ask so many questions."

"If you're going to keep me here you might as well entertain me. Come on, Vampire, tell me a story." I said the words casually but under my skin my heart was racing. I loved a good story even if it was bound to have a pretty unhappy ending, which it was obvious my own was destined for.

Owen sat still for a while and I didn't think he was going to talk. Then slowly, quietly, he did. "I fell in love with a woman I thought I would die without. Instead, it happened that to be with her, I had to die."

"You became a vampire for love? Then why isn't Mrs. Vampire still around?"

"She died centuries ago."

Oh. Sympathy for him filled me, although I didn't want it to. "I'm sorry. I thought you vampires were immortal. How did she die?"

Owen moved off the bed and turned away. "I killed her."

What kind of guy killed the love of his life? Vampire guys. That's what he was. And I couldn't forget what my ultimate goal was. Escape.

Dawn showed its full face in the glass of the doors. Thin streaks of gold lay on the carpet, and Owen turned back to me with a look of such heartbreak that I felt the pang deep in my own chest. One second he was standing there looking down at me, the next he was gone. I saw a blur in the corner of my eye, and heard the door open then close, but that was all.

I lay there, confused and wrung out. The sun rose above the horizon, followed by a band of clear blue sky that showed in the distance. Birds sang loudly, and I rolled over on my back.

"I really have to get out of here," I said to the ceiling, but it didn't bother answering.

11

Time began to blend together. I found myself sleeping during the day more often and staying up with Owen at night. He would feed me then feed from me, coming in as a monster, and leaving as a man.

He was gentler now when he fed, and the newer bites didn't leave gory marks like his earlier ones did. But still, I felt my health waning slowly, as though every time he drank from me, a few days of my life were sucked away.

Having the cuff around my ankle instead of wrist made it a little more out of sight, out of mind, but I still regularly tested its strength. No new chances at escape emerged, and some days I almost gave up any hope of freedom in my future. My thoughts and emotions grew so conflicted my insides were at war.

The emotions spilled out, making me a teary, giggly, snappy mess. Mood change extraordinaire, that was me. The fact that Owen, on the other hand, seemed to be growing more and more patient, caring, and sensitive in turn was strangely infuriating.

One night, Owen brought me a simple, but truly delicious, meal of handmade ravioli filled with whole egg yolks, coated in crispy sage and burnt butter sauce. He wandered out to the balcony, staring at the stars while I ate. When I finished, I followed him out, figuring it was his turn.

The long chemise from my costume I still wore hung off my shoulders and trailed behind me on the carpet.

Instead of biting me, Owen asked, "Do you swim?"

"Yes. Why?"

"Would you like to?"

"Uh, I guess?"

Without another word, he gathered me in his arms, released the shackle off my ankle, and leaped to the top rail of the balcony. I screamed. I wasn't sure if vampires could commit suicide by falling to their death and I didn't want to find out either. I *did* know I was very fragile and breakable even if he wasn't. We took flight. Terror had me in its grip and I screamed all the way down.

He landed featherlight on the concrete below.

"You still don't trust me," he said.

unLife

I was shocked that he could talk given that my arms were locked in a death grip around his neck. I could have killed him if he wasn't already dead.

"I trust you as much as a drunken frat boy, pulling stunts like that," I snapped.

With a troubled look, he placed me gently onto my feet. It struck me how different he had become. His flashes of coldness still happened, but he rarely seemed inhuman.

"Go, swim. Enjoy some exercise." He nodded toward the water.

There was an exit gate to the side. I stared at it for a moment, knowing there was no way I could outrun Owen. With a sigh, I turned my attention to the pool.

The naturalistic style of it was stunning, and I couldn't resist wading slowly in. The chemise spread around me like a cloud, and I enjoyed the way it moved in the water, but it tangled too much around my limbs to allow me to swim. I ducked under the water and slipped it off. I felt a little self-conscious in my lacy underwear in front of Owen, but the water was dark, cozy, and concealing. My black hair hung down long, swirling around my chest, and the waterfall played a soft tune as it dripped and dropped at the other end of the pool.

The water was blood warm, the moon above sent spangles across the tiny little wavelets created by

my movements. The flowers planted around the pool gave off a heavenly smell of rose and jasmine.

I plunged under, gliding through a few leisurely laps, then swam over to the side where Owen sat, watching me silently. I folded my arms on the edge.

The vitality of being immersed in water in this dreamlike setting left my philosophical.

"How do you see the world? Is it different to when you were human?" I asked.

"As a vampire, your senses and emotions become different. Some are stronger, and some fade away entirely … But it's been so long I can hardly remember. How do you see it?"

I stared around me. Everything was sharp and angular, black and gray with occasional splashes of color. The roses were scarlet but the dark shadows behind them made the blood red of them seem even brighter, arterial even.

The sky was an immense dark bowl with bright pinpricks of stars, and the moon hung wafer thin and bright in one corner. The mountain was cloaked by darkness, making its edges softer, kinder.

I described what I saw in halting tones. I was used to reciting other people's lines, not putting my own thoughts into words. It was a strange feeling that left me unsure and self-conscious. He sat on the lounge chair, leaning forward to listen, elbows on his thighs.

"No. I do not see the world the way you do. Maybe I never did."

He seemed softer tonight, less intense.

"Do you miss the day?"

"I can see sunlight from afar."

"I know, but do you miss it? I mean, being out in it and feeling it on your face, getting a tan, or hanging out at the beach, that kind of thing."

"I never really *hung out* at the beach." His tone was a bit sarcastic. "I do miss riding though."

"Riding? Like on a bike or something?"

"No, on horseback." He stared out into space. "I used to love to ride."

"Why don't you do it anymore? I mean, can't you ride a horse at night?"

"Animals tend to shy away from me now."

Oh. I had forgotten for a moment he was a monster. He seemed so human tonight. Pity filled me. I fought the sensation. He didn't deserve my pity. But his face was suffused with a kind of longing I had never seen on it before. I wasn't sure what to say, but he spoke, saving me from having to say anything.

"The first woman I fell in love with I met riding. Rather, I was riding, and her horse had spooked and was running away with her across Hyde Park."

A tiny smile ghosted across his lips. "Her hat had come off, and she had slung her leg across the horse in a decidedly unladylike manner, which hiked her

skirts up almost to her thighs. Still, she managed to get the stallion under control."

A haunted kind of happiness crinkled the corners of Owen's eyes and he shook his head, staring across at the waterfall.

"She sounds like one hell of a horsewoman."

"She was a lot of things."

A coyote howled from somewhere and I flinched, a movement he saw though I hadn't thought he was paying attention at all.

"There's nothing to fear. They can't get past the walls."

Owen stirred again and sighed, a heavy sigh that sounded hurt and tired all at once.

"I wish time had not moved on so much."

"What do you mean?"

He laughed but there was no humor in it. "I mean, I don't know how to live in this time. It wasn't something I thought about before I was turned, that time would march on and leave me behind."

"Progress can be hard to adjust to," I agreed. "I guess most of us don't really notice it too much until we look back and think about it. My mom used to talk about the microwave, how she never had one growing up until she was a teenager because they just weren't around, or because they were too expensive. She barely uses hers now because she never got used to it. But for my generation, well, I can't imagine not having one."

Owen nodded. "Every time I think I adapt, something new comes along. Sometimes so fast it has already passed to the next thing before I have had a chance to catch up."

I swirled a slow three-sixty in the water, looking at the vast mansion behind me, full of expensive modern appliances. "You don't seem to be doing too badly. Why did you turn vampified then, if it's so hard? I mean didn't you think about forever being such a long time?"

For a minute I was sure he would tell me to mind my own business but then he spoke, "At the time being with her forever seemed like the proposition of paradise and I had no idea of how little like that it would be."

I didn't have to ask. I knew she was the girl on the runaway horse. The woman he had at some point, for some reason killed. The breeze ran across my body. My hair dripped down my back and the scent of chlorine grew stronger. I shivered.

"Adelle St. Delaurents. She was the daughter of a duke and I was the second son of a mere baron, an officer in the military whose entire pay went to support myself in what was hardly a high style. The match was impossible. Adelle's family already had her betrothed to a very wealthy man when we met."

I gaped slightly. Talk of dukes and barons made

my head spin in a very not-in-Kansas-anymore kind of way. It was so far outside my field of experience, like something from a period romance, not something someone brought up in a conversation about their ex.

Owen continued, "She had to wed. Back then, women were little more than commodities, even the ones born into privilege had little or no control over their lives. A beautiful daughter was often sold off to the highest bidder. They were given huge wardrobes and trotted out to balls and fetes and soirees so they could have a chance to make the best match possible for their family. It was all done with little, if any, consideration to their heart or desires."

The bitterness that lay in his words stirred sympathy in me. The lack of freedom women of a past era suffered cut close to home, especially given my current situation. "Why didn't you two run off together?"

"To run away would have meant causing the ruination of her entire family. She married the man she was betrothed to. It drove me crazy. Her husband was thirty years older, and he was cruel. He found her too headstrong and outspoken, and he spared no mercy in his attempts to change her."

I shuddered. I could well imagine the methods he employed in his attempts at reeducating Adelle.

"We managed to see each other at times, but it was never enough. Soon, we got careless, and her husband became suspicious."

There was a lengthy pause. I did my best to wait it out but after a minute I couldn't stand it anymore. "You totally got her pregnant, right?"

"No. Regardless, he took her away to France for a year and my company went to India. When I came back, she was ill, close to death. She recovered slowly, but she was never the same."

I didn't ask what her illness was. Back then, even the common flu could be deadly. But also, part of me worried that if I knew, I'd care more, and I was doing my best not to care.

"She became terrified of dying. More, she was afraid of getting old. Adelle was well aware that her only commodities were her youth and her beauty. She had begun to take all sorts of weird little cures. I suppose in retrospect it was no odder than what people do now—facelifts, having botulism shots, and getting their skin sanded down—but at the time it seemed very strange. She would take these long baths in milk and roses. She coated her body in honey and had her maids wrap her in muslin strips. She used sand and sugar to wash her face. It became an obsession."

"Did it keep her young?"

"No. No, Strawberry, that did not keep her young."

His tone didn't change but there was something, a faint twist to his full and ridiculously kissable lips, a subtle movement that expressed sorrow. I could almost see the young man he had been, madly in love and unable to do anything about it. *He's still a vampire. Still your kidnapper.* I didn't have to care about his story. I didn't have to care about him. I was trying my very best not to. But the least I could do was listen. I wanted to know more of the story, and he seemed to want to tell it.

"After France, her temperament also changed. I thought merely that she was still agonizing over her illness and her brush with death, but she was longing for something, or someone else. I wanted more than anything to save her. But she wanted something I could not give her."

He took a long breath and rubbed his elegant fingers across his forehead. "I learned later that she'd met Rene, a vampire, in France. She coaxed him into coming to London, and then she began to coax him into turning her. I had no idea. I thought … I thought she no longer loved me. I thought she had gotten bored with me and had simply taken on a new lover. Rene was wild and dashing. He was always turning up at the strangest hours and was always full of life latest at night while the rest of us were yawning in our cups. I thought it was no wonder she had turned her affections away from me." Owen paused, staring up at the stars.

"I thought it was over, and tried to move on. One night, I noticed Adelle and Rene, out late on the street. He was being violent with her, and I saw red. I followed them as they went into her townhouse, and I heard her screaming. I ... I was so naïve. I thought that was my chance, to save her as I'd always wished I could. I burst into the house, and when I saw Rene on top of her ... I killed him. I ran him through with my sword."

A hush fell again. The only sounds were the crickets in the grass, and the tinkling fall of the pool's waterfall. I was breathless, tingling with anticipation, eager to hear more, but it was obvious the telling of it was hard on him.

"She looked up and her face was ... she was deathly pale, and at first I thought I had struck her as well, that my sword had run them both through. Then I realized she was bleeding from a wound on her breast that had not been made by me, but rather by Rene's teeth."

I reached up and brushed my fingers over the closed wound beneath my collarbone where Owen had bitten me.

"He ... evaporated. I can't describe it any other way. He turned to dust in front of my eyes. I was horrified and repulsed. I knew ... I had heard the stories of vampires, but to see it, I thought I would go mad."

I scoffed softly. *I could relate to that.*

"I wanted to save her, to keep her from that fate,

but there was no going back for her, she had turned. She told me she needed blood or she would die. Rene had given her enough of his to turn her, but she had to feed. Part of me knew the best thing to do would be to kill her. Just run her through and allow her soul to be judged, but I couldn't do it."

His voice actually broke, and I saw a glint on his cheek that couldn't be anything except a tear. "I loved her too much. I could not kill the woman I loved."

A huge, salty lump rose in my throat. My chest felt tight, and my heart literally ached. I had never loved anyone that much, and it didn't seem like I would ever get the chance given my circumstances, but I wanted to. I wanted to love so much that impossible choices made sense.

I should have stopped the words that came from my mouth next, but in the usual fashion, they spilled anyway, making a mess. "But you did. You did kill her."

Owen's head swung around to glare at me. "Out of the water. It's time to go back to your room."

I stood, dumbstruck. I would have kicked myself if my foot wasn't already wedged in my mouth.

Owen reached down and grabbed me under my shoulders, hoisting me out of the pool and onto the pebbled edge in one swift motion. Water ran off me, pooling under my feet. Owen still gripped me, standing before me like a vengeful god.

I reached up to touch his face, a motion of comfort, of apology. He snatched my hand and squeezed it between us.

I stammered and shook my head. "I'm sorry. I was just more confused than anything, I mean, about why. Thank you for telling me your story, for opening up to me. I can't imagine what you've been through, what you've suffered. To still be this much of a man, a good man—kidnapping aside—is a miracle. I just wish I could understand you more, maybe heal anything in you that hurts." I didn't even know what I was saying, words spilled out of my mouth as my heart ached in unwanted sympathy for him.

So many emotions flashed through his expression. He seemed so human now. Not just from him revealing his past, but from the level of emotion and compassion and vulnerability I saw in those dark eyes.

His voice was a tortured whisper. "I did. I did kill her." His eyes closed, and he buried his face in my neck. I thought for a moment he would bite me, but instead, he just rested his face there, cool cheek against my skin. His fingers reached up and twisted into my hair. And he held me like that as time stood still around us.

The water dripping off me, and the cool air left me chilled. Owen's lifeless body did nothing to warm me. A succession of shivers shuddered through me,

encouraged by my confused emotions.

"What if this is my curse, to kill the women I—" His body tensed around mine then he backed away. His face was a mixture of fury and confusion which left me shaking even harder.

His eyes landed on my almost naked body and softened. "You're cold."

I nodded, teeth chattering.

Silently, he lifted me up, my body limp and limbs heavy as he carried me upstairs to my bedroom.

I resisted kittenishly as he laid me down, hiding my wrist. But he did not try to cuff me. Instead, he laid down beside me, drawing me into the hollow under his arm.

He nuzzled into my neck, and his teeth sank gently into the skin. I relaxed, allowing it to happen. That slow languor that was left over from my swim drifted into something else, something so sweet and golden edged that I embraced it. The soft heat of blood flowing from me to him was such an intimate connection, a crimson thread connecting us.

His teeth left my flesh, but he remained curled around me. He whispered, "Thank you, for listening."

His cool body wrapped around me and I faded into sleep. In the hazy, dreamlike moments before slumber took me, he whispered again, so softly it felt like the wind from the distant mountains. "Strawberry. I don't know what to do with you."

unLife

I woke up several hours later.

Owen was still asleep beside me, and dawn peeked under the drawn curtains, a blaze of pink and gold. I blinked, feeling a bit disoriented, and then I moved my leg that had been tucked under Owen's.

The chain rattled. I stared at it in utter disbelief. He had chained me again, despite the fact he was in the bed next to me. Anger swelled under my skin, flaring red hot.

I didn't know what to think, what to do. I went and locked myself in the bathroom until I heard him leave, then returned to bed to sleep out the daylight. I blinked back tears that made no sense as I settled back under the covers that still smelled like him.

12

I awoke around midday. Lying in bed, staring at the ceiling, I played through what had happened last night, and what in all-mighty fuck it could have meant. Who cuddled up to and slept with their captor? This idiot. I had tried to remain detached, but Owen and his damn heartbreak edged in under my armor, and the thought of pushing him away after that had felt too hard.

I *liked* having him next to me, holding me tight. I grunted and kicked at the sheets. I did *not* care about him. I just needed to release the pent-up energy and angst brought on by the vampire opening up to me like some tragic Victorian romance hero. It probably didn't mean a god damned thing. Still, I didn't know where I stood anymore. Had our relationship changed?

When I finally sat up, the room, at least, had changed. I stared at the wide-open armoire, not quite sure that my mind wasn't playing tricks on me. Clothes overflowed from it, heaps of silk, satin, and lace in exquisite colors. My eyes couldn't turn away.

I got up and went to the wardrobe, my fingers stroking the garments lovingly. They all looked incredibly expensive—the perfect cut and exquisite fabrics gave that away. When I had first arrived in Hollywood, I had been wearing designer labels head-to-toe. The clothes I had worn then had names screaming from their back pockets, or across the chest. I wore them until a producer told me that wealthy people never wore such garish things. Very wealthy people wore clothes that were incredibly expensive due to the cost of the workmanship and materials, not the cost of the giant letters emblazoned on them. By wearing those clothes, I was marking myself as a rube.

I had learned to scour the thrift shops and consignment stores, looking not at names of designers on the outside of the clothes, but the things that most people never thought to look for. I had a small amount of incredibly good stuff that was pre-owned, which Lisa always seemed to get her mitts on, but I had never held anything brand new in my hands before.

Alongside the couture fashion were some equally quality comfy clothes; organic cotton singlets, yoga pants and merino hoodies. *How strange.*

There was a heavy white envelope on the dresser. I opened it and pulled out the elegant stationary within. A man's strong, back-slanting handwriting met my eyes, and I traced the letters with one finger, knowing it could only be Owen's.

These are for you. Over the years I have developed a taste for the luxuries in life. I can most certainly afford the finest of things, and I have been remiss in not providing you with clothing and other necessities. I ask your forgiveness for that oversight. Immortality has also taught me the value of comfort, so I hope you will find some comfort in this selection. The emerald green and gold dress is the one I would like to see you in at dinner. Please be ready at exactly eleven pm. This will be a formal dining occasion.

I read the words twice, and then found the gown he had referred to in his note. It was a marvelous confection of dark green silk that I knew would cling like a second skin. The top was a corset type thing, woven through with metallic gold thread. The laces tied tightly on the back, but closer inspection revealed a tiny and nearly invisible zipper on the right side that would make it easy for me to dress myself.

I went a little crazy pawing through the selection. There were not just outer garments but undergarments as well, lacy bra and panty sets, sheer stockings, and even shoes of all different heel types and styles.

I hugged a swimsuit to my body and danced around a bit wildly in a burst of exhilarated joy.

All the clothes were just my size and for an hour or so I delighted in trying them on, preening, and primping, caught up in the excitement of it all. I mostly tried on the dresses, which made up the bulk of the clothing. I wanted to put some new panties on since I'd been wearing my old ones for far, far too long, but had no idea how I was meant to do that with a chain around my ankle. It took me half an hour to work out I had to feed the fabric through the gap between the cuff and my skin. That was when reality crashed in.

I was still chained up. I had not won any freedom.

I hadn't succeeded in making Owen see me as human. I had simply succeeded in earning the status of a spoiled little pet, a comical little pooch, or ... I shuddered, remembering Loretta calling me Meow Kitty. I was no more cared for than one of those little dogs toted around in a specially designed purse. I was just a belonging to Owen, still a prisoner. A prisoner with comforts, but no less a possession.

My happiness deflated as though it were a leaky balloon. I crumpled onto the bed, head flopping over the side, and stared at the heaps of gorgeous things, feeling my humanity slipping away. What hurt the worst was that I *had* started to care about him, despite every effort not to, despite him being a

vampire. It was the human-ness he had displayed lately that made me care about him. Yet he seemed determined to turn me into a mere object, a prettily dressed and plated meal, a pet who would eventually give her life for his.

The chain was a hateful but visible reminder of how little I should trust him. I was no better off than a cute Chihuahua that was dressed in a funny suit then tethered in the yard so it didn't run for the road.

The darkness inside me grew more complete and I had no energy left to reach for the light. Depression weighed me down so much that I literally sagged into the mattress. How did I put a screeching halt to this before I gave in entirely? Before I let my life be taken from me, one way or another?

With my head tilted back at that angle, a reflection of light behind the side table caught my eye. I looked again, my heart doing little jumping jacks when I realized what I saw.

Loretta's cleaver.

It lay hidden under the bedside table, only a thin wedge of its handle showing. She must have dropped it there before going feral and chasing me to her death. Owen had cleaned the room afterwards, but he must have missed it. It had been lying there, hidden from both of us for all this time.

I dropped to my knees and picked it up. It was real and solid in my hands. A giggle, born of hysteria, bubbled out of my mouth.

I tested the edge with my thumb. *Ouch, sharp!*

I caught my breath at the enormity of the possibilities. I could hack my way through the chain or try to hack out the section of bedpost that the chain was attached to. If it came to it, could I cut my foot off to free my ankle? Or could I just kill Owen when he came to have dinner, stick the cleaver into his neck and cut his bloodsucking head right off his shoulders?

That last thought made me go cold. *Could I do that to him?* No. I didn't think I could. I wanted to hate him, to think of him as only a heartless monster, but the truth was some part of him was human. I had seen it with my own eyes. I could not kill that person.

I set to work on the bed, figuring I might need my foot at some point for a successful escape. Half an hour later, I stared at the barely splintered post in disbelief wondering if I really did need my foot. It would have been easier and likely less messy to simply chop it off. The post was solid as a rock, ugly gouges and deep scars marred it, but it still held.

I attacked it again, grunting and trembling with exertion. There was a strange groan and hunk of wood fell away. It was taking too long. I could sense the hours slipping away. I could almost feel the night, and Owen, approaching. I hit the post with the cleaver again with renewed vigor, only to have the cleaver fall apart in my hands. The blade fell to the mattress and I stared at the useless handle, wondering if this were all some cosmic joke.

The sky was warming outside, turning from blue to syrupy orange, dipping into night.

I tossed the handle and blade to the floor, then lay on my back. With a battle cry of frustration, I used both feet like a battering ram, kicking, even though it sent waves of pain through my legs. The post cracked, creaked, and then it toppled down, almost braining me in the process.

I sat up, tugging the chain at my ankle. It swung free against the bed and I shouted out, "Yes!"

The cuff was still locked firmly around my ankle, and the long length of chain attached to it, so I had to scoop it up and carry it. I was still wearing a shirt from my earlier dress ups, but no pants. There was no time for pants. Daylight had almost gone.

I didn't stop for anything. I ran down the stairs, pelting for the front door. I could see it right in front of me and I reached it, opened it, and almost cried at the sight of the front lawn, turned golden by the strong final rays of sunlight.

I had one foot out the door when an arm snaked around my middle and yanked me off my feet. All the air whooshed out of my diaphragm and I fought, flailing and kicking, beating at the hands that were tangled around my torso.

A soft, hissing sizzle filled my ears, and I choked on the smoky fumes clouding my eyes.

Owen cursed, but still held tight.

He dragged me back into the house.

"Let me go. Please, just let me go!" I howled and kicked at his shins.

Owen turned me around to face him. His skin showed signs of ash and burns, but healed before my eyes.

I had been so close. With freedom so near within reach, every fiber of me yearned for it. But at the same time, I felt at home within his arms. Confused, appalled, and at home. A rough sob tore out of my throat, and I wept loudly.

He dropped his forehead onto mine, still holding me tight, arms wrapped fully around me. "You can't leave, Strawberry. You can't leave me. Please don't leave me."

13

He held me until I ran out of tears. Then led me back to my room, and re-attached my chain to a different bedpost.

"Dress, and we will dine." His voice was commanding, but gentle.

I had nothing else left to do but obey. I moved like the living dead, all spirit and fight gone.

I discovered that the bathroom also had some new additions. High end organic hair products, and a few pieces of jewelry that matched the green dress he had asked me to wear. I found a clever little makeup kit, expensive as all hell and brand new. I would have killed to have it in my former life. Now, I just stared at it, empty and uncaring.

I showered, taking my time. I felt no need to

rush. I wasn't going anywhere. Owen wasn't going anywhere. I was stuck in this house with him forever and couldn't even bring myself to hate that outcome anymore. I'd all but given up.

I dried my hair and pulled it up. Looking in the mirror, I saw a vague and indefinable difference in my face. I was thinner, yes, but there was something else there too, something I could not put a finger on. Something like defeat.

I dipped the make-up brushes into the little pots of pure mineral pigment, smudging shadows around my eyes, and coloring in my lips. I plumped out my eyelashes and daubed blush on the apples of my cheeks.

I took the green dress off the hanger and shimmied it on over my head. The green and gold silk clung to my body like wet cloth, and the corset pressed my breasts into a perfect shape, rounding out the tops and accentuating the small puncture marks in them.

I put on the matching emerald earrings. *Those aren't real emeralds, are they?* But I couldn't bring myself to put the bracelet on. I couldn't have something around my wrist again.

I stepped out of the bathroom and found Owen waiting patiently in the middle of the bedroom.

My ire and sadness evaporated like mist before the sun. He looked splendidly handsome in an ebony suit with a scarlet silk shirt below it. His thin, black tie was perfect, his shoes shined to nearly nuclear glow, and his dark hair swept up and back from his forehead, accentuating the high angular planes of his face.

"You look beautiful," he said.

"You too." My voice sounded weak and thin. My heart fluttered like a schoolgirl's, and I could not stop looking at his broad shoulders, the way his fingers lightly rested against his thighs, and the long sweep of his lean legs. There was a little color in his cheeks, just a hint of rosiness high on the cheekbones, and his eyes were paler than I'd ever seen them.

"I like your hair up."

I touched it self-consciously. I was way overdue for a trim and I had not had access to a straightener in ... *How long had I been here?* My hair had returned to its naturally wavy state, and even though I had pinned it up, small curls escaped to frame my face. I had outlined my eyes dramatically, using long sweeps of eyeliner and a rich gold-green shadow, as well as a lot of mascara. His eyes said he approved of me entirely and I felt a flush of pleasure at his obvious desire.

Here he stood, the monster who'd robbed me of my freedom, who'd caught me and crushed my hopes of escape just moments before, and we were playing out some dress up fantasy like kids on prom night. I felt

strangely hollow, like all my emotions were happening on my skin but not actually reaching inside me. I think he noticed because his smile faltered.

He walked up to me and scooped me into his arms. "Trust me."

I nodded, absently. I did trust him, in a way. He held my life in his hands every day since he'd stolen my freedom. I knew he would protect my life, if nothing else.

He moved so fast, all I sensed was a rush of speed and blurring landscape.

One minute we were in the house, the next, we were standing on a mountain top. A few tall trees created a wall on one side, and the scent of pine hovered thickly in the air, mixing with the smell of ocean drifting from a cliff down the rocky slope.

"Where are we?" My eyes darted left and right, hoping to see a house, or a car, or any sign of civilization, but it was just us high on a windswept peak.

"Come, sit."

A table stood to the right, draped in fine white linens, laid with china so thin it was nearly transparent, and a selection of wine bottles formed a centerpiece. French champagne, a rich, deep red, and a bottle of German ice wine, accompanied by appropriate glassware for each. Silver domed trays covered the table, and I walked to it, numbed and uncertain. Was this real?

Had he put me under a spell? The last time he'd tried, it didn't work. But I was still confused. He had no maid anymore that I knew of.

"Are the catering staff hiding behind the trees? Or …"

He grinned, a boyish and charming quirk of his lips that melted my heart. "I did this for you. I have always cooked for you, Strawberry."

Oh, that figured. Gorgeous, rich, and a good cook. Of course, he was a bloodsucking kidnapper and killer; he had to have some kind of fucking fault.

His hand was cold on my back as he pulled out my chair and seated me. How ironic that a vampire had better manners than most guys I had dated. I gratefully accepted a glass of sparkling champagne, the fizz bringing notes of apple and oak into my nose.

Owen extended an empty glass to mine, chinking gently, before serving my dinner.

"What's the occasion?" I asked. Don't get me wrong, I didn't want to look a gift vampire in the mouth, but I wasn't used to being spoiled like this. Ever. Even with human men.

Owen paused with my plate in his hand. I wished I hadn't asked the question at that moment because I wanted that food. Now.

He smiled softly and replied, "You provide me with delicious sustenance. I simply felt the urge to return the favor."

"I would say aaaw, but it's not a favor really, now is it, if I have no choice in the matter?" I snapped at him, but was smiling as well. A mischievous mood had taken over. *Holy hot dogs. Am I flirting with him?*

The thought was wiped away by the appearance of sea scallops ceviche. The dish was bursting with the flavors of the citrus marinade that cooked the scallops, leaving them tender and supple. Maybe it was the food, but I felt my hollowness beginning to subside, drowned out by an eagerness for fine dining, good company, and my own desire to be normal, or at least pretend for a little while.

The bread he sliced and put on my side plate was crusty outside, fluffy and filled with air pockets inside. The butter melted into it and I sopped up marinade with the tail end of the bread, not caring about my manners.

Owen watched me curiously.

I spoke through a half-full mouth. "I bet your fancy old-fashioned girls ate all pretty like."

"They did. They even took classes to teach them to eat properly."

"What did they even eat back then? Potatoes? Gruel? Put a plate like this in front of anyone and I dare them not to lick it clean."

Owen laughed. "I do enjoy seeing the pleasure you take in your meals."

Ditto. The thought hit me with shock, remembering

a time when Owen sunk his teeth into my thigh. I fanned my heated cheeks and shook the thought away.

Next up was a salad with grilled peaches and goat cheese as the main flavor points. I was on the verge of proposing long before the duck confit showed up. I was beyond sated. Owen had poured the wine generously into my glass throughout the meal, and I was tipsy from alcohol and the surfeit of food.

Placing the last bite of juicy duck into my mouth, I let out a long, low moan that sounded truly sexual. Good food really did turn me on.

"Enjoying yourself?" Owen asked, an eyebrow raised.

"Uh huh," I murmured, leaning back in the chair, basking in the fullness of my stomach. "Some entertainment would have been nice with the dinner though. You could hula dance naked on the table for me."

I thought dinner was done, but with a truly wicked smile, Owen retrieved the final dish. He bent on one knee and opened the dome in front of me, like opening a diamond ring box. I squeed and said, "Yes, yes, yes!"

The chocolate soufflé was light, high, and so beautiful it seemed almost a sin to break its surface. Not that I minded being a sinner. I certainly wasn't going to let its looks, or the fact that my belly was protruding horribly, stop me.

I raised a bite of it to my mouth and he said, "Tell me how it tastes."

I tried to, but I wasn't sure he understood. How many years had it been since he'd had real food? I felt pity for him again, not being able to enjoy things like chocolate and wine must truly suck. I felt myself stumbling over my words the same way I had the other night at the pool, and I blushed at my own incompetence. He didn't seem to mind though. He just watched me, his eyes full of a shimmering, vulnerability that seemed far too human.

14

The meal ended and my belly felt swollen and too full, but it was a good feeling. The wind had picked up. It rustled through the trees and sent tiny leaves shivering down onto my shoulders. Under my bare feet the earth was still warm from the day. My toes dug into a loamy layer of dead leaves and pine needles gone soft from rain and wind. The small tendrils of my hair that had escaped the knot I had pulled it up into, lifted from my face and neck. The sky was ebony, a few clouds scuttled across its surface, and the bright stars pricked the sooty colored down with gleaming sparkles of light. It was so exquisite that a lump rose into my throat.

Owen helped me up from the table and we wandered down to the edge of the cliff. I gazed at the jumble of boulders and the shimmering motion of the tide far below. A ledge sat about halfway down the mountainside, a glittering streak of mica running through it. Dread coiled into my belly. What if I fell? My toes curled into the edge and I heard tiny pebbles rattling and sliding down the sides of the mountain.

Owen wrapped his strong arms around me. The intense cold coming from his body made me shiver as I leaned against him. I rested my head on his chest, hoping to hear a heartbeat, but there was nothing, just the feel of his body beneath mine.

"Trust me, Strawberry," he said.

Then he jumped.

We went over, and that time I didn't scream. I had learned to trust him, to know he wouldn't let me fall. That trust made me immensely sad. The first guy in my entire life that I trusted was not only going to hurt me but eventually kill me. I tried to ignore the tightness in my chest, forcing myself to take a breath, and hoped my shudders would be mistaken for nerves rather than sorrow.

Owen floated easily to the ground with me still clasped in his arms. The tang of the sea was tangible. The sound of the waves slapping the shore, and an occasional caw from a nocturnal bird, fired up my emotions. The ragged remains of the depression lifted, and I laughed loudly as we landed in the sand.

unLife

The mountain loomed over us and the lights of a jet plane winked red overhead. I could hear a faint music—a sign of life existing far beyond the confines of the world that only included Owen and me.

Owen carried me easily. My arms were still wound around his neck and his scent came to me, a little musky and coppery. The smell of blood and cologne.

He let me down and we stood together, watching the waves nip at our toes. A swell ran across my bare feet, awash with shells and sand. As the salt water rushed over my skin, it stung the light abrasions left on my ankle from the cuff. Again, I was reminded that I was nothing more than a pet on a very long leash. Hatred flared inside me. Even now, I wore the evidence of my imprisonment.

I stepped away from Owen, folding my arms against the sea breeze which suddenly left me chilled. I knew that the look I wore wasn't kind or happy. I could have been a queen in exile. Really, I was just a woman with nowhere to go, too stubborn to give in.

Owen asked, "If you could do one thing right now, anything, what would it be?"

"Escape." The word came to my lips instantly. I didn't even need to think. It was the truest answer I could give. No matter how attractive he was, how beautiful the clothes were, or how amazing the dinner, I was always going to try to escape. I wanted to agree to go to dinner, not be forced. I wanted to

buy my own clothes. I wanted to be free.

"That isn't possible for you."

"It is if you turn your back and let me run like heck," I said. I faced him, stalking him down. Every step forward I took, he took one back. "I'm never going to stop trying to get away. Until the day you kill me, I am going to want out. I will never be happy being a vampire's prisoner."

He stopped suddenly, before I could halt myself. I started backwards but tripped on the hem of the dress. One of his strong arms caught me around the waist as I dipped back, like the whole thing was choreographed. Our lips came close, so close I could feel a puff of cold air leave his and land on mine.

He brought me slowly up to my feet. His gaze was turned down, and brows lowered. "I see."

He lifted me into his arms but didn't speed us through the air in a flash. He walked at a regular, human pace along the beach. Cradled against his chest, the sound of the waves, the steady rock of his footsteps, and the heavy food and wine filling my belly, lulled me.

I awoke in a comfortable position, semi-reclined on a leather couch. It wasn't my room. Was it Owen's? The furniture was similar, but there was no window, and the bed had black sheets, shimmering like dark water under the low light. I didn't need to check to know I was chained to the bed. Owen sat at the other end of the lounge, holding a full glass of red wine, staring at it as though it was about to reveal the secrets of life itself.

"You're drinking wine?" I asked, skeptical of the scene before me.

"No. It turns to ash on my tongue. I don't know why I even tried, why I thought it would be different ..."

He set the glass down on the table beside him.

When he turned to me, his eyes were glossy, as though they were close to tears. He held me in his gaze.

"I've said how I feel you are changing me, how I didn't know whether I liked it. I know now. I do like it. I want this. But it torments me, as though something miraculous lies just out of reach. It torments me, because I feel the wrongs I have done you, but I cannot let you go."

He lifted a hand and stroked his fingers down my cheek, so softly I barely felt it. The touch made sparks leap between us—sparks neither of us could deny though we both knew we should. The moment hung suspended, rife with possibilities. I wanted him, and I could see it on his face—he wanted me, too.

Words shook from my lips. "You have changed. You seem so different to the vampire who first locked me up. He was cold, distant. Not anymore."

There was no accusation in his voice, only pain. "And yet you only want to flee from me."

Heat stung in my nose, and tears threatened.

I couldn't deny it any longer. I couldn't fight it. "I want my freedom. But I don't want to flee from you."

I had never seen him so open, so warm. His hand cupped my jaw and he leaned close, touching his forehead to mine.

"Kitty," he whispered.

I almost sobbed. "Owen."

Our lips met in a kiss that left me shaken to the cells of my being. He always elicited a primal response in me, one that was as thrilling as it was frightening. Sensations broke out along my nerve endings and my skin raised with gooseflesh. My tongue met his and tangled, slid away, met again. Passion left me dizzy.

His fingers brushed across my skin, tracing lines of desire over my bare shoulders and arms. I slowly worked to free his tie, slide back his jacket. I took time to caress each button of his shirt as I pushed it open, revealing his chest inch by inch.

Owen tugged at the lace up binding of my corset. I was about to reach for the hidden zipper when he took the strong layered fabric in two hands and tore it off me. I threw myself back into his arms, pressing my bare chest against his. When I licked along his neck and sucked at his earlobe, he groaned deeply, pulling me into his lap and running a hand under the silk skirt, up my legs. My mouth opened in a silent, helpless plea of longing.

unLife

Desire built through my body to an almost unbearable ache. He pushed me back, flat onto the lounge, hands running across my chest, belly, hips, gently torturing me with his cold touch on my skin. He kissed his way down between my breasts, looped his tongue around my navel, then kissed the soft skin of my inner thigh. My eyes rolled with pleasure and I wanted nothing more than Owen, Owen, Owen.

He stood up, taking me with him, and placed me on the bed, laying me down so carefully. I felt fragile and cherished all at once. It was a giddy moment, made more so by the rush of lustful longing when he whipped off his belt and let his pants fall away.

He moved over me, bringing his weight down carefully, his dark eyes seeking mine for consent, for assurance. I nodded, wrapping my hands into his hair and kissing him deeply.

We cried out together as we joined. Pleasure shattered all of my defenses. I had no reservation, no hesitation. All I knew was the incredibly powerful need that built up inside me at his every touch and caress.

I kissed his neck, right in the hollow where his shoulder and collarbone met, and slid my hands up his back, relishing his weight and the reality of him. Our bodies rocked together in a slow, gentle, intense rhythm, and I whispered, "Take my blood, Owen. It's yours."

I had never before surrendered to his teeth, not truly. I had merely tolerated the bite, as a means to an end. Now, I offered my blood, my life, willingly. I was his.

His teeth slid into my skin. He drank and kissed and sucked at my neck. My eyes closed, and I gasped. A sweet ache spread from my toes to my scalp. A powerful need was obvious in his touch as he pushed into me, filling me, drinking my blood deeply, his arms wrapping me so tight I thought I would break. Something was happening. His body was growing warmer than it ever had before.

That shift from cold to hot within me knocked me senseless, and my body shuddered and locked tightly as pleasure hit me like a wall. Owen also cried out, clutching wildly at his chest in a gesture that scared me witless. A gesture full of pain, and terror, and disbelief.

He stumbled off me, backing away across the room. His fingers were interlocked over his heart, and his eyes had gone a strange shade of … blue?

I stared at those eyes, at the terrified expression on his face, speechless and confused. He fled, literally fled from me, and I could only stare in total bewilderment as he streaked across the room and out the door.

"Maybe there was too much garlic in my blood, and he got heartburn?"

The joke fell flat, a desperate and failed attempt

to keep myself from falling into despair. My voice quavered, and tears slid down my face. I felt naked and exposed, not only because I actually was but because shame and confusion had set in.

Daylight splashed in through the open door, and from somewhere in the house there was a wounded howl. My skin prickled, and I crawled under the covers, smashing myself flat and as small as possible. Fear broke out along my spine. I shivered, while the rich food roiled and tumbled in my belly.

I lay there, looking up at the ceiling for what seemed like an eternity, waiting for him to come in and kill me for seducing him. Or to find out my blood had killed him, and I would die here alone, chained in this room. Or that he'd decided he didn't like the way I was changing him, and it was time to finish this. I waited for the end of the world I knew.

It didn't come.

The tension drew out nearly unbearably, but eventually my mind and body could take no more, and I drifted off into a dream-filled and restless sleep, marked by nightmares of Owen burning in the sunlight.

15

Sometime in the afternoon, I crawled out from under the covers, threw on Owen's shirt that had been left in a crumple beside the bed, and began to prowl around the room. The shirt still smelled like him. I clutched the silk tight around me, rolling my shoulders in it to feel it slip against my skin, shocked at my body's immediate, visceral reaction to the smell that I associated so closely with the man. The vampire. The man. The vampire.

The chain yanked me up short every time I reached its boundaries, and I screamed in anger and misery. The screams ripped from my throat and chest, leaving a pain in my body but clearing my mind.

The room had few to no personal effects. Just clothing, some cologne in the bathroom, and several

ancient books stacked on the bedside table. But the ghost of his presence burned me. I kicked the wall and tossed a lampstand over, shattering the stained-glass shade. I felt like a rock star trashing a fancy hotel room. Everything just piled up and I couldn't help it, I needed to destroy. The wine glass and bottle on the coffee table were the first victims, shattering on the wall and staining the thick carpet. I pulled the bookcases down and flipped the couch over.

It was when I tossed the bedside table to one side that one of the books popped open, catching my eye. The book had a fake interior, and a small purse tumbled out. I got on my knees and looked at it. It was a lovely little thing, with silver clasps and gold embroidery. The name stitched into it made me catch my breath. *Adelle St Delaurents.*

I opened the purse with trembling fingers to see a diary, bound in leather and marked in place by a silk ribbon that was a mottled, faded gray. It was so small, it must have been made to be carried in a tiny bag, or in a small pocket. A lady's pocket.

I opened the diary and began to read.

Adelle's handwriting was rounded and flowing. It was also tiny, and when I closed her journal, my head ached fiercely from the strain of it all.

Owen had been right about her. Adelle had loved an adventure. She had seen him as one as well, a young and handsome man she could kiss and flirt with, ride at full gallop next to, dance wildly until dawn with, but long before he had ever seen her, she had been betrothed to her husband. A husband she never had any intention of ditching. But Owen had been exciting, and the fact that he fell in love with her just made her giddy. It made her feel important to have him lusting after her. It gave her an incredible feeling of power, that she could manipulate him so blindly.

Where Owen had gotten it was wrong was in assuming she wanted him just as badly. Adelle wrote of her manipulations and flirtations, always finding them amusing. Like the other men she kept on her string, Owen was nothing more than a flirtation, a way of passing the time and ensuring her dance card was always full at the countless balls and parties she attended. She never let any of her beaus go any further than kisses and groping up her legs, because she was shrewdly and acutely aware that to do so would be to ruin her prospects for marriage.

When she did wed, and realized she no longer had to stay a virgin to ensure her place in society, she began to take on numerous lovers, of which Owen was just one.

He had no idea. She dangled her love in front of him for her own amusement. Her husband was indeed a cruel man, who treated her with little more than contempt or rage at her inability to produce a child, but she was cruel as well. More than cruel, really. She seemed to accept her husband's treatment as normal, not going to any great lengths to avoid the punishments. Indeed, with delight she wrote about the color of the bruises that blossomed on her skin, and how the marks enraged Owen and the other lovers she kept on with lies of love and faithfulness. How she so enjoyed seeing the fury and passion it provoked in them, she made sure she always had some mark upon her skin.

When she was whisked away to France, she became infatuated with Rene, a handsome man with *'ebony hair and eyes, a walk that makes me shiver as it speaks of danger with every step, and an endless hunger for life nothing seems to assuage.*

'From the moment we met I could feel a need for him, a starving and thirsting need that would not, has never, let me rest. I adore him, despite his odd ways and violence in lovemaking. Just a fortnight ago he kissed my bosom so fiercely that he left a bite there, which made me so weak I could scarcely stand for days. The weakness passed but the bite remained in full view, making it necessary for me to stay in bed for days playing at megrims and other illness in order to keep anyone from seeing it, especially my hardly beloved husband. He would kill me if he knew I was once again cuckolding him, but I think Rene would be worth dying for.

'He manages to come into the house at all hours

of the night, unseen by the servants or passersby on the street. He always smells of wind and places that I have never been. Oh! To be with him there and forever!'

If Rene were anything like Owen, I could understand the attraction. But not wholly. When Owen was a vampire, that turned me off completely. What made me care about him was his human behavior: his kindness and vulnerability. It was when he was at his most unvampire-like best that I …

Oh shit …

I blocked that thought before it could work its way into my head. I could not possibly be in love with him. It just wasn't possible. Not even if he was great in bed and a damn good cook. No way.

I turned my attention back to Adelle. Rene had bitten her, and she had gone into a serious depression when she was hauled back to merry old England. Bored and lonely, she had turned to Owen, feeding him tales of her love for him. She claimed that she had been unable to see him, abed with excuses of ill-health, and that she had gone to France to see a doctor. All these lies and stories she'd concocted, I don't know how she kept up with them. If anything, Adelle sounded like a more accomplished actress than I was.

There was a sharp shift in her writing around then as well. It was as though Rene's bite had made her somehow terribly aware of her own mortality. Was it possible she had known that he was a vampire? I believed she had, and she longed to be young and beautiful forever as well, to be able to keep her lovers enchanted and on her strings.

When Rene came after her, she was ready for him, seducing him and using him just as she did all men. Together they had turned her husband into a thrall. He was seen in public and acted as normal as could be managed. He rode in carriages and attended balls for short amounts of time before pleading illness and leaving. Rene and Adelle kept him prisoner for nearly two months before she managed to convince Rene to bite her. I think she had some idea that the two of them would float through high society, with wealth and power, together. I think she may have really loved him, despite how she tried to use him. Though I didn't know much about Rene, what she said of him made me wonder if he was playing her as much as she was playing him.

That was when things got very out-of-control. Owen came upon them together. Everything he had told me about the night he had been turned had been true, with one exception. Adelle had been a vampire for weeks. She had simply lied so he would not kill her too. She promised him that her love was still true, and drank from him as greedily as if he were a giant-sized cherry Slurpee.

But Owen had bitten her back. He had known,

somewhere deep down, that she was a liar, that she meant to simply drain him and dispose of him. He had bitten her wrist in a frenzied moment, and she had been too caught up in feeding from him to stop him until it was too late. Adelle had been amused by his biting her, by the sudden and startling rebellion against her pretty lies. She had also thought it sexy as hell.

So, she kept him around. While Owen was busy searching for a cure for them, Adelle began to hunt, not just for food, but also for sport and to increase her wealth. Owen drank but never killed. Adelle saw that as a weakness. She thought it was just because he was still new, and that as his humanity was left further behind, he would become like her. She always killed her prey, often haunting the places where men with money went, so she would have cash on hand to support her ever-increasing love for luxuries. They had argued about it more than once. It was clear she began to tire of the rules and boundaries he tried to lay, and his attachment to being human. In some of their darker moments as a couple, they discovered the law that vampires could not kill other vampires, not without receiving an even worse punishment from others of their kind.

Over time, Owen drifted away from Adelle, and started to build businesses on his own labors and small inheritance. He began running a tavern, only

open at nighttime, so it would seem natural he only appeared then to manage the business.

Dark Raine. Duh. I mentally face-palmed. He must own the club the LARP was at. More than that, I was sure it was a worldwide chain.

Owen annoyed Adelle with his constant need to be returned to his human state, and his ongoing love for her only made her angry. She viewed him as a weight, and since her husband had died while still in thrall, she set out to find a lover that would be willing to kill Owen.

I could have killed Adelle for that. She bewitched a wealthy man, then told him that Owen was a vampire. He raised a mob and they came after Owen. Owen managed to escape and, in fury, Adelle killed her latest lover for failing.

The diary ended there; the next few pages torn out.

I threw it at the wall in frustration.

16

"I see you are reading."

Owen appeared behind me. I spun around and my mouth dropped open. His face was positively glowing with warmth, and his eyes were still that same light shade of blue. He was wearing jeans, something I had never seen him wearing, and a plain white shirt.

A very different presence radiated from him, but I couldn't put my finger on what it was. Some emotion on his face, hard, but human, relieved, but desperately sad. Still, he didn't seem pissed at finding me digging around in his dead lover's belongings, so I answered honestly. "Yes, I was."

He bent down and retrieved the diary from where it had fallen. He stared at it for a long time. "I suppose you think me a fool."

I huffed. "I've done some crazy shit because of love, too."

A smile turned the corners of his full lips upward. "Really?"

I deflected, playing down any meaning to my words. "Who hasn't?"

He leaned over and his shirt pulled up to reveal the smooth flesh above his waistband. Owen slipped the diary into the purse and then back into the fake book.

"I am guessing you want to know what happened."

"She tried to have you killed, then it just ends."

"Would you believe I had loved her for more than a hundred years at that point, and was still blind to her nature? She was cruel and corrupted, but when I looked at her all I saw was beauty. All I saw was the one I loved, once, when I was human. I held onto my love for her as I held onto my humanity, or at least, the pretense of humanity. I hadn't been human for a long time at that point. I had forgotten how to truly feel anything. I couldn't love, couldn't show compassion or empathy. I had set myself rules and morals which I stuck to, but not for any form of kindness. Only to be clever, for self-preservation. And she did not agree with those rules. When I confronted her, she laughed at me and said she had never loved me, that she would never love me, and that I was weak."

He closed his eyes, lost in the memory, and I found myself longing for them to open again, so I could stare at that new shade of blue.

"I wanted to be horrified by her actions, but I could feel nothing. I left, going to my offices to get some peace and to think. All the blood, all of those years, my mortal life, wasted. All of the killing she had done, all the people no longer on the earth for no purpose but to serve her selfish need to be beautiful, to be wealthy, and powerful, and worshipped. And yet, I couldn't feel. The smallest hint of sadness came to me for all I had lost, and then it too was gone. Only clear, emotionless decision remained."

I took a step closer to him, as though drawn in. He opened his eyes again, stepping back.

"A mob showed up with stakes and torches, they swarmed through the tavern and into my office, killing two of my human bartenders—good men making a living for their families. The mob dragged me out into the street and beat me, stabbed me with their stakes. They narrowly missed my heart and I had just enough strength left to flee. I staggered away, bloodied and dying. The first human to cross my path was a child. *A child.* I almost killed her trying to regain some strength and then, *then*, I didn't even care. I've committed too many inexcusable acts in my time."

I reached out a hand to Owen's, but he pulled away before I could touch him.

"I grew even colder and harder inside. I travelled abroad, seeking answers. I discovered that while vampires cannot kill one another directly, there is an ancient death curse for those who are corrupt. It was held within a silver ring that was possessed by the spirit of a vengeful ghost; a young woman killed wrongly."

Owen's gaze roamed around the room, anywhere but to me. His mouth grew tight. "I found the ring. The old Romani man who held it told me he could not give it to me, that the ring found those who deserved it. I told him of Adelle, and he said if she deserved punishment it would come.

"I went back to see Adelle. I had no plan, other than to try to make her see what she did was wrong, hoping time had changed her. Even if we as vampires couldn't feel, we could still decide how to behave based on the world around us. We didn't have to be monsters. When I opened her door, she was lying there on a chaise, her hand in the air and the ring on her finger. It could be no other, with an immense ruby cut like a drop of blood, the silver setting tarnished to black. She was admiring it, and I wanted to tell her to take it off, to save herself, but it was not up to me. That ring chooses its wearer.

"I said what I wanted to, then turned away. She

laughed at me but then she stopped. I did not turn around to see her die. I didn't need to. Her ashes drifted across the room in a stinking cloud. I dispersed her wealth to the poorest of the area, and left England for a new … *life*."

"I'm so sorry." My heart ached for him, but he brushed my words aside.

"It's over now. I promise you, if I had not found your blood so sweet, so bewitching, I would never have held you prisoner. That has never been my way. I had my rules. Harvey sends porn actors to many a game at my club, and I've often taken them to feed from after the night has ended. But I have never killed any of them, never showed unneeded cruelty, nor kept them prisoner before, until you."

I choked. "I'm sorry, did you just imply I'm a porn actor?"

"What?" He blinked, looking clearly confused by my objection.

"Oh god, you think I'm a porn actress." I stared up at him.

His blue eyes bored into mine. "You're not a porn actress?"

"I'm not a porn actress!"

He put his hands over his face and laughed, huge gusty laughter.

"But you're so …" He bit his bottom lip, looking over my body. "I just mean …"

I considered the way I've acted under his captivity. I almost couldn't blame him for thinking that way. "I'm not, I'm really not. I am an actress, but I have never done porn. I'm the girl that always dies in the horror flicks before the hot blondes even start getting naked. It's sort of the formula, you know, geeky dark-haired girl with small tits gets chain sawed first, while the blonde with the giant bolt-on tits survives until the shower scene."

He looked completely nonplussed. "Bolt-on tits?"

Leave it to a guy to focus on that.

He shook his head. "I'm sorry I assumed you were. Kitty French sounds somewhat like a porn star's name."

Ouch. I glared at him. "Not hardly. I mean … okay, it might, maybe, a little …" It did. *Shit.* I had taken to using Kitty instead of Kaitlyn when I first moved to Hollywood, to be a new me, and all I did was make myself sound like a porn star. "That does not mean I am though."

"He said you were."

"Who?" Even as I asked, I knew the answer. *Harvey! That bastard.* He had sent me on a porn job after all. I wondered if he knew the real fate he was sending those girls to? A bit of role playing, and a quick bite from a real-life vampire. Owen must have had his pick of hot bodies to drink from. My stomach gurgled with jealousy.

UnLife

"You didn't, you know, sleep with all the porn actresses as well as bite them, did you?"

Owen glanced at his feet, a gorgeous, bashful motion that made my heart backflip. "No, you're the only one."

We stared at each other, and I couldn't get over the shade of blue his eyes had turned. Like ashen cornflowers, or a dusky winter sky. His face grew solemn, and in that frown, tiny lines of age showed around his eyelids.

"Your eyes, they're … You've changed." I reached up toward his face, but he took a step back before I could touch him.

"Can you ever forgive me, Strawberry?" There was something strange about his voice, so sorrowful. I didn't understand, but it made my soul ache.

"Forgive you for what? I'm sure girls are confused for porn stars all the time. I mean, there was the whole kidnapping thing …" I tried to make it sound light, but I could see a darkness closing over Owen.

The dim light from the hallway stroked the planes of his face while he paused for a moment, then said, "I am so sorry, Strawberry. Maybe one day you will find it in your heart to forgive me, but I don't know how you ever could. You shouldn't. Not for what I've done to you."

Owen left me there and didn't come back, though I waited for hours. I lay on my back, staring at the

shifting shadows on the ceiling, and alternating between wanting to scream, cry, and laugh hysterically. It's a good thing I couldn't get to the kitchen since I was ripe for a peanut butter jar and a spoon kind of moment. I missed ice cream. I really, really did. To keep myself amused, or maybe just to add a little salt to the wound, I thought of gelato, Italian ices, and waffle cones. Rainbow sprinkles and hot fudge poured liberally over soft serve. I dreamed about mint chocolate chip, and the delicious texture of cookie dough ice cream. Eventually, daydreaming turned into real dreaming. I welcomed the escape of sleep gratefully.

$\mathcal{I}$ woke up in my own bedroom with the sun shining through the open balcony doors. Funny how I'd come to think of it as mine when I was just being kept prisoner there. It was like possession made it better somehow. I rolled over on my side, prepared to face another day in captivity. My feet hit the floor and I pushed myself up so I could head to the bathroom. Apart from a few birds chirping, the house was strangely silent.

I was halfway there when I realized what the silence meant. I had grown so used to the clatter and chatter of the chain that I no longer heard it, until I didn't. I looked down and stared at my ankle. It was red and chafed, the skin abraded in places, but it was free of the cuff. I shook my head and pinched

myself. Surely, I was dreaming still.

But I wasn't. I glanced at my wrist. It still showed some abrasion marks from the cuff, though it was mostly healed. On my other wrist, marks from Owen's fangs were only small, red dots.

Confusion set in, and I felt fear creep over my thoughts. What if this was all some sick game, like where the predator pretended to let a prisoner go just so they could capture them again for the thrill of it? I really did think in movie terms, but it came with the job.

There was a neatly folded slip of paper on the dresser. My hands shook when I opened it. The words made my stomach clench into knots.

You are free of me, Strawberry. Go. Do not try to come back or find me, I will not be here, and I do not want to see you again. Enjoy your life, Kitty, may it be better than you imagined it could be.

I read over the note three times, carefully taking in the words.

I was pissed as hell. How cowardly of him to break up with me in a note! Wait, did I just think that? This wasn't a breakup. It was the release of a prisoner. I should be grateful, and I was. I'd gotten what I'd been fighting for. I longed to be outside of the walls of this house of horrors, but another part of me was saddened by the prospect, and more than a little scared. My feelings about Owen were still so conflicted, a mingle of desperation, fear, love, and anger.

Below the note was a small black bag. I opened it and a stack of hundred-dollar bills greeted me. Hello! I had a vivid image of myself throwing it on the bed and rolling around, but it quickly faded. I counted one stack then estimated the rest—there had to be at least ten grand there. What was this? Some kind of victims' compensation?

I needed to leave, but I just stood there feeling incredibly uncertain. As weird as it was, that was the first time I didn't want to run away. Last night had been amazing. Owen's humanity had shone through, past any monster in him, and the sight had been incredible to behold. I wanted to talk to him, learn more from him. I wanted to touch him, and comfort him when he got that lost look in his eyes. Those new, incredible blue eyes.

I was free, but I could not leave. There was a pile of new clothes on the dresser, too—jeans in my size, a pretty top I would have bought myself, and a bra and panty set decorated with strawberries. The set was almost childish, but it made tears burst from my eyes. He had left, but I was still his Strawberry.

Stockholm syndrome much? The nasty little voice in my head startled me and I spun around, looking to see if there was anyone else in the room. That voice sounded nothing like the voice I used to talk to myself. It sounded older, cynical and tired. My shoulders

slumped. I was all of those things, and heartbroken to boot. I felt much older. Or maybe just wiser.

I got dressed, brushed my teeth and hair, and stared at my face in the mirror. My first neck wound was healing, but would leave a scar. On the other side, two tiny red marks from last night showed. My skin had regained a bit of color but not enough. I was eerily pale. Under my eyes there were slight lavender-colored circles, and my cheekbones had hollowed. I still had bruises on my arms and shoulders from hitting the wall while escaping from Loretta. There were also the marks of the cuff, but otherwise I looked … damn good. Like a beautiful woman suffering a terminal illness and suffering it well. I would have been believable in the part of a tragic young woman at the end of her life. Had I really come that close? I didn't feel like I was dying, even though my heart ached. I felt painfully alive.

I slid my feet into some strappy sandals. I was confused and feeling sick from hunger. I had no idea how long Owen had held me. The days had blended together in a long taffy-like string of dawns and sunsets and nights. The walls of my cell seemed to press in on me. My chest tightened and I closed my eyes, a sudden moment of panic overtaking me. Then a long, lonely bird cry called out from outside my window. I forced myself to take a deep breath, and slowly opened my eyes. First, I looked out over the balcony, then let my gaze wander back through the room.

The clothes in the dresser caught my eye, and I stroked the ruined dress I had worn the night Owen had taken me to the mountain to have dinner. The last place I'd seen it was in tatters on the floor of his bedroom. I tore a piece of silk off the edge of the skirt and used it to tie my hair into a ponytail, then I left the rags where they were. I tossed the other clothes onto the bed and tied the corners of the sheet together to form a bundle. I went to the bathroom and tossed all the fine toiletries and make up into the cash bag. When I hoisted the cumbersome lump and walked toward the door, I felt like a kid running away to join the circus. It seemed petty to take these things with me, like a tourist stealing soaps from a hotel, but damned if I was going to leave it all there. Bag of cash aside, I felt more than entitled. I had no plan and no idea of how I was going to get out of there. I was just leaving. I had freedom, and I wasn't sure I still wanted it.

Well, I mean sure I did. I wanted my life back. But I didn't want my life back alone. I wanted Owen with me.

The doorknob would not turn for a moment my hands were so slippery with sweat, and I started to panic, but it finally did. I walked out the door. It was the first time I had not been carried or fled too fast down the hallway to appreciate the place, but

as soon as I got to the third door, I knew what was wrong with it. Only a few rooms were furnished. The rest of the house was unused and empty.

I wandered into the kitchen, trying to recall exactly where he had stood the first time I had opened my eyes to see him standing in the shadows. The wall showed a slight repair where he had manacled me that first day. Kneeling, I could see a small dark stain on one base board, a missed spot of my blood. There were still the remains of food in the fridge, bacon, eggs, spinach, and a number of different cheeses, cream, and what looked like a fish fillet wrapped in paper. I made myself breakfast, taking my time to leisurely explore the kitchen and eat. I was stalling, hoping he would come back. It felt weird, eating at a table I'm not sure had ever been sat at, looking out the picture window at the sea. I'd pulled back all the block-out curtains, filling the dim rooms with sunlight.

The silence echoed endlessly around me. I sighed and took one long breath, then another. I closed my eyes and waited in the red veined darkness, hoping to find one last trace of him, to smell his particular smell, or to hear a soft footfall, but there was nothing but the dry wind outside tapping lightly against the windows.

I found two rooms on the lowest floor. One had no furnishings, except a tiny nest of blankets curled into a corner that had a rank wild smell. A single tube of lipstick lay in the rags. This must have been Loretta's lair. The other was Owen's room. His wardrobe had been cleared out. No clothes left, no books. Owen was gone.

His smell lingered in one of the pillows though, and I clutched it to my chest.

"Come back, you cowardly bastard!" I screamed, but there was no answer. He had left me.

It was late afternoon when I decided I might as well go. Shouldering my hobo sack of clothing and sheets, I stomped out the front door, slamming it behind me.

In the driveway sat my car. I stared at it, disbelieving. It was mine all right, the same dinged fender and fading paint job. I put my hand on the hood, certain I was hallucinating, and the metal scorched my fingers. I yanked them back and stuck the burning tips in my mouth to cool them. I wondered for a moment how long it had been there. Had he been keeping it at the club or in a garage, or had it been there the entire time, just steps from the door? I couldn't recall seeing it on my last desperate bid for escape, but all I really remembered was blinding sunlight, and then the strength of Owen's arms around me, pulling me back.

My windows were open, the keys in the ignition. I really was free. I got in and cranked the engine, expecting to hear the usual nothing I got from the old and faulty battery when the car hadn't been started

for a while. It rumbled easily to life, running smoother than it used to. My purse was on the passenger seat, and beside it my cell phone blinked on. I stared at it, stopping there in the apex between the drive and the street. I'm not sure how the phone even still had battery. Had Owen charged it for me, too?

I lifted it up. Five messages, three from bill collectors, one from a girl I knew asking if I wanted to go out to a club that night, and one from my mom. The date showed me I had been with Owen for more than three weeks. Three weeks, and all I had were two personal messages. How sad. And to be honest, I knew the motives behind all of them. The girl was someone who liked to have a big entourage along wherever she went, and cared little who was in it. The message from my mom was just a guilt trip about not remembering to call on her birthday. I would have, if I hadn't been chained up by a vampire at the time. Tossing my phone back onto the passenger seat, I decided I would call her later. I really needed to concentrate more on people—real, living people—and forging friendships in the future.

Then maybe if I was abducted again for three weeks, someone would care.

I clicked on my navigator and headed back to the city.

18

My roommate and landlord, Lisa, stared at me as I walked in the door.

"Where the hell have you been? We were just about to toss your stuff into the living room and have a free-for-all with it."

Her eyes swept down my body, taking in the quality of my outfit, and I glared at her. Lisa was a clothes thief of the worst sort. She would wear other people's stuff and put it back reeking of cigarettes and beer and sweat, then swear she had never touched it. She had ruined more of my clothes than I could count. I'd taken to keeping my good clothes in the trunk of my car, because it was the only way I could keep them safe.

I gave her a level smile. "Oh, you know…" I waved

a hand in the air in a casual gesture. "I met this guy ... He had this awesome motorcycle, and was headed down to Mexico for a few days ..." I added a half-embarrassed titter. It was a pretty terrible lie, but I'm an actress. Making terrible lies believable is what I do.

She shrugged before answering, "Yeah, that happens. You got some shit bad bruises there. You guys take a spill?" She didn't bother getting up from the couch she was lounged across, smoke curling lazily from the cigarette between her fingers. The whole house reeked. There were dishes in the sink that were there from before I left, the walls were yellowed from smoke, and everything stank of pot and alcohol.

"You could say that. You know how it is, there's no fun unless it's dangerous." My tone was light but the words felt wooden. Her bird-bright eyes drifted to my wrist, then back to my face, a catty smirk saying she knew I'd been up to raunchy things.

"You have to pay your rent today, or I really will boot you out and keep your clothes." She got up, swaggering toward me. I stood my ground, though normally I would have ducked away and scurried to my room. I was done with that now.

I answered her with, "I'm moving out."

"You still owe from last month," she parried quickly. She thought I was leaving because I had

a sugar daddy or something. I could tell from the way she eyed me. Lisa had never been able to keep her mouth shut or her nose out of other peoples' business.

I gave her a tight smile and handed her the four hundred bucks that was my share of the rent. She counted it, her slender and calloused fingers running across the bills expertly. "You still owe utilities."

"Take it out of the cost of all my clothes you fucked up," I said. I could feel a hardness surfacing in my eyes. She must have seen it too, because her tongue stilled, and she took a long step back. Normally she would have used sixty-seven swear words by now. I walked past her and grabbed my things, stuffing them into a couple of battered suitcases. I discovered my roommates had changed and that all of my stuff was in a box under a bathroom cabinet. Since I hadn't been there using my cupboard-room space they had rented it out to someone else. They all had just figured I had got a big gig and moved on or something. To see first-hand how little an impression I made on the world had opened my eyes in a big way. That was my life, or rather it had been. I had settled and half-stepped as long as I was going to. I had my life back, and damned if I was going to keep living it in half measures.

A tear crept out of my right eye and slid down my cheek. Owen had taught me to trust that even

if there was nothing below my feet, I could survive a fall. I was still afraid of what was going to happen next, of what might happen if I failed, but I wasn't going to let it keep me from doing it. I had to try.

I walked out with my head held high. I never looked back.

It was time for me to soar.

Harvey stared up at me, his moon like face registering first shock, then dismay, then a leer that made me want to shower immediately.

"Damn, Kitty, you look great! Did you get a facial, or your teeth professionally whitened, or something? Hey, I got your money from the LARP game here." He reached into his drawer and pulled out his check book, hastily scribbling one out. I took it from him. He didn't need to know Owen had paid me that and more. The jackass agent owed me.

I shoved the check into the pocket of my jeans, tapped a foot, and glared at him, "You mean I look great for someone you thought would be dead by now?"

His face went pale. "Aw c'mon, what's that supposed to mean?"

"You were the *only person* who knew where I was,

Harvey. Did you report me missing? Tell anyone? No, you were just damned glad one of your troublesome clients was gone. You send a lot of the porn girls out to those games, don't you? Or worse? How many never come back?" I slammed my hands down on his desk. "Don't try to be cute Harvey, I don't have any fucks left to give."

His lips twisted. I could see the wheels spinning in his head while he tried to think of something to say that would keep him out of trouble. "Always knew the games could get a bit rough, vampires have that whole snuff fantasy vibe. When you didn't come back, I kind of figured … hey, it's not my fault all right? I'm just a guy trying to help new talent get a start in this town. I didn't want my name getting dragged into some investigation." He spread his thick hands out and gave me an insincere smile. The thing was, I knew he was telling a partial truth. He honestly didn't think it was his problem. He had no concern for the welfare of the girls he sent. I'm not sure he knew exactly the danger he'd sent them into, but he knew it was dangerous. I answered by spitting in his face.

He rocked backward in his chair, and his eyes narrowed down to slits. "That ain't nice, Kitty. You could get hurt playing like that." His voice lost some of its oily charm, a hint of a rougher tone creeping in as his composure slipped.

I saw his hand just then. He had a new ring. Black tarnished silver with a bloody tear-drop shaped ruby twinkling malevolently.

I blinked. Could the cursed ring be real? And did Harvey really deserve it? If the legend was true, then he did. Maybe he did a lot worse than sending porn stars to rough games. God knows what fates he's been sending girls to. Or could its appearance here have something to do with Owen?

I almost considered warning Harvey, but I'd just sound crazy if I tried. It made me pause though, and he started talking again. Like I really cared what he had to say.

"Kitty, Kitty. It's all water under the bridge anyway. You're here, you're fine, and I think I got a part for you," he said, leaning back in his chair so hard it creaked. He must have decided we were still friends after all. Of course, he believed I was there to see if he had any other work for me. He thought I still needed him. His arms lifted to reveal sweat stains under his pits. Large yellow tinted patches that made me curl my nose. Had I ever been so naïve as to think this guy had my best interests at heart? He shuffled through some of his papers and started telling me about some minor gig, the same D-list crap he'd always given me. I wasn't listening anymore.

"I'm getting a new agent, Harvey," I said, and walked out the door. "Enjoy your evening."

Unlife

The door closed behind me, cutting off his retort, and I leaned against it. My heart was pounding, and a goofy grin creased my face. It had been an odd day, to say the least. I had left my prison, and left my home and roommates. And now, Harvey was dealt with.

I dusted my hands and headed out into the twilight. It felt like starting over, a fresh new try at life. Owen might not have bled me dry, but he had killed the old me. I was still getting to know the new one. I think I liked her. As I was getting into my car, I saw a thick clot of shadows gathering around the doorway to Harvey's office. I stared at them in horror, remorse filling me. Then I cranked my engine. Harvey would face the ones he hurt, as we all do eventually. I had not brought that on him, he had done it to himself.

19

It only took a week for me to make the decision to go to Owen's club to try to see him. The façade was boarded up, under renovations. The large chrome letters reading *Dark Raine* were being taken down, replaced with a new neon sign. A banner pasted across the front of the boarding said, "Under New Management. Re-Opening Soon."

I went into full-on stalker mode. I hunted down any information about Owen Raine I could find online. There were a few basic entries about his business life, and one new article which did little more than say the reclusive businessman had recently become more reclusive. There was nothing in public records revealing what property he owned. It was as though he hardly existed at all—just a

ghost passing through. I spent a whole weekend pouring through the vast archives of the internet, filing away any snippet I could find. And I eventually found more. I dug further back, collecting scans of old articles, obituaries, anything where his name was mentioned. There were small notices from old newspapers announcing the business being passed on to a 'son' or other male heir, and an obituary for the old man saying that he had died quietly at home in the company of his only family. Owen, trading in one identity for another, father to son, as he lived through the centuries. It wasn't much to go on, but I obsessed over every scrap. Even though I was the only one who used my laptop, I hid it all in a folder called 'whatever' and pretended it didn't exist unless I was putting something in it.

I told myself to get over it, to forget him, move on, and consider myself lucky he was gone. But I couldn't. God, I missed him so much I thought my chest would implode. Every night as sunset fell, I waited for him, expecting him to walk into my life again. Maybe I just needed counseling, but it felt like more than that. Besides, what would I say? Hi, my name's Kitty, I fell in love with a vampire who kept me prisoner because he loved the taste of my blood? Fat chance. I hadn't known love before, but if this wasn't what it felt like, I don't know what it would.

Nights stretched long and lonely, and I had trouble

sleeping. I took to swimming in the pool of my new complex. It kept me fit at least, even if it didn't keep the dark circles at bay. I missed the smell of roses and jasmine.

I drove by Owen's house every day. It was always empty and abandoned. It had begun to take on a sort of derelict appearance by the time I saw a man outside of it. I pulled into the drive, eager to find out what was going on. He came to meet me, his eyes taking in my crappy car with something like dismay.

"Hey there, Walter Longbow," he said, reaching out a friendly hand.

"Kaitlyn French."

"Are you here for the house sale?"

"I'm sorry, I wasn't aware it was on the market."

"Oh well, it's still a private listing," he hastened to add, his face saying he doubted I was there to buy.

The house was being sold. Another tie to Owen severed. "I was actually here to see Owen."

"You know Mister Raine?"

"Sort of. I don't suppose you know where I could find him?"

Walter shook his head and raised an eyebrow skeptically. "I wouldn't be able to share his private address, even if I could."

I tried to laugh casually and not seem like a stalker. "Oh no, I didn't mean like that. I meant right now, like, if he was just around the back or something."

"No. I only deal with Mister Raine by email. I handle a few of his properties for him, and to be honest, I was surprised he decided to sell this one. It's been in his family a long time." Walter loosened up. "You know Mister Raine's great-grandfather built this house in the nineteen-twenties. He was a heavy player during the prohibition, then one day, he just retired. He retreated to this house and shunned everyone. Nobody knew why."

Because he was not aging would have been my guess as to why he'd retreated from the world. Because the isolation suited him. Because he had grown weary of trying to fit into a world in which he did not feel he belonged. I said none of those things. I could only guess, and know that all of them were partly true. And there were probably a dozen other reasons I couldn't fathom.

"Anyway, he left it to his son, who left it to his son, not that they ever came here, except on the rarest of occasions. The house was only used a few months of every year, which seems a shame given it's so lovely. But Mister Raine has properties all over the country, and abroad. This one was renovated just last year. It was a bit in need of it, but he took care to make sure the original character of the place remained. I understand he did much of the work himself, and he takes as much pride in his work as the man who built it."

He is the man who built it, and he could be anywhere. Anywhere in the world.

I stared at the mansion, using it as a distraction while I fought to hold back tears. It was lovely, in a stark and forbidding way. I wondered, briefly, if the tennis court was still stained where Loretta had fallen. I had never dared look down to see what he had done with it. I tried my best not to think about it at all really. "It is an amazing house."

Walter touched one hand to his too-perfect-to-be-anything-other-than-fake hair. "Since you're here, would you like to look at the inside of the home?" He was putting on his best realtor face. I assumed it was habit for him, just like it was habit for me to pretend that Owen didn't exist, despite the fact that I looked for him in every brown-haired stranger.

"I've seen it. I lived here for a short time."

Walter perked up, leaning toward me conspiratorially. "Is it really haunted like they say?"

"Not anymore," I said, and climbed back into my car. I gave the house one last look, because I knew I would never come back. There was no longer any need to. All hopes I had that Owen would return had been dashed by a real estate agent in a toupee and off-the-rack suit. Dreams get killed by the most mundane of things sometimes.

20

Six months later, I was walking in a farmer's market, basking in the smell of flowers, and freshly baked bread, and a last few moments of anonymity.

It had been a hell of a time for me in many ways, both good and bad. I had marched into the office of Jenny Kurtz, the best agent around, darting past her security and secretary like a ninja. I made it into her office, where she was talking with a well-known director.

I looked at them both and said, "I'm Kaitlyn French. I'm your newest client. You may not remember taking me on, because you haven't yet. But I know you will."

Jenny had laughed out loud. The intense little man sitting in the chair across Jenny's rosewood

desk had asked me to stand in the bright sunlight coming from the windows. I had, and he had gotten very close to my face, surveying it like it was a work of art and he was looking for minute cracks. Then he handed me a script and asked me to read a few lines with him.

I did. The part called for me to be angry, and I was plenty that. It called for me to be hurting, and I damn sure was. It was a role made for me. When I'd finished reading the few lines he'd asked for, I was shaking from adrenaline and emotion. The looks they gave me had been cautious, like they weren't sure if I was crazy or not. So, I pushed all my feelings into a little box, and put on my best, winning actress smile. The director handed me his card. Jenny shook my hand and told her secretary to get the necessary paperwork.

The very next day, I was screen testing for that role. They wanted to see how I looked on film, and lo and behold I got the part. It was a supporting role, but a major one, in a major film. It would be released in cinemas worldwide tomorrow.

Filming had been exhausting. Because of the time crunch, I had been on set pretty much non-stop. In the beginning of the movie, I had just played a bitchy goth girl. Easy enough. It was the end that had been hard, playing too close a parallel to my real life. The screenplay had my character falling in love, as it turned out, with the villain of the story. She disappeared for half the movie, and when the main female and male leads found her again, she'd been used and abused, imprisoned, and driven insane so that she believed she was still in love with the man who had hurt her. The director praised the complexity I brought to the role, the character's struggle to know what she really wanted or needed. *Yeah, I wonder where I pulled that from?*

It had only taken a few takes to get it down, and for that I was grateful. I wasn't sure I could do it again without breaking apart completely in front of the whole cast and crew.

I'd kept to myself for a while after filming ended, but now I was finally starting to feel better. I was starting to feel more myself, and damn if I wasn't excited for the premier. That, and Jenny had me working hard. The work kept me from dwelling on my past too long. From dwelling on Owen, and the hole he'd left in me.

Things were good. I had a brand new agent, one of the best who was determined to push me to new heights. I had just finished filming four television appearances, and Jenny was already negotiating my role in three new films. More than that, I liked her. She seemed like a genuinely good person. She'd called me up once or twice when filming was over, asking how I was doing and checking if I was ready

for more work. I never had to ask, as long as I said I could take it she always had work for me. And I wanted the work. I wanted to be busy. I was living more comfortably than I had in a long time. I still hadn't told my parents that I thought I was going somewhere. I didn't want them to say 'I told you so' if I failed. Still, I was making the effort to call them, and to mend some of the relationships I'd ruined when I left home.

Harvey, on the other hand, was found dead in his office. The coroner ruled it a massive heart attack, which could easily have been true. Whether it was really caused by a cursed ring was something I tried not to think about. Some things you can't explain or find logical little boxes for. Some things you don't want to have to answer. Or answer for.

Life was mostly normal though. I still jumped at shadows, but I hadn't seen anything supernatural since my release. I sometimes felt like I was being followed, particularly at night. I often thought I saw people who looked like they didn't belong in this world, but to be honest, it's hard to tell in Hollywood. I don't ever try to get close enough to look in their eyes. I'd started to see all kinds of things in the dark, now that I knew vampires were real. That meant anything was possible. It was enough to make me jumpy after dusk, and sometimes kept me awake at night. Not that I could sleep anyway. I was always too busy waiting for the night to bring Owen back to me.

I still have a scar on my throat.

"Strawberry?"

The single word knocked me from my reverie. I turned back to see a grocer holding up a tray of strawberries to sample. "Try one. Best you've ever tasted. Get two punnets for the price of one."

The man standing in the stall held out the plump and juicy fruit. I stared at it, my heart aching. He called again to another passerby, and my eyes closed, remembering the way that word had fallen from Owen's lips.

Had anything ever been as sweet as that? In all that had changed in my life, in all the good I'd found, I still missed him. My eyes opened to see the stallholder looking at me carefully. He held out the sun-warmed fruit. "Here, try it."

I placed the ripened berry between my lips. It broke open between my teeth. Juice spilled across my tongue, filled my mouth, and tears hung in my eyes.

"It's so sweet." I licked the juice from my lips, savoring the flavor.

But I wasn't going to buy from him, not today. Maybe tomorrow I'd return and pick up enough to make something divine. Or perhaps I'd just eat them as they were, while I read a book in the bay window.

Truth was though, I just couldn't eat strawberries anymore without crying my eyes out, wishing Owen would come back to me.

I turned away quickly so I could wipe my eyes, and I caught sight of a familiar face, staring at me through the aisle between stalls. My heart stuttered to a standstill.

I'd had false sightings too many times before. Owen haunted my dreams, and my waking life, too. I thought I saw him everywhere, but when I chased him down it would be some perfectly ordinary guy looking back at me. One of them had asked me out, one had given me a look that said I was nuts, and one had been so startled he had dropped his bag of groceries.

The man turned away in an instant and headed off through the market. It was broad daylight. I knew it couldn't be him, but I had to follow him anyway.

His hair was a lighter shade than I remembered Owen's being, and shorter. He was muscular without being bulky and moved with a lithe grace. It was the way he moved that inflamed a tiny bit of hope in me, and impossible desire. Owen had always moved with such precision. He was never clumsy or out of sorts. The set of his shoulders, and length of his strides, just seemed too familiar. He wore a grey shirt rolled up to the elbows that showed his tanned arms off to perfection. Tanned? It wasn't him. It couldn't be.

There was no forgetting the pallor of Owen's skin.

I almost left it at that, when the man turned his face around quickly to check behind him, meeting my gaze.

It *was* him. My heart clenched like a fist then bloomed back open. My head spun. *It was him!* There was no mistaking it, no mistaking those lips or the high angles of his cheeks. Even from a distance, I could see the blue of his eyes. I remembered how they had faded away from black to periwinkle. It was him, of that there was absolutely no doubt. He was as magnificent a man as ...

He was *human*. That thought hit me and staggered me. That was what his grabbing his chest had been all about, his heart had begun to beat again for the first time in centuries! My blood had restored him to his human form, and what had I gotten in return for that? Ten grand, a new wardrobe, and abandoned like a one night stand? I have lousy taste in guys. I should have known he would be no better than the rest of them. Anger suddenly ripped through my heart. It didn't override my desire for him, it just made me want to smack him as much as I wanted to kiss him. And I really wanted to kiss him.

Why was he here? It had looked as though he had been following me, but as soon as I spotted him, he had turned away. Had he been keeping tabs on me? Was it possible he missed me as much as I missed him?

He was walking away faster than before, his arms swinging by his sides. I couldn't hesitate, because if I did, I would lose sight of him, perhaps forever.

I pushed through the crowd, throwing apologies over my shoulder to those I bumped. He crossed the hot parking lot and I ran after him, my heart beating so hard and fast I was sure I was going to topple to the ground.

I wet my lips with my tongue and called out. "Owen!"

He kept walking. My heart plummeted. I caught up and grabbed his arm. He swung around to look at me, his face carefully blank and his eyes inscrutable. I faltered a little, but I knew it was him. Unless he had some progeny he'd never told me about that was his spitting image in human form ...

"Can I help you, Miss?"

"It's me." I ran my gaze over his face, the face I had once hated to see and had missed so much since it had been gone from my sight. "It's me, Kitty."

"I'm sorry. I think you have me mixed up with someone else." He withdrew his arm gently.

"The hell I do. I know it's you, stop pretending it isn't."

"I'm not who you think I am." His voice held an aching tenderness. His eyes were kind and warm, but there was hurt underneath, I could see it. Why was he hurt? He wasn't allowed to be hurt when he was the one who left me! I was hurting too, dammit. Couldn't he see that? Didn't he care?

Tears as corrosive as battery acid sprang to my eyes, and my throat filled with a salty lump that would not let me speak, let alone refute his words. I had been mistaken before, but not this time. I knew him, knew him all too well.

He turned away, reaching for his keys. I heard the locks on the sleek black sports car disengage, and I knew this was my only chance. If I let him drive away from me, he would likely leave LA and my chances of ever finding him again were slim to none.

I said, so low that I knew those around us couldn't hear but he could, "Don't you turn away from me. Face me, dammit. You owe me that, Vampire."

His shoulders slumped and he turned toward me. Guilt creased his features, and he met my eyes. "Strawberry," he sighed. "You always were too persistent."

I fell onto his chest, swallowing away the sob that rose in mine. The solid warmth of his body met me like a wall, and I welcomed it. He was real, he was there, and I hugged him so tightly I could hear his back creaking. The warmth of him was what really struck me. Every time I had touched him before I had expected it, only to find his skin cold and inhuman. Now, it was hot, sunbaked. I could even

smell a faint whiff of sweat and leather, probably from the car seats. Good smells, living smells.

"It really is you," I said. "And you're really human?"

He stiffened in my arms but I held on, not letting go. Like hell I was going to let him go again.

He breathed out a long sigh. "Yes. Something in your amazing blood transformed me. I had felt the change coming, the slow progression of my humanity coming back to me, but almost didn't believe it until that morning after we made love. I walked into the daylight, and I did not burn. You made my heart beat again, and you gave it something to beat for."

I looked up into his eyes. "Then why did you leave me?"

"When I found myself human, I also found that I had fallen in love with you. In that moment, I realized the tragedy that had befallen me. How could you ever forgive me for what I'd done to you? How could you, when I could never forgive myself? I had kept you, against your will." He looked truly horrified at the memory. He turned away and wouldn't meet my eyes, but for that moment it didn't matter. I rested my cheek against his chest, listening to the soft, steady thump of his heart.

"You … fell in love with me?" Trust a girl to focus on that part.

"Heart, body, and soul." His voice was barely a whisper, like his confession pained him, stealing

his breath. "But I knew you could never love me in return after the crimes I had committed against you. I had done you such wrong … I had to let you be free of me. I had to leave."

"You were a monster," I said. He flinched and looked away again. I reached a hand to his chin and turned him back to face me. "*Were* a monster. I love the man who was trapped within. I love Owen Raine, not the vampire that possessed you for so long. You are human again, and it doesn't matter what the cost was. I don't love the monster that imprisoned me. I love the man who set me free."

He held me, crushing me to him as though afraid I'd disappear. My face pressed into his chest and I could hear it, his heart, drumming a steady beat. I loved the sound. Closing my eyes, a hundred days and nights seemed to flick before my eyes, falling asleep bathed in moonlight to the sound, and waking up to the brilliant morning sun with it still steadily beating by my ear. I picked up one of his hands and held it to the sun, the sunlight turned it red, outlining the veins below his skin.

He smelled of cologne, something subtle and expensive, but the coppery scent of blood had left him. He was a human, a man, and the one I wanted to love forever, for the rest of our natural lives.

"What are you even doing here? I mean, why? Why have I found you again now?" I asked, breathlessly.

"Can I make a confession?" Owen said softly.

"Confess away."

Owen's eyes darkened with concern. "I've been keeping an eye on you. I'm sorry, I know that's not the done thing these days, and I don't want to seem strange, or overprotective, or possessive. I had reason to be worried about you. If your blood was at all as appealing to other vampires as it was to me, I considered you could be at great risk if you ever crossed a vampire's path again."

"I suppose that makes sense," I rolled the words slowly off my tongue. I had often wondered the same thing. It made me feel special, and safe, to know Owen had been worried about me. "Except that no vamp is going to steal me away from a daylight market, now are they?"

Owen grinned bashfully. "Mostly I've had some men I hired keep you under surveillance. But when one reported some suspicious activity, I had to come myself. I needed to know, after all you'd suffered, I just needed to know you were okay. I needed to see you. Perhaps the more honest truth was that I just could never let my Strawberry go, as much as I knew I should.

"I'm sorry. I didn't want you to see me, too," he said, pressing his lips into my hair. I could feel the warm trickle of a tear on my face but it was not mine, it was his. "I did not know how to handle

the emotions that came with being human again. I did not know how to be a good man, maybe I never did. Your blood changed me, made me something far better, and I can't believe you would ever be able to look at me and not see the vampire that had harmed you."

I leaned back to look at him. He seemed confused, and I felt a mischievous smile steal across my face. I stepped away, feeling his hands clutch at me for a moment before reluctantly giving way and allowing me to move freely.

"What if we just start over?" I held out my hand to shake his. "I'm Kaitlyn, Kaitlyn French. I'm an actress, and I'm not doing too badly at it. I like food, especially good food, castles, and happy endings."

He smiled a lop-sided smile that sent arrows of lust slicing into my heart. "I'm Owen Raine. I'm a multimillionaire businessman who currently lives on a ranch with horses. I like grocery shopping, because every time I go, there is some new and wonderful food to try. I just learned how to use a computer in order to keep up with the world better. I googled you, just so you know. I recently began to 'hang out' on the beach, and I have learned to like dining in restaurants."

"It's nice to meet you," I said, shaking his hand, both of us laughing.

He twined his fingers through mine. His smile

was full of the boyish ruefulness I'd only seen once before, and I cherished it. In the touch of his fingers, his skin hot against mine, and the way his blue eyes saw into me, I knew that he felt the same way about me as I did about him. He'd said it, sure, but neither of us were the best with words. Our souls resonated with each other though, proving the truth in both our hearts.

The day shone down on us as he pulled me in for a slow, tender kiss. I wanted to keep that moment forever, but knew I didn't have to. I had Owen again, and he loved me, and I loved him, and everything was right in my life.

Never before had I felt so loved.

Now and forever, I belonged to him.

His strawberry.

He whispered in my ear, "I'm glad you're going by Kaitlyn French now. I like it. Sounds less like a porn star."

"Oh, bite me."

Remortality

HeartsBlood
BOOK TWO

1

"Death won't part us. You hear me? Fight this. Fight for me!" I cried, tears streaming down my cheeks.

Kneeling before me, a man with the face of a Greek god looked up with hooded eyes, his blond ringlets shiny and wet from the light rain that fell. The love and desperation in his expression was as clear as the blood spread across the chest of his civil war officer's uniform.

I cupped his face in my hands, feeling his rough stubble.

His head swayed weakly. "You are everything I wanted. To be with you. To be yours. And you mine. I have fought, and I have lost. I fear you will lose me now ..."

"No. I can't lose you. We belong together." I leaned down and planted a soft kiss on his lips, tasting his tears. "Wherever you go, I go too."

I slipped the knife easily from his belt and plunged it just as easily into my heart.

I fell into his arms.

"Cut! I think we've got everything we need." The scene finished. Applause broke out. I blinked rapidly, so lost in the part that for a second, I couldn't remember where or even who I was. Cameras and lights surrounded me in a warehouse-sized studio.

Getting to my feet, I handed the prop knife back to Miles, the leading man, to reset the scene. We held our places, waiting to hear from the director whether we were going to do another take. Make-up came to spritz us with water again to simulate being wet from the rain that would be added in post-production. This was the last day of filming, doing pick-ups and capturing some final takes for the big moments. This scene was the most important. It had to be perfect, moving, painful.

I had plenty of painful memories to draw upon.

How things had changed. My nerves tingled, and a wide smile spread on my face. No matter how many times I told myself this was real, it still felt like a crazy dream. I was an actress, and rapidly becoming a successful one.

There'd been a time when I'd been sure it would

never happen. Not just because my agent back then had been a slimy weasel unable to get me good roles. But because that same slimy weasel had sent me on a job that had nearly ended my life. It was supposed to be an evening with make-believe vampires. Only— surprise!—there'd been a *real* vampire there, and he had imprisoned me in his house of horrors, feasting on my blood again and again.

I'd been sure I was going to die, that I would never escape the torment of having my blood taken against my will. Of being chained and deprived of my freedom. Of being some *thing's* food. Or the fear that eventually, he would stop just sipping at my veins and open them up to drain me dry.

He only hadn't because my blood had changed him. It made him more human. It made him feel things he hadn't felt for centuries. And then my blood had somehow cured his vampirism completely.

Owen was human now, and he was the man I loved. And who I'd been missing like crazy.

I'd been kept apart from Owen by this fantastic role my new agent had gotten me. He was an amazing agent, but really, anyone would have been a step up from the last guy. An agent willing to send you to your death is not the person you want representing you. That's Hollywood 101.

Spencer, the director, was busy going over the dailies with the director of photography, checking

over the last footage, confirming they had everything.

"That's a wrap!" he called.

People whooped around the set which still buzzed with activity. The night wasn't over for most here, not yet. The few extras on set cleared out, but all around, the crew were busy with their tasks, and I marveled at the human machine we had become, all the pieces ticking away together to create a work of art. A story in motion.

But for me, my job was done.

Stepping off the set, I grabbed my dressing gown from the back of my chair. I stifled a yawn. This shoot had run late and been taxing physically and emotionally.

Miles joined me, grabbing a bottle off his chair and taking a long swig of water.

"It was such a pleasure working with you." He extended his hand, grinning warmly. I took it, but after a brief shake I pulled him in for a firm hug. He had been awesome. I had been awesome. I was so excited for this film.

"See you at the premiere." I shook his hand again and headed off.

"Principal actors leaving set," the assistant director called.

Movement around the room did stop then, briefly, as everyone paused to applaud. I blushed, and smiled at the throngs of people who made me feel as though

I truly belonged there, on that set and on that film. That I'd earned my place here and I did it well.

I opened the studio door to rejoin reality outside. I knew it was late, but the darkness of night still surprised me. On set it had felt like it had just been daytime.

Spencer caught up to me on my way out. He beamed. "Excellent job, Kaitlyn. Excellent. I love your work. Love it."

Kaitlyn. The name change had been Owen's idea, and it had been a good one. I used to be known as Kitty, and looking back, I could see now why I got so many casting offers for low-budget slasher flicks and porn.

I said, "I love your work too. Although, I know that's obvious, and I've said it about a million times, every time we talk."

He chuckled.

"I'm so grateful you decided to cast me as your lead. It means everything to me." And it would mean everything to my career. Spencer's like or dislike of an actor had big repercussions in Hollywood. If he told other directors I was good, they'd ask to have me sent a script for their projects. But I didn't have anything lined up off the back of this shoot yet, which made me anxious. The old struggling actress inside me wanted to take any offer that came my way, but my agent had assured me it was best to wait, that some amazing roles would be coming …

if I impressed Spencer.

The way he beamed at me like a proud father, I felt confident I had.

"I don't know where you were hidden away before this" he said, and I choked back a small laugh. "But don't go hiding again. You're made to act."

He hugged me, then I turned away and headed for my trailer. I was dying to get out of this rigid, scratchy, but admittedly gorgeous, period gown.

When I opened the door, I had another reason to get out of this dress.

"Owen!"

He stood in the middle of the trailer, wearing a casual gray suit, and twirling a single rose cheekily in one hand.

I hadn't seen him for three weeks. Three long weeks, while I filmed on location in Virginia. Coming with me would have meant he had to hide out in my trailer all day, every day. Despite being human now, he was still avoiding the sun, and any kind of publicity. He worried about the news of his return to humanity getting back to the wrong people. He was still playing the part of a vampire, and sometimes I also wondered if he avoided the sun in case the cure wasn't permanent.

Even with how far we'd come, we were still a few blocks away from Easy Street, but I didn't care. The sight of his beautiful face and smitten eyes left me breathless.

Remortality

I rushed into his arms. He bent to kiss me then paused, a frown appearing. His thumb wiped across my cheek and came away red.

My heart flopped. "Oh no, it's prop blood. Fake. Not even *my* fake blood. Someone else's fake blood. Everything is okay."

Blood was a bit of a trigger for him, given our pasts.

He nodded as though he understood, but the frown remained.

The moment had cooled, and while I longed to press my lips against his and have him rip this bodice from me, I satisfied myself with a soft, slow kiss on his cheek.

He breathed in deep as I did. "You're not wearing the perfume I gave you?"

"Must have forgotten." I shrugged. It was a beautiful, unique scent, and I normally wore it every day because it reminded me of Owen when we were apart, but I'd been so focused on the shoot. "What are you doing here? I didn't think I'd see you until I got back to the ranch next week."

He ran a finger down the side of my face and looked at me with those cornflower blue eyes. "I've arranged a special gift for you."

"Oh?"

He smirked, devilishly. "A secret surprise."

I regarded him. Owen loved to give me presents. He often cooked for me, and since he had been

unable to eat regular food for centuries, he had now become almost as much of a foodie as I was. *Almost.* But his resources never ceased to surprise me, nor his creativity. He'd taken to being human again with a thirst for new and beautiful things as unquenchable as his thirst for blood had once been. And he loved to share that with me.

I purred, "You'll tell me now though, right? Don't keep me in suspense."

He just laughed and took my hand. "Come on, we have to go."

"Fine, be secretive then. But I have to change, real quick. This dress belongs to the set. My reputation can't afford being labeled a wardrobe thief. Also, it's itchy as hell."

Owen shrugged, a small smile on his face. "I don't mind watching."

I didn't mind him watching me change either. Once upon a time, he had kept me without access to much clothing, and I'd hated him for that, but he was a different man then. Not even a man—a monster. Now, as I undressed before him, deliberately taking my time to undo each button before allowing the bodice to fall away to the floor, I loved that he let his eyes wander up and down my body, and didn't hide the desire he had for me.

He wanted *me*, and not my blood, and there was a huge difference.

Remortality

The early spring weather was crisp and cool in the evenings, but I felt bright and happy so chose a light sundress, regardless of the sun having been down for hours. I didn't bother with a bra, just slipped the dress over my body with a flirty wiggle.

Owen stalked up to me, desire heavy in his eyes.

I leaned into him. He had body heat now, and I couldn't help but remember how cold his skin had been when we'd first met. Cold as the grave. I smiled as I soaked up the warmth of his humanity.

My head tilted back so I could look up at his face, and his lips claimed mine in a dizzying kiss. He tasted like red wine, and I drank him in. My breasts flattened against his broad chest, and my hands rested along the strong curves of his shoulders. The reassuring thump of his heartbeat against my flesh grounded me, even as his kiss swept me away.

My eyes fluttered closed. When I opened them again, I saw us in the mirror, kissing. I stared at the sight, mesmerized. I never did see vampire-Owen in front of a mirror, to discover if the old myth was true, but every time I saw him in one now, it came home to me all over again that he was human. That we had a life together.

I parted from his kiss but didn't leave his arms. "So, now what?"

Owen grinned. "I hope you're ready for an adventure."

2

OWEN

The door of the trailer banged shut behind us. Kaitlyn giggled as I led her along by her hand toward a shiny black limo. She skipped, light on her feet, but her body swayed and her eyes stayed closed a moment too long each time she blinked. It was late, and she'd been working hard. I should have waited until the morning, but no. I couldn't have. I couldn't wait a moment longer to see her again.

I opened the door for her, and she scooted across the back seat to let me in beside her. She kicked her shoes off and dug her toes into the soft carpeting, smiling blissfully.

I put my arm around her shoulders and tapped on the closed partition. The driver got us moving, and Kaitlyn sank into me. The adrenaline from being on

set, which I could tell had kept her going until now, must have worn out. The heat and weight of her head on my chest felt so right and perfect, so real. We sat silent together, content in each other's company.

It was late at night, more morning really, and barely anything could be seen through the nearly-black tinted windows. I hadn't requested a car with such dark tinting like I would have once done, but I'd received one anyway. It was like a relic from my sunless past. One I wished I could shed, like so much I had left behind since then, but one that still provided a privacy and anonymity that was convenient.

The driver took a hard turn and the small regional airport came into view. Kaitlyn raised her eyebrows at me. "Just how far away is this surprise? Because I only have my purse."

"Don't worry. Everything is sorted." I gave her my smuggest grin, then pulled her in closer, feeling a sudden surge of protectiveness for her.

I'd missed her while she was on location for this new film. Honestly, I'd wished she wouldn't go. That she wouldn't leave my side. But I could never again control her freedom as I'd done before. Ever since I'd been cured, I've had to keep a low profile. I couldn't let the other vampires know I was human any more than I could let humans know I had once been a vampire. I was existing outside both worlds.

Remortality

I had to avoid her places of work, or even being seen with her in public, lest a photo of us together was taken and shared in this new world of social media, online content, and facial-recognition software. I found the new technologies of the internet and intelligent software useful for business, but social media held little interest to me. I liked my privacy, now more than ever.

And I worried about Kaitlyn's career. The more famous she got, the harder it would be to hide our relationship. To keep me, and her special blood hidden. So far, she had been mostly off the paparazzi's radar, just another up-and-coming starlet. But with Spencer's film, things were already changing. Yet, I could never say a word that would come between Kaitlyn and her dreams.

She probably knew the risks as well. At least in part. But I wasn't helping by holding back so much information from her either. So much about the world of night I had left behind. Of how I had to dismantle the life and businesses I'd developed over centuries and make Owen Raine disappear. Of how much danger Kaitlyn might still be in, just for the scent of her sweet blood. I wished she'd wear the Nemexia perfume more often, but I didn't want to explain to her why.

We were waved through the gates and the driver took us right onto the runway, up to the small

jet I had chartered. I used to have my own plane, complete with blackout windows safe for flying even during daylight hours. But like so many of my possessions from that time, it was gone. Most of my assets had been liquidated, and the wealth that remained was hidden under various new names and corporate entities. Sacrifices had to be made. I didn't mind. Despite some remaining limitations and fears, life felt fresh and new, and I had Kaitlyn by my side. That was enough.

I did miss the strength and speed that I'd had as a vampire, but this body was still strong. I got out of the car, and when Kaitlyn followed me, I scooped her up into my arms. She giggled delightfully, and I carried her up the steps into the jet.

"I've never been in a private plane before," she said. I put her back on her feet. She seemed more awake now, alert and excited as she explored the interior, then flopped down with a happy sigh into a wide, cream leather seat. "This is lush."

The only details I paid much attention to were the crystal-clear windows. Sunrise would come while we were in the air. A chill ran through my bones. Part of me still worried that one day, while I stood under the warmth of the sun, the cure would wear off and I would burn to ashes.

I buried that fear and sat down beside my love. "You've seen nothing yet."

Remortality

The captain's voice came over the speaker to announce our departure, so we buckled up as the jet began to taxi around and build speed. Kaitlyn sat back in her chair, closed her eyes, and squeezed my hand as we lifted off the ground and zoomed for the sky. Once the sensation of acceleration slowed and the seat belt light went off, she sighed and stretched.

She propped herself up on her elbow on the armrest between us, her nose brushing softly against mine. "Just how private is this plane?"

She took my hand, bringing it up onto her breast as she brushed her lips over mine. I groaned into her mouth. I had missed her body as much as I'd missed the rest of her.

Our mouths met fully, desire pressing us into each other, an undeniable force. Kaitlyn pushed the armrest up and threw her leg over mine. Her silky sundress slipped right up to her hips, her thighs bared, smooth and milky. I grabbed at her, pulling her off her chair and into my lap, moaning as she pressed against me. I tangled my fingers in her dark hair, placing kisses down her neck and across her cleavage. As a vampire, I'd sunk my teeth into her there, and the temptation to do so again came over me like a wave, but for an all-different form of desire. Her breath was a gasp as my hands ran up between her thighs.

The rustle of the velvet partition curtain opening

broke us apart just as the flight attendant appeared, pulling a trolley through after her.

Kaitlyn sighed dramatically as she moved back into her seat and re-adjusted her dress, but I knew she wouldn't be upset for long. The trolley arrived beside us. On it, champagne cooled in a silver bucket filled with heart-shaped ice, with two very fine-stemmed glasses set to one side. Chocolate-covered strawberries were piled high on a wooden board between a range of cheeses, small triangles of crisp bread, Russian caviar, and cured meats sliced so thin they were nearly transparent.

"I may not be familiar with private planes, but now we're in territory I know all about," Kaitlyn said, eyeing the food with a lust akin to how she'd just looked at me.

"Excuse the interruption." The attendant smiled pleasantly, a glint in her eye showing she knew full well what she'd just put a halt to. "If there is anything else you need, just press the call button. I hope you both have a wonderful flight."

She had a sweet face and blond hair in a perfectly trimmed pixie cut. Well dressed, well mannered, well kept. An opposing image of my thrall, Loretta, in her grimy rags, came to me. As a vampire, I'd still had feelings, of a sort. Anger, desire, even sadness to some extent. The one aspect of humanity that vampires truly lacked was empathy. With my empathy returned now, so too came the guilt for keeping Loretta as I had done. She was the only thrall I had kept. For the most part, how I had employed people was very normal in the running of my businesses. Normal humans working normal jobs for a reclusive CEO they never met, or only saw at night. I only used my enthralling powers on people who discovered too much and needed the memory of those discoveries removed. Like those I'd fed on.

But Loretta was different. She had begun as one of my normal employees, until I discovered the depth of her violence and psychosis. I'd kept her as a slave more to keep her from other humans than because I needed her. Even still, the misery of her slavery, and how it had ended, still haunted me thanks to my new-found empathy.

So did the knowledge that other vampires often kept a whole stable of enthralled humans for far more unsavory uses.

Kaitlyn waved a massive strawberry under my nose. The intoxicating scent drew me from my thoughts, and made my whole body tingle and my mouth water.

I ran a finger down her cheek and said, "There is no strawberry sweeter than you."

She made the cutest cooing sound before the glint of mischief returned to her beautiful green eyes. "And there's no cheese cheesier than you."

I opened my mouth to quip back, but she silenced me by sliding the strawberry between my lips. I bit down. Tart and tangy juice filled my mouth. Dark chocolate coated my tongue with its bitter decadence. The flavors met and melded and I let them rest on my tongue. As a vampire, food had turned to ash in my mouth. Strawberries had been my favorite food before I'd been turned, and they still were. But the small, wild strawberries available back then could not compare to the massive, succulent fruit available now. Being able to taste such beauty would alone have been worth becoming human again for.

The sticky insides of the soft cheese Kaitlyn had just placed in her mouth coated her fingers, and she licked them sensually. Her expression of indulgent happiness made me smile as well. She rested her head back, closed her eyes, and then did not open them again.

Her breathing slowed and I realized she'd fallen asleep. Her head slipped a little to the side, exposing her long neck, and the scars there of my first savage feeding on her. They were covered by make-up from the set, but I could see the raised lines and marks beneath. Scars that would never fade.

I called the attendant for a pillow, and tucked it between her head and my shoulder.

I watched the darkness outside the window for a long time, until the sky slowly brightened. Soon,

the rising sun's strong rays turned everything pink and gold, the sky pale and serene, patterned with puffs and ribbons of cloud, tinted peach.

At that moment, my heart was so full I honestly thought that nothing could ever mar the perfection of my new life.

I should have known better.

3

KAITLYN

The bump of the wheels hitting the runway woke me from my sleep. It had been the deep sleep of total mind and body exhaustion—the result of completing the grueling shoot. I peered groggily out the window as the roar of the jets firing up in reverse slowed us down.

Sunset.

I turned to Owen. "Where on Earth are we that it's sunset already?"

He chuckled. "You slept through the whole day. Which really is the best way to fly if you can. Although, I don't know who is more vampire right now, with these hours you keep."

"You still didn't answer my question. Where are we? Where are we going?" I didn't want to nag, but

the mystery was becoming a bit too much when I'd been flown to who knew where for a whole day. Obviously, I knew we were flying *somewhere,* but I'd thought it was maybe back home, or at least in the same country. I still felt half asleep, and disoriented, and being taken somewhere so distant without my knowledge was starting to rub me the wrong way.

Owen became serious. "We're in Slovakia. It's not much farther to your present now. Please trust me, Strawberry."

Slovakia? I looked out the window again as the last golden edge of sun slipped away behind craggy mountains.

"Okay already. Let's get this adventure started then."

I still didn't have a clue where we were going next, or what the present he was determined to surprise me with was, but I would try to be patient. Knowing Owen, it would be worth it.

The plane came to a stop and we got off into a crisply cold evening, filled with shadows and the scent of wood fires. The airport was small—one runway, a few hangars, our plane, and only one smaller jet were in view. An older-style town car trundled toward us.

"You could've given me a little clue about our destination when I put this skimpy dress on," I said, shivering.

Owen didn't reply. His head was turned to one

side, and when I glanced over at his face, caught his eyes scanning the distance, and his lips had compressed flat. His body went rigid with tension and his nostrils quivered. Fear flared along my spine as I tried to see what he was looking at.

A shape separated itself from the deeper shadows beside the other plane. My heart pounded as I watched, a primal, animal fear shivering through me for no apparent reason. It was a man's figure, but he was too far away for me to make out much else.

"Owen? Who is that?"

His body relaxed as the man walked toward the tiny administration office.

Owen turned to me again and did a double-take, as though he'd forgotten I was there. "You're freezing." Without another word, he stripped off his jacket and draped it over my shoulders. I could feel the lingering body warmth he'd left in it and hugged it close to me.

Our luggage was loaded into the car, and I saw that Owen had packed my set of suitcases from home for me. We were driven to what counted as a terminal and passed through what counted for customs with a cursory glance and a few quick stamps in our passports, which Owen had also packed. There was only one man in the tiny building that I could see, and he was a very large man, entirely not the shape of the shadow-man we'd seen outside. The

other man could have been a security guard, or a groundsman. There were a million other plausible reasons why he wasn't this man we saw now, but I still felt unsettled.

Before I knew it, we were back in the car. For a while, nothing but darkness flashed by our windows. Then a town came into view, all stone houses and fairy tale cobbled streets, filmed over by a thin fog that crept along the sides of the road as we climbed ever higher along a tall mountain. The lights of civilization dropped away behind us, but the car crept higher and higher yet, the headlights picking up a terrifying drop on my side of the road. My whole body tingled with anticipation, as though I stood on the edge of a great adventure, and the night invited me to leave everything behind.

Tall trees stood thick on the other side of the road, their tops pointing at a sky that held more fine veils of obscuring mist, and a bloated white moon, full and ripe. Stars pricked against the velvety black. The sense that we were leaving the world behind strengthened as we passed an old church. It stood alone, framed by moonlight and glowing with an unearthly, silver pallor. A large cross riding atop it shimmered like a portent.

The car halted before massive wrought-iron gates. They were abutted by a high stone wall on either side, topped with fanciful little curlicues and scrolls

of more iron. I heard the driver buzz us in, and the gates swung open with a soft clang. We drove along the driveway, which swept through an alley of trees with long and skeletal limbs, holding only the tight buds of new spring leaves, still unopened. Coming around a tight corner, I nearly dislocated my jaw when it dropped so hard and fast at the view before me.

It's a castle!

I mean, I didn't know the exact definition of what counted as a castle, or palace, or chateau, or whatever, but this thing had god-darn princess towers. And it was bigger than any mansion I'd ever seen. I was calling it a castle.

I gulped. "Um … is that … is this yours?"

"No." Owen leaned across me to look out my side of the car as well. He landed a soft kiss on my cheek then said, "It's yours."

"It's *WHAT?*"

His eyes lit with passion. "It was mine. It was the first thing of great value I bought for myself once I became wealthy. I haven't lived here for centuries, but have visited on and off every decade or so. When I was having my properties sold to remove Owen Raine from this world, sentimentality took over and I couldn't part with this one. So, I came up with this solution. This castle, these lands, and the trust which funds the maintenance of them, are all now in your name."

What did a girl say to that? I had no words. The only thing my mouth knew to do then was kiss Owen in the deepest way I could.

Owen smiled beneath my lips. Between kisses, he said, "You gave me back my life and my heart. Giving you a castle is the least I could do in return."

"Well, when you put it that way …" I mumbled back.

Gravel crunched under the car's wheels as it braked in front of a wide stone staircase which led to two tall wooden doors, carved with blossoming fruit trees. The moment the car stopped, I was out. It was significantly cooler than it had been back in Virginia, and the mist, running low and thick, clung to the grass and flowerbeds. It gathered near the feet of a tall statue of a goddess-like woman, surrounded by shorter statues that looked like something between cherubs and demons.

Owen appeared by my side, and we headed to the entrance. The doors had large, brass knockers, covered with verdigris, except the base of the rings which were polished bright through use. I looked from the door to Owen, wondering if we were supposed to knock. *Did one knock at one's own castle?* My question was answered when the door swung open and a gaunt face appeared atop an equally waiflike body.

The woman was incredibly tall, and incredibly old. Her face was seamed and marked by age, but her eyes were sharp and clear. She wore a finely cut gray dress, covered by a white apron neatly tied at one side of her narrow waist.

"Dobry wieczór, Owen," she said.

Owen tilted his head to me. *"Po angielsku proszę."*

Eyeing me, she nodded. She spoke in a low voice and heavy accent, "Hello, and welcome home. Please to come in. Shall I present for you some foods after your travel?"

I was too busy being surprised about Owen speaking—crap, I felt so ignorant, I didn't even know what language—to answer. I wondered how many languages he may have learned in his centuries-long life. Inadequacy punched me in the gut.

Owen replied, "Thank you, Marianne. We're good. Please, you and your husband can finish up and head home. We will be fine alone for the night." Owen nodded to our driver as he walked past us, taking our luggage in. "Thank you, Tomas."

Somewhat shorter than Marianne, stocky, and just as old, the man smiled at Owen as though bestowing a blessing on him, then bowed himself away.

"He doesn't speak much English," Owen whispered to me.

Marianne curtseyed, sharp and to the point. "You'll find everything in order. Kitchen is stocked as your wishes. I collect my things and go. Good night to you."

She headed off down the hall. When they were

both out of earshot, I said, "Aren't they a bit old to be working here?"

Owen's eyes crinkled at the corners. "Oh? I didn't notice."

"You didn't notice?"

He shook his head, putting an innocent expression on his face that I wasn't buying at all. "They've been working here a long time—long enough to think I'm the son of the previous owner. They practically live here, and still do good work and seem happy to do it, so I haven't thought to replace them."

"Well, they are certainly much nicer than Loretta."

Hurt flashed across his face.

"I'm so sorry," I said, realizing my mistake the second the words were out of my mouth. Now that Owen was human again, the last thing he needed was for me to point out his misdeeds from when he was a vampire.

He shrugged it off. "No, it's okay. I have a lot to make up for in my life. Come on, let's go inside."

I hesitated. The last time I stepped into a place all decked out like a gothic castle I'd ended up as a captive to a vampire. This place didn't just look the part—it was set in a landscape that could have been hijacked from the set of some old horror flick I never wanted to see because, hell, I'd already lived it. But really, what were the chances of that happening again?

Remortality

Owen's hand met the small of my back, and he gently pushed me inside. To my relief, the interior was bright and classy, nary a gothic candelabra to be seen. LED downlights made bright, polished marble surfaces sparkle. An enormous, glittering chandelier hung between a double staircase, that swirled in elegant symmetry up both sides of the foyer. The carved spires and railings ran upward and then formed lovely half-turns that eventually led to the second floor. Amid the decadence, there was a modern elegance to everything that I found comforting.

The banks of windows were draped in burgundy velvet which pooled on the white marble floors. Gold leafing accented the hand-carved wooden furniture, which were either antiques or fantastic reproductions. A subtle brocade wallpaper led the eye upward to the ceiling moldings, filled with frolicking cherubs and winding roses.

"Would you like a tour?"

My stomach grumbled audibly in reply.

Owen laughed. "Let's start at the kitchen then."

We left our shoes in the foyer, and I delighted in feeling the heated floors under my toes.

It wasn't a long walk through the main hall to the final door on the right. The kitchen was contemporary and fresh, so much so that it surprised me. It could have easily appeared in *Modern Chefs Magazine.*

Gleaming granite countertops, stainless steel, top-of-the-line, catering-class appliances, and restored hardwood floors.

Owen opened the fridge and revealed a tray of cute, and very appetizing, sandwiches cut in triangles, scrolls, and fingers.

I popped two in my mouth at once, then picked up the whole lot on their porcelain tray. "Marianne is quite thoughtful to have prepared mobile snacks. Can we keep exploring?"

"Of course. However, Tomas is the cook, and driver. Marianne maintains the house and grounds. She's quite the skilled topiarist and does a spot of game hunting as well, if you're ever in the mood for pheasant."

"And there I was calling her old No wonder she stays so fit."

We headed out of the kitchen. His hand remained on the small of my back, leading me as we strolled side by side along the wide corridors and I nibbled on asparagus sandwiches. There were some small living spaces, simple and yet with the same elegant gothic personality as the rest of the castle, arranged along the lower floor. We climbed the staircase upward, the steps, covered in red velour carpet, soft under my feet.

There were several bedrooms behind solid oak doors, with antique hinges and locks of wrought iron. But most exciting were the bathrooms. Huge soaking tubs, pebble-floored rain showers, and marble countertops sat under the warmth of modern heating and golden light. And we hadn't even reached the master bedroom yet.

Owen watched me explore. "Do you like it?"

"Do I like it? This oh-my-freaking-god castle I've just been gifted? Do I like it?" I repeated with my eyebrows lifted. "Let me think for a minute."

I tapped my finger gently against his firm chest, as though it helped me to ponder this difficult question. "It is beautiful. Incredible, really. Totally decadent. But also, just gothic enough to clearly be the home of a vampire," I teased, my smile a dare.

Owen's gaze became hard as he peered down at me with a cheeky sneer. In a flash, he bared his teeth and hissed.

I jumped in surprise, the tray of sandwiches falling from my grasp and shattering into a mess. Neither of us mourned the lost platter or sandwiches as Owen growled at me again, a dark lust in his eyes, and I sped off squealing and giggling down the hallway. His jacket that I'd been wearing, too large for my narrow shoulders, slipped right off and fell to the ground behind me.

My heart pounded as I raced to get away from him, all the while desperate to be caught.

He wrapped his arms around my waist just as I reached some stairs going farther up. Our momentum folded us forward and I fell on my hands and knees on the steps, his weight on my back. His mouth came down, warm across my neck, kissing hard as he ran his hands down my sides and lifted me so my ass was pressed firmly into him.

Owen's hands grasped at the bottom hem of my sundress and pushed it up my back, exposing me. He traced kisses across my bare skin, then I felt him straighten up and away from me, whip off his belt, and unbutton his pants.

He froze there, hesitating. "Wait. Um, I need …"

I knew what he meant. "No, you don't," I said. I turned myself over, wrapping my legs around his hips where he knelt just below me on the step. I pointed to the thin, firm lump under the skin of my upper arm. "Contraceptive implant, remember? I got it last month."

His fingers traced up my arm. "Of course. Sorry, keeping up with modern contraception previously hadn't been a priority for me before."

I opened my mouth to say something, but before I could his lips came back down on mine, and I forgot about technology and immortality and fertility and everything else but the feel of him in my arms, against my body. I lost myself in the sensation of my hot flesh meeting his. My dress was off over my head and flung somewhere up the stairs. The cool air brought goosebumps to my bare skin.

I showed no respect for the fine tailoring of his suit as I tore away his shirt. He slid my underpants down with reverent care, then his hands moved to undo his belt.

He stopped again. A frown creased his forehead. "Did you hear something?"

I clung to him, desire making me shake and pant, unwilling to stop. I could hear nothing but my rampant heartbeat and the kisses I spread over his skin. But the serious expression on his face cooled me down.

I listened hard. A slight creak came from somewhere. I sat up, away from Owen. He moved back too, his chest muscles becoming rigid under the light sheen of sweat. He stared down the hall we'd just run along, and his eyebrows met.

I waited but heard nothing else. "Maybe it's just the building. Aren't these old castles supposed to be all creaky and scary and stuff?"

"Maybe." The frown stayed on his face.

The creak came again.

I crossed my legs and folded my arms over my chest to cover myself, as a chill shook my whole body. I strained to hear anything to indicate what was happening.

Owen stepped quietly away from me, sneaking toward the source of the sound. I began to follow, but he held a hand up to tell me to stay. A queasy feeling grew at the base of my stomach. What was going on?

"Owen?" My whisper broke the silence, shattering it into a thousand pieces. Owen tensed, the muscles in his bare back standing in stark relief under his skin. He looked like he was poised to pounce on something, and he didn't even acknowledge that I had spoken.

Owen spoke in a low and deadly growl, "I know you're there."

The hair on the back of my neck stood up. Who was he talking to? My mouth opened to ask that question but my brain screamed at me to stay quiet. Fear froze my whole body.

The creaking came again, then I heard the definite sound of a slow, deliberate footstep. The smell of musty earth and old blood filled the hallway.

Owen tensed, his voice full of disbelief. *"Lance? Why are you here?"*

A voice came from the hallway, masculine and very deep, with a faint trace of an eastern European accent. "You've changed somehow. I smell it all over you. You smell ... human. How can this be?"

A heavy shudder rolled over my body, rippling my skin.

Owen whispered, "Kaitlyn, get dressed."

I really don't even know why he had to tell me. There was a strange man in the hallway who could

smell human flesh. That should've been my first clue to get some clothes on.

I scrambled to find my dress on the stairs behind me and tugged it over my head. I didn't care about finding my underpants. Primal instinct formed words in my mind. *Just run. I have to get away from here. RUN.* But my only escape route was up. I'd been in enough slasher flicks to know what happened to people who ran upstairs. And I couldn't leave Owen.

From my angle on the stairs, I could see him, but not who he spoke to down the hall.

"You're not welcome here," Owen said through gritted teeth.

"Dear Marianne seemed happy enough to let me in on her way out." A mocking mirth filled Lance's voice.

A surge of protectiveness made my hands clench into fists. He better not have hurt Marianne.

Lance seemed to respond to my thought, but more likely to a look from Owen. "She's fine. I let her go on her way. You are who I've come to find. But to find you like this … I hear your heartbeat. I see your undarkened eyes. I can almost taste your warmth. How? How are you human again? How is this possible?"

My legs trembled and I pressed my back to the wall of the stairwell, hiding myself from the view of the man in the hall, although I was sure he knew perfectly well I was there. And I knew, without a

shadow of a doubt, that he was a vampire.

"Leave here, Lance. I've wanted nothing to do with you for centuries, and what I am now hasn't changed that."

I groaned internally. Great. Not only did we have a vampire in the house, it was one Owen didn't get along with. I also didn't think being outright rude was the best tactic when we were frighteningly overpowered.

"Poor Owen. Now you're human, insults are all you have left to defend yourself."

I almost stepped in between their bromance-gone-wrong to tell them to cool off, but doubted it would be a smart move.

Lance said, "No, I'll be going nowhere. There is something here. Something … delicious."

My stomach quivered and bile rose in my throat. I had no doubt that he meant me.

Air rushed by me and then on the stairs, right in front of me, stood the vampire.

Lance was older than Owen. An eternal silver fox, he had a thick mop of hair the color of bright steel, and his eyes were deep pools of black, the same as Owen's had once been before he drank from me. The dark jeans and black shirt he wore seemed too mundane for the creature he was. He had a V-shaped torso and a long, lean body, as if he'd just stepped out of an anime. A lazy smirk gave his features a roguish touch, but my body only responded to his handsome appearance as it had to Owen when I'd first seen him. With primal, animalistic fear.

I shrieked and dashed to Owen, hiding behind him.

"Don't you dare touch her," Owen growled.

Lance said, "I see nothing here but weak humans. How *ever* could you stop me?"

I gulped and pressed closer to Owen. His body was so tense that the muscles along the base of his neck had corded up, and his hands had balled into tight fists. I tried to breathe but could take in no air. I buried my face in Owen's back. I tried to think, to find an answer to Lance's teasing, rhetorical question I could slap him back with. To know we had any way of stopping him. I had nothing.

"I will kill you, Lance. Make no mistake, whatever friendship we once had is gone, and whatever ties I had to the vampire community and its laws are gone. If you lay one fang upon her, I will make you pay. She is mine. I have claimed her."

I chanced a look at Lance. His face had an almost drugged look of lust, his lips curling open with each breath, revealing sharp fangs. His gaze was on me, as though Owen had said nothing at all.

"Your claim over this delicious morsel would only mean something if you were a vampire. You've turned into a human and a fool. Maybe *I* should claim her. I must taste that blood."

"Lance, listen, there are consequences. Her blood isn't normal. It will change you," Owen warned. But I knew. It was true before, what Lance had said. Words were all we had, and they weren't working.

"You just don't want me to drink from your woman. But I will, and you will watch her blood flow into my mouth."

Owen threw his whole body at Lance.

A scream dislodged itself from my throat as they collided. Owen was larger than Lance, wider, thicker, more muscled. But that would have only given him the advantage if they were both human, or maybe even if they were both vampires. They smashed into a hall table. A vase of flowers fell, shattering with a sharp musical jangle. The scent of crushed freesias and lilies filled the air.

Owen shouted back at me, "Get to the luggage, get the blue bottle!"

I didn't know what he meant. But I ran. I couldn't do anything there. The only hope for us was for me to get away, to get a weapon. Maybe that was what the blue bottle was. Then maybe, maybe I could save Owen and myself.

The length of the hallway passed by me in a blur.

My feet slipped on something sharp. A broken piece of the sandwich platter met the sole of my right foot, slicing into it. A harsh yelp came from my throat. Pain shot upward from my foot into my ankle. My arms waved in the air as I groped for something, anything at all, for balance.

I fell so hard that my teeth clicked together and met on my tongue, bringing up the coppery taste of blood to my mouth. My head went backward, cracking against the hard marble floor.

Blackness hovered on the edges of my vision. Down the hall, Owen and Lance fought, their bodies a blur through the graying fog that tried to take me down into unconsciousness.

Lance was a vampire.

Owen was a very new human. It wasn't a fair fight at all.

Owen charged toward Lance again. Blood streamed down Owen's face, his nose likely broken.

Lance tossed him across the corridor like a wet rag. He landed with a sickening thud and didn't move.

"No! Owen!"

My hand closed around the largest shard of porcelain I could reach.

Lance came toward me, terrifyingly fast, but all the horror that I felt wasn't for myself. It was for Owen.

He lay still, an unmoving heap of bloodied flesh.

Lance stood over me, his hand tangled into my hair. He lifted me to my feet with a ripping, searing *pain as some hair tore away from my scalp.*

This was meant to be my home, my fairy tale castle, and it had become a nightmare. My home …

Lance said Marianne had let him in. Did vampires need invitations?

"I uninvite you!" I cried out.

Lance's lips quirked up, amused. "How are you with Owen, yet know so little about vampires?"

Defiantly, I stabbed the jagged piece of porcelain right at his face.

Lance snarled. He knocked the shard from my hand. He clamped down hard on my arms and I hovered there in his unrelenting grip. I had barely broken his skin, that hard, vampire skin.

But I had made him angry. I could see it all over his face. Angry, hungry, and lustful.

I panted out, "You don't want to eat me. You don't know what you're getting yourself into."

His fangs glistened, long and sharp. He inhaled my scent and growled.

Before I could say anything else his teeth were in my neck. Rough, deep, tearing. He drank in vast gulps that would take all of me. He was just as savage as Owen was the first time he drank from me, or more.

I struggled and fought, but Lance's hands held me like iron manacles. A sensation I knew too well.

The pain in my neck grew and grew. The icy yet hot sensation spread through me like lightning. Revulsion set in. That violation, that entering of my body with his teeth, that taking of something that was solely and wholly mine, my blood—it was something I had thought I would never have to feel again.

Tears ran down my face and dripped off my chin. The roaring in my ears grew louder, as though my heartbeat echoed there, the weak thumps growing slower and slower. But his frenzied devouring of me didn't slow at all.

The room spun as blood loss overwhelmed me.

Just before I faded away, a strange and terrible clarity came, briefly, with the thought that this time, I might not wake up again.

4

OWEN

Light, a faint and flickering glimmer, woke me. It got brighter and brighter with each second. With it came pain.

My eyes watered as the sting in my nose, back of my head, and shoulder all returned in force. I blinked the tears away, my eyes searching, taking in my surroundings.

Lance knelt on the floor, his eyes glazed and forehead wrinkled in confusion as he looked down. Kaitlyn lay there before him, unmoving. Even from a distance I could see her lips were blue. My heart leapt into my throat.

"What have you done? WHAT HAVE YOU DONE?" I roared.

My screams woke Lance from his stupor. He

glanced at me, frowned, then back to Kaitlyn. His pupils had lightened to a warm gray. Down one cheek, a thin, red scratch healed rapidly.

"She's alive. She's … what is she?"

"She's in hypovolemic shock, that's what she is," I hissed, crawling my way to be by her side. I ran my hands over her cold face and felt her slow heartrate. I shook her gently, called to her. She would not rouse.

Lance just stared at her, then at his own bloody hands.

"Help me. Help me save her," I begged.

Lance did nothing for a painfully long moment, and then nodded.

"There are first-aid supplies in my luggage."

Lance stood slowly, glanced at Kaitlyn again, then disappeared in a blur. I groaned, my shoulder protesting as I scooped Kaitlyn into my arms. I took her to the closest bedroom and laid her on the bed, elevating her legs.

I wasn't sure Lance would come back, but he did. He brought a bag of IV fluids, bandages, and epinephrine. All vampires who cared to keep their food alive knew how to treat blood-loss. And these days, I still kept around what I could, just in case. Easy to acquire, long shelf-life supplies only, but hopefully they would be enough. Once I was in control of my vampirism, I had always been careful not to drink so much my victims suffered from blood loss. Kaitlyn had been the first since modern medicine with whom I couldn't control myself. And I hadn't been prepared. All I'd had was coconut water. I was lucky she was tough.

I hoped she was tough enough to survive this.

Lance dumped the supplies listlessly on the bed beside Kaitlyn. I moved quickly, hanging the IV bag from a post of the bed's canopy and running the line down into one of Kaitlyn's veins. I gave her a shot of epinephrine to get her heart pumping faster again, then began bandaging her neck. Lance stood silent and still beside me the whole time.

My mind was split between doing everything I could to save Kaitlyn, and finding a sharp piece of wood to stab into Lance's heart.

Kaitlyn stirred. The smallest movement, her blue lips parted.

Lance turned away.

"Lance," I started, not sure what to say next.

He glanced back over his shoulder, his face a scary mix of emotions. Then he walked out, closing the door behind him.

I heard the click of the lock.

I cursed him. And I cursed myself for ever knowing him, for ever being a vampire, for ever being part of that bloody world. For everything Kaitlyn has suffered because of it, and was likely to yet.

But when we got free from this room, I would

have my revenge on Lance. If I could only get to my luggage and get the Nemexia, or to the hidden vault where I kept my even deadlier weapon. I still had my secrets.

It felt like hours I knelt beside that bed as though in prayer, watching Kaitlyn for more signs of life, waiting for her to come back to me.

Then I stood, pacing the room in long, thumping strides, rage building on hopelessness.

It was a long time before Kaitlyn's voice, soft and rough, reached me. "You're not dead."

I raced to her side. "No. I'm still here, and so are you."

She tried to sit up. I put my hand on her shoulder and gently pressed her back. "Don't. You lost a lot of blood, and you really need to stay lying down."

Her eyes drifted closed. "I thought he killed you," she breathed out.

Tears ran down the side of her face, and while her eyes were still closed, I let just one of my own fall. We were alive, and as long as we were, we could work the rest of this mess out together.

I wiped my thumb across her temple, wiping away the tears. "That makes us even then. I thought he'd killed you as well."

"I think it was a really close thing there for a second. It felt like he was never going to stop."

I looked back at the locked door. "But he did."

Remortality

Her hands sought out mine, her fingers chilled and shivering. "Where is he now?"

"He let me carry you in here. But he's locked us in."

"Ugh," she groaned. "You know I hate being a crab."

I frowned. Maybe she wasn't as lucid as I'd thought. The blood loss must have her confused.

"I mean," she continued with a *don't look at me like I'm crazy* expression. "How you once explained how people yank their legs off, toss them back into the ocean and let them grow new ones only to take them out again and snap off another one. I don't like feeling like a crab. Sure, this Lance guy stopped now, but maybe he just stopped so that he could save me for later."

My face fell. That was exactly what I'd done to her. When I'd first compared her to a crab it was to explain that she was only food to me, nothing more. As though *she* were the fool for not being able to understand her role.

"I won't let that happen. Not again."

"Then how do we get out of here?" she asked.

I surveyed the space we'd ended up in. It was the corner room, built into a tower. The ceiling was incredibly high, rising to form a conical point. There were a few windows, slim slits with stained glass that were fixed in place, and too narrow to fit through anyway. We were on a four-poster bed, designed to look old, but quite modern with a quality mattress.

Being a guestroom, it was devoid of any personal effects or decoration. The adjoining bathroom had the most basic toiletries, and no way of escape.

The bedroom door was thick, heavy wood. The old-fashioned two-way lock required a key that could be used on either side. The kind of lock where you could slide a piece of paper under the door and push the key out onto, if you were lucky enough that the key was left in the other side, and you had paper, and something to push the key through with. Lance had taken the key from the inside where it was normally kept. I looked through the keyhole, but he hadn't left the key in. I wasn't surprised. It was the oldest trick in the book, and he was just as old.

Kaitlyn looked around too, taking in the room first and then the IV line to her arm.

"Why do you think he stopped?"

"Given the look of utter horror on his face, I imagine the same thing happened to him that happened to me when I drank from you. I think your blood changed him."

"Do you think he's human now? He drank a lot."

I shook my head. A strange jealousy grew within me, that another vampire could taste Kaitlyn, could be changed by her. "No. He drank a lot, but the truth is, I drank much the same amount from you that first time too. While it changed my emotions immediately, it didn't make me human then. It took more … much more." My voice cracked, and I looked away, studying the IV line and avoiding Kaitlyn's eyes.

"Owen." Kaitlyn's voice grew stern. "I forgave you for that. But my forgiving you doesn't mean it didn't happen. We can't spend the rest of our lives tap dancing around the subject, and I'm not willing to hate you for it, because it wasn't you. You are no longer that monster. But you have to stop hating yourself too. I can't do that for you."

"I know. The things I did when I was a vampire … I may have been a different person then, a different creature, but I still did those things. I will always have remorse and regret, and I don't think that's a bad thing. I think for me to stay human I need those feelings."

Kaitlyn smiled up at me. Her eyelids fluttered, and I knew staying awake, and talking, were a struggle for her.

"You should rest. Sleep if you can. Recover while I find a way for us to get out of here, so you have your strength when the time comes."

"Tell me about Lance, how you know him," she said in a whisper. "Knowledge is pretty much the only power we have right now."

"Lance … He was my best friend, once. Older than me, both in human and vampire age, but he's never told me how much older. When I was free of Adelle, and trying to find my way, he was my mentor."

Kaitlyn lay still. Her hands squeezed mine lightly.

"All those years ago, Lance was a different type of being. He used to get angry at me for not always making the moral choice. He taught me that although we … *they* do not have the same compunctions or empathy as humans, that doesn't mean you can't use logic to decide which course is the better moral option.

"Lance was always on the side of doing the right thing. The thing that would cause the least harm to humans. Vampires may see humans as food, but you can still treat your food well before you devour it."

I paused for a long moment. Kaitlyn's breathing was steady, and deep. I smiled, knowing she'd recover. She was a survivor. I thought she'd fallen asleep when she squeezed my hand again.

"So, what happened?"

"I'm not sure exactly. Something did happen though. He changed, grew cynical, hateful, outright violent toward humans. I always wondered if perhaps it wasn't so much a case of him being cynical as it was a case of him becoming bored. Tired of trying to do the right thing when it went against his nature. You can't live as long as him and not get bored."

"Sure. I get bored occasionally, and I've hardly lived at all."

I looked at her face, her eyes still closed, but a cheeky smile cracked her lips, which had regained some color. Still so young, so few years she'd had to experience this world, this life. "I never should have brought you here. I never should have returned to this place from my past. I should have sold it and moved on, buried Owen Raine completely. I am so sorry."

Her eyes opened then, reprimanding me with a look for my expression of guilt. "If it didn't happen now, here, this was likely to happen anyway. Wasn't it?"

I couldn't answer. It had been my biggest fear every moment since my Strawberry had walked free of the home I'd held her captive in.

"Me and my damned tasty blood. It's why you had me followed, after you set me free. It's why you hired bodyguards for me while I was on set. I thought you were just being protective. I thought maybe, maybe chances of coming across another vampire were low."

"Not low enough. The perfume I gave you, it was for your protection too. It was based on Nemexia, or corpse flower, a fragrance that can knock out a vampire. Things like holy water are a myth, but Nemexia, wormwood, and a few other botanical extracts can be quite effective. I have some more of the perfume in my luggage, if we can somehow get to it."

"Why didn't you tell me? I would have worn it always if I'd known."

"I should have. I should have told you all these

things, but I didn't want you to always be scared. I wanted you to have nothing to do with that world." I shook my head slowly. *I wanted to protect her from all of this. From the truth of what is out there.*

"How many ..." Her voice choked off and started again. "How many vampires are there out there? I mean, really, how many could there be?"

I couldn't lie anymore. "Tens of thousands. Hundreds of thousands. Maybe millions. A whole society, all across the world. One with a long and bloody history, with its own standards and laws. One with every facet of vampire character. Those who follow the law. Those who follow a spiritual path. Solitary ones, and those who form communities. Those who only kill to eat. Those who let their food live. Those who kill for pleasure. A world I wanted to keep you free from, and failed."

Kaitlyn looked away. She stared at the wall, her lips parted. Fresh tears pooled in her eyes.

A faint opalescence hung in the corners of the windows; a tinge of light that said dawn would come soon. A dawn I could only see because of her. She had changed me. Maybe she could change Lance as well. Maybe we still had hope.

"What do you think will happen to Lance now he has had my blood? I mean, can we use him having drunk my blood to our advantage? If he had enough, maybe he gained some ... you know, some feelings.

Perhaps we could work on those feelings to try to get him to release us."

"I was thinking the same thing."

It was, in a way, what she'd done to me. I know she'd played on my growing feelings as her blood changed me. I couldn't blame her; she was just trying to stay alive. Now, I found myself questioning whether I'd be able to watch her seduce Lance in the same way if it meant her living. I didn't want to answer. I wanted the inhuman strength and lack of remorse I once had back so I could rip Lance to shreds.

The pearly glow in the windows was diffused by a golden-rose-colored blush. I stared at it.

Kaitlyn did too. "Help me up."

"Why?"

"The sun's rising," she said softly. "I want to see it, and so do you."

I did. I needed to see the sun, to hold onto my humanity and all it meant.

The IV was empty, so I removed it from her arm. I helped Kaitlyn from the bed and then carried her to one of the windows. I held her as I settled into the window seat, cradling her, and we stared out through the thick glass.

The view was magnificent from that room. A view I had never been able to enjoy until now, my first time in this place as a human. The high and jagged peaks of the mountains lit up and glowed, as though

someone had set them on fire. The sun, coming up between two peaks, hung there, framed by the stark rocks, a glowing orb whose color changed from rose to carnelian to beautiful gold. Little tendrils of color hit the sky, and those fingers stretched and raced across the heavens, sending the blackness of night fleeing before their reach.

The sun escaped the cage of the peaks and rose higher. The trees took on distinct shapes. The greenery of the pines stood in stark relief to the black rock. The sky lightened, and lightened again.

My head dropped as exhaustion came.

Kaitlyn sighed. "I know it should come as no surprise, but I'm starving. I should have pocketed some of the sandwiches instead of trying to stick Lance in the face with a broken plate. That would've been the smart plan."

An unexpected laugh coughed out of me. "I was wondering how he got that scratch."

I cuddled her closer. The thought of food made my stomach growl loudly, and Kaitlyn giggled.

She snuggled into my body. "I could really go for some outrageously cheesy pizza, and maybe a few garlic knots. Some creamy sauce for dipping, and extra—"

"Stop. I'm going to die if you don't."

She grinned.

I kissed her forehead. There was some small comfort

in the shared misery that was being hungry. Being hungry meant being alive, and we were, together.

The sun crept farther into the room, spilling broad bands of light across us and the floor. My eyes closed and I drifted off, Kaitlyn's arms around me, and the future hanging menacing and uncertain around both of us.

5

KAITLYN

I slept like the dead. Or at least the near dead, which I was sure I literally was.

Sleeping the whole day away felt like a waste. But I'd done this dance before. I knew what it was like being held captive by a vampire and drunk nearly dry. Our chances of escape were low, and even lower while I was still so weak from blood loss.

At some point, Owen had moved us back to the bed. He lay curled around me, protective, and warm. A few times through the day, I was woken by him as he got up and paced the room, tested exits, searched the bathroom, or tried to break the side-table into pointy stakes. Unsuccessfully.

I let myself sleep. Even the sound of wooden furniture being flung against the stone walls wasn't

enough to keep my eyelids open. I hovered between consciousness and the void of exhausted slumber, noticing what happened around me in a dreamlike way.

Owen returned to bed and laid beside me.

Night returned, darkening the room.

The steady creak of the door opening echoed around us.

Owen's body tensed against mine.

I woke fully, galvanized by fresh terror and the will to fight.

Owen sat up, shielding my body with his as Lance entered the room.

He flicked the light switch. His skin was a warmer tone, his irises slightly brighter than before. His expression hadn't warmed or brightened though. It was hard, thoughtful, but angry.

His hands twitched. "It's her blood, isn't it? How you became human?"

Owen shook his head. "You're mistaken. There is nothing special about her blood."

Lance laughed heartily. "Boldfaced, and ridiculous lies. It's too late to try to hide it now. There is something very special, and very delicious about her blood."

I cringed. My blood was like potato crisps. Once you slurped you couldn't stop. He was going to keep me just as Owen had. Owen had fought hard against taking more of my blood, but his willpower had faded before it every single time. I really had to get my hands on that vampire repellent perfume. I really wished Owen had told me about it before. Did he think I was too weak to know these things? He should have known better.

Owen was up off the bed. Without his shirt, I could see every muscle in his chest ripple and strain in anger. "Don't even think about biting her again. You won't get another drop of her blood. I will kill you first."

Lance remained amused. "I don't want another drop of that blood."

My jaw dropped.

"Have I hurt your feelings? Thought you were too tasty to deny?" Lance asked.

I broke eye contact. I did think that. I didn't know whether to be upset or relieved.

"You're delicious, sweetheart, but so is chocolate. It is possible to say no to chocolate."

"Says you," I muttered. Chocolate from some four-or-more hundred years ago had no chance of comparing to modern chocolate. He had *no idea.*

"Especially if you know it's bad for your health," he said.

I looked him in the eye again, trying to gauge his current motivations. He seemed serious. He had no interest in my blood.

The thought chilled me. I'd always believed Owen treated me as he did when he was a vampire because

he literally couldn't resist. That the monstrous part of him had an unstoppable thirst for my blood.

But he could have stopped. Lance was choosing to stop.

The truth was, Owen chose to keep feeding from me. To keep me prisoner. Because he wanted to, and he could.

Lance had more information to make his choice. He knew the consequences of continuing to drink my blood. Maybe if he didn't know that, like Owen hadn't, he'd make a different choice. But still, I knew now that it was, indeed, a choice.

Owen sat back beside me on the bed and put his arm around me protectively. I had the strange urge to shy away from him.

He's different now. He's human now. He's not the monster that chose to keep me as food—he's the human who set me free. I tried to remind myself of all those things, but the lines felt too blurry and confused right now.

Owen's body softened, shoulders dropping. His whole posture changed from aggressive to submissive, but the small muscle twitching in his jaw told me the effort he put into making that switch. He pleaded, "Old friend, let us go. Don't get involved in what her blood could mean. Forget you saw me like this. Forget her."

Lance nodded, but just as my hopes rose, they fell again.

"I will let you go. Only I cannot free you entirely. What she's done, what you are—you can't keep this hidden."

Lance looked back at the open doorway and said, "I had to tell the council what has happened to you, and to me. You shouldn't have come here, Owen—not with nothing but human in your veins. Had I not found you, they would have scented you out fast enough. They were already looking for you anyway, with your suspicious attempt to disappear."

That's when I realized we weren't alone. I saw them moving, but didn't hear a sound, as two people—presumably vampires—dressed entirely in black came in to stand behind Lance. Their clothing matched, a uniform maybe, but more ninja-like than soldier. Long pants and full-length sleeves in flowing black silk, cowls that covered their head except their black eyes, and thick, black armor protecting just their neck and chest.

I peeked up at Owen's face. His jaw was tight. "I gave them no reason to watch for me. I was nothing to the vampire world, their politics. I never broke their laws."

Lance raised his gray eyebrows to that comment. "Whatever you may or may not have done in the past, you were a long-lived and wealthy member of both vampire and human society. Trying to make all that disappear was a mistake. Of course, they

would look into it. Of course, *I* would look into it. We may not have been friends for a good century, but I was curious what happened to you. I had to look for you. Why do you think I'm here?"

"And now they know where I am, and what I am. Thanks to you," Owen growled.

Lance's shoulders lifted, then dropped. His hands opened and closed. A confused look crossed his face as he glanced at the silent black warriors flanking him. "It's out of my hands. You have been invited to the estate of the Synedrion."

Owen's eyes narrowed. A red flush of blood spread along his cheeks and forehead. "You mean we are to be taken there. That is no invitation, and you know it. Don't try to dress it up as one."

I had no idea what the Synedrion was, but it didn't sound good at all. It sounded downright terrifying in fact, as did the mention of a vampire council. I had never imagined vampires to be so organized. Then again, I'd imagined that we'd be able to avoid vampires for the rest of our lives. I clearly didn't know anything about vampires.

Lance turned away from us. "Get up. You have thirty minutes before we go. I wouldn't try anything. Joss and Ash here have been sent to make sure you both arrive at the Synedrion estate, alive."

He left the room. Left us to the cold stare of our two new jailers.

Remortality

I stood beside Owen. He pulled me under his arm and whispered, "They are Ebonguard. Vampires, but you don't have to worry about them coming after you, unless those are their orders. If their orders are to get us to the Synedrion alive, that's what is going to happen."

"And that's just the tip of the explanation iceberg I need right now. I know enough to tell we're in deep trouble. I'm going to need you to catch me up on the rest."

Owen nodded. "Come on. We need to do what they say, for now. We have little hope against a regular vampire. Let alone an Ebonguard."

I shivered. I hated being helpless. Head on confrontation would get us nowhere. We just had to wait for an opening, a chance, and there wasn't one now.

My first step forward almost dropped me to the ground. I hadn't realized how weak I still was. Owen caught me and supported me through to the adjoining bathroom. We weren't allowed to close the door. We showered quickly and at the same time. Under other circumstances that would have been sexy. Instead, it was frightening and tense. I carefully washed away the dried blood around my neck. The warm water helped bring my body back from the deathly cold I'd been feeling, but it didn't stop the shakes.

One of the Ebonguard had brought our suitcases

up into the room while we showered. It seemed like a thoughtful, almost human gesture. They probably just wanted to hurry us along though.

I met Owen's glance with the same look of hope when we saw our cases, mine still unopened from our arrival the day before, Owen's riffled through for the first-aid supplies. Before we could reach them though, one Ebonguard unzipped and worked through each bag, their hands flashing with speed as they searched. I held my breath, and almost groaned it out when the Ebonguard held up a tiny blue vial. Lance must have told them about it.

And buh-bye, there went that plan.

We weren't left alone to dress, so Owen blocked me as best he could from the view of our guards. I dug out some purple fleece tights and a chunky-knit, ivory sweater dress. I didn't care who we were seeing or how I should dress for the occasion. I needed comfort clothes right now. Owen put on navy-blue suit pants and a pale gray t-shirt. We both grabbed our warmest coats and zippered up our luggage which was taken away again by one of our ninja-like companions.

Owen checked his watch. We had less than ten minutes, so headed quickly to the kitchen. I could have eaten a twelve-course degustation with a few large pizzas on the side. But we didn't have time for much more than a scant meal, whatever we could grab. We scarfed down thickly sliced creamy brie on crusty sour-dough bread, and a couple of cups of hot, strong coffee. There was a bowl of fresh fruit, and I grabbed an apple for the road. I tried to slip a steak knife into my pocket too, but an Ebonguard snatched it back from me with a chiding shake of their head.

The thundering hum of a helicopter landing out the front marked the end of our stay.

"Time to go," said one of the guards. I was stunned to hear a woman's voice. The cowl, armor, and loose uniform hid most of their body shape. Looking again, I supposed it wasn't too unclear it was a female form. Maybe both of them could be. The names Joss and Ash could go either way.

I downed the last sip of my coffee and we were led outside.

Black shadows crept around the statues on the lawn and clung to every corner of the grounds. We were loaded into the helicopter, and I was glad to see our luggage coming with us. A small sign that they didn't intend to kill us right away. That maybe we really were going to be treated like guests rather than prisoners. Joss and Ash took the seat opposite us, our knees touching theirs in the small space.

Lance was in the front, across from the pilot, another Ebonguard.

When he saw we were all in, he said something inaudible. He and the pilot wore headsets that they could speak to each other through, but the roar of the engine and blades was all I could hear. I tried to say something to Owen, but even my own voice was only a dull hum.

I wanted to ask so many questions. Who were the vampires we were being forced to go see? And where were we being taken? What would they do to us? Would they kill us? Would they see my blood as a threat to their very nature? Or as a savior?

There was no way to know.

The helicopter rocked on its feet as it lifted from the ground. We bobbed about in the air, the sensation of flight so much different than in a plane. Then the pressure of acceleration pushed me back into the seat, and the details of the world below us vanished into black.

I stared out the window, my hand clutched in Owen's, and tried to just breathe.

I looked over at him. He gazed back at me.

I mouthed, *"I love you."*

He kissed my forehead in return.

Far below, small towns and cities passed by beneath us, their lights like glittering streams in the darkness.

We continued onward through the gloomy night, through a darkness as deep but not nearly as restful as the grave.

6

KAITLYN

I checked my phone during the trip. The Ebonguard kept an eye on me, although didn't try to take it off me. There was no reception as we flew anyway, even if I thought I could call anyone for help. I could just imagine how that call to 911 would go.

"Hi, what's your emergency?"

"Well, I've been kidnapped by vampire ninjas and I'm in a helicopter who-knows-the-fuck-where."

Even if emergency services could help, I didn't know what country we were in at this point. I didn't have enough reception to send a message or get online. I ended up playing a tower defense game, just to kill time and take my mind off the anxiety that swirled as fast as the helicopter blades. I ate the apple I brought along, sharing with Owen bite for

bite, and wished I'd pocketed the whole fruit bowl, and some chocolate bars, and the coffee machine.

We'd been in the air for about two hours when we finally descended to land. I was ready to be on solid ground again; the whir of the helicopter felt embedded in my bones like a strange vibrating sickness. It worsened the fear I already felt about this enforced invitation into the vampire world.

The helicopter went down, down, as though descending into the pits of hell. Darkness rose on either side of us as we flew low between two mountain ranges, deeper into a valley where even the stars and moon above seemed out of sight.

Then light flared around us as we reached the flood-lit landing pad. Vampires may have been creatures of the night, but they didn't seem averse to having well-lit spaces.

The helicopter landed with the crunch of gravel underneath and the whump, whump, whump of the blades winding down.

"We're here," Owen said, and squeezed my hand. Hearing his voice was like I'd been deaf and suddenly learned to hear again. He spoke low, although I imagined the vampires around us could hear him anyway. Did they have super-hearing? I added that to my list of vampire information I needed.

"Where *is* here?" I whispered back. My voice didn't want to work.

"Romania. Umbravallis, the Valley of Shadow."

"Cheery," I said.

Owen rushed his words, as though trying to catch up on what he hadn't been able to tell me during our flight. "It is home to the Synedrion, a powerful vampire council who oversee a large vampire community, and imagine themselves the rulers of all vampires. Umbravallis is a valley so deep it only gets direct sunlight in summertime. This is where vampires go when they prefer to live only amongst their own kind, by their own rules, rather than living hidden alongside humans. There is a town, a number of private estates, and the estate of the Synedrion."

"Great. So, it's Vampireland. We're in Vampireland. Are we the only humans here?"

Owen's expression became grim. "No. There will be thralls too. Food sources, slaves, some willing victims, some not."

I shuddered at the thought.

The Ebonguard on my right slid the helicopter door open. Outside lay a barren, rocky landscape, as though we'd just landed on the moon. Nothing seemed alive out there. A soft wind blew through the night, bringing the earthy scent of dust and dryness.

We were ushered out almost politely and loaded into an awaiting car. Joss and Ash got in the back with us. The divider between the back and front

was clear glass, and Lance got in the driver's seat. He tapped at the dash of touch screens and the car moved without any further action from him. Driverless technology. So the vamps here were up on modern luxuries and had the money for it too. A self-driving car would be very handy if you had to black out every window.

The road was smooth and well-made, despite the sharp, craterous landscape around us. We glided along, soon passing wider areas filled with walled estates and immaculate mansions. Not many gardens though. Only a few misshapen plants grew here with so little sunlight: potted plants of varieties I'd never seen, and a few leafless, tortured trees. Estate grounds were mostly paved, decorated with fountains and statues. One we passed had fake trees in colors of gold and silver. And all those homes had vampires inside.

"We're going to be seeing more vampires, lots of vampires. This doesn't feel safe at all. What if one decides my blood is just too delicious?" I looked to Owen for assurance, but Ash, or Joss, whichever one it was, beat him to the answer.

"That's why we are here. To ensure your safety. You will be under guard for your protection throughout your stay."

For my protection and imprisonment, I wanted to argue. But didn't. I was starting to learn to keep

my mouth shut. Sometimes.

Joss and Ash were all business, and appeared to have no interest in my blood, which comforted me a little. Neither did Lance, now he knew what it did. That didn't mean I was safe. The Synedrion wanted to see us because of my blood and what it was reported to do.

Once they'd seen for themselves ... best possible outcome? They could like the idea of having the choice to go human again and we become lab rats. Worst possible outcome? The end.

I couldn't see any way out of this, but if these vampires could be reasoned with, I was preparing myself to do as much reasoning as possible. Vampires could be intelligent, and they even had emotions of a sort. They just lacked empathy. I imagined myself about to deal with a room full of sociopaths. Could be a bit like some days in Hollywood.

We passed through a small town. Historic buildings mixed with occasional modern shops and apartment towers, the roads all lit with elegant streetlights designed like hanging bell-flowers. People ... *vampires* moved about, as though it were a normal day, shopping, chatting, drinking at a café. Probably not coffee though. I had the oddest sensation, the strangest little thought that this was all some fantastical movie set and that at any minute the director would yell "cut," the lights would go up, and there would be normalcy just beyond

the car's closed doors and windows.

I blinked hard and then bit my lip. The slight pain grounded me, snapped me out of the disorientation and disassociation that I had been floating toward. I knew how dangerous that was, and just how seductive. I had to keep my wits about me no matter how much I would rather pretend this was all some dream that would blow away the moment I awakened.

My eyes widened as we drove into the largest cavern I had ever seen. The road went right in, lined with those same ornate streetlights. Floodlights lit the cave, showing off the impressive limestone falls, columns, and stalagmites and stalactites, all old-bone yellow, like the cave had its own skeleton and teeth.

We passed through massive iron gates, onwards toward a palace that had been built of the same stone that surrounded it, up against the back of the cave itself. Three stories in height, the palace was lined with columns cut from dripping limestone, and elegant arched windows that shone brightly from within, accentuating their pointed gothic style.

The circular entrance drive looped around a huge fountain created from a spiral-shaped lime-stone column. Parked cars crowded the front of the building. I imagined that gossip had already spread, and hundreds of black eyes looked down from the windows to see the vampire turned human and the woman who had made that happen.

We pulled up amongst the row of cars. A blank and silent human came to take our bags. Her pale, blue eyes held no expression, and the modern, gray housekeeping uniform she wore hung loose over her malnourished frame. She didn't have the same stink of crazy about her that Loretta had had. I wanted to reach out to her, shake her from her slavery and see her run free, but she ignored me entirely.

Drips from the fountain plinked melodically, but its music was offset by the shriek and chatter of bats in the cave ceiling high above.

Joss and Ash led the way inside. Owen's arm wrapped around me but brought me no comfort. Lance walked ahead, then dropped back to be beside us.

He opened his mouth, hesitating for a moment before he actually spoke, "If it's worth anything, I'm sorry about this. Just after drinking your blood, I was flooded with feelings, with anger and confusion at so many things. Mostly at myself. I contacted the Synedrion before I had the clarity I have now. Before I considered what it could mean. For you, Kaitlyn and Owen, and for all of us. I fear I've made a mistake."

He seemed sincere, almost sad. His skin tone had barely anything left of the warmth it had held after drinking from me, and his eyes were pure black again. But here he was, expressing regret.

"A mistake?" Owen grunted. "You've doomed us."

Lance's eyebrows furrowed, then he rolled his eyes, as though chasing that expression away. "You're over-reacting. I'm sure the Synedrion will treat you well."

Owen snorted in disagreement.

"It's done now. What are you going to do to help keep us alive if they don't treat us well?" I challenged.

Lance's head bowed. "I'm not sure what your experience with vampires has been like in the past, but we can be perfectly reasonable. Some may see your blood and what it can do as an offense to our kind, but I'm sure they will be a minority. Having tasted it … having known these human feelings again, even if they fade from me and I never drink from you a second time, you've changed me. I used to be a better man in the past. I had forgotten those emotions. I had forgotten the reasons why. But I've been reminded."

He looked Owen in the eyes then. "I want to be that better man again. I don't see how that can be a bad thing."

Owen held his gaze and nodded his approval.

Yay. A new vampire friend, I thought, not without sarcasm. If it takes every single vampire on Earth drinking from me to turn them to my side, that might be a bit much.

We stepped into a three-story-high entry hall hung with two rows of brightly lit crystal chandeliers. Not the black wrought-iron, filled-with-bright-red-candles cliché I'd been expecting. Whoever these vampires were, they had beautiful taste.

"It's all so bright," I said.

"Expecting it to be dark and gloomy?" Lance said, raising a silver brow. "Vampires see well in the dark, but only a dull, black and white view of the world. Color and warmth is still appreciated, even if it's not necessary."

A huge casual area, almost like you'd find in a hotel lobby or bar, lay beyond the entry hall. Black satin and rich leather armchairs filled the generous space.

You know what else filled that space? Vampires. Vampires filled that space.

As we walked in, almost every one of them paused to stare at us. Some bared their fangs. Others sneered and whispered to each other.

My feet were working on their own, walking backwards. An irrepressible fear had taken over my body and I had to get out of there. It's not safe for a lamb to be in a place with so many wolves. Every instinct I had screamed *GET OUT!*

One of the Ebonguard grabbed me by the shoulder, halting my progress. "You are safe," he said, simply. *He.* The distinction between him and the female Ebonguard shocked me out of the fight-or-flight instinct. I still didn't know which was Joss and which was Ash though.

Owen and Lance took their positions on either side of me again. My small entourage improved my spirits, and I faced the room again.

The vampires stared at us like we were the new kids at school. Scattered between them, dozens of human thralls moved about. Some fawned over their vampire masters, but in a dull, drug-hazed way. Others were being fed on, right there in the open, their faces blank to the pain. Some stood motionless simply awaiting their next command. I wanted to help them, but didn't even know how to help myself.

A vampire with slick black hair and a carefully trimmed beard suddenly appeared before us. His hand was outstretched to grab Owen, but was held mid-air by the male Ebonguard. I hadn't even seen any of it happen. One moment we were walking, the next, there he was.

The female Ebonguard stepped forward. "These guests are under the protection of the Synedrion."

They stood like that for a moment, sizing each other up. Long enough for me to take in the situation, before the black-haired vampire submitted and backed off a step.

I heard Owen let out a long, slow breath. "Dante. Haven't seen you since—"

"Since Adelle," Dante spat back at him. "Since you killed her."

I raised an eyebrow. I knew the story of Adelle.

Owen had told me how vampires weren't allowed to kill each other, and that a cursed ring had found its way to Adelle. Seemed Dante had heard a different story.

"You know that's not true," Owen said. "I was cleared of any suspicion regarding her death."

Lance flicked his chin up. "Bugger off, Dante. We've got no time for your drama."

Dante grunted. He leaned in dangerously close to Owen, hissing in his ear, "I was there when she died. She hid me from you, knowing how jealous you were, how you'd killed her other lovers in the past. I don't know how you did it, but I saw you take something from the dust you turned her to, and one day I will prove your guilt."

My eyes widened. Before I could fully process what Dante had said, a tall female vampire stepped up behind him. She placed her French-tipped fingernails lightly on Dante's shoulder. His lips twitched closed as he turned to her. Silky blond hair fell around her moon-like face.

She smiled through lips painted a perfectly glossy nude-pink. "Playing nice, Dante?"

His response was to growl and stalk away.

Owen greeted the woman with a formal embrace and European-style double-cheek kiss. "Night's greetings, Niamh."

"To you too." She looked him over and grimaced. "It looks like you've done it this time." She leaned close

again and took a sniff of him. A spike of jealousy hit hard. *Vampire or no, how dare she sniff my man like that?*

In a voice filled with wonder, she said, "It's true. You … you changed back to human!" A blood tear ran down her face. Her hands shook.

My own lips parted. I didn't know vampires could cry, that they could feel much other than hunger. There was something so powerful about that single tear of blood. I wondered if it were a happy tear, or a tear of mourning.

"Night's greetings, Niamh." Lance kissed her in the same way Owen had. I wondered if all vampires knew each other, or if this was a select circle, the vampire upper-class, which I could imagine Owen would have at some point been part of.

Then Niamh's gaze fell on me. I smiled, thinking for a moment to try to win her over. But her nostrils flared and her tongue swiped across her bared fangs. Her voice was thick. "Well, hello there. I was warned you would smell delicious." Her eyes darted briefly to Joss and Ash standing by me. She blinked and offered a polite smile. "Come. I'm to show you to your accommodations."

Niamh led us out. I tried to catch Owen's eye with a WTF expression, but it was like he was avoiding looking at me.

The opulence of the palace we walked through

rivalled that of Versailles. Thralls hurried about their tasks, none of them speaking a word to anyone. The sound of music, baroque and stringed, drifted from somewhere. Many vampires we passed eyed us with unhidden repulsion.

"Ignore them," Niamh said. "It's natural some will see Owen's change as an abomination. Some simply see him as a curiosity. But there are some who see him as something else entirely, a hope long ago lost."

Owen didn't react when a male vampire, wearing a well-tailored black suit with a dark dress shirt, paused, hissed, and raced away from us like we were carrying the plague.

Well, okay, maybe I was carrying some kind of vampire changing plague, but Owen wasn't.

Or was he? He didn't have the yummy scent I apparently had, but we had no experience yet with a vampire drinking from him. I was sure this would be something else the vampires here would want to know, maybe even to test.

Niamh stopped at a door, smiled, and punched in some numbers on a keypad so fast her fingers were a blur. The door clicked open.

Lance bowed very slightly. "I'll see you again soon," he said. Clearly being our friend didn't mean being trapped in our "accommodations" with us.

"You'll have some time to rest before the council meet. You'll be provided with food and medical aid

shortly. I must also ask now that you surrender your phones and any other connected devices to us."

We both reluctantly handed over our phones.

"There is a laptop in their luggage as well," said the male Ebonguard.

Niamh narrowed her eyes at us, and Owen just shrugged. Hey, couldn't blame him for not mentioning it, right?

The laptop was collected by one of the Ebonguard, then Niamh stood back from the door and waved her arm for us to enter.

Owen ushered me inside and the door shut, the click of the lock unmistakable. My shoulders tensed. *I'm getting real tired of vampires locking me up.*

"At least the room's nice," Owen said.

I rolled my eyes. A pretty prison was still a prison, but I could imagine a rat-infested, muddy, medieval dungeon would be a lot worse. I guessed I was grateful for that.

"Owen, you do know they could decide to eat the both of us at any moment."

"I do."

I saw real pain written on his face then, torment showing in the wet gloss of his eyes and twitch of his jaw.

"I … I have never wished so much to be a vampire before. If I still was, we wouldn't be here. Lance wouldn't have dared to take your blood back at the castle, as it was claimed as mine."

"I get that he wouldn't have done it because … I don't know, maybe stealing another vampire's blood vessel is like the human version of double-dipping chips or something, but you know I prefer you as a human. Mostly because I didn't much care for you sucking my blood."

Owen's shoulders dropped lower. His voice was a throaty growl. "You're still my Strawberry. The one thing I can't live without. I wish I still had the strength to protect you."

My heart beat a little faster. I loved him so much, and I hated to see him so torn about being human. I hated it, and the guilt that crept over me at that helplessness he felt due to being human, a state I caused him to be. Being human was a weakness we shared now, and that weakness might see one, or both, of us dead.

"I can't live without you either." My hand grazed his shoulder. I turned to him, and my mouth caught his.

The kiss was long and lingering. My body arched into his and he wrapped me tightly in his arms. My eyelids fell closed as I clung desperately to him. I still reacted to him with such a primal, fierce longing. My cheeks flushed and hands roamed. I wanted him so badly that I shook with the heady mix of desire and fear.

There was a knock on the door, and we both

tensed. The door opened and a thrall entered, bearing a tray of food hidden under silver domed lids. Joss and Ash stood outside the door, and had probably been there the whole time. The food was placed down on a table and the thrall left as a new vampire arrived. He carried an old-fashioned doctor's bag, but was gangly and looked too young to be a doctor. With vampires, though, visual age meant nothing.

Joss or Ash, I still didn't know which was which, followed him in, closing the door behind them.

"So, are you a human doctor or a vampire doctor?" I asked.

"I'm a vampire doctor to humans. Vampires generally have no need for doctors, but their thralls do," he said, his voice blunt.

He put his bag down on the table next to the food, and clicked it open.

"Quite the oddity, you two," he said, failing to introduce himself again. Doctor Vampire pulled a modern-looking blood-pressure monitor from his bag and took my arm without even asking.

"Um, excuse me?"

He didn't react to my objection either as he continued checking me over, flashing a light in my eyes, cleaning and redressing the wound on my neck, and injecting me with something. I looked to Owen in alarm.

"Probably antibiotics, for the risk of infection,"

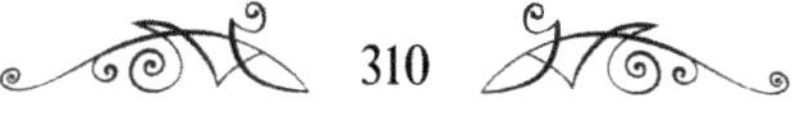

he offered.

"Blood-loss medication," the doctor corrected. He didn't bother with more details.

Apparently finished with me, he checked Owen's vitals as well. He noted all down on a slim tablet computer, then just like that, packed away his gear.

"Eat the food. Drink lots of liquids," he ordered.

I realized that was probably how he was used to treating humans, if thralls were his main customers. Bedside manner from a creature with no empathy who only treated brainwashed slaves was probably too much to ask.

Then he left, the Ebonguard at the door following him out and giving us some privacy again.

"Food it is then," I said.

Owen opened the room service, to reveal two bowls of a very thick, unappealing gray stew and glasses of room-temperature water.

"Wow. I guess human food isn't a big priority around here."

"It is dull, but nutritious, full of iron. It is what the thralls eat."

I sighed.

We ate in silence. My mind swirled like a tornado, but instead of dust and debris it was filled with fears and all the things I'd learned so quickly about vampires. I had so much I wanted to ask Owen, but the darker thoughts, the doubts, started creeping in.

Wondering what that Dante man had been getting at. Wondering how every vampire here had been able to resist me, but Owen chose not to. Wondering too many hurtful things, so I dared not open my mouth for fear they would all burst out.

The stew was thick and sludgy, like a mix of veggies, porridge, and ground meat. There were no spices or salt to improve the flavor, but it went down easily enough and settled well in my empty stomach.

I had almost worked up the nerve to ask Owen some questions when the door opened again. Niamh and Lance had returned, and Joss and Ash came in after them.

It was time to meet the Synedrion.

7

KAITLYN

We marched down the long hallway in silence. "That's it. I can't bear it anymore." I gave a melodramatic, exasperated sigh. "Which of you is Joss and which one is Ash?"

The ninja-like Ebonguard, one on either side of Owen and me, kept walking silently.

Then, "Joss," said the woman.

"Ash," said the man.

"Making friends with the Ebonguard now? I'm impressed. They aren't generally the friendly type. You're a special one indeed." Lance laughed, slowing to walk closer to us. The Ebonguard didn't seem to find it funny.

"Yeah, and maybe you monsters are too busy being monsters to care what each other's names are," I snapped.

Lance seemed almost hurt. "You might be right there. You know, it's Ebonguard tradition, during their initiation, to shed all but a single syllable for their name. And no, most don't speak to them. They are, even among us vampires, a bit intimidating." He shrugged, and picked up his pace again, moving ahead.

Me and my big mouth. I should have been trying to make friends here as much as possible. It was my only chance.

"Sorry," I muttered. "I'm a little out of sorts. Blame it on the blood loss. And being kidnapped. And held prisoner."

"Those things are likely to dampen your spirits." He slowed, returning to my side. "I'm sure things will be fine, but I wish there was something I could do to ease your concerns."

"You can," I said promptly. "You can hold off Joss and Ash—no offense guys, I know you're just doing your job—while Owen and I make a break for it. Easy peasy, done."

Joss and Ash didn't react to my open plotting at all. Talk about confidence in their role, or in how hopeless our escape attempt would be.

"Not so easy peasy. Firstly, I doubt I'd be physically able to hold off Joss and Ash. I'm not that powerful. Few vampires would be. Secondly, vampires are everywhere, and there is nowhere for the two of you to hide now."

"A very sunny part of the tropics sounds good to me. A small deserted island. I'm sure Owen could swing it. Or I'll sell the castle and trade up. On a side note, are you looking to buy a castle?"

"Aren't you charming?" Lance said. "Ready to make a real estate transaction out of a bad situation. I like that about you."

I had a feeling he liked my blood way more than my humor and charms. I also felt a really uncomfortable sensation set in at the words as I pondered the possibility that Lance was actually flirting with me. Right here. In front of Owen. Right after he'd almost killed me. The fucking nerve.

"What I like about *you* is that you're not drinking my blood. Let's keep it that way so I keep liking you. How about that?"

He put a wounded expression on his face, and played it up. "I already said I don't want any more of your blood. I will not hurt you again. Some of us can control our hungers."

We rounded a corner in the maze of corridors and were met with a mob of vampires blocking the way. We came to a stop.

"And some of us can't," Lance finished his thought.

"Clear the path," Niamh commanded.

One male vampire let out a low groan and I shrank

away, my arms tucking tightly to my sides. He jostled closer. "Soon, the council will decide they don't care for whatever you are, and stop protecting you. Then you'll be fair game. Then we'll all be drinking from you, taking turns, tasty thing."

Owen tensed, but before his slow human body could act, Lance stepped in front of me, shielding my body with his in an alpha male display of aggression. His stance screamed an ownership of me that neither I nor Owen appreciated, but the other vampires stepped back. Another warning from Niamh and the Ebonguard had them fleeing in a blur of speed.

Owen glared. He grunted, whispering in my ear, "He's acting like he's claimed you."

Lance heard this and turned to look Owen right in the eye. Like a challenge. Then he smiled. "Just a show. It will help keep her safe."

Owen clearly didn't like the idea either way. Neither did I.

I would not be some vampire's possession.

Before I could say anything, or maybe make a break out a window, a low ringing bell sounded. The bell, deep and timorous, made every vampire stiffen. Owen pulled me closer. His eyes looked into mine. "The council is waiting on us."

We followed Niamh through echoing hallways and past empty rooms. The place had a strange deserted feel despite the things living inside of it. A dry, bitter smell hung over everything.

We exited one corridor into a much wider and taller hallway. In the shadow beside me, a man stood, poised to attack. His fangs were bared, his arms outstretched.

I gasped and stumbled back into Owen. The man standing to the side of the hall made no other move. No move at all—nor would he ever, I saw. He was a statue made of charcoal-colored stone.

My heart still pounding, I saw more hideous statues lining each wall of the hallway. Owen steadied me as I looked around at them. Some were frozen mid-attack. Some cowered or begged. One appeared to be asleep. Some were women, some men. All were vampires, and all had an expression of agony on their faces.

What a way to welcome people into the council chambers. A nice little reminder of the consequences of possible verdicts, I supposed.

Owen squeezed my shoulder but offered no explanation. We moved down the strange gauntlet of horrifying statues.

We reached a set of double doors at the end of the hallway and Niamh opened them.

Lance, Owen and I went through; the others remained outside. As the door behind us closed I stopped in my tracks. My eyes went wide.

There was a raised dais that led up to a massive fall of limestone, like a waterfall made of melted bones.

Seven thrones were carved into the rock, each equal in size, and the falls were spotted with candlelight. Rivers of wax dripped from them, blending into the ivory limestone underneath. Tapestries in dark bloody colors hung from the other walls. Velvety red carpets covered the floor and steps leading to the thrones.

The ceiling was high, at least three stories, right to the top of the natural cavern. There were no windows. It was stifling, not only because the air was thick and heavy either, but because that color scheme, which should have been decadent and opulent, felt oppressive and too-heavy. It appeared to have been unchanged for centuries.

A herald of some kind was announcing our entrance and making long and tedious introductions and instructions in a droning thrall voice.

But my only thoughts were on the seven who sat on those thrones. I didn't want to look. I somehow knew, on a primitive and cellular level, that monsters sat there. Not just monsters, the rulers of monsters. No matter how much I told myself to keep my head down, my curiosity got the better of me. I looked up, then openly gawked at the seven vampires seated in the chairs that ranged along the raised dais.

Five were women. One had hair the color of flame. Her skin was so pale and so perfect, and her neck so long and slender, that she could have been a pre-Raphaelite portrait that had somehow had life breathed into it. Okay, maybe not life, an animated un-death. She wore a jade-colored gown made of a heavy brocade fabric, and an emerald and ruby necklace that encircled her neck like a high collar.

Owen saw me looking. "That is Delphine. Next to her is Shirina, Milton, Lin, Viatrix, Toren, and Bertha."

Putting names to the faces didn't help make them more human. Delphine had a regal, imperious demeanor, and as her eyes locked with mine, the corners of her mouth, lips as reddened as a ripe raspberry, lifted upward slightly.

I hastily looked away to the next in the row.

With hair that fell like a black waterfall all the way to the ground, and an elegantly curved nose, Shirina wore a tight royal-blue gown with a very low neckline that showed off her other elegant and abundant curves. Sapphires winked and flashed from her throat, her hands, and her ears.

The man next to her, as golden as she was dark, looked at me with black vampire eyes that were in stark contrast to his glowing god-like appearance. Milton's ivory blond hair, and a light, honey tan, were played up by an all-white suit. *How on earth does he have a tan?* It had to be a spray-on.

Lin seemed the most normal. Uncomfortably normal, like she could have stepped out of an office

meeting, with her neat, mousey brown hair, her pant-suit, and her smile that was both disingenuous and frightening.

Viatrix was the one furthest from normal. It was like there was no color at all in her skin or hair. She sat still, like part of the stone around her, her eyes closed, her ashy dress of dripping lace giving the impression she was crumbling to dust right in front of us.

The male vampire next to her, Toren, looked as I would imagine Merlin, or some other ancient wizard, to appear. His body was old, his skin crepey and translucent, his hair white, but he had no stiffness or stoop that came with age. He sat tall and alert, strong and clear.

I knew vampires could be any age, whatever age they were turned, and stay that way, but I'd always imagined them young. And Bertha was at the youngest end of the age spectrum, a teenager by appearance. I wondered if there were younger vampire children out there, or if turning children was taboo even for these monsters.

My mouth hung slightly agape as I studied Bertha. She appeared to be no older than eighteen, but her petite form was dressed in a way more suited to an adult. A white silk shirt in a modern cut was worn casually, collar loose, under a herringbone blazer. Her blond hair was trimmed short in a no-nonsense pixie-cut.

As I observed her, the teen vampire yawned widely, not bothering to cover it either.

The vampire with the flaming red hair spoke in a sharp tone, "Bertha, if you cannot concentrate on your duties, perhaps we should relieve you of them."

The herald, who had been continuing his droning announcements about the glory and honor of the original seven, halted, and his last words echoed throughout the chamber.

Bertha gave Delphine an insolent glare. "There's nothing wrong with my concentration, thank you. I just wish you would dispense with the boring ceremony and get on with it already. We're here to discuss Miss French, not bore her to death with pompous speeches." She looked over to me then. "Loved you in *The Way You Do*, by the way."

I opened my mouth to say thank you, but my voice had been stunned silent. That was the movie I'd had a role in right after being freed by Owen. I guess it shouldn't have been surprising that vampires watched movies too, but it just seemed such a human thing. I warmed up toward Bertha a little bit.

"I agree. About this meeting, I mean. Let's get to the matter at hand," Milton said, his smooth and debonair voice insinuating itself into the conversation. "We do have much to discuss, about some rather concerning developments."

Delphine sat rigid. Her lips twitched around her words. "We honor the original seven by continuing the traditions which they started. We hold their seats only until they return."

Bertha snorted. "They won't return. It is ridiculous to keep believing silly myths. We are in the twenty-first century! Yet you insist on continuing to embrace the past as if it were a lover you cling to, despite them having long since turned into bone and ash."

Silence filled the chamber. Behind me were rows upon rows of pew seating, all empty. Maybe these meetings normally had a crowd of spectators which hadn't been allowed in this time. I wondered if the council would talk to each other like this in front of a crowd of their peers rather than just our small group of two humans and a vampire who had a close call with humanity.

"This is the vampire made human then?" Lin said, her voice loud and firm, ignoring any pettiness around her.

Lance went forward a few steps and knelt before the seven. "It is. Owen Raine and I were old friends. I had been seeking him out. I saw him at the airport and was taken aback by the sight of him, because all I could sense and smell was human. Nothing but human, yet he looked like the one I once called friend."

He rose again, continuing, "I followed these two to their home, and confronted them. I was shocked to discover that it was true. Somehow, Owen had become human, but I was overcome by the desire for the woman's blood." Lance bowed his head. "After tasting her, feeling the effects of her blood, I made the connection and drew the confession from them, that she was the cause. As you can see that one feed has not managed to strip me of my immortality."

Toren nodded. "The doctor's report confirms it. Owen Raine is completely human. Lancelot Ferland did have a marginally higher core temperature than normal, but no other side effects."

"Physical side effects," Lance qualified. "I have also felt a change in my emotions since drinking from her. That is worth noting."

"Oh, interesting indeed," muttered Shirina. "Shall Raine remain human forever? Will he return to his vampire form? Does he crave blood even though he is human? Will he live longer, or will the years spent as a vampire accelerate his aging now he is a human? Does his blood now carry the affliction that would turn vampires human if drunk? There are too many variables. How are we to make a decision here until we have done more research on the subjects?"

"We can decide that it is clearly an abomination," spat Milton. "We must put it to death. Both of them. The once vampire and that ..." His dark eyes held nothing but disgust, "... *thing* that would bring so much strife and discord to our lives. Let's be done

with this nonsense."

I tried to speak up for myself, but Lin's firm, business-like voice beat me. "Somehow, as much as we tried to keep this quiet, news of the changed one spread before they had even arrived in Umbravallis." All eyes in the room turned briefly to Lance before Lin continued, "Our vampire kin know this is now a possibility, and some may even want it for themselves. If we simply dispose of this potential cure without even considering its uses, there will be a lot of anger."

"Cure?" Milton tensed on his throne, as if he were about to jump out of it and right at me. "We have nothing that needs to be cured. We are perfection immortal. Choosing to become a weak, finite human again is like choosing euthanasia."

"Which some would argue is a valid choice," Lin returned.

"And some would argue it is not," Milton spat back.

Wow, I thought. Politics were politics whether you were dealing with humans or vampires, it seemed.

Delphine, who had been seething silently as her companions had their free-for-all debate, finally spoke again, "Tell me, human, how do you do it?"

I swallowed, my mouth suddenly dry, knowing now was the time to try to talk my way out of this, and knowing I was not the person for the job. My mouth generally talked me into trouble, not out of it. "My name is Kaitlyn, Kaitlyn French," I offered, trying to buy time. "And I have no idea how I do it. I'd say we know it's something about my blood. Drink it, and it makes you more human. Drink enough, you're human for good. That's what happened to Owen, and started for Lance. But I'm not really working with a large sample size."

Crap. Did I just give them a reason to start drinking from me to test the theory? Realizing that, I added, very quickly, "What I mean is, we don't know enough, and I honestly couldn't say what would happen to any other vampires if you tried it. If I have some kind of weird vampirism-killing virus in me, it could affect different vampires in different ways, like a bad allergic reaction or something." I let out a *whew* under my breath, hoping I'd said the right thing.

Lin eyed me for a moment, and with a small, sly smile, said, "It's a correct enough assumption without any further evidence. We could die from that blood. Not only because it could potentially turn us human, and humans are weak and frail and die, but just from the act of drinking it."

"All the more reason to put it to death. It's a danger to us," Milton said. "Its very presence disgusts me."

Fury sizzled and spiked along my spine.

Oblivious to my emotions, Toren asked, "How many times did you drink from her, Owen?"

Owen shook his head. Shame coated his face. "More times than I would like to admit. I could feel the change, but never understood the final consequences of my actions. I kept her and drank from her for weeks."

My heart felt heavy at the memory, but I reached my hand out to his and held it, offering again my silent forgiveness.

Bertha eyed our hands with an intense expression. "Just look at his human sadness, at their joined hands. I do so miss that connection of empathy. As much as I struggled to hold onto the memory of how it felt, it is all gone from me. If we decide that they may live but are too dangerous out in the world, I would keep them as my pets to be voyeur to such feelings."

Did she just put dibs on us? I stared, speechless. Any warmth I might have felt to Bertha before was gone.

"You may find she's already been claimed," Delphine murmured with a sly smile.

A deep frown marred Owen's face as his gaze traveled between Lance and me. His lips thinned, and I could see that he was still angry enough to kill if he had to. The idea chilled me, that even now as a human, to kill seemed like a natural response for him.

Lin said, "Could it be genetic? We'll have to test other members of her family."

"What?" My thoughts flashed to my poor, simple, country mom and dad. "No, this doesn't have anything

to do with anyone in my family. I mean, wouldn't you have known? Wouldn't this have surely happened some time before in history if there was a whole family tree out there of irresistible blood that turned vampires human?"

"Not if a single feed isn't enough to bring the change. Not if the vampire couldn't control themselves and killed during the first feeding. Have you ever had family members disappear before?" Toren asked.

"No. My family is as boring as boring can be—no missing bodies, no scandals, no vampires. I'd like it to stay that way."

I didn't get a reassurance there either way. They didn't seem to care for my opinions or negotiations at all. I had no leverage.

Lin looked to Shirina. "Oh, I can't wait to get some samples into the lab."

Shirina nodded enthusiastically.

Guess my lab-rat fears were founded.

Shirina tossed her shimmering black hair. "I, for one, can't wait to drink from the cup of her neck. That blood smells so sweet. Whatever price is involved it will be worth paying. I crave a taste. There's something so tempting about her smell, like fresh, ripe berries. It has been so long since I've had a berry in my mouth. I have to taste her, at least once."

My limbs froze. And there I thought she was the logical one.

Toren gave me a long, assessing look. "I would suggest that none drink from her until we know more, even though she smells so delicious."

"Or from Owen," Lance cut in. His expression had become drawn, and his already pale skin seemed nearly white. "His blood was made human by hers, and who could know what effects it may have?"

Delphine's hand lifted and silence fell. Her eyes locked onto mine yet again, and I thought I saw that smile lift her mouth once more. Yet she was not smiling at all when she spoke, "We will now vote on this matter. You have been brought here because your deaths have been called for. Regardless of what your blood can do, we are to decide if you live or die. The Synedrion shall vote now."

That was it? We didn't get to make our case or anything? We didn't have any say?

Shirina said, "I vote they live. What this human has done is not a crime."

Milton's vote was obvious. "I vote for death. She has, in essence, killed a vampire. Our laws are strict about such matters."

Toren waved a hand. "Our law only calls for death for vampires who have killed other vampires."

"And for humans who dare hunt us," Milton snarled. "They carried Nemexia."

Delphine glowered, a sparkle in her dark eyes.

Toren shrugged. "Troubling, but not a crime

for a human. It's been confiscated, and there's no evidence it was used on a vampire. The woman didn't hunt Raine, nor has she yet killed him. Our law says nothing of humans who inadvertently cause an inevitable death to a vampire through a return to mortality."

Delphine spoke again, "We vote. Those against death, raise your hand."

My heart literally shook in my chest as I surveyed the hands lifted for keeping us alive. Lin, Shirina, and Toren. Only three of the seven. We were dead.

Delphine said, "Those for death."

Surprise, surprise, Milton's hand was the first one in the air. Then Delphine's. Then Viatrix, who'd remained with her eyes closed and so still I thought she may have been asleep through the whole meeting.

Delphine surveyed her companions with a look of distaste. "You abstain, Bertha?"

Bertha's forehead creased in a frown. "We do not know that she is dangerous. But we do not know that she is not. It may be that some vampires wish to become human, and if they had that wish they should have the antidote within her blood. It should be a choice. So many of us weren't given a choice. We were turned wholly against our will." She looked down at me, head tilted ever so slightly. "On the other hand, her blood could be a weapon. It could be used to decimate our ranks. If our enemies came

into possession of her blood, they could use it against us, steal away our power with it, to the point where they could exterminate us entirely."

Silence settled on us like a blanket. It lay heaviest on me, its weight crushing. Bertha was right. When she put it like that, my blood could be a huge threat to their whole kind. To their ways, to their continuation as a species. I wasn't sure if that was a good or bad thing, but it was a dangerous thing, for me.

"We have three who wish for death, three who do not, and one who has abstained." Delphine sighed. "We do not have a majority. Until we can break the tie, nothing shall be done with them. We must consider all the things that Bertha has mentioned, as well as many others. We must spend more time to truly consider all the points that we should before we make our decision. We will deliberate, and return."

Sweat broke out along my hairline at the uncertain verdict. We would live, but for how long?

8

OWEN

The Ebonguard met us outside the Synedrion's chambers, and we were escorted back to the palatial suite that we had been in before. Kaitlyn tried to make small talk with our guards, to no response, on the way. I could see the nervous energy filling her and felt the same myself.

When the heavy door shut us in and locked, she stared up at me. Tears sprang into her eyes. I watched her fight them back.

"You were quiet back there," she said.

My jaw twitched. "I was so angry. If I'd spoken, it would have been to threaten their deaths, and that wouldn't have helped us at all. But I would burn them in their beds if they touched you."

I reached for her hands and she shied away from

me, so my fingers wrapped in on themselves instead, making fists. If I were only still a vampire, I would have the strength to break down these walls, and how I felt now, I was almost ready to try, vampire strength or no.

No natural light reached the windows of our room with the palace too far in the back of the cave, in the deep, shadowed valley, but it must have been near morning. I was exhausted, and Kaitlyn's eyes were rimmed red with gray smudges beneath.

She turned her face from mine before I could kiss her tiredness away.

"What is that smell?" she said.

An appetizing aroma met my nostrils, and I stepped back, my head turning as I tried to figure out where it was coming from.

A table had been set with the finest china, heavy and well-polished silver, crisp white linen, and heavy crystal. A far nicer spread than had been provided before.

Kaitlyn almost skipped over. Her unending, joyous curiosity for food always pleased me. But a lump formed in my throat. I wondered what this meal had been left here for, why we were being given more than the gruel afforded the thralls. Was this meant to be our last meal?

I said nothing to Kaitlyn though. She deserved something to take her mind off our situation.

I pulled a chair out for her in a courtly, gentlemanly gesture.

We lifted the lids to find a stunning array of fresh fruits, and no less than six different varieties of cheese in generous serves. Crackers and sweet biscuits were also arranged around the fruit and cheese on the tray.

The door opened as Kaitlyn took her first bite, and Lance entered.

"Not only are we imprisoned, we also have no freedom as to who enters our chambers and when," I muttered.

Kaitlyn tsked at me and whispered back, "He's trying to be a friend."

And we needed all the friends we could get right now. I knew that too. But I didn't know how long I could stay friends with some*thing* who looked at Kaitlyn the way Lance did.

Along with him, one of the Ebonguard entered to stand guard on the inside of our room. Apparently, even Lance wasn't trusted to be alone with us.

Lance pulled up a seat at our table. He smiled, but lines around his eyes and eyebrows gave away his concern. "Please, don't let me interrupt you. In fact, I was hoping to enjoy watching you eat."

Kaitlyn's nose wrinkled with embarrassment in a way that was far too adorable.

She kept eating, although less at ease than when

she'd begun. My appetite was gone, replaced by a seething hatred like lava inside me.

"So, old friend," I said, "how do you see our chances now?"

Lance had been watching Kaitlyn lick the juice of a pear off her fingers, but turned away and sighed. "Yes, I was wrong. I truly didn't expect such hostility against you. I wish I'd made a different choice yesterday, but I was so distraught over what Kaitlyn's blood had done to me that I didn't think. I contacted the Synedrion because I couldn't contain the immensity of what had happened within myself. I should have said nothing, and let you go. I'm sorry."

Before I could reply, Kaitlyn said, "We might be more willing to accept your apology if it came with the keycode to this room, and a key to a fast car."

"Or return our perfume of Nemexia to us," I grumbled.

"You know that's illegal for a vampire to possess. If I had taken it from your luggage myself, I would be just as imprisoned as you and no help. What you had is probably destroyed. I will help you as much as I can, but it is not simple. Now that they know of the two of you, they will track you and they will hunt you anywhere you go. Ebonguard put your human Mounties to shame in that regard. And if you escape from here, it will make their verdict decided and they *will* kill you. Stay. Be patient. You do stand a chance. The Synedrion deliberates, and you have powerful allies upon it."

He was right. I tried to calm the anger in me. It was hard. I didn't remember if it had been this hard to control my emotions when I was human before, or if I was struggling because I had had to relearn it all again within a few months. "I understand, Lance. I, too, was torn and confused at the taste of her blood. I, too, suffered from the sudden onset of things I hadn't experienced in a great many years. I had what I could only refer to as terrible mood swings."

Kaitlyn nodded vehemently in agreement as she chewed.

Lance said, "If there was a way to release you, I would. They don't trust me now either, and while I'm free to move around, I doubt I'm free to leave this place. They have declared me to be something … in between. Not human, but not vampire either. I have no idea what I am now." There was a very real sorrow in his voice.

"I'm sorry," Kaitlyn said.

I slammed my fist on the table in a way that rattled the cutlery. "Don't be sorry! It's not your fault. How could it be? He chose to drink your blood, and you had no say in the matter. You tried to warn him not to. You tried to fight him away. Don't give him your sympathy for the consequences of his actions."

Kaitlyn frowned at me, frozen. She blinked, then said to Lance, "Maybe, as long as you don't drink

anymore of my blood, you will go back to being the same old vampire you were before. Until you change completely, I doubt it's permanent."

Lance's fingers twisted around each other. "I don't know that I want to go back to being what I was before."

I growled in a low whisper, "You may not drink more from her, Lance."

Lance recoiled. "How many times do I have to tell you that I don't wish to? The last thing on Earth I want to be is human. I've come to accept and appreciate my immortality. Even after all these centuries, the idea of a final death is a terror I don't want to face. But I don't mind the sensation of these emotions that have resurfaced in me. I feel I have been reminded of who I used to be, who I wanted to be. A little bit of guilt can be a good thing."

A long, awkward silence fell around the table. Even Kaitlyn had stopped eating.

I stared down at my fists, and worked to release and stretch my fingers. Why could I not contain this anger in me? Was this who I was? Had I always been this hotheaded? The last few months with Kaitlyn had been so blissful, despite worries at the back of my mind. I hadn't been under any stress close to this level. I barely knew how to start dealing with it.

A man cleared his throat at the door. "He may not want your blood, but I do. Under the Synedrion's orders, of course."

Lance looked over his shoulder. "Ewan. Lin and Shirina worried these two won't last long enough to get their precious blood samples to the lab?"

The same doctor who had seen to us before walked in, set his bag right down next to our food, and began prepping sample tubes. "You know how they love some interesting blood samples."

Lance grinned wryly.

"I don't suppose I have any say in this?" Kaitlyn said, her hand wrapped around her inner elbow as though anticipating the needle.

I glared at Lance, hoping he would intervene. Neither Kaitlyn nor I had the strength to match a vampire. I didn't want this. However small the sample of blood, it was a theft, an intrusion, an abuse against my Strawberry.

"Neither of you do. I'm to get samples from both the … humans." Ewan drawled the last word, looking me up and down with curious disgust.

I slammed my arm down on the table, offering myself first. The doctor moved quickly, drawing three vials, before strapping Kaitlyn's arm and drawing two from her.

He tapped her veins at her wrist and gave her skin a soft pinch. "That's all from you. Still need to replenish. I told you to hydrate."

And with that, he clipped his bag closed and

walked out.

Kaitlyn cleared her throat softly and asked, "You said that we had some allies? You weren't counting Lin and Shirina, were you?"

Lance smiled in an embarrassed sort of way. "At least their scientific interest in you is enough that I believe they would protect you at all costs. There are many against you, however. To some, this is a matter of the greater good, and they don't have the ability to care about you and your needs if they wanted to. They fear, and rightfully so, that our enemies may capture you and use you as a weapon against us."

"What enemies could vampires have?" she asked.

I offered her an answer, trying to let the facts clear my emotions. "The Synedrion lead the largest group of vampires, but there are others, those with different leaders and different values. Extremist groups, vying for a greater share of power and more influence."

"Enemies to all of us," Lance added. "Then there are those who would see themselves as human again. Who would accept that gift willingly. They will fight for your lives, but only if it benefits them."

Kaitlyn lifted her hands as though weighing the options. "And here we are, between extremists who want us eradicated from the world, and those who want to keep us and our special blood in their labs."

"Where do you stand, Lance?" I asked.

Lance's head lowered. "I stand with you, Owen. You were like my brother once, and I feel that bond again anew. And I stand with Kaitlyn, not only because I know that you love her. There are plenty of reasons to love her—even I can see that."

Kaitlyn blushed.

Just as I start to feel for Lance again, he says something like that, right in front of me.

I hid my anger under a smile. "Ignore his attempts, Kaitlyn. He always was a flirt. It seems some things don't change."

"I recall it was you who decided it was a good idea to tell women that I really was Lancelot of Arthur's court, an immortal knight come to woo them. Quite the wingman, you were."

I paused, my mouth open. I had forgotten that. When our friendship had ended, I left him behind and blocked out the memories of our good times together. He'd been there for me, helped me, from my darkest moments after Adelle died, when I almost became as bad as her. That was when he found me, taught me his ways. Taught me a vampire could be more than their urges, that even without empathy we could make the right choices.

Kaitlyn was looking between us. "I have literally a million questions."

Lance chuckled. "She says, hyperbolically."

My smile became sincere. Maybe I did still hold

some love for my friend. "How long until they come up with an answer?"

"They are likely going to rest now, so we know you have at least the day."

"A day." Kaitlyn almost sobbed the word. Her head shook, dark hair shimmering in waves around her. "What if we did escape? Really. There must be a way we could go underground, just … just …"

I said, "Kaitlyn, no. You deserve the life you have worked so hard to have. Even if we could live in hiding, I wouldn't ask you to live your life that way."

"Any life is better than no life at all!" she gasped.

I felt the same. But I had to keep up the appearance that we had some hope. What else could I do? I had some ideas, but we would have to be patient.

I stood from my chair and kneeled beside hers, wrapping my arms around her. She was shaking. She leaned into me.

Lance stood abruptly, the legs of his chair scraping across the floor with a loud racket. "I, too, must rest. I have no answers to the when and how the Synedrion will decide your fate. I shall endeavor, however, to send a thrall out to fetch you more food."

"You got this for us?" Kaitlyn asked.

"I arranged it to be delivered while you met with the Synedrion. There is no more food here other than the poor stuff they feed the thralls. I wanted to prove that vampires could be reasonable, even hospitable." Lance shook his head softly. "Even if the others proved me wrong, I shall continue to make sure that your stay is as comfortable as possible."

I could hear the sound of him walking away, the door scraping open and closed again, and then we were alone.

"We should rest, too," I said.

Kaitlyn nodded weakly, no doubt as physically and emotionally drained as I was. I bundled her up in my arms and lifted her from the chair. I carried her through to the adjoining bedroom and put her on her feet. We removed each other's clothes slowly, lovingly, and climbed beneath the sheets. She curled into my body and I wrapped myself around her like a shield, listening to her heart and mine, beating together.

Our precious lives.

I wouldn't let anything end those lives yet, not yet, not when we had spent so little time together.

I would kill anyone and anything that tried. I may not have been a vampire anymore, but I still had a way. A way I could remove anyone or anything that threatened us.

I still had the ring.

9

KAITLYN

I woke up feeling dehydrated and aching all over. The stresses and injuries of the previous days were taking their toll. Owen lay beside me, his bare chest rising and falling with the slow breath of sleep. He seemed so calm now, so peaceful. It was hard to remember the rage I'd seen in him not long ago.

I wasn't sure how I felt about him right then. He had such anger, such darkness in him. He reminded me too much of the monster I thought he'd left behind when he became human again. Had I been so naïve as to think those violent emotions were all gone now? Humans were capable of that much and more. Maybe I didn't know Owen, vampire or human, as well as I'd thought.

I slipped out of bed and stretched my body. A

grandfather clock read five o'clock, but I had no idea if that was AM or PM, or what time vampires kept in their cloistered little land here. International travel, vampire schedules, long sleeps, and long meetings had screwed with my body clock, and I couldn't place a bet if it were day or night.

I unzipped my luggage, wincing at the loud sound, worried it would wake Owen. I pulled out some clean underwear and a simple fuchsia-colored slip dress. The palace was cool, but not uncomfortably cold, either naturally because of the cave, or kept at a living temperature for the sake of the thralls and other humans on-site maybe. Certainly the vampires themselves didn't need it.

I had just pulled the dress over my head when Owen curled his arms around me from behind, smothering my neck with gentle kisses.

I held his arms back, and warmth filled me. With him I felt safe. I felt at home. Of course he'd been angry. I was angry too, at the unfairness of all of this.

I turned to face him and pressed my head to his chest. "They're not going to let us live, are they?"

"Someone once told me I should hope for the best but expect the worst. I suppose that's what I'm doing."

"They hate me so much," I whispered. What they thought about me shouldn't matter in the scheme of things, but it did. "Even the ones who want to keep me alive so they can find their own humanity again. I bet they despise the fact the cure came from a human, rather than one of their own."

"We have to play along until we can find a way to escape."

I nodded. "We have to get the F out of H."

I held Owen's hand as I turned to look around the room. I pointed to the windows. "We could shred the sheets, make a rope ladder. Break one of these windows and climb down."

It all sounded a bit fantastical, but the act of laying out a plan, even a crazy one, lifted my spirits. "There are probably still cars out the front. We grab one with a thrall driver so we can get the keys. We can't take out a vamp, but we could get past a thrall. We do it when the vamps are sleeping."

Owen had a very small smile on his face, but it faded almost as soon as it appeared. "Ebonguard never sleep. They are probably listening to this conversation right now, and would be upon us the moment the window broke."

"Only one way to test that theory," I offered, hopefully.

Owen shook his head. "Where do we go after that? It's a long drive out of Umbravallis, and some vampires can travel on foot as fast as a car can drive. Neither of us know how to fly a helicopter or plane, if we could even hijack one. If we could get back to Slovakia ... there is something in the castle

that could help us, but only against a single enemy at a time, not against the hoard of vampires that might come after us."

My curiosity and hope spiked. "What could help us?"

Owen's eyebrows lowered, and he looked down. "It would be the first place they would look for us though. We can't go back there. Not yet."

I wanted to ask again what it was, but his glower made me stay quiet.

"We just have to hold out a bit longer. We have to cherish every moment we still have," he said, and pulled my chest into his, pressing his lips to mine.

Just like that, my temperature spiked about five degrees. It seemed impossible, maybe even a little wrong somehow for me to be so turned on, for me to want him so badly when our lives were in so much danger.

Perhaps that was exactly why it was so right. We had no idea if this was to be our last day on Earth. If it was, I didn't want to regret not knowing his body against mine, the feel of his lips on mine, and the touch of his skin against mine, one last time before I died.

I slid my hands down the rippled muscles of his bare back until they reached the silky satin of his boxers. Owen's mouth found my neck, laying down a trail of kisses. Even as a human, he was still very much a neck guy.

Remortality

Time coalesced to the distance between heartbeats and nothing more or less. My breath caught in my throat and my fingers wound into his hair. Our mouths met again in a wild and passionate kiss that said everything we could have ever tried to say to each other in our final moments—words of love, and desire, and hope, and despair, all of it written by our tongues. The things left undone and unsaid that may never get the chance to be spoken, or put into action, all the things we had hoped for, and still hoped for, even as we knew they may never be.

My legs wrapped tight around his waist, and I let my hands move from his hair to his shoulders, relishing the strength in his muscles. His breath washed over my neck and cheek as he spoke, and I shivered. It was still hot when he called me Strawberry, even if his reasons for it had changed.

A loud thump came from the living room of our quarters, freezing us in place.

Owen gently let me go and crept to the door. He held his hand out to warn me back, but I had to peek out too.

One of our Ebonguard lay motionless on the carpet inside the entrance door.

Our second Ebonguard was being dragged inside by Delphine. She dropped them to the ground with a second matching thump before clicking the door closed behind her.

"What the actual fuck?" I whispered.

Her black eyes glared at me. Her mouth turned to the same small smile she'd given me in the meeting.

Horror threatened to topple me toward the floor.

She moved toward us, her body swaying elegantly. "It is time to die, humans."

I shook my head. It didn't make sense. If the council had come to a decision, why had she turned our guards into ragdolls?

Owen must have had the same thought. "Taking matters into your own claws, Delphine? The Synedrion hasn't yet ordered our deaths. You will be stripped from your position and worse if you touch us."

"Yeah," I shot over Owen's broad shoulder. "I thought you were all about tradition. You can't kill us until you've got your damned majority."

"By killing you both I am saving tradition. What if what you have is a virus, spread through contact rather than blood? You have to be destroyed, now. What I do will save all vampires. I would take the risk for that." Delphine traced a finger down the side of her face, brushing back her flame-red hair. "But no one will know it was me. I used a thrall to scent your guards with Nemexia—thanks for bringing some with you, by the way. Now your guards will awaken to find you dead with no evidence of who killed you. They will likely take the blame themselves, if, say, there were someone on the council who could push that motion." Her grin was terrifying.

She stalked closer. The aquamarine couture gown she wore was at odds with her menacing prowl. I thought she could have dressed a bit more appropriately for murder, but if this was what she normally wore, it might have aroused suspicion if she started wandering the halls in black-ops gear.

She didn't rush. Her slow confidence held every threat of the truth of how powerful she was compared to us.

She seemed surprised when Owen picked up a chair and swung it at her. The chair hit hard enough to knock her off balance, but not enough to fell her. The chair splintered into pieces, and I grabbed a large and wickedly jagged chunk.

I didn't hesitate. I lunged straight for Delphine's heart.

She twisted her torso away and swiped her clawed hand at me.

I inhaled sharply as I ducked under her attack, jabbing out with my other fist. My agent had set me up with hand-to-hand combat training, hoping to score me some lucrative action movie parts. I sent a silent thank you across the world to him.

I landed that punch in Delphine's lower stomach, but it felt like punching a concrete wall covered in silk.

Obviously unharmed, she swatted me with one quick flick of her arm, and knocked me completely back across the room and into a wall. The stake flew from my grasp.

My back hit the wall so hard that all the breath escaped from my lungs, flying out of my mouth with a loud squeaking sound.

Owen snatched the chunk of wood from where it had landed. He stalked Delphine around the room. Her hand casually swept furniture aside, blocking Owen's path to her. Her smile remained. This was a game for her. She would kill us in a flash when she was ready.

Owen jabbed the stake at Delphine and came very close to impaling her. Not close enough, however.

Run, get help, I begged Owen silently, because I didn't have enough air in my lungs yet to speak, or follow those instructions myself.

Owen flipped the stake around and used it like a baseball bat, hitting Delphine so hard that the wood splintered again and left Owen holding two smaller stakes.

I looked to our Ebonguard, lying lifeless on the ground not far from me. I wished they would wake up. I had no idea how long the Nemexia stuff would last. I felt a strange sort of betrayal that they hadn't protected us.

My elbows, and then my hands, found the wall, and I worked my way up it into a standing position. I ran to the door and tugged at the handle. Locked.

Remortality

I hammered at the door. Surely someone would hear the commotion, notice our missing guards. Would no one help us?

I turned back to the fray.

A scream of fury ripped from my mouth as one of Delphine's hands came out and her claw-like fingernails left bloodied furrows along Owen's right cheek.

It was as though my scream shattered every window in the room. Glass exploded around us, and hooded figures poured in, too many of them to count.

Has help arrived at last? Are we saved?

Delphine hesitated, but Owen ignored the chaos, taking his chance to lunge with a small stake in each hand. Before he could drive them home, Delphine's attention snapped back and she knocked his arms aside with one hand and pushed him away with the other. Owen landed on an overturned lounge, then rolled to one side, landing on his feet with the stakes still held in both fists. I ran to his side.

Delphine looked at the figures in the room, advancing on her, their tattered brown robes swishing around them like whispers of death. She roared at them.

An all-encompassing terror overwrote everything else that I felt. The figures overwhelmed Delphine. One lifted her into the air, then with a casual, effortless

motion, ripped her head right off her shoulders.

Blood, a disgusting fountain of it, spouted from the stump of her neck, dark and thick. Her arms and legs twitched in a grotesque parody of a dance, and the scent of decay filled the room. Blood splashed across the ceiling and then rained back down, falling onto the floorboards and the broken and scattered furniture.

My mind went completely, utterly blank. I simply couldn't process what I had seen. It was too horrific. It was so horrific that there was no way it could be real, only it was.

The hooded figures came toward us. I shrank back, tears running down my face. I had hoped that the enemy of my enemy must have been my friend, but they proved that was a lie within seconds.

These new creatures were not our saviors.

Two of them grabbed me. I screamed, but a rough, dry hand covered my mouth. Wild-eyed, I looked for their faces to identify our new attackers, but every one of them was covered in a leathery mask shadowed by a heavy hood.

More of the robed figures grabbed at Owen. He fought hard, managing to stake one of them. I didn't know what it was that Owen had killed, but it wasn't human. A yellow-brown dust rose from the staked corpse as it crumbled away, smelling like mold and something else, something gruesome and *dry*.

Remortality

Five more of the hooded figures were on Owen. He disappeared beneath a pile of flapping robes and leather masks that covered the entire heads and faces of the new arrivals. I could hear his anguished cries until a final crack sounded that destroyed my heart, and he was quiet.

I whipped my face free of the muffling hand on me. I screamed so long and so loud that it tore up my vocal cords.

Something hit me in my temple.

Darkness swam in and took me down.

10

KAITLYN

I awoke to the sight of crumbling cave walls moving past me. My vision was blurry, and a thick pain gouged into my belly, making it hard for me to breathe. I blinked a few times, trying to figure out what was happening.

I was bent over the shoulder of one of the robed vampires. He moved fast. My head banged against his lower back. I smelled a disgusting *wormy* smell on the brown robes that flapped around the creature's body.

Vomit rose in my throat. The ache in my temple intensified, making my head spin. My fists raised and I brought them down onto a body that felt like gnarled wood.

My screams echoed down the hallway. I heard Owen's voice, coming from somewhere ahead of me.

It lifted into curses and promises to kill every single vampire that had taken us hostage. I could hear the sound of his fists striking against the cold flesh of the creature who carried him through the dim tunnel. We went deeper. Goosebumps rose on my skin as the temperature dropped. Mucky, musty air filled my lungs.

Were we still in Umbravallis? In the cave of the Synedrion palace? Or some other cave in some other place entirely? Only an occasional sconce with burning oil lit the way.

Soon, the crumbling dirt walls changed to bricks of stone, creating neat hallways which branched out along the way.

The air got thicker and even harder to breathe, the claustrophobic sensation taking me right to the edge of full-blown panic.

Owen's voice, raised in yet another curse, and the sound of a vampire hissing in pain, brought me back from that abyss. He was still here, somewhere, with me. I shuddered all over but was ready to keep fighting again.

I wrenched my body around, kicking off the vampire who had me over his shoulder. I fell away from him, right into another. Hands grabbed at me in the darkness and I hit them away.

My skin tightened into goosebumps and tears filled my eyes, but I kept fighting, no matter how repulsed by their touch and terrified of them I was.

Remortality

I had to fight back, had to. No matter how uneven the odds, I intended to fight for my life.

My life.

The life I had almost had right there in my fingertips. The career that had just started. The roles that might have followed.

I fought for Owen.

Owen and all that we could have had.

Tears ran down my face as I managed to claw my fingers under one vampire's leather mask and yanked it away. It satisfied me, as though I'd ripped its very skin from its face.

The sound of seams tearing was loud, but it vanished beneath my screams as I finally saw the face below the hood.

My heart stopped for a full second. I choked on hysteria as every horror movie I had ever seen, as the terror of that LARP game that had landed me with Owen, as the memory of having woken up hanging on the wall like a trapped butterfly, as every vision of every twisted creature of darkness all came rushing in at me, threatening to snap my very sanity.

I was shoved back and landed on a cold, slippery floor that stank so badly I heaved.

Just enough light showed the bars of the cell locking me in, and the face I'd torn the mask off.

Another scream ripped from my mouth and my sanity fled into the dark.

11

KAITLYN

"Wake up. Wake up, Kaitlyn. Strawberry, Strawberry, answer me. Wake up."

The words drifted in and out of my mind. My eyes opened and closed.

Sickness hit at the same time the smell did. I rolled over and retched pitifully, thanking my stars that there was nothing in my stomach to add to the stench. I may have complained that a prison was a prison while being kept in palatial comfort, but now I understood that everything was relative. This wasn't just a prison. This really was a dank, dirty dungeon.

Owen's voice reached me again. "I hear you. It's okay, it is. I love you. I love you, and I'm so sorry." I heard the slam of flesh against metal. Owen growled,

"If I were still a vampire, I could break these bars and save you right now."

I made it to my feet. My hands felt gross, and I wiped them on my filthy and bedraggled dress. Owen's cell must have been next to mine, but we were separated by a stone wall. I went to the bars and turned my head, hoping to see him. His hand came out and I extended mine. Our fingers could touch, only slightly, but that touch reassured me.

"Owen, don't. Don't do that to yourself. If you were still a vampire, there'd be no need to try to save me because I'd already be dead. We would never have been together if you were still a vampire. So don't. Don't do that. The only things to blame are ..."

The memory of the face I had seen when I yanked that mask off came flooding back to me. That horror, seared into my brain.

A shriveled face, so shriveled that the outlines of jawbone and eye sockets had been visible under the yellow-gray leathery flesh. Wrinkled lips were sewn shut with thick thread, the ragged stitches so clumsy and large they looked childish. Bulging black eyeballs surrounded by gray pouches of flesh sagged toward the sunken, dark hollows that once were cheeks.

My voice quavered, "What are they?"

"The Starved."

I gulped. "Say what?"

"The Starved. A cult of vampires that don't feed. They sew their lips shut so they can't. Not that some haven't. At times, the hunger gets to the ones who pledge themselves and they have ripped out the stitches in order to drink."

"Oh." I closed my eyes, trying not to imagine that. "Why don't they feed? Do they think it's wrong?"

"No, they don't value life. They think humans are filthy animals, that their blood taints their purity."

The words I had hoped to hear were, 'they sure do think it's wrong,' and, 'no worries they are our friends!'

I managed to drag a long breath into my lungs. "We've been kidnapped by a cult of perpetually hangry vampires?"

The small grasp Owen's fingers had on mine tightened. His voice echoed off the stone walls. "Damn Delphine. If she hadn't scented our Ebonguard, they could have protected us from this. And damn me for providing her with the Nemexia."

"What exactly is it, this Nemexia stuff?"

"Perfume of a rare corpse flower. The scent renders a vampire unconscious."

"Nemexia, wormwood, what else? What other weapons are there? What else don't I know? You should've told me these things, all of them. I should've known and been able to defend myself. At least known to wear that perfume you gave me every damn day!"

I grew frantic, hating that I took it out on him, but needing to vent all the same.

Owen was quiet for a moment. No other sound reached us, only a heavy, foreboding silence. "There's a lot about vampires you don't know. I simply haven't had the time to tell you everything. But I also purposefully hid things that I could have shared. You deserved to know. I should have told you more."

I felt his fingers slipping away from mine and pulled them back. "I get it, okay? You thought you could keep it all from me. That we could just be regular, oblivious humans together. But here we are. Just promise me the truth now. All of it. I need to know everything."

Two deep breaths of silence passed, then, "I promise."

"Okay then. The Starved, how do they stay alive if they don't drink blood?"

"I don't know. It's said they don't drink human, animal, or vampire blood. They take nothing. It's dangerous to go too long without; it destroys the body and the mind."

Insane vampires. I let that thought settle into my stomach like cement.

"No one knows exactly how long the Starved have abstained. Some break and drink before fasting again. Some shrivel away to nothing and die. But there are rumors some haven't fed in decades."

"It destroys their bodies? Does that mean they're

weak?"

"Weaker than a vampire who feeds? Yes. Weaker than us? No."

That didn't sound so good. I shifted, trying to reach farther, but there was no way.

The corridor outside my cell was empty and dark. My thoughts were equally bleak and dim. "What happens to us now? I take it they aren't exactly our friends."

"No, they aren't. I don't know what they would want with us."

"They probably won't want to eat us though. So, there's that."

Owen coughed a small, desperate laugh that quickly faded.

The silence spread out. I looked around, my eyes blurring with fatigue and hunger. There was so much pain in my heart. Tears leaked and dripped off my chin, but I made no sound. I had to be strong, and not just for me.

"When we get out of this, I want you to know, I'm okay with doing whatever we have to do to survive." The words wrenched their way from my throat. "Being an actress, having roles in movies, being in the public eye—I have to accept that is incompatible with who I am, what my blood can do."

"Don't lose hope for being who you want to be," Owen whispered, but despite his words, his conviction

sounded weak. He knew it was true, too.

My destiny had been tied to the vampire world from the moment Owen tasted my blood. Here I was now, wondering how I'd even survive the next day, let alone what my life would mean if I could keep that life, but not the dreams and desires that made it worth living.

Owen's fingers moved, brushing against mine in a soothing gesture. And him. Could I stay with him, the one who had brought me into all of this? Would I continue to love him if we had to live on the run, as the resentment of my crushed dreams built in me? Could I be happy to be alive and with him as my one love, giving up all else?

I shivered, not from the cold, but because deep inside I didn't have an answer. I didn't want to choose. I wanted him, I wanted our love, I wanted my career, and I wanted our lives. Why couldn't I have it all? It wasn't fair. I was strong. I'd been through so much. I was …

"I'm valuable," I said, stunned by the revelation.

"Of course you are," Owen replied.

"No, I mean, I'm valuable to vampires. I am my own bargaining chip. If we can get out of this hellhole, and back to the Synedrion, I can leverage that value. I'm sure of it."

Owen seemed to ponder that for a moment. "You always were a clever one, Strawberry. Now, let's focus on getting away from the Starved, and whatever it is they want with us."

"Looks like we're about to find out," I said.

A small group of Starved stood before the bars of our cells. They had arrived silently, and the dim light and tattered brown robes camouflaged them until the last moment. The leather masks that covered their faces and heads were clearly hand-stitched, and the leather was badly cured so it was hard and cracked rather than soft and supple. The pieces that formed the hoods were crudely cut and stitched, much like their mouths. I shuddered.

One very large figure stepped forward, easily seven feet tall, and burly. He wore neat, black robes with gold embroidered edges, and no mask covering his bald head.

His skin had a strange ashen cast but wasn't desiccated like that of his brethren. No stitches bound his mouth. His eyes were the strangest part though, a bright, burning red rather than the pitch black all other vampires that I'd seen had. He clearly wasn't starved the way the others were, but they followed him like he was a leader. I wondered what he ate. I heard Owen inhale sharply at the sight of him.

"Bring her," he said, his voice like gravel.

My cage was unlocked. Masked Starved came for me. A hand, so skeletal it didn't resemble anything living, lifted and reached for me. I screamed and

scrambled away, but that arm caught my hair and yanked me forward. Pain traced along my scalp.

"Leave her alone!" Owen shouted.

They dragged me out. I bucked, but couldn't free myself as more hands grabbed and lifted me. My eyes turned to the stone wall that separated my cell from Owen's. I heard him thrashing against his cage.

"I'll be okay. It will be okay. I'll escape and find you," I cried out my lies, not knowing if they were for him or for myself, as I was dragged away.

12

KAITLYN

Tunnels turned this way and that as I was carried aloft by the Starved, led by the larger one. I tried to keep track; memorize the turns we took. Left, then right, then right again, then I was lost. The thought I couldn't find my way back to Owen if I had to filled me with helplessness.

We reached a huge cavern, lit by dozens of flaming torches. At least a hundred Starved filled the room, some still coming in from a number of other entrances. As we entered, they parted, and I saw what was behind them.

I wished I hadn't.

A monstrous stone statue of a giant demonic creature stood at least two stories tall. The face carved onto the creature was the stuff of nightmares:

bulging eyes, an obscene, lolling tongue, a horned forehead and an uneven grin, all made from a chalky, bone-colored stone, stained with patches of muddy red.

It had a bulbous body, and huge, gnarled claws, out of proportion with the rest of its size. Its misshapen feet were planted solidly behind a long stone altar. I gagged and turned away, not sure what it was I was seeing but knowing it was evil. So evil that there was no way to deny the darkness flowing from it.

I was dragged before the altar. The leader stood beside me on the raised dais, holding me up by the scruff of my neck to display me before the legion of Starved.

His grimy thumbnail moved along my face. I fought, my hands balling into fists, wanting to strike away that thing, but I was still restrained.

A thin sliver of pain came to my cheek. A wet and warm fluid dripped down my face. Blood! I cried out, despair and fear causing me to lose my courage.

The leader sniffed and the others leaned in, a low moan rippling across the room. The hoods showed their eyes but not their noses or mouths, and I watched with disgust as those leather masks moved up and down, and their eyes closed as they inhaled the aroma of my blood, like wine lovers sniffing their favorite vintage.

He spoke. "Yes, it is she of the strawberry blood."

A strange howl arose from the crowd, muffled by mouths stitched closed.

"Kissare's chalice always delivers truth. Though others have long since lost faith, we remain. They succumbed to the thirst like fools. We remained, and here, now, is our reward."

If I thought that sounded bad, what he said next left my stomach on the floor.

"We have found the strawberry blood and the cured one. We have found the ones who will give us the child that will cure our thirst forever."

That throaty howl called out again, louder than before.

My instincts said to run, but there was nowhere to go. Nowhere to escape to. No way to break the hold of the hands on me.

I stammered, "I'm not planning on having kids anytime soon, so I'd say you would be better off letting me out of here and checking back in about ten years, you know, when my career's more stable and I'm ready to do the parent thing." I had no idea what he meant or even what I was saying. I just knew I wasn't pregnant and had no intention of being, either. And as for curing thirst, my blood could already do that, in a way, child or none, but I wasn't sure that was information these guys already had, or I wanted them to have.

My words were ignored regardless.

A Starved entered, carrying high a large chalice made of tarnished silver inlaid with blood red agate. The hair on the back of my neck stood up as I watched the hooded figures of the Starved suddenly animate and then bow. They crowded close to each other, their robes pooling onto the floor by their bent legs and feet.

The red-eyed leader took the chalice when it was presented to him. It held a small amount of liquid, and the leader wiped his finger up my cheek again, collecting my blood he'd spilt and dripped it into the water.

A red glow shone from inside the cup.

He stared into the light. I was too short to see whatever it was he saw, to know whether this was some sort of stage trick, or if this chalice really spoke some truth only he could see. I feared what truth my blood might be telling him.

The leering grin on his face when he finally looked away was like the worst news I could hear. "Place her on the altar," he said.

The Starved that held me followed his order with swift obedience.

I was laid down on the cold stone. My feet and legs were held by too many hands to kick. My hands and shoulders were held down by more. Tears ran down my face as the leader ran his hand up my leg, over my thigh, pushing my dress up to my ribcage.

Then he revealed a wickedly sharp blade in one hand.

The ones holding me muttered and chanted. I hated them. I hated them so much, and when the blade found my arm, every one of my muscles tensed and waited for it to open my veins.

Only it didn't. It cut the contraceptive implant from within the soft underside of my upper arm. I ground my teeth at the pain as the leader moved away and another Starved applied a tight bandage.

The leader looked upon the blood covering his knife with a lust that curled his lips back.

He wiped the blood with his finger, then with rough swipes he drew something onto my bare abdomen.

"Three days," he declared to a reply of howls. Then he left.

The Starved lifted my battered and aching body. I was too numb to fight anymore. They carried me to a cell and then closed the door.

I sobbed silently. I had an idea forming in my mind, but it was awful, so incredible I couldn't manage to make it shape into the thing I was sure it was.

"Strawberry. Kaitlyn. Please, look at me."

I lifted my head. I could see his face! They had put me in a cell next to his on the other side than I was before, one that had no stone wall between us,

only a grid of rusted metal.

I sagged forward. Owen's arms came through the bars and held me up. My face pressed into the space between them and tears rolled down my face.

He wiped my cheeks, stroked my hair. He didn't ask what had happened. I knew he wanted to know, that I needed to tell him, but I wasn't ready.

A single Starved appeared and pushed a metal tray through a horizontal slot in the bars. I guessed if I didn't move to take it, he would let the miserable-looking food fall to the floor, and once it did it would be entirely inedible.

I moved to the front of the cell and took the tray. The Starved left us. I brought the food back to where Owen stood. I said, in a shaking whisper, "It's just bread and … and maybe that's … I don't know what that lumpy orange thing is."

"Eat."

I shook my head. "Not if you don't."

Owen looked at the small meal. "You need it more than I do."

"The hell I do."

I broke the bread into two pieces, then took a share of the oddly-shaped and bright orange thing, which, as it turned out, was some kind of pickled vegetable. It wasn't good, but it filled the hole in my belly. The rest I pushed through to Owen.

Owen spoke softly, "I heard … some of that, down

the halls. What did he mean by three days?"

"I don't know exactly, but if I had to guess I'd say he thinks that's about how long it will take the birth control hormones to leave my system." I showed him my bandaged arm. His eyebrows dropped into a deep frown. "They said something about us, me, and the cured one, giving them a child to cure their thirst. Did a magic show with a glowing chalice and all."

Owen inhaled so sharply his chin lifted. He stepped back from the bars, his food untouched, and paced like a caged wild-cat.

"A glowing chalice?" he repeated.

"Yeah. Crazy, right?"

"A child?" he growled.

I could only nod. I'd acted brave, but my whole body felt wrong. My toes curled and my thighs felt greasy and dirty, and I wanted to wash the feeling of unwanted hands away.

Owen whispered, "I won't, Kaitlyn. I won't do that to you. I won't. We just won't."

I swallowed hard. "The leader, with his red eyes, whatever that's about—"

Owen grunted.

"He also did this." I lifted my dress. Owen bared his teeth as though terrified to see what I meant.

My stomach came into view and there, on it, my blood made the shape of an upside-down ankh, roughly covering the area and shape where my

ovaries and womb would be.

"A symbol for life. It's probably ... probably just symbolic," Owen said, his head shaking. "But that leader, he's ... if his appearance is true, he is something else. Something even vampires consider a dark fairy tale. A vampire who is able to feed on other vampires. And if the chalice you saw is Kissare's chalice, we're past the realm of even normal vampire lore. These are things from myth and legend."

My own teeth clenched, and I spat on the hem of my dress and scrubbed the blood off my belly. I sank to the ground, sitting on the moist dirt.

"Just when I thought things couldn't get worse with the Synedrion, here we are with magic chalices and a cannibal super vampire who wants me pregnant." My forehead bumped the bars. "I mean, really, we're not even near rocks and hard places and frying pans and fires anymore. We're way beyond that."

Owen's hands came through the bars and my fingers wound around his.

I picked up the remaining bread and brought it to Owen's mouth. I knew it was the only way to make him eat. Even then he turned away at first, but finally took a small bite. He took it off me, feeding the next bite to me, then taking another for himself, the two of us sharing nibbles at the stale crust until it was gone.

Time ticked by, but there was no way to measure it. It drew out and on. The light stayed the same, and the stone walls had no chinks we could find.

We did look. We tried everything we could to escape. Not just because we wanted out of there but to pass the time. I knew, deep down, that the three days the shaman had given us would come to an end far too soon, but I still needed to keep my mind and body distracted.

Owen tried to dig at the softer parts of the rough walls with the metal tray our food had come on, and I used a rock that came loose to try to bash open the hinges of my cell door. We searched every crack in the stone and weld in the bars for weaknesses. Our only hope came when Owen unearthed a short length of partially rotten tree root in the back wall of his cell. It took him half a day of sharpening the side of the tray to be able to cut through the inch-thick wood and extract it, and another day of cutting and whittling to create two stubby wooden stakes. The wood was split and soft, barely long or rigid enough to form a point, but it was something.

Those pathetic stakes were what kept me from thinking about what would happen to me, to us, when the three days ended and whatever it was the Starved had planned for us came. I held tight to mine, and to one desperate hope.

Owen, my human, non-vampire Owen, would never force himself upon me. Never.

13

KAITLYN

I woke to a hollow gonging sound. My eyes snapped open as the sound infiltrated first my dreams and then my waking mind. The pungent, rotting, muddy smell reminded me exactly where I still was.

I was worn down by hunger and the filthy conditions of the cell. My body was a welter of bruises, and so was Owen's. We had no beds, only hard stone benches, and we were often blasted out of sleep by nightmares and fear.

The only thing I'd been able to think about was what if I did get pregnant. Or how long it might take to fall pregnant, and if this torture would not stop until I was.

And then what?

Would they hold me here in this filthy cell until

I birthed a child? Our child?

I couldn't stop imagining nightmarish futures. My heart twisted painfully as I wondered what they would do to that helpless infant once they had it. Surely, they wouldn't kill us, not until they knew for sure that whatever purpose that infant was intended to serve would be fulfilled, but once they knew that child was what they wanted, then our use would be finished.

And our baby? Would it be some kind of blood sacrifice for them?

My eyes closed to try to block off the image of my child, our child, being drained dry by those creatures. I couldn't escape the vision though. It stalked me even in the darkness of sleep. I could see my unmade child's feeble fists waving, hear its pained screams, feel its terror and misery.

My eyelids parted. Owen stared at me through the bars. I looked at his face, and I knew those visions of our potential future tormented him too.

We both were victim to the same nightmare, and we both understood exactly why we had to fight again, and again, and again to stop them getting what they wanted from us.

If only we weren't so weak.

We weren't fed often or enough, and I might have given up and cried over that hunger if Owen hadn't whispered to me wonderful things about the food we would eat when we finally escaped. Of handmade gnocchi drenched in burnt butter and sage sauce. Of lavender crème brûlée and light-as-air meringues. Of pork crackling, spiced with fennel seeds, so puffy it crumbled on our tongues.

It should have made me hungrier, his speaking of food when I was so famished, but it didn't. It soothed me because those things were so close—all we had to do was get out of that house of horrors.

And we would get out. We had to. I just didn't know how.

We had tried to overpower one of the Starved who brought our food, and Owen still wore a violently purple bruise on his cheek for that, while I had several shallow cuts in my left forearm from the loathsome creature's nails. Still, that attempt had given us fresh courage, even if it had failed.

The gong sounded again. The Starved arrived. They had come for us. Three days had passed, and it was time.

The leader stepped to the front, stood in front of Owen's cell, and a smile, one of sheer triumph, filled his face. His red eyes flashed, and Owen swayed on his feet.

I shouted through the bars, "Owen! No. He's enthralling you. Fight it!"

Too late. It was fast and easy, too easy. Owen had never stood a chance. I didn't even know if humans

could resist being mesmerized. I'd managed to with Owen once, but they were extenuating circumstances. Still, I'd expected more from a man who knew all about the dangers of a vampire's power.

One of the Starved opened his door. Owen, obedient as a thrall, stepped out.

The leader came to my cell next. I blocked off my mind, refusing to be compelled. Maybe I could beat it when Owen couldn't. My anger would be like a fire that burned away the Starved leader's attempts.

My lips pursed. Spit flew out of them and landed on his face.

The leader's fingers flicked it away casually, but I saw a glow of anger in his eyes.

"Bring her. Let her be aware for what is to come. We only need him to act."

Owen stood there, his face as smooth and blank as the visage of a statue as I was dragged from my cell, all attempts at mesmerizing me done and over with that spit bomb I had hurled.

The moment both I and Owen were out of our cells, Owen roared and launched himself at the Starved holding me. My heartrate soared with hope and adrenaline.

Wow. I wasn't the only one with decent acting skills.

There were only four Starved there, plus the leader. We were both free from our jail. We had a chance.

Owen pulled his stake from where it was held in the back elastic of his boxer shorts.

I reached under my dress and pulled my stake from the hem of my underwear and plunged it into the Starved dragging me from my cell. His dry flesh was hard, and splinters bit into my palm as I forced the stake in.

I was let go. The Starved stumbled back from me, then crumbled to dust, leaving my stake on the floor a few steps away. I dove for it, but I was snatched away by the burly leader. He scooped me up as though I were nothing. No matter how I bucked and struggled, his grip remained firm.

I was dying to stab this guy. I'd lost my stake, but Owen still held his.

I searched for him in the melee. He fought like a raging tiger, jamming a thumb into the eye of one of the Starved. It made a sickening popping sound, and sludgy blood flowed out of the mask. Still reeling from that, Owen staked him.

Two dead Starved was a good thing, but not enough.

Both my wrists were caught up in the huge hands of the leader. I struggled but couldn't free them. The leader didn't seem concerned about any of this.

Owen managed to drive the stake right into the back of another Starved, and I screamed with both joy and disgust before I was dragged away toward

the ritual chamber, toward that baleful statue.

More Starved poured down the hallway behind us toward Owen. He was up against a full dozen now, and alone.

I thrashed in the leader's hands, helpless as I lost sight of Owen. I could still hear him fighting as I landed on the altar, my arms bloody from the leader's brutal nails.

Starved filled the large cavern. Some moved to take over restraining me as the leader let go.

Owen was half dragged into the chamber, half fought his way in, trying to reach me.

I heard the blows he landed but I was held in place, spread-eagled and helpless, on that stone altar by both ropes and hands, and unable to assist him. One of the Starved made the mistake of getting too close to my mouth and I bit the bastard through his robes, sending him scrambling backward with a yelp.

I twisted and heaved my body up and down, hoping to slip through their fingers. My heels drummed against the stone slab.

Owen was fighting a losing battle, and he was tiring now. He no longer had a stake in his hand. His shoulders were slick with sweat and his chest heaved, but when the leader approached him, again Owen's fist came up and out and he delivered a devastating uppercut that stunned the leader for a moment.

Remortality

As much as the idea of being alone terrified me, a moment of clarity hit me. I shouted, but it came out like a hoarse whisper, "Run, you should've run!"

I managed to get one wrist up and off the table a few inches. I grabbed the hood of the nearest Starved and yanked him toward the stone altar. His head hit it with a satisfying crunch, but it barely affected him.

The leader brought a hand down hard on Owen's shoulder. Owen's knees buckled under the force, and he was pushed onto them. The leader stared down with a force so powerful I could feel the energy coming off him in palpable waves that battered against my mind and body.

Owen went lax and limp under the leader's hand.

I began to weep because I knew this time it wasn't a ruse. I knew what was going to happen.

I could take it.

I could.

But could Owen?

The guilt of what he'd done to me in the past weighed so heavily on him. And he'd vowed, over and over, to never wrong me like that again. This could crush him.

I was pinned fast to the table. One of the Starved fastened my neck, strapping it down with rope so that I couldn't lift my head even an inch.

My teeth clenched together so hard they ached.

The leader drew closer, bringing Owen with him. Even though I was bound fast I could feel myself retreating from him. Not physically. But in every other way possible. My mind wanted to go blank. I wanted to disconnect as much as possible, and find a place where I could hide from the things that were about to happen to me, and to Owen.

I didn't allow myself that comfort. Owen needed me, more than ever. Now that he was human, he was ruled by the empathy and guilt that vampires didn't have. Humans couldn't deal with their emotions well, and a centuries-old vampire who had suddenly found himself human and burdened with human emotions again so recently was even less likely to be able to handle the guilt and confusion that this ritual would place on his shoulders.

So I didn't escape. I stayed with him, focusing all of my will and attention toward him. They would not break us. I wouldn't let them.

After the chaos of fighting, the space had stilled.

A low, muffled chanting rose in the room. It grew louder, and Owen climbed up onto the foot of the altar. His features shimmered as though caught under a heat haze, twisting and reshaping themselves. He was fighting, trying to break that spell. To save me from the ritual that would be forced upon us.

He jerked and moved like a puppet trying to fight its master. His fingers worked and he removed

his only clothing, his boxers, as docile as a lamb. I pleaded with him, trying to help him escape the enthrallment. My words didn't even provoke so much as a blink from Owen.

I might as well have not even existed.

He stood above me, the outside of his feet touching the insides of my calves. The leader shouted at him to begin, but Owen didn't move. He was still fighting off that spell, and while I knew he would eventually lose and surrender, my heart swelled with love for him.

His courage gave me courage. His strength gave me strength. He made me want to keep fighting too.

Tears ran down my face. "This changes nothing, Owen. Can you hear me? I still love you. I know you aren't doing this because you want to. I know you wouldn't do it if you had any choice at all. This is not you or me right now, not really. I love you, and I will always love you."

Tears rolled down his blank face and splashed onto the altar.

The Starved paused for a moment, the chants falling away into a pin-drop quietude. The lull made goosebumps rise all over my skin. An expectant tension, heavily weighted with something else, something indefinable, fell over the gathering. My eyes rolled back and I stared up at the carved stone face of the demon statue that I lay at the feet of. I was so sure the thing was coming to life, that for a moment, I could've sworn I saw it move.

Owen's teeth bared in struggle, and more tears leaked from his extraordinary blue eyes. The taste of salt lay in the corners of my mouth.

"I love you, Owen. I love you. I know you can hear me. This is not your fault, and I don't blame you, not for this. Never for this."

With a strange, wobbling, struggling motion, he landed on his knees on the altar.

Screams, earsplitting screams, rang out.

My heart stopped as those screams filled the room and I stared up at Owen, frozen above me.

Liquid splashed onto me. A cold liquid fell over my body, slick and sticky. That liquid touched my lips, and my mouth opened both in thirst and confusion.

Sweetness and the tang of anise met my tongue. *Absinthe?*

The Starved who held me down recoiled, screaming hard enough I could hear their stitches popping.

I turned my head to find out what was happening.

Heavy gray-green tendrils of smoke rose from the Starveds' robes, and one, who had been caught directly on the hood by the water, screamed and beat his head with hands that clicked and chattered like bones.

The leader snarled, stepping away as spots of wormwood-infused alcohol splashed his face and hissed and sizzled.

How did it just start raining absinthe inside? I looked for the source. The Starved whose robes were in flames whipped them off to reveal corded, sinewy flesh pulled over muscle that had shriveled and wrapped around hard edges of bone.

A few of the Starved lay dead on the ground, their robes wrinkling as their bodies crumbled away beneath them. More were falling back from a second explosion of green liquid, clearing away completely from the altar. I tried to swivel my neck to see where it was coming from but couldn't because of the way I was bound.

"Owen!"

That cry had not come from my mouth. My eyes went to the left, and a fierce, triumphant joy battered its way through my heart as I saw Lance striding through the altar room, a plastic container in one gloved hand and a hose that was attached to the container in the other. He pumped the handle again but nothing came from the tube.

The Starved also saw that he was out of ammunition. They were regrouping, like a swarm of ants.

Lance half jumped, half flew, to us. He yanked Owen down, and off the altar. His eyes flicked between the ropes binding me, and the Starved that were advancing on us. Owen, lax and unresisting, hung there in Lance's arms. Lance looked at him and cursed under his breath.

The Starved growled and hissed, creeping closer to us again. The leader stalked forward in huge strides.

When Lance saw him and his glowing red eyes, he froze momentarily. "That better not be what I think it is."

I wrenched at the remaining ropes that still held me down. "Get me out of here!"

"What do you think I'm trying to do?" Lance said. He ripped the ropes binding one of my legs free, then looked again at the horde surrounding us. He was clearly stronger than them individually, but not all of them together, and once that massive, over-powered leader joined in, he'd be finished.

Lance took a step back from the altar. "There's too many. I can't carry both of you. I'm sorry."

Ice grew inside my heart.

I couldn't run fast enough on my own to escape this place. I knew what Lance had to do, and so did he, yet he hesitated.

I looked him in the eye, my jaw shaking. "Go. They won't kill me. Just get him out of here. You can't let them have us both."

Lance nodded firmly, holding Owen tight under his shoulder. He made a leap for the exit, carrying Owen with him.

They landed in a clear section, halfway to a tunnel leading out. The Starved pivoted, moving for them immediately.

"Run!" I screamed.

Owen jerked as though he'd heard me. He looked back at me, his teeth clenched. In control of his own body again, he fought against Lance. He struggled within Lance's grip, fighting with the same desperation and rage that he had fought the Starved with. He screamed, "We're not leaving her! You can't do this!"

"We have no choice!" shouted Lance.

Owen tried to break free. He did, once, and raced toward me, toward the wall of Starved between us, but Lance caught him in a bear hug and tugged him away. Lance was relentless, and far too powerful for Owen. He dragged him backward. He leaped again, and they disappeared down the tunnel.

"Kaitlyn!" Owen's final cry held sorrow so vast that it echoed along the walls and made my heart clench painfully.

Owen had been saved. Our potential child had been saved.

I was alone.

14

KAITLYN

I lay there on that altar, as still as the stone it was carved from.

My heart raced fast enough to cause a loud thrumming in my ears. But I barely even breathed. I stared with wide, dry eyes up at the cavern ceiling, willing myself not to cry.

I'd told them to go. It was their best chance, *our* best chance. It made sense.

I wished they didn't go.

The leader yelled in his coarse and guttural voice, "Go after them. Bring them back!"

I didn't move, but I heard more and more of the Starved dashing down the tunnel after Lance and Owen. Lance was faster than them, but dragging an unwilling Owen along with him had to slow him down. I didn't even know if they went down the right tunnel. I didn't know which of the three tunnels into the chamber was the way out. I didn't know where we were. I didn't know anything.

I could only hope they would escape. And that they would come back for me before it was too late, before whatever horror was going to happen next.

The room grew quiet. Almost all the Starved were on the chase, but the leader stood above me, brooding.

I drifted my gaze down to meet his and found the ability to smile, a wild, triumphant smile.

"You can't do anything without him. You might as well let me go." I managed to inject some real authority into my voice. "Once Lance and Owen get back to the Synedrion, tell them what's going on here, you're going to be in big trouble. I hope they stake you out in the sunlight on top of a fire ant hill."

His burning red eyes looked down at me. Firelight glistened off his hairless scalp. He calmed, and that calm was more frightening than his rage. His huge hand with those filthy, sharp nails, wrapped around my throat.

"You will not escape your fate. You cannot. It has been seen by Kissare's Chalice as truth."

His hand clenched, enough to make me wince as breathing and swallowing became harder. "This setback means nothing. Either the cured will be captured and returned, or we use another way. There is another way. One of much greater sacrifice. Regardless, when the moon rises again, the child will be conceived."

I didn't like the sound of sacrifice. Surely they weren't going to kill me. They needed my uterus too much, didn't they?

In a cold, logical way, I considered that they could cure another vampire from my blood. But that took time, if it worked the same way again at all. I'd be safe from that outcome, for a while at least. They had to be planning something else.

The leader released his grip and left me lying there, bound on the malevolent altar.

The chamber was empty now except for me.

Now they all were gone, tears and a very real fear washed over me, and I screamed and sobbed for myself until my throat was raw.

Owen would come back for me. I knew that. He wouldn't leave me there to suffer. He knew now where the lair was and he would come back. I clung to that thought, because it was the only thing I had to comfort me. The stone of the altar bruised the hard points of my shoulder blades and tailbone. My ribs ached from not being able to take a deep and satisfying breath past the uncomfortable constriction of the ropes they had bound me with.

The sweet absinthe that had fallen into my mouth

had merely awakened my thirst. I concentrated on that thirst, reveled in it, because it meant that I was still alive.

I was alive and Owen had escaped.

There was hope.

There was worry too, of course. Would the Starved catch up to Lance and Owen? Would Lance be caught in the sun? Where would Owen and Lance go? Back to the Synedrion? Would they listen to Owen's story, or decide it was time to kill him after all? Would they come to help me, or come just to be sure I was finished off as well?

Owen did have some friends among those vampires. Perhaps, if he couldn't talk the Synedrion council into a rescue, he could convince some of those he had once called friends into helping us. Maybe he could even get the ones who wanted a taste of my blood on our side by offering me up to them in some way.

If they would rescue me, I'd be happy to fill a punch bowl with my cursed blood. They could have some, by all means. I'd rather lose a little than all of it, and what was a little blood between friends? They would be my friends too, if they would just come and get me out of here!

Despite telling myself that Owen would come back, that he would never leave me, no matter what, desolation set in. I tried to fight it back. It came anyway, and with it came a sense of deep loss.

I could feel Owen's absence. Not just because I was now alone in that torture chamber, either. I felt the loss of him as keenly as though Lance had removed my left arm and taken it with him. All doubt was gone. I loved Owen with a depth that ached for every step he was away from me.

I couldn't just lie there, dwelling on how bleak things were. I had to try to get out of these bonds. I kept trying to yank my neck forward enough to loosen the rope, reasoning that I might be able to chew my way out of one of the straps holding down my hands if I could. And if I could get one hand out, I might be home free.

Eventually, I realized that the bonds holding my shoulders and neck in place were not coming loose, and my tugging and pulling at them was only resulting in chafed and painfully abraded skin. Talk about a pain in my neck.

I concentrated on the ropes around my arms and wrists. I kept tensing and loosening my muscles, hoping to feel even a slight slip. I braced the foot of my free leg against the top of the altar and pushed against it. Every move hurt. I knew when I had done too much because small trickles of blood began to pool around my wrists.

I kept going anyway. Maybe the blood would act as a lubricant.

There was a small yielding in the ropes.

I closed my eyes to the pain, gasping out harsh screams each time I strained against the rope, and it cut farther into my wrists. But they were moving, becoming looser. I almost had one hand free.

Then something rough touched my neck.

My eyes snapped open.

One of the Starved leaned over me, the hood hanging close to my neck. Her mask was off, and I could only just tell through the flaking and dehydrated skin that it was a her.

The Starved sniffed me and moaned with desire.

"Oh no, you don't. You can't. You're not supposed to drink. You'll be punished."

With pinched fingers, she tugged away the stitches in her lips, each one making a snapping sound as it broke. A reptilian tongue, dry and scraping, darted across the blood on my neck. A long, indrawn breath followed, and my insides froze as I looked sideways to see the Starved one licking her lips and shivering with the same sort of greedy abandon I knew I had displayed at fine restaurants.

Her tongue came back out and licked at my neck again. I pressed myself flatter into the altar, my throat knotting with a scream it was too sore to utter.

Despite my revulsion, I realized this could work for me. I hoped she did drink from me. I hoped she fed on me and felt some human emotion that would make her let me go, let me live. That would make her help me instead of the group she was part of, and if she had to bite me to have that happen, so be it. I braced myself for the touch of her dry lips against my skin, for the feel of sharp fangs puncturing my flesh and blood being taken.

A shout rang out. "How dare you?"

The Starved was yanked off me, thrown backwards.

The leader's hand lifted the one who had licked my neck off the floor and shook her like a ragdoll. The female Starved went limp. "Great Scarl, Forgive me. Her blood calls, you know it does, even more than normal. I couldn't resist. After so long in hunger, I couldn't resist!"

Scarl? Is that his name, or the name of what he is? He was definitely something ... different. A vampire that drinks the blood of other vampires, Owen had said. A monster to the monsters.

Scarl dropped the Starved one onto the floor. The surreptitious licker whined and groveled for a few more seconds.

Scarl gestured to a tray with a bread roll and bottle of water on the ground beside her. "I sent you here to do a simple task, and this is how you go about it? You do not deserve to be one of us."

He hauled the Starved woman up off the floor and said, "I banish you. You cannot resist hunger, and if you cannot resist her here and now, then how will you resist centuries of starvation?"

The woman stuttered, her voice rough from who knew how long without use. "But with the child we shall never know hunger again. It shall slake the thirst forever. We will be immortal and without hunger. We're so close. Please, do not send me away now!"

My blood turns vampires human. Would my child's blood somehow allow them to still be vampires—but vampires who did not crave blood?

Immortal, all powerful, and no need to feed to stay 'alive,' for lack of a better word? I didn't know if that was a good or bad thing.

Owen had told me that many vampires sought ways to end their thirst. Many did not kill in order to feed, either because of moral reasons or because they didn't wish to risk turning a human who they drank from into a vampire. But they needed human blood, thirsted for it, and could only take that blood from living humans. Not the dead, not animals, not blood banks. No artificial method had yet been found.

The Starved didn't drink because they thought humans were below them, tainted. But they'd been promised a cure, through me, through my child, by some damned magic cup.

I had never wanted children. I wanted a career. I had never imagined having children before, and I wasn't sure I wanted to imagine it now, either, all things considered.

But the thought of bringing a life into the world, only

to have that life stolen by vampires, was unbearable. A motherly instinct that I didn't even know I had swelled inside of me.

Not all the Starved were on the chase, or perhaps some had returned, because a group of a dozen came at the leader's call. He spat out what the Starved woman had done, and they dragged her away.

My insides churned as Scarl cut away my bonds, then forced me back into the dungeon. He clicked his fingers, and another Starved appeared behind him, carrying the tray of food. He took the tough bread and tossed it at me like I was nothing more than a dog.

I caught it, because that bread was life, and there was no way in the world I was going to let it land on the filthy floor. I had to eat it if I was going to have any strength at all.

"No tray for you this time," he said.

I held my composure. "I need the water."

A small contemptuous smile tilted his lips into a sneer, and he threw the plastic bottle into the cell through the locked bars. I winced as it landed in the filth with a thump.

He left without another word. I wondered where the Starved woman was then. I had no idea if she was gone forever, or if she was somewhere in the place still begging for her spot in the cult. Or if they disposed of those who failed them in a more permanent manner.

My teeth closed on a hunk of bread and tore it away. I chewed, my jaws working hard and my teeth clicking and clacking, as though taking out my anger on them.

I picked up the plastic bottle from the ground. It was slick with mud, and I shuddered at the smell of it. I wiped the bottle as clean as I could with the hem of my also filthy dress, now a dark maroon rather than the bright fuchsia it was before. The bottle still felt wet despite being wiped and I stared at it, confused. Giving the soft plastic a gentle squeeze, a spurt of water came out from a pinpoint hole in the side.

My first thought was frustration. I needed every drop of water I could get. I unscrewed the cap and took a small swig, careful not to squeeze any more liquid out the puncture hole. It brought cooling and relief to my parched throat.

I stared at the bottle in my wet hands, and the tiny hole jabbed in the side.

It must have happened when it landed on the ground. But how?

I crouched over the area where the bottle had landed, and held my breath as I dug into the thick layer of filth with my broken fingernails. If my manicurist could see my hands now, she'd absolutely faint.

Something hard and smooth met my fingers through

the mud. A shard of glass. Pointed, and sharp down two sides like an arrowhead. I considered it a small miracle that I didn't slice a finger digging it out. And it was just the right size to conceal in the palm of my hand.

This was something. Something I might be able to use to cut through the ropes they bound me with if I was taken back to that horrible altar again. If I was left there alone. Something I could jab eyes or cut throats with. The idea left my hands shaking.

Get a grip. It was awful to consider these things, but I had to. I had to stay alive, and I had to get away from these monsters.

The glass shard gave me some hope, something to cling onto both literally and metaphorically. I used my loudest inner voice to tell myself I could use it to survive, trying to talk down all the other voices telling me I had no chance, even if I were armed to the teeth.

Hours passed. I had no way to know exactly how long. It felt like both an eternity and no time at all, but I knew night must come again soon.

I wound up on the floor with my arms dangling through the bars and jutting into the cell that Owen had occupied. His absence hit me again, and tears rolled down my cheeks. I needed him so badly. A hollowness had grown in my heart like a dark void, one that whistled a haunting tune inside of me.

I bowed my head and pretended that he was there, right there, that his lips were on the crown of my head, and he was whispering to me of ice-cold botrytis Semillon, handmade ganache truffles and sfinci fried ricotta filled with coffee cream.

I didn't know how long I sat there pretending. I did know that it probably saved my sanity in that moment. I had every reason to go insane. Every single reason.

And only one not to.

Owen.

15

OWEN

I came back into awareness with a jump. My blood pounded through my veins as I sat up, taking in my surroundings.

Stone walls, low thatched roof, moth-eaten curtains drawn shut with a faint glimmer of light showing through the gap in the middle. Dust on all the surfaces. Some abandoned farmer's cottage, maybe.

A scratchy woolen blanket had been thrown over my naked body.

Lance crouched beside me on the wooden floor. "I'm sorry I had to subdue you. You were fighting too hard. Slowing—"

He dodged my first fist and caught my second.

I roared at him. "You left her behind!"

Lance dropped my fist and ran his hand through

his silver hair. "I know. I hate it too."

"You have no idea ..."

"We only barely got away ourselves. Now we can get help."

Help. He just means our other imprisoners.

I wrapped the blanket around my waist and stood up, tearing through the room, throwing drawers and fabric aside until I found some old pants. I tugged them on. Too big, but they'd do.

Doing up the buttons, I said, "Where are we?"

"About halfway between Umbravallis and the Starveds' nest. A half hour's drive, or run, to either. No one knew they had an enclave so close."

"Then how did you find us?"

"I've fed from Kaitlyn. It made her easier to track." Lance didn't meet my eyes as he said that. "I would have come sooner, but I was suspected of helping you escape. They locked me up for two days, questioning me about it and Delphine's death. But Joss was half awake during your capture and saw the Starved take you. It took her a long time to shake off the full effects of the Nemexia, but once she did, she let me know who took you. She freed me so we could make our case to the Synedrion, but I ditched her and came on my own."

"They aren't going to like that," I said.

"The hell with what they like. They would have been still arguing now about what to do. Seems to

me I barely made it in time."

A deep, aching chill ran from the crown of my head all the way down my body to my toes. I hadn't been able to control what I was doing, but I'd been there. I'd experienced it all. I'd fought against it, and I still hadn't been able to stop.

I picked up a dust-grayed ceramic pitcher from the table and smashed it against a wall.

"You were under a thrall. What you were doing, whatever *that* was, it wasn't you," Lance said softly.

"Did you see their leader?" I asked.

Lance nodded slowly. "Do you think he really is a Scarl? A red fiend?"

I shrugged. "He has the traits supposedly possessed by one. He also has Kissare's chalice."

Lance's jaw dropped then clenched. "You have to tell the Synedrion. Between the value of Kaitlyn to them, and the chalice, they will come to our aid."

"Screw the Synedrion." I turned to Lance, taking a fistful of his death-dusted shirt in my hand. "Turn me, brother. Make me one of you again. Give me the strength to save her."

I saw my own reflection in the black pools of Lance's eyes, my skin scratched and bloody and covered in grime. I saw my desperation. How I shook with despair and fury.

Lance saw it all too, and still he shook his head. "I will not. You have something precious. These feelings,

this love you have for her, and her love for you. You want to fight for that, but you'll lose it all if I turn you."

"They want her pregnant, Lance." I half sobbed out the words. "They want her child, prophesized by the chalice to take away their thirst. Do you realize what they could be doing to her?" *What I almost did to her?*

Lance gently detached my fingers from his shirt and held my hand in his, strong between us. "We'll save her. You don't have to tell me she is precious, that she's worth saving. I *know.* I want to save her too. But we need help. We need more than the two of us. That's why you're going back to the Synedrion, and you will convince them to help us."

"They won't," I said.

"You will have to find a way to make them. I'm stuck here for the day now. If the Starved were still on our heels, they would burn out there too. Whether they took shelter as well or went back, we're all stuck."

"I'm not," I said.

Lance watched me, warily. Dawn brightened the sky outside the cottage. If I ran, Lance couldn't follow, or he would burn out there.

"Take this time to get help. I've already called Joss; she's coming to collect you."

On cue, I heard the rumble of a car out the front. I cracked the curtain to see one of the Synedrion's driverless cars with opaque black windows.

Lance shied back from the shaft of light that lit the floating dust in the cottage.

If Joss was in that car, she wouldn't be able to come out to get me. Lance couldn't take me out to the car. Once outside, between the two of them, I could run.

But where? I couldn't even find my way back to the Starved without Lance, and I was helpless. Lance was right; we needed more help. I had to try to convince the Synedrion to send us aid. Somehow.

"I'll bring back help."

I opened the door carefully, and Lance stood behind it, guarded from the sunlight that streamed in.

"Tell them what has happened, about the Scarl, the chalice, their plans for Kaitlyn. They *will* listen this time, I'm sure," Lance said. "And remember, you killed the Starved that are dead back there. I killed none. Because the Synedrion will ask."

I nodded. Regardless of who it was or why, it was a serious crime for a vampire to kill another vampire. Serious enough to warrant being bound to the sun. To take an immortal life was considered something far worse than taking a mortal one.

Lance grabbed my shoulder. "I will stay here till night, but take comfort that one way or another, with or without the Synedrion, I will be going back for Kaitlyn."

I clapped my hand on his, then stepped outside. One way or another, I would be too.

16

KAITLYN

Anxiety conspired to turn me into a bundle of nervous energy. I paced the floor of my cell for hours. I couldn't sleep, despite knowing I needed it. I didn't know how long I had been awake at this point. It felt like days.

With every footstep or scuttling sound, my head swung to look. I kept expecting Owen to be thrown back into the cell next to mine at any moment, his escape failed.

My dark hair hung in scraggly matted sections, itching my skin. I pulled it back from my face, winding it into a bun as tight as the knot in my stomach.

The stale air of the cavern never felt like enough. I stared at the ceiling, wondering if there was a whole mountain above me.

I heard the key clanking in the lock, and looked over my shoulder.

The Starved had come for me again.

I hid the glass shard I intended to use to escape in the palm of one fist.

The door opened and they entered. My eyes went from one hooded and cloaked figure to the other. They seemed a somber bunch tonight. I could see the tension in their bodies, and they reeked of something reminiscent of old sweat and leaking batteries. It was weird and upsettingly familiar. It was the same way I had smelled when I first realized I was held captive by a real vampire who desired my blood.

That was the stink of fear.

The smell unsettled me so much I almost dropped the glass. Just in time, I curled my fingers around it, safe and concealed.

I sized up the group. When in the past they might have only been a few, this time, there was a full dozen to escort me. I didn't fight. Not yet. There were too many. It would be futile, and I'd lose my makeshift weapon in the process.

I walked out of the cell before they could grab me. They seemed happy to keep their hands to themselves. Maybe news of the banished one had spread. They led me through the long tunnel to the ceremony chamber.

The torches were all lit and flaming bright, but

the cavern was nearly empty. There weren't as many Starved as before. Around twenty or thirty. Maybe I'd have a chance, if the right moment came up.

I searched the raised area with the altar, where the leader stood. No Owen.

They hadn't caught him. Maybe they were still out looking. But those remaining seemed to be going ahead with Plan B regardless. Whatever that was.

I expected them to take me to the altar and tie me down upon it, the way they had done the last time they had trotted me out for a ritual.

But they paused. Other than the shuffling of feet, they remained quiet. No chanting, no howls of victory.

It was eerie, and it was frightening. They stood there, holding me by my arms but not moving. The hands clasping my flesh never warmed no matter how long they stayed against my skin, and no matter how long they were against my skin I could not seem to accept them being there.

My brain kept dancing around the question—if Owen wasn't here, what were they planning to do?

I felt the way I had the night of the LARP game that had delivered me into Owen's possession.

A deep gut instinct that something was wrong.

Something that was right there in front of my face, and if I could just clear my head, really focus, perhaps I could see it.

When I'd agreed to take the LARP job, I'd been too busy worrying about how to get a part, how to make something out of the nothing that I had. I'd only thought of the money promised for that night's work, and the need to find a new agent. I had been worried about my broken-down car, and the fact that my rent was late, yet again, and I was facing eviction.

I'd been too busy focusing on all the wrong things. I didn't listen to my gut telling me the job was going to get me into trouble, that it was the kind of job girls might disappear from. But back then, I didn't have the knowledge to realize the risk wasn't one of sexual harassment, but rather ending up as vampire food.

Owen had told me it hadn't been his intention to drink so much from me, or to take me prisoner. He had said, a trifle sheepishly, it was not uncommon for him to arrange those reenactments so he could snack on the players and actors. He would always wipe the memory of those he drank from, but something of the emotion sometimes remained. And something of a nasty-looking love-bite. Taking his meals from those who'd been at a vampire re-enactment made things easier to explain.

It probably would've been business as usual if he hadn't sniffed my blood out. But it was my fault I was there at all. I let all those distractions cloud my focus and distract me from the truth that was lurking right beneath the surface.

And there was a truth here, now, as well.

A dangerous truth, that churned deep in my gut.

I was being distracted by the unusual quiet, the glass sliver in my hand, and my hope to use it as an escape plan, the feel of the Starved one's grip on my flesh, and the aching loss of being here without Owen.

There's a truth here, I said to myself. *Open your eyes to it right now, because whatever it is, if you don't see it coming before it happens, it may be the death of you.*

It had something to do with the ritual.

It had to, but what?

They wanted my child to cure their thirst.

They needed the cured one to impregnate me, but Owen was gone.

Owen was the only cured vampire.

My blood had made him human.

There was a connection there somewhere, I knew it, but I wasn't able to see it. I had been rendered punch-drunk by physical abuse, hunger and thirst, fatigue and the sheer mind-numbing amount of evil I had been subjected to.

Metal ground against stone, clattering down behind me. The tunnel we had come along had been closed by a thick gate of gridded, rusty bars. Each of the three tunnels that led into this chamber had been closed off.

Did they expect Lance to attack them again? Was this a precaution?

There was already movement behind the bars. A crowd of shuffling, silent bodies.

That was where the rest of the Starved were. But why were they locked out, only a fraction of their order in the ritual chamber?

The small crowd of Starved around me knelt in a neat line before Scarl.

He drew his ceremonial dagger and sliced down the pad of his thumb. Walking along the line, he anointed each of the Starved in the room on their foreheads with the bright red blood he let run.

Electric tension struck as he walked past me. I clutched my small piece of glass and wondered if it would be far better to plunge it right into Scarl's throat now, even if it meant my own death. With the whole room barred, and Starved inside and out, maybe death was my best option.

Scarl finished dabbing his blood on all the Starveds' foreheads. He took his central position and boomed in his crackling voice, "For your sacrifice, we are eternally grateful."

The anointed Starved placed both hands over their mouths then reached them toward Scarl. The Starved outside the chamber howled wordlessly.

They hoisted me up to the altar, and right past, to the huge, grotesque statue behind it.

Remortality

Ropes had been tied to the stone figure, and I was lifted into the air between them.

My wrists were bound by the two ropes hanging down, then the two ropes beneath me were lifted up, tying my ankles. I was suspended from my wrists, like a butterfly caught in a spiderweb. I was facing away from the statue, but leaned back enough that my view was filled with the disgusting hollow of the demon's mouth and its long, lolling tongue.

An uncontrollable, rattling fear built in me as it occurred to me that maybe, just maybe, they were going to attempt to bring that statue to some kind of impossible life, and have it impregnate me.

Struggling got me nowhere except re-opening the torn skin around my wrists. The wounds there burnt like the ropes were made of lava.

One of the Starved who'd bound me paused for a moment.

He took a long sniff of me, and a low growl began in his throat. It was the sound that a starving dog might make when it was about to fight for food. It sent spirals of cold radiating out from my center. My eyes went to my fist, curled around the glass so hard my skin broke. The warm sting of blood on cut flesh filtered into my awareness.

Had they seen it?

The one who had growled ran his dirty fingers over the abraded patches on my wrists and growled

again. He thought the smell was coming from there and hadn't noticed my only weapon. I still had hope there would be a moment I could cut these ropes to free myself.

They worked again at the ropes at my ankles, pulling the tension tighter. The one who had growled seemed as disconcerted as I felt. He worked fast, sloppily, and every motion told me he was eager to get away from me. It was apparent that my blood was testing his hunger and thirst in a way he could not handle.

Good. As long as he was driven to hurry by the temptation of my blood, and the fact that it could cause him to break his vow and be exiled, he would continue to be sloppy while tying me up to the demon statue.

My hope strengthened when the Starved stepped away. I gave my wrist and ankle on the growler's side a quick little wriggle and found the ropes weren't as tight as the others. If I could get that hand and that foot free while they were busy with whatever ritual they were planning, I might have time to saw through the rope on the other side and free that hand too.

The leader spoke, "It is time for us to claim our destiny."

The sickening howls raised through the echoing cavern again.

Remortality

"I sacrifice myself." Scarl looked around the room at the Starved inside, and then at those outside the bars. "Those who die now, and the death I take, do so that our kind may never have to crave the unworthy blood of a human ever again. We die so they may live eternally, and live without hunger. We die so they may live in pureness and wholeness ..."

Giddiness, or maybe temporary insanity, set in. All of the Starved in the chamber with me were going to be some kind of sacrifice? Including the leader?

And I was, what? Hanging here to be some kind of spectator?

Whatever. I would be cutting myself free as they offed themselves.

I snarled at them. "Get on with it then. I'm more than ready to see the end of you all."

Despite being bound in the air a few feet off the ground, Scarl was tall enough to look me in the eyes. The blood red glow of his unsettled me. "You will not be free of me yet, vessel. I take the long death tonight, for my brethren. I take the death of mortality."

Bile rose in my throat so fast it made my eyes water.

The truth I didn't see. The truth I wouldn't see, hidden behind my foolish hopes, behind my own denial.

They didn't need Owen. They would use my blood to make another cured one.

And that cured one was going to be Scarl.

17

KAITLYN

My legs went weak, and had it not been for the ropes I would've fallen.

The starved leader planned to make himself human with my blood, to be the one to impregnate me. Acid filled my mouth and eyes, but hope came too. He would drink from me, he'd have to, again and again. It could take weeks. I had time.

But what were these other Starved for?

Scarl raised his arms high, and the twenty or so Starved within the room formed a circle around the statue. They climbed, one at a time, to the top of the statue's head. I couldn't see them once they got up there; I could only see the underside of the demon's face. But I heard horrible sounds. Cutting sounds, howling, slashing.

The demon's tongue seemed to move.

I blinked as something splashed onto me in a thin stream, cold, thick, and a dark, off-red.

Blood.

The demon statue wasn't moving. The appearance of movement was the blood, flowing through a channel in the demon's head, along its tongue, to create a waterfall of blood down to Scarl and me. The blood moved slowly, a thick slurry of scarlet. It flowed onto my arms and ran over my belly, soaking into the fabric. The tangy, earthy smell was overwhelming. The horror was equally overwhelming.

"No, no, no," I stuttered. But my denial couldn't stop it from happening.

The blood of twenty Starved dripped onto and around me.

The leader reached up his hands, chanting, catching the falling red rain. He cupped his hands, drinking their blood. It was true. He did drink other vampire's blood. His eyes lit with an inner glow, as though that blood set him on fire inside.

Throwing his shoulders back, he dropped his cloak away so it hung from where it was belted around his hips. He stood there painting his bared chest, face, and scalp with the blood of his brethren until he was red all over.

I stared, transfixed by terror. With a mental slap to the face, I shook myself out of it.

Remortality

A cold voice, a steely determination, spoke up in my head. *You can live through this. You can. It will be awful, but you can live through it. You lived through Owen when he was a vampire, and you can live through this too. You have to. You have to live, because death is the only other alternative.*

With Scarl busy chanting and finger painting himself, and the other Starved in the room bleeding out on top of the statue, it was probably now or never.

I worked my fingers into my palm to try to get a useable grip on the glass.

The glass slipped in my sweat. I grasped hard to catch it. The sharp tip jabbed into my skin, but I didn't drop it. I let out a silent *phew*.

My hands shook, numb from being tied so high over my head. My heart raced as I forced them to work. I pinched the glass between my thumb and forefinger and got it to the rope. I sawed furiously. Sweat broke out on my forehead and streamed down my cheeks. I licked it away from my lips and kept going, blinking back stinging drops of perspiration from my eyes.

The rope barely frayed.

My wrist and arm ached, seized up, and I hadn't done much more than cut away a few strands of the rope.

The leader roared. I thought he'd seen my escape attempt, but he paid that no attention. His fangs

were bared, his muscles straining and obscene under their coating of red gore.

The Starved outside the barred entrances were going crazy, clamoring against the gates, howling and grunting through sewn lips.

Scarl ripped my dress open down the front. He placed his hands on my stomach, leaving bloody handprints there, and then with a growl, sunk his teeth into my neck.

I cried out, horror and pain making the edges of my vision dance and blacken.

He detached himself quickly, and I wondered for a moment if he'd changed his mind. If my blood was changing him. But those thoughts vanished when he chanted more words, then stabbed his fangs back into the other side of my neck, drinking deep.

His lips already felt warmer. He was becoming human much faster than Owen had. This ritual was somehow speeding up the process. The part of me that had hoped I had time was crushed, but the fight didn't leave me.

I kept sawing at my bonds. Scarl was too focused on drinking and chanting to notice.

Blood flowed down from both sides of my neck as the leader paused to chant then drink again, over and over.

Those locked out of the room were going nuts, the smell of my blood flowing, and their leader, quickly becoming human, too much for their craving, empty bodies. They threw themselves at the bars, wrenching at them, clawing at the stone. The sound of groaning metal and crumbling rock made me work my piece of glass faster.

If the Starved out there broke through, it was only me and an almost human in here. They would overwhelm us. They would tear us to pieces in their hunger. I could hear it in their frenzied howls.

Only the leader showed restraint, drinking from me bit by bit between the dark, incomprehensible words he spoke. I wondered if he hated it, if it disgusted him, having to drink from a thing he thought so little of.

Or maybe he was just being very careful to keep me alive. All of this would be for nothing if I died.

At least it meant I remained lucid enough to keep fighting. One of the larger strands of rope snapped under the glass, my arm jerking almost free. Just one thin fiber to go.

Scarl gurgled out a deep cry, and staggered a few steps. His head fell back, exposing the long curve of his throat. He bellowed, an undulating howl that made the hair on my arms and the back of my neck stand up.

Scarl's skin rippled, then it went shiny and glowed bright red. His arms shot out and his fingers flexed and curled. The nails he had retreated, growing backward right into his nail beds.

He fell onto his knees, clutching at his heart. His body shuddered. Blood spilled from his mouth and nose. His head came back up, red streaming down his face. His chest moved, his ribs expanded and contracted as he took deep breaths in newly working lungs.

I looked into his eyes, hoping to see a shred of humanity there, something I could speak to. His eyes were hateful, a bright red-brown that looked at me with contempt. Regaining his humanity had done nothing for his personality. *Once a fanatic, always a fanatic.*

He rose to his feet with a look of determination. I met his stare, equally determined. The two of us alone in the center of the room, both drenched in blood. He was still huge, stronger and larger than me, but we were both human now.

I put all my strength into one final tug at the rope I'd been cutting, and my arm swung free.

I cried out in pain as the movement ripped at my bleeding wrists and throat. I fought through the pain. I had to, while I still had the advantage of surprise.

I slashed at Scarl with the blade of glass, aiming for his vulnerable, human throat.

He moved at the last second. The glass went deep into his cheek, exposing a vast flap of muscle and tissue below his skin. It also cut the skin between my fingers, and blood flowed down my hand onto my wrist. My fingers went slick and I lost my grip on the glass. It dropped away, my only weapon and my only chance gone with no way to get it back again.

His shock turned to wild fury. He backhanded me in a way that made my head ring.

A loud cracking sound followed by an enormous crash of thunder struck the air.

My thoughts blurred. *How can I hear thunder down here in the cavern?*

Stars in my eyes, thunder in my ears. My thoughts dulled then cleared.

It wasn't thunder.

It was the sound of the Starved breaking down the bars.

18

KAITLYN

 eal fear filled the leader's eyes as the Starved flowed into the chamber.

"Stop this!" he roared. "Fight your hunger! It will ruin everything when we're so close!"

And I did see fighting. The crowd of Starved tumbled over each other, fighting to be the first to reach us, fighting each other. Some appeared crazed for a taste of blood; others tried to hold them back. Black shadows darted between them, strange blurs like moving darkness that made me distrust my eyes.

Two Starved broke free of the crowd and rushed at the altar. They ripped off their hoods, their nails tearing the stitches out of their skin with sickening popping sounds that turned my stomach.

Scarl reached into his robes hanging from his

hips, and drew his ceremonial dagger. I bet he was wishing he had some stakes right about now.

I knew I was.

I didn't even have my glass shard anymore. And I only had one arm free.

Scarl sliced the throat of one Starved right through, decapitating it. Its headless body stumbled back from him and turned to dust.

Another reached me, fangs first, tearing deep into my thigh. I beat at his wrinkled face with my free fist, but was too weak to detach him.

Then he became a shower of dust that stuck to the tacky blood on my skin.

Behind that dust stood a figure all in black.

An Ebonguard? My heart burst into breakneck pace. Then stopped, when I saw who stood there as well.

Owen.

I sobbed in sheer relief, sagging and hanging from the ropes.

His hands cupped my face. I could not lift my eyelids to see him. From the corners of my vision I saw Scarl, wrestling a Starved across the altar.

"Strawberry. Kaitlyn. Savior of my life. You're safe now."

My body didn't move but I mentally shook my head, denying what he said. Seeing him here, amongst all of this, snapped something inside of me. I wasn't safe. I would never be safe. He would never be safe. *We* would never be safe. This couldn't be true. I could feel myself tumbling into the yawning abyss of insanity. I could touch that madness. I could see its deep and seductive darkness right there, so close, hear it whispering that all I had to do was let go and this horror would go away.

But Owen's voice called to me, "Look at me. I'm right here and I love you. Come back to me. I'm begging you."

My lips cracked as I used all my last energy to whisper, "I love you too."

His fingers moved along the ropes binding me. Was I dreaming? Was any of this true? His body, so warm and alive, pulled me closer. I could feel the steady beat of his heart against my chest.

It was real.

He was real, and I was still alive.

He came back for me. Of course he did. And he brought help.

Ebonguard filled the room. They were the black blurs I'd seen before. I didn't know how many; they moved too fast to follow.

"Joss," Owen grunted, anguish all over his face. "Cut her down."

Joss nodded, and the ropes were sliced before I could blink.

I collapsed into Owen's arms. He caught me, and

bundled me up.

He almost toppled backwards as more Starved reached us, clawing at him. The room was in chaos, a bloody free-for-all. Joss's arms flashed, fighting three to her one. One Starved dragged its fingers across the armor around her throat, making a sound like nails on a chalkboard. It lashed out at her face, tearing away the black cowl she wore, revealing dark skin and bright pink hair.

Joss lashed back, her limbs an elegant flow of motion as she flipped two of the Starved to the ground. They were pinned there with metal stakes, right through their abdomens and into the stone. I was confused why they weren't being killed, and saw throughout the room more Starved pinned down like insects in a gruesome collection.

Owen ducked away from the third, still holding me. I wrapped my arms around his neck, pressing my body to his, as though I could melt into him, be shielded by him entirely.

The Starved who reached for us was grabbed by a hand on each shoulder, one from Joss, and one from Lance, who threw him onto the ground and pinned him down as well.

Joss and Lance formed a barrier between the Starved and where Owen held me. I wanted to press my face against his strong chest and not see what was happening in the room, but the clash of combat drew my gaze.

Blood and ash and screams filled the chamber. Some Starved tried to flee, but they were no match for the Ebonguard. Brown-robed bodies filled the room, pinned to the ground, squirming for freedom.

Still, the Ebonguard were not killing the Starved.

The Starved were killing themselves.

They were driving stakes into their hearts, or using ceremonial knives to release their thick, dark blood into the air and onto those nearby instead of being captured. I wept, not only out of horror but out of a kind of shocked pity at the sight. The Ebonguard were trying to capture them, but they were choosing to end themselves instead.

A movement near the altar caught my eye. The leader was there, sheltering himself behind the stone block. But he couldn't hide the scent of his now human blood. A group of his followers dogpiled him, and I heard his pained cries.

Lance broke away from us, throwing the skeletal bodies of the Starved off the leader into the crowd, where they were taken down by Ebonguard. He wrenched Scarl to his feet, his new human blood flowing freely from scratches and bites over the dried blood he'd painted on himself.

"You're not getting out of this that easily," Lance spat.

Joss surveyed the room. She whipped a black scarf from her belt and wrapped it around her face to replace the cowl she'd lost. She signaled to another Ebonguard, who came and took the leader off Lance. In two blurred leaps, the Ebonguard and Scarl were out of the chamber.

"Give me Kaitlyn," Joss said. Owen hesitated, then nodded and passed me over like a child. Joss nodded to Lance who took hold of Owen. "Let's go."

19

OWEN

I wanted to keep hold of Kaitlyn. I never wanted to let her go again.

But there were still Starved and Ebonguard fighting out there, still Starved who could be lurking in the tunnels. And I was only human, too weak and slow to carry Kaitlyn out of this hellhole. So I handed her over.

Air rushed past as Joss and Lance sped us from the cavern, out of the stinking blood-addled darkness.

The air freshened as the cave tunnels became stone stairs, leading up through a house then out into freedom.

Cars lined the weedy dirt driveway. I turned my head to look back.

The house was plain and small, nestled in front of a rocky hillside, made of mud-bricks and with a thinly

thatched roof. It could have been any picturesque cottage sitting in a pastoral countryside.

How could such evil lurk beneath such an innocent-looking exterior?

Joss handed Kaitlyn back to me without ceremony. I thanked her silently.

A slim band of moonlight lay across the overgrown grass, full of singing insects.

I could feel Kaitlyn take a big lungful of that fresh air. I breathed deeply too, the tight compression of stress around my chest breaking as though it had been bound by leather straps. The smell of wildflowers, and something else, filled my nose.

"Look," I whispered to Kaitlyn.

Her gaze followed my pointing finger and stopped, staring at a low stone wall hung with leafy runners that bore ripe, red wild strawberries.

Tears washed trails through the grime and blood on her face.

Those strawberries said life existed beyond this death, and blood, and terror. That something beautiful and life-giving could grow even out of soil darkened by misdeeds and horrors.

"We're alive. We're really still alive?" Her voice was half sob, half whisper. Her hands reached for my face, as though trying to confirm I was tangible.

"We are," I said. I eyed the Ebonguard around us, preparing to take us back to the Synedrion. *But for how long now, I don't know.*

We had been delivered from this pit of horrors back to a cold, calculated verdict that would be made by the council.

Kaitlyn nuzzled her face into my chest, wetting it with her tears.

Joss waited by a black van, the back door open. I carried Kaitlyn over and stepped up and in with her. Inside was laid out like an ambulance, and the Synedrion's doctor waited, first-aid supplies at the ready.

I placed Kaitlyn onto the stretcher on one side. I had to pry her arms gently from around my neck.

Joss banged on the wall between our part of the vehicle and the front, and the van got into motion.

Kaitlyn lay flat with a sigh and opened her eyes. Looking at Ewan, she groaned. "It's my favorite doctor."

"I should be," he replied. "I'm probably going to save your life right now. Unless you'd like to die of blood loss and infection."

She deadpanned him. "Hmm, blood loss and infection, or your bedside manner. Both deadly. Do I really have a choice?"

"No," he said, and got to work. He moved as fast as he could, as fast as a vampire could, his arms a blur as he dressed Kaitlyn's wounds. She winced as he washed them with saline solution, and the sharp smell of antiseptic followed. He applied padding and pressure bandages around her neck, crisscrossing her torso so it didn't restrict her breathing, then saw to her other abrasions, cuts, and puncture wounds. I noticed, as he flashed with motion, sample bottles being laid out behind him, blood wiped from Kaitlyn's skin.

Within a few minutes, Kaitlyn's wounds were all cleaned and dressed, and she was hooked up to fluids, antibiotics, and pain relief.

"Okay, maybe you are my favorite doctor," she said, as the codeine hit her system. Despite the clean patches around open wounds, her skin and clothes were stained in a layer of grime and dried blood. "Now I just need some water, a good meal, and about sixteen showers in a row."

I took her hand, kneeling beside the stretcher so we were eye to eye. I swallowed a hard lump that came into my throat. "I'm so sorry I left you there."

"Don't be. We might have both ended up dead, or worse, otherwise. And I don't think Lance gave you much choice." Her tears had stopped, and her breathing was strong and even again. *That's my Strawberry, so strong.*

I took some spare saline solution and gauze, and wiped the blood from her face where tears had left clear rivers in the dirty red layer. "I should have brought you clean clothes. I'm sorry I didn't think of that."

Remortality

"You brought the cavalry. Way better." Kaitlyn tilted her head with a wince, looking for Joss. She reached a hand out, as though to touch her, or shake her hand, a gesture Joss ignored. "Thank you," Kaitlyn said.

"Just doing my job," Joss replied through the black scarf that covered the bottom half of her face. She looked away, as though staring into the distance, like she had no interest in us at all. Then her eyes flickered down to meet Kaitlyn's, and back away again. "You're welcome."

I couldn't help but smile. My Strawberry always did have a way of winning hearts, even the blackest of them.

I hoped that would be enough for what was to come.

20

KAITLYN

When our van pulled up outside the Synedrion's palace, my first response had been, "Oh, hell no! They want to kill us! They want to kill me! You rescued me just to take me back here?"

That was until I got inside, and got into the shower.

I must have stood under the hot jets of water for an entire hour, letting them wash away every last trace of the Starveds' torture cave from my skin, and hair, and soul.

Owen offered to join me, to help wash me since my arms still ached so much, but I wasn't quite ready for that kind of intimacy again. Not yet.

So I stood there, alone and still, under the running water, letting the warm stream wash me clean like tears of life.

When I finally emerged, I found Owen had left some clothes for me in the bathroom. Thick, fluffy socks, a soft merino hoodie, and comfy yoga pants. I gingerly peeled off the waterproof covers for my dressings that the doctor had provided, then slipped the clothes on. I cuddled the soft, clean fabrics to myself. They were like heaven.

A bath would have been heaven too. I'd planned on one at first, but Ewan said showers only, doctor's orders, as a bath would soak all the contaminants on my skin back into my cleaned wounds. I didn't like the sound of that much either. He said he had orders to draw new blood samples from me too, but would wait until I had recovered a little. He reminded me to hydrate, *again*.

Tomorrow I would have a bath. If my luck kept up and I was still alive then. Maybe being captured and tortured by hangry vampires, then held prisoner again by bureaucratic vampires, wasn't the kind of thing I'd normally consider lucky, but I still lived. Against all odds, I was alive. There had to be some kind of miracle work involved in that.

I stepped out of the bathroom and went through the bedroom into the living area. These were not the same quarters we'd been in before, which I was sure were undergoing a major clean and renovation after what had happened in there, but they were laid out in the same fashion. A huge and luxurious living area, and a separate bedroom and bathroom. I almost considered staying in the bedroom, lying down, and sleeping for days, but I could smell food beyond.

Owen had cranked up the heat in our room and I cuddled myself again, relishing the warmth and my still beating heart under my clothes.

Lance and Owen sat at a table together in front of one of the domed room-service-style trays. They both stood quickly when I entered the room, both moved to pull the chair out for me.

I walked to Owen, and Lance re-adjusted, reaching to open the food coverings instead. He cleared his throat. "I'm afraid, with all the time spent on rescuing, I wasn't able to bring in any more fine food for you."

Under the dome were two bowls of the thick stew given to thralls. "I will make sure you have better for breakfast tomorrow."

I didn't even blink—just grabbed a spoon and started eating. Right then, it was wonderful. Better than truffled triple brie on artisan lavash. Better than prosciutto-wrapped lamb backstrap, or stuffed and deep-fried zucchini flowers. Hell, right now, it was better than deep-fried anything, and that was saying something.

Owen had waited until I started eating, then joined me. Lance watched, his expression sharing both a small smile and a small frown. I noticed then an Ebonguard standing by the door, their

usual policy when it was more than just Owen and myself in the room.

"Joss?" I asked. I wasn't sure, but she looked to be the right height and build.

She gave a small nod.

"Come and join us," I said, patting the fourth chair at the small table.

I had warmed to Joss. She may have been some kind of cold vampire ninja, and maybe she was only doing her job, but I liked having her around. Partly because she'd saved my life, and partly because of her wicked cool hair. It made me wonder if there was a little party animal hidden under her strictly-business personality.

She hesitated a moment, then came and took a seat. She sat there, still as a statue as we ate, her face and expression covered by her cowl.

"Are there a lot of female Ebonguards?" I asked out of curiosity. It was honestly hard to tell.

Joss didn't reply, but Owen nodded. "Gender equality is one thing the vampire world has gotten right. Vampirism tends to even out physical strengths, and removing reproduction from the equation means there are less reasons to oppress or discriminate."

Lance leaned back in his chair. "Women also outnumber men as vampires. Maybe two to one. Women are much more likely to be turned, for one reason or another."

Realization hit me. "There were five women to two men on the Synedrion council. You'd never see that in the human world. Not yet."

"Four to three now," Owen grumbled.

"Oh, of course, Delphine is gone," I said. I tried not to vividly remember how she went. "A man replaced her?"

"Dante de Silva." Lance looked at Owen, and Owen looked back, their expressions concerned.

"That same creep who attacked Owen, jealous-lover style, when we first got here?"

"The very same."

"So we're screwed?" I put my spoon down. "He's not going to vote on our side, is he?"

Lance shrugged. "It was looking that way, until Owen came to beg for the Synedrion's aid in saving you. They had all but decided before then, but now they are debating again and still haven't made a decision. That might be a good thing."

"Really? Why?"

Owen shook his head. "I'm not sure. Maybe because the information we brought them meant taking down those who killed a member of the Synedrion, and it also meant recovering Kissare's chalice, an important relic long thought lost."

"A relic that can read the future? Although not necessarily accurately," I said. Despite the best efforts of the Starved and their leader, here I was, not pregnant. A small shiver ran through me, knowing that it didn't necessarily mean the prophecy wasn't true. Just that it hadn't happened *yet*.

"What's going to happen to the Starved that were caught?" I asked.

"The punishment for murdering another vampire is to be bound to the sun." Owen stabbed at his stew with his spoon, then left it alone, as though his appetite had gone. "There is a shrine on a low peak here in Umbravallis, where only a thin band of sunlight can enter. The Starved will be bound in there, and each day they will burn, inch by inch, not enough to kill them but enough to make them wish it did. Then each night they will heal, ready to repeat the process again."

"Yikes," I said. "That won't work for Scarl, though. He's human now."

"No." Owen looked down at his food, deciding to eat again. He mumbled through a mouthful, "It may be Alam's dagger for him."

"You vampires and your fancy terms. Alam's dagger, bound to the sun, Kissare's chalice ..."

"The dagger and chalice are some of our most sacred relics from the original seven." Lance leaned back in his chair and eyed Owen. "Along with other items, like Tiamat's Ring."

I looked at Owen too. "If we get through this, you're buying me a vampire history book so I can get caught up." Then I looked over at Joss, sitting deathly still. "If it's so bad to kill other vampires, how come the Ebonguard can?"

I wasn't sure she'd reply, but she spoke before anyone else could answer, "We are allowed only when given the order. Our mission was to retrieve you. Any who stood in our way could be killed. But whenever possible we were to capture and return them for punishment."

"Ebonguard are renowned for their adherence to orders," Lance said. "They are very strict about it all. Failure is a three-strikes-and-you're-out sort of system." Lance said this so nonchalantly, but Joss's dark eyes twitched when he did.

Softly, I asked, "Did what Delphine do to you, and how we were taken, count as a failure?"

"I'm on my second strike," was all she said, her voice blank.

"And what does *out* mean?"

No one answered me that time.

I watched Joss for a few silent moments. For how little she moved, she could have been nothing but stone covered in black silk. But I found myself worrying about her.

Lance pushed his chair back from the table and dipped a tiny bow. "I had better let you two get some rest. I'm sorry. I forget how much human bodies need it. I will see what I can do for your cause.

Keep up hope."

He left, and Joss shadowed him out the door without a word, locking it behind them.

Owen and I ate our food, each of us quiet. There was so much to think about, so much to ask, and so much to say that it overwhelmed my fragile state. I shut it all out and just sat. Just ate.

When my bowl was licked clean, I pushed it back with a huge and happy sigh.

Owen asked, "Better?"

I sighed. "If they're going to kill me, let them do it now. I'll die full and clean and happy." Although, I was still tired, thanks to the blood loss and sheer lack of sleep that had been the norm for too long. I was delirious with exhaustion. Maybe that was where the incongruous sensation of happiness came from.

Owen stood and came over to where I sat. He reached for me, and I placed my hands in his, feeling a slight tremble there. I didn't know if it was mine or his. He guided me toward the bed and pulled back the covers. I tried to give him a smile but it didn't quite want to form. There was still so much left to say, and I was too tired to say it.

The mattress was heavenly soft and comfortable. Every one of my aching muscles tingled in delight as I stretched out horizontally between the warm, silky sheets.

Owen slipped under the covers next to me. My

hands found his, and we curled together.

He tucked me into the hollow of his body, and that whistling emptiness inside me closed up like it had never been there at all.

21

KAITLYN

From the moment my head hit the pillow until I awoke who knew how much time later, I knew nothing but oblivion. I jolted awake, confused and unsure where I was from the fog of bad memories from the passed days. The room was dark, and all was quiet and still.

We are still in the Synedrion estate. They are deciding our fate. They could come for us at any moment. My eyes snapped wide open with terror.

A panic attack hit me, and my hands patted the bed, trying to find Owen beside me. I couldn't find him, and then … there, his warm, resting body. His smooth, firm muscles.

My arms wrapped around him with a primal urgency. I pressed my face to his, my forehead against his cheek. I clung to him with greedy fingers. I needed him, to be with him, here and always.

He stirred, slowly at first. Then his arms came around me, drawing my chest tight into his. His face turned, and warm lips met my forehead.

His hands stroked along my flesh, touching me and finding the spots where tension had gathered the hardest—the points below my shoulder blades, the flesh of my lower back, and the base of my skull. His fingers went deep into strained muscles, and the rigidity loosened and let go like the air I moaned out.

My eyes closed. Sensations met and melded in the red-tinted darkness behind my eyelids. My pulse quickened. His hands moved over my flesh, touching me in a way that made me want him wildly.

He kissed my forehead again, sending vibrations through my body like an electric shock. My back arched. I sought his lips like they were an antidote to poison. The kiss lengthened and deepened, rough, craving kisses, drenched in desire, full of the frenzy of life and the panic of death. He took hold of my top and pulled it over my head, and I did the same for him. The muscles of his chest rippled under my fingers.

His head lowered then, first to my breasts and then lower, his hands sliding off my pants.

Lying on my back, I clawed my fingers into the sheets as waves of pleasure built inside me, filling me from my toes, zinging up through my heart, and tingling across my scalp. I cried out with an overwhelming fierce desire to fill myself with Owen until I burst into pieces.

I pushed onto my elbows, reaching down to Owen and he responded, crawling back up my body, laying down kisses all the way.

We moved together with a sense of urgency that changed and shifted and grew ever more intense, that left me gasping. My nails bit deep into the skin of his back, desperate to bring him closer, even though we couldn't physically get closer than we were.

"I love you," he breathed into my ear. "You're my Strawberry, always and forever."

Heat, and pressure, and a delicious aching need for release, for Owen, for relief, for more, grew so strong I screamed, holding nothing back, as though weeks' worth of tension and terror and unrequited desire, love, and loss exploded through me.

My hands grasped for him, my whole body driven my maddening passion and desire to crush him into my being until we were one and could never be separated again. "I love you too. I love you so much."

Owen let out a roar of pleasure. My eyes closed as he collapsed on top of me, his breath coming in and out of his mouth in a fast rhythm that slowed and then normalized as mine did. Our heartbeats found a calmer pace together. We stayed locked in that tight embrace, two halves of a whole, unwilling to let go, as sleep took hold of us again.

It felt like hours later, hours of blissful, restful slumber, when I awoke to the smell of coffee.

That smell awoke a different kind of desire in me. COFFEE.

It had been so long. I glanced at Owen in the half light, and decided to let him sleep some more. Emotionally, he'd been through almost as much as I had. And he was still learning how to cope with having emotions again. Even regular never-been-a-vampire-for-a-while humans weren't good at dealing with their emotions. Life was hard. Life being imprisoned, tortured, and with the one you loved held at the mercy of vampires was even harder.

I slipped out of bed and into a fluffy, white dressing gown.

Tiptoeing into the living area, I found a mouth-watering breakfast laid out for us. Tea, coffee, milk, and a choice of juices. A dozen different breads, pastries, cakes, croissants, and pancake options. Poached eggs, crispy bacon, sausages, and potatoes roasted in butter and rosemary. Sliced watermelon, guavas, and blueberries. It could have been room service from a fancy hotel, but a small folded note in the middle of the hot and cold beverages had "From Lance" scrawled across the front. I took a sip of orange juice, remembering how important vitamin C was in helping iron absorption, as I poured out a coffee and stirred in way more sugar than I really should.

My first sip of coffee was like inhaling liquid life.

I unfolded the note. It read, *No outcome yet. They are still not ready to vote. I remember good food as being one of the best ways to pass time. I'm not the chef Owen is, but I hope you both enjoy what I could scrounge up.*

I smiled, wondering where he got it all. Did he do a run to the nearest human town for some groceries? Or did some of the vampires here spoil their favorite human thralls? And were the chefs here humans or vampires, if they had any at all? Owen explained to me once that he'd learned to cook after he became a vampire. Mostly to learn more about the restaurant industry, since he owned a number of restaurants and bars, to be able to better communicate with his chefs. But he could never taste the food he made. It became an abstract sort of art form for him, creating foods and flavors scientifically, analytically, visually without ever knowing their flavor himself. It was one of the reasons he took such great pleasure in feeding me when he first held me captive. To see the food he made being savored.

I slathered a croissant in butter and filled it with blueberries and maple syrup. I had never done it before, but it felt like a good idea. And if that was the biggest risk I took today, it would be a good day.

I was enjoying my first mouthful when the door

opened. I stiffened, my breath held, wondering if this was the moment.

Ewan, the doctor, entered. He had promised he'd be back for more of my blood. In a doctorly way rather than a vampirely way.

I held up my coffee to him and took a sip, demonstrating myself hydrating.

He shook his head. "Coffee? Not coffee. Drink water."

I snorted. And drank more coffee anyway.

I let him take his blood without resistance. I didn't see the point. He popped and swapped vacuum sample tubes, filling three of them.

"What's happening to all of these?" I asked, pointing to the samples.

"Tests," he said.

Duh, I wanted to reply, but waited, and he continued without prompting.

"The first samples were inconclusive. Apart from that you're an incredibly rare blood type, Rh Null. Which is why we've been unable to give you any blood transfusions."

"And here I thought there were only As, Bs and Os." For someone who had been vampire food more than once, I was shocked at myself that I'd never known my own blood type before. I'd never really had the need, in normal human medical terms. I had never even heard of Rh Null type before.

Remortality

Ewan gave me the kind of look you might give an imbecile, clipped his bag closed, and left.

I finished my blueberry croissant and coffee, then snuck back through the bedroom and into the bathroom, carrying my luggage with me.

My eyes went to the massive tub. It could probably hold a dozen people. The outside was carved marble that made little steps up into the tub, and on each step were scented candles and pretty little vases filled with colorful bath salts and delicately carved soaps.

I wasn't allowed a bath yesterday, but I was clean now, and had waterproof dressings. This might be the last bath of my life, so to hell with Doctor Vampire's rules.

I got the water running and spent some time sniffing the different fragrance options, settling on one that smelled of a fresh spring day and green grass, with the lightest floral tones and something that reminded me of sunlight. I shucked off my robe, applied a few waterproof dressings to my worst wounds, and entered the tub with a happy sigh. I floated there for some time, enjoying the ebb and flow of the water and the scent rising from it. I could feel months' worth of tension melting away.

After the bath, I stood in front of the mirror, combing out my matted hair, black and dripping. I figured that vampires maybe could see their reflections, since all the bathrooms here had mirrors. I stared into my own eyes, rimmed in dark shadows, and at my sickly pale skin. These weren't my most glamorous moments, but there was a defiance in my expression that felt more beautiful than make-up could ever manage. The rebelliousness of life. After a good breakfast, good bath, and great sex, I felt ready for anything.

I dug through my luggage, seeing what Owen had packed in there. No comfort clothes for me today. I was ready for war. I found a classy yet sexy rose red gown, and matched it to black pumps with a red heel, and my richest crimson lipstick. I twined my hair into an elegant rope braid down the side and wrapped the length into a French twist in the way a helpful hair-stylist on set had once shown me how to do.

I removed the bandages from my torn throat. It was ripped and bruised in blotchy yellow and maroon patches on both sides, from the base of my ears right down to my collarbones. I left it uncovered, so the Synedrion could see what had been done to me. I knew vampires didn't feel empathy, but it made me feel as though I were being rebellious, letting it all be visible. The ugliness of it stood in stark comparison to my beautiful dress.

Owen opened the door behind me. Wearing just his boxers, he came up and held me from behind, placing his chin on my shoulder, careful to avoid touching my neck.

Remortality

"You look beautiful, Strawberry."

I smiled wryly at him in the mirror. "What I am is ready to hear what the damned Synedrion has decided. And ready to deal with whatever their decision is. If they won't give us their verdict soon, then I will burn this place to the ground, Owen. I will."

"I'll light the match myself," he replied.

We smiled at each other. Resolve hardened between us. We were done being pawns in this vampire game. We were done being held prisoner and waiting for vampires to decide if we should live or die.

It turned out we didn't have to wait much longer.

By the time Owen had dressed, choosing a suit and red shirt to match my gown, and we'd both eaten some more breakfast, there was a knock at the door.

The sound of a deep bell ringing in the distance followed it.

Our time was up.

Dread came in but so did courage. I was finished being jerked around by these vampires. Live or die, I wanted an answer, and I wanted it then.

Lance appeared. His face was grim. "They have finished debating. They are ready to vote on your fate."

22

KAITLYN

Every step I took reminded me that I was alive, and I wanted to stay that way. My muscles flexed and rolled. Long, determined strides carried me quickly to the council chambers, past the creepy statues, through the heavy, carved doors.

This time, the chamber was full. The Synedrion hadn't managed to keep me and my blood a secret, so obviously didn't see the point in keeping this meeting private as they had the last one.

No one made a sound as we entered. My eyes roamed across the crowded space and to the seven on their raised thrones. The sound of my breath and heartbeat seemed very loud in this quiet, lifeless place.

We were met at the door by Niamh who led us to the front of the dais.

Owen held my hand, and I kept my head up, leading with my chin. Refusing to look down or away, or to be cowed by what might be our sentence and fate. I was ready.

The thrall who gave the announcements seemed to be near the end of formalities, having started before we arrived.

Bertha gave me a smile, but she also licked her lips like she wanted to eat me. Lin and Shirina leaned toward each other, whispering enthusiastically. Dante's fingers gripped the armrests of his throne with blatant aggression. I wondered how he made the cut for joining the Synedrion. I honestly had no idea if this was some kind of monarchy or democracy, or something else entirely.

After the thrall had finished, Toren said, "We rule here today on a matter that concerns all vampire kind. With either outcome, there will be ramifications. Heavy ramifications. The Synedrion has deliberated on all concerns surrounding this issue and spent many hours debating."

Viatrix no longer seemed to be asleep. She looked down upon me, her head tilted and owl-like. She remained silent. Milton snarled and turned his face away, disgusted.

I began to sweat, my fingers shaking inside Owen's grasp. He squeezed them gently.

"We have spoken long on this issue, we have

made our decisions, and we are ready to vote," Toren said, standing to look down upon us with his dark, wrinkled eyes. "Those in favor of death for the humans."

Milton, Viatrix, and Dante raised their right hands high, as though summoning down lightning. I waited for more movement, my heart drumming like the thunder that should follow.

I couldn't breathe.

"Those in favor of allowing the humans to live."

Toren, Lin, and Shirina raised their hands. A moment after, Bertha followed.

Four to three. We were to live, four to three! Breath rushed back into me in shaky bursts.

I looked up at Owen, and saw hope and relief shining through his eyes, as I'm sure it did in my own.

A roar came from the crowd, a cacophony of applause, disbelief, and dissent. It was clear not everyone in attendance was thrilled that we weren't going to be murdered. Voices rang out.

"Give them Alam's dagger!"

"I want the cure!"

"Death to the vampire killers!"

I shrunk away, my relief short-lived. Regardless of the vote, of the verdict, the population was split, violently, in their opinion of us.

"Quiet!" roared Lin. The room settled. "We are not savages. Not animals. You must understand

this human is important to our whole society. Her blood could offer a method for those who wish to become human again to do so, and based on our recent research, may offer even more."

Dante grunted. "Forget the woman. Raine deserves punishment for his recent and past crimes."

I turned to look up at Owen, but caught Lance's gaze on the way. He stood still, frowning, watching from the side of the room.

"You could provide us with no proof of these alleged crimes, and the vote has been made," Toren said. "Being as they are humans who aren't held to vampire law, and that they acted in self-defense, there is to be no punishment for them for the vampires, the Starved, they killed."

A cry came from somewhere in the crowd. "Destroy them both! They will bring a plague of final death to us all!"

Milton turned his anger toward Shirina. "If you're going to keep your lab rat, you should keep her locked up as one. Humans are food or slaves. Letting her go free is a mistake."

A clamor of agreement rose from the crowd.

"If you don't give me my freedom, if you keep me as a slave, I will kill myself, and you'll have no blood for your tests," I threatened.

The crowd cheered, as though they liked that idea.

Shirina's eyes narrowed. "Then I would simply keep

you under thrall and have total control of your actions."

I narrowed my eyes in return. I wouldn't be beaten by these vampires. But I could play by their rules. "You don't have the right to keep me in thrall. I don't belong to you."

Owen's hand tensed in mine, and I squeezed it in return before letting it go. I hoped he understood what I was doing, that it was only for our freedom, and nothing more.

"I've been claimed by Lancelot Ferland, as has Owen. We are his, and he alone can choose what form our freedom now takes." The words were hard to say, but Owen had explained to me how seriously being claimed was in the vampire community. It would mean we were Lance's property, with very similar laws protecting that.

Lance seemed surprised by the announcement at first, but with a quick nod, he showed he understood. He came to stand by my side. "It's true, I have claimed them."

"Thank you," I whispered under my breath.

I wrapped my arms around his and hung on his side, dropping my gaze subserviently, as though I were his obedient and fawning property. I hated doing so, especially with Owen right beside me. How fake it felt compared to our real love. But I was an actor, after all.

I could feel the intensity of Owen's emotions. I

prayed that he wouldn't act on them. Being perceived as under Lance's ownership was a hell of a lot better than being a vampire scientist's thrall.

"It seems as though you have claimed her." Lin's eyelashes fluttered in a perturbed way. "So be it then. They will be your responsibility. You'll be expected to keep your property safe and under control."

"Of course," Lance said with a bow.

Grumbles rose from the crowd.

Toren boomed over them, "What this human can give us, through her blood, is of remarkable value. Not only for those who want to become human again, but all vampires. She and her companion, the vampire remade human, have our protection and the protection of the Ebonguard. That is the Synedrion's ruling."

That only made the rabble louder. Lin spoke up, "Beyond the ruling of us seven, Kissare's chalice shows her to live free."

That shut the room up. Apparently, this chalice was something to be taken seriously.

"And we have only regained the chalice, thanks, in part, to the humans," she followed up. Soft murmurs replaced the fanatical yelling.

She eyed Lance again next. "And of course, there are conditions to her freedom."

Still clinging meekly to Lance's side, my lower lip trembled but I bit it, defiantly, then spoke for myself. "Conditions?"

Shirina nodded. "We have already discovered much from your blood, but will require fresh samples for the foreseeable future to continue our work. You are to make these available to us as needed."

"Do we have to stay here, in Umbravallis?" I asked, my hope deflating.

"That will depend on your owner, human," Milton snarled.

Shirina waved his comment off. "We can have the samples collected anywhere and couriered as needed. We aren't relying on messenger pigeons," she said, with a tiny eye-roll. "Wherever you and your owner do go, however, you will always be watched by the Ebonguard. For your protection."

Bertha said, "Those are the terms we can live with."

We can live with.

We could live.

We would live!

And we would be free. Thanks to Lance, and my acting skills. And Owen for checking his jealousy. Maybe putting up the appearance of being claimed wasn't complete freedom, but it was a hell of a lot better than the alternative.

Elation made my heart sing, and my blood run hot through my veins. Tears filled my eyes. "Thank you."

Lin gave me a regal nod and clapped to the thrall who stood at hand, who announced the end of

proceedings and signaled for the crowd to leave the hall.

The crowd swirled, and heated conversation sprang up all around as the chamber cleared. I stood there, unable to move, as though my feet had grown roots like a tree and bound me to the ground.

Lance stepped out of my grasp. "Clever," he said.

Owen inhaled deeply, and his voice came out as a low growl. "As long as you don't take advantage of the situation."

"I'm sure he won't," I said. "And thank you for going along with it. I hope it won't mean too much trouble for you."

Lance smiled for a brief second only. "You? Trouble? Never."

We stood in our small triangle, silent for a moment.

Lance cleared his throat. "Don't worry about keeping up appearances of any kind regarding your relationship with Owen. Being with a human does not discount my claim over you, if I allow it. Only your obedience to me is important to display, in public, of course."

He patted Owen on the shoulder then, and left to speak to Niamh.

Owen put his arms around me, and we stood in a still embrace until the room was quiet again. When we split apart, I saw only Bertha, Lin, Lance, and our Ebonguard escorts remained in the chamber.

Remortality

Bertha and Lin studied us with bright, interested eyes. I imagined Lin's was a scientific interest, but I wasn't sure about Bertha's.

"You know," Lin said, "beyond the rare blood type, we could find nothing remarkable about you or your blood ... at first. We even sent agents to track and test others with Rh Null-type blood. We sent for blood samples from all those related to you by blood. There was not a thing we could find or replicate about your ability."

A painful fire lit inside me. "Did you ... are they alive?"

Lin waved off my concern. "Our Ebonguard are very good, unlikely to be overcome by a desire for sweet blood. Not that any of the other candidates were found to be so desirable. We knew you were unique, but we didn't know why. Then, something very interesting happened.

"The blood sample that was taken after your return from the Starved has some significant changes. It now contains somatic cells that behave and replicate like pluripotent cells. It's incredible. Not only might we be able to create a cure for vampirism, but your blood might also hold the key to creating artificial human blood. The moment we found that, we called for the vote. That was all we needed to see to know we had to keep you alive."

"My blood ... changed?" My voice cracked. Did it

change from the ceremony the Starved had held, their weird blood magic? Or something else afterwards? The lowest parts of my stomach churned. The Starved had wanted a cure for their thirst, a way that meant they didn't have to drink from humans, and they'd said my child would do that for them. But if Lin and her scientists could create an artificial blood, wouldn't that be fulfilling their prophecy, in a different way, without a child?

Lin was speaking again, but my thoughts blocked her out at first. I finally focused.

"… no special indicators, no passed-on traits. Owen is apparently purely human now."

Bertha tilted her head at that, blinking at us with her large eyes. "Owen saved you. You should know that."

I reached for his arm, clinging tight. "I do know that. If he hadn't brought help—"

"I don't mean bringing you back from the Starved," Bertha said. "Honestly, had we known where they were, we'd have sent for them sooner. They did kill a Synedrion member, after all. We just didn't know where they were. We've had no real reason to hunt them before. Despite their extremist fervor, their unwillingness to drink the blood of humans has generally been seen as unproblematic, no threat to other vampire activity. Owen did tell us where to find them, and that they possessed Kissare's chalice, but that's not how he saved you."

Bertha stood from her throne and walked down to us. Oddly, she seemed even smaller up close, fragile and sylph-like, forever caught in a gangly teenage growth spurt that made all her limbs seem too thin and long to support her modest height. "What I mean, is that Owen swayed my vote. When he came to plead for help, he told us how much he loved you. He begged to be turned again so he'd have the strength to fight for you. I wasn't sure before, when I first saw him. I thought maybe the change was only cosmetic. A surface thing, just a glamor of warmth and clockwork heart. But I saw then that the change was real, something deep and profound. You didn't just give him back his human form. You gave him back his humanity."

I looked from her intense gaze up to Owen, who stared back at her, his mouth parted but silent.

And it's his humanity that I love in return. But I didn't think a spoken declaration of love to Owen was a smart idea so soon after I'd announced I'd been claimed by Lance.

I looked for him again then, but he must have left the room.

"I still fear the very many things that may happen with you in the world. I fear our enemies using you. I fear that you will bear a child as the Starved saw visions of in the chalice, but I also fear that child and its powers may not be what they believed. The visions of the chalice are notoriously true yet open to mixed interpretation. I fear much, but what I fear most is war within our ranks."

Owen's hand came back to mine. "I can understand all those fears, and no matter what your reasons, I thank you for voting for us to live."

Bertha smiled. "How could I not? Your humanity was wonderful to see. That you could love in such a way, a way so many of us have forgotten even exists, made my decision easy. It also gave me hope. Reckless hope. And I have made the decision I will be one of the first to take the cure, when Lin and Shirina confirm it is safe."

I didn't know what to say. Owen bowed to her then, a sign of respect at her decision that seemed so right, I joined him.

Bertha smiled in a wistful sort of way, then turned from us. She met with Lin at the door, then both left without looking back.

Owen and I stood in the center of the huge chamber, alone except for the Ebonguard, who were to be permanent shadows in our lives. I could deal with that. It was a better outcome than I'd been imagining in my nightmares.

I looked at Owen, and swung my arms up around his neck, swaying as though slow dancing with him. "You saved me. You wanted to be a vampire to save me, but it was because you're not that we're alive. It was your being human that saved us both."

His eyes shone. His lips curved upward. "I think you're right."

I was, and he knew it.

"I want to go to the beach." Tears lay in my eyelashes. "As soon as we get back to the US, I want to go to Malibu and go to the beach. I want to swim and lie on the hot sand and … and forget. I want to forget all of this, Owen."

His hands reached around my waist, his fingers clasping at the small of my back. He rocked side to side with me, our cheeks together.

"Me too," he said. "There's so much I have to learn about being human again. I was scared I had only just begun and was about to meet my end." His forehead creased, eyebrows low over his pale blue eyes. "It's been so long since I felt really alive, Kaitlyn. I spent so much time just watching time pass. There was always so much of it, that it didn't seem to matter. Now I have … I don't know how much time I have, and somehow that makes it all so much more precious. I want to make each moment really count."

I let my tears of relief spill down, wetting both our cheeks. "I don't know how much time I have either, Owen. Death is the bill we get handed when we're born, and no human escapes having to pay

it, unless they become a vampire, I guess."

"I don't mind knowing I'm going to die. I'm happy knowing it, in fact. If I could live five hundred years without you or five minutes with you, I'd take those five minutes and squeeze every drop of living I could out of them and be content that it was enough. No, not enough, because I *could* live forever with you, but … but even five minutes is enough, in its own way. Does that make sense?"

I squeezed my eyes closed, but tears still poured freely. "It makes perfect sense."

It did. I felt exactly the same way. I had been willing to die, as long as I would die at his side, but I would equally be willing to live with him for all eternity.

I couldn't live without him.

He was my whole heart.

Time passed, but we stayed there in each other's arms, just being together and being alive. We had a future coming and we had no idea what it would bring, but we would explore it together until death took us.

23

OWEN

The lies I spoke stung my heart, and made my lips taste bitter.

They told me it was my humanity that had saved us, and it was my humanity Kaitlyn loved, but fear had crept into my soul. Fear, and a loathing of my weak, mortal form.

I hadn't saved Kaitlyn. Everyone else had. Joss, and Lance, and the Ebonguard, and the Synedrion, and Kaitlyn herself—they all saved Kaitlyn. I hadn't even been able get to her fast enough without being carried like a damn child.

I spoke of only desiring to spend every precious moment with her. I didn't know if I really believed that was enough. The idea of watching her die, whether now or of old age, filled me with a primal fear that ate painfully at my insides. We had a future again now. We'd been given a reprieve, but the future terrified me. I was terrified I would fail Kaitlyn again.

I was failing her right now with my thoughts.

I couldn't win.

Part of me thought Kaitlyn knew how much I was struggling. She showed me how to do ten-minute meditations to help calm myself when my thoughts spiraled.

I found them useful when the Starved were delivered their punishments.

We were expected to be present at the trial of the Starved leader. He was quickly judged as guilty of Delphine's death, and being as he was human again, he was to take Alam's dagger, a sentence reserved for only the most wicked.

There was little mention of him being a Scarl. Some thought we'd been mistaken, that he couldn't be, that any physical indications were a trick of our minds. Either way, there was no proof left to speculate on. He was only human now.

He was held right in the middle of the council chamber, between two Ebonguard, as the dagger, a curved thing of jagged, black metal and a fire opal hilt, was brought out of its ceremonial case, and plunged into his heart.

Kaitlyn gasped beside me as his body and his

clothing transmuted into stone before our eyes, starting at the point the blade struck his heart, and travelling outwards. He screamed until his lungs were hard rock and he breathed no more. His head and limbs drooped, his death faster than the change, and he became an odd and disfigured statue.

Kaitlyn buried her face in my chest. "All the statues out there, is this what they are?"

I nodded, stroking the back of her head, as though my hands could wipe the memories and trauma from her mind. "I think this is only the second time it's been used on a human. Vampires don't die from it until they are completely stone. Some believe they don't die at all. But there's no way to know."

"That's terrible," Kaitlyn whispered.

"Not as terrible as what is to come next."

It was before dawn that the rest of the captured Starved were taken to the Sun Shrine for their punishment.

It wasn't often vampires were bound to the sun. We ... *they* generally respected the law not to kill each other. I'd only ever experienced one receiving such punishment before, so I knew what to expect.

Seeing, and hearing, what happened to that vampire that one time, was enough to make me know I never wanted it to happen to me. That was back when Adelle was still with me, and I with her, and I had been looking for any possible way of being free of her. I think

she knew. She was the one to arrange being present at the sun binding ceremony. She wanted to make it clear I'd never be free. A vampire couldn't kill another vampire. Not without suffering a fate worse than death.

Even then, I was a man of resources, and I'd turned every one of them to finding a way to end her and the torment she'd caused me. I'd learned about the original seven, about their relics and the powers they were said to have. About a ring that would bring an untraceable death to those who received it.

The story I'd told Kaitlyn, and others, and myself, all those years wasn't the complete truth. Even if I began believing it myself. The ring didn't find its way to its victims on its own.

It was hidden now, in the safest place. It wasn't the kind of thing one could carry around on their person. But if anyone ever found out what I'd done with that ring, or even the fact that I had it, that I knew where one of the seven most sacred items in vampire culture was, then I'd be out there in the Sun Shrine myself. I had no doubt they would turn me again just so I could suffer that death.

Kaitlyn and I didn't have to be spectators to the Starveds' punishment, and we didn't want to be. But the location of the Sun Shrine, right near the entrance to the Synedrion's estate cavern, sat in a way that amplified the screams from those being punished throughout the valley.

Remortality

The anguished howls of the Starved reached us, even within the closed rooms of the Synedrion estate. We tried to sleep through it, but their cries were as relentless as the pain they suffered. It would take days, or weeks, for them to succumb, for their bodies to finally give in and be unable to heal themselves. Until then, all of Umbravallis would be in a state of mourning. Even vampires didn't have the stomach for this.

But Kaitlyn and I would be leaving before then.

We awoke the next evening, grim and pale, as the haunting cries of the Starved ceased, the night bringing them a reprieve before their torture began anew.

I slid out of bed and took several long breaths. Kaitlyn was already up, drinking coffee at the window and looking out at the artificially lit cavern that surrounded the palace.

She said, "They want to draw some of my blood today, and afterward, we will be allowed to leave, with Lance's permission, of course."

We were well and truly on vampire time. Even Kaitlyn spoke as though the days were nights and nights were days. But the silence from the Starved was all I needed to know the sun did not shine. I kissed her forehead. "Are you ready to go home?"

"Any version of yes I said would be an understatement." Her brow wrinkled. "It feels like we've

been here forever, but it hasn't really been that long at all. Maybe two weeks? I don't know. Time went funny so long ago." She shrugged. "Would you like some coffee?"

"I would. I'll get it, and I'll get you a refill on that one. Just let me get dressed first."

When I came back into the living room, still buttoning up my shirt, Lance was there. In Kaitlyn's hands was a book. Something small and bound in old leather with gold patterning. Had Lance given it to her?

"Thank you," she said. "About time I got caught up on some more vampire history."

I frowned. I didn't like that she needed, or wanted, to know vampire history, or that Lance had given her a book about it when she'd asked me for one. I still didn't like that for all intents and purposes, he now owned her, and me. At least under the eyes of vampire law. I still worried he would take advantage of that. All I could do was hope he wouldn't. But if he did, I knew exactly what to do to him.

"A little going-away present. I wanted to give you something, since you've given me, given *us* so much," he said. He looked down at his feet, then to the window. "I've also come to escort you to the lab. It's on the way to the airport."

"Can't Doctor Bedside Manner take the blood?" Kaitlyn asked.

"Lin and Shirina would like to see you again, so they prefer you come into the lab on your way."

Kaitlyn huffed. We were already packed, just waiting for the official word we were free to leave.

"Let's get out of here already," she said. She hopped up, and I admired the spring in her step. "Oh, one more thing."

She dashed off to the bathroom, and returned with a few bottles of bath salts and toiletries. She quickly unzipped her suitcase and stuffed them inside. "What?" she said, in response to my laugh. "A girl's got to get some perks from all this."

When we reached the car waiting for us in the driveway, two Ebonguard were there as well, loading heavy black duffle bags into the back. I'd been told one of our shadows was Joss, although Ash had apparently been assigned to some other task, so I didn't know our new second bodyguard.

Lance carried our suitcases for us with ease and loaded them in too. I noted that he wasn't using thralls anymore. He really had changed.

It was a short drive to the lab. Part of a large complex slightly away from the main town, it was a black, block-like building with smooth, clinical walls, and high-tech security. Floodlights lit the area all around, making it hard to see the stars in the night sky above.

In the foyer, Lance spoke through the intercom,

and the door opened for us automatically. We walked down the long white hallway, past rooms where scientists worked away at high-end sampling and analysis apparatuses. Lin and Shirina headed this research institute, but science was an area I'd never held an interest in, and what they did here was beyond me.

We reached a lab where Shirina sat looking into a huge microscope. Lin came in through a back door. They both wore white coats, protective glasses and gloves, and smiled to Kaitlyn, waving her over. Kaitlyn settled into a chair and chatted with Lin and Shirina, as though they were everyday human pathologists drawing her blood.

Lance and I waited at the door. I looked over at him as he continued to watch Kaitlyn, and her blood, with an intense expression. His gray hair always made him seem older and wiser than I had ever been, although he didn't have many more years on me. But he had been wiser, for a time. I'd looked to him for guidance for centuries.

"Will you take the cure, when it is ready?" I asked.

Lance raised an eyebrow. "It certainly has some temptations. But I don't think I will. I still hold a fear of mortality that is greater than my desire to see the sun again. I can protect Kaitlyn better if I stay this way too."

I watched his expression closely. He spoke of fear,

but he didn't seem to experience it in the raw, primal way in which I now did. He didn't experience any emotions in the way I, or any other human, did. Yet, he seemed to feel them more than a vampire would. "You have changed, though, since you tasted her. You sound more like the vampire you once were. The vampire who was my mentor. Do you still have the feelings her blood brought to you? Or has it all faded?"

He frowned. "Mostly faded now. That sensation of empathy, real empathy, where I hurt to even see the pain I'd caused the two of you, it's all gone. But it acted as a reminder to me. Of what it was to be human, of why I'd chosen to follow a moral path even as a vampire."

"You'd forgotten, at one stage," I said.

"I did. Something happened, and, I guess the anger I felt for humankind made it hard to remember why I'd ever cared about them. Maybe that's the true curse of being a vampire—not having a sense of guilt or understanding of the frailty and preciousness of human life."

We both watched as Shirina finished taking her blood samples, and checked on Kaitlyn's other injuries, making sure they were clean and healing properly.

Lin held Kaitlyn's hand, then spoke something quietly into her ear. I couldn't hear it. I wondered if Lance did.

Lance stiffened slightly. He sighed and said, "I

never told you that I had a family."

I frowned, unsure exactly what he meant. Vampires couldn't procreate.

"Before I was a vampire," he clarified. "I'd had children, before I was turned. And those children had children. I had two beautiful great-granddaughters of my own blood, even when I knew you. In a way, that's what kept me on a moral path for so long, and what knocked me right off that path."

"I never knew," I admitted.

"I kept it secret. My secret joy. Until one night, a man whose life I had spared, who I'd drunk from and set free, as was our way, went on to attack my descendants. He did terrible things to them. And so I did terrible things to him. I took the revenge that they couldn't. But that revenge had a cost. What happened to him was blamed on them. Because of my actions, my great-granddaughters were burnt as witches. They burned under the midday sun, and I watched from the shadows, unable to go into the light to save them. After that, I could no longer find any reason to spare human lives."

I didn't know what to say. I'd known something had happened, something that had changed him within the space of a week from a logical and moral man to a violent animal. Something that had destroyed him and our friendship.

Kaitlyn arrived back with us, looking both pale

and flushed.

Lance nodded to her. "Until now," he said. "Thank you again, dear Kaitlyn, for making me the man I once was."

"I'd say no problem, but, well …" She gestured to everything around us, as though it summed up the trauma of the past two weeks.

"Maybe one day I'll be able to make it up to you." He reached for her hand and placed a kiss there.

I inhaled sharply, jealousy spiking unbidden. I tried to fight it away. He was my friend. *Our* friend. "Is everything fine? What did Lin have to say?"

"Huh?" Kaitlyn seemed distracted. "Yes, fine. Nothing. Let's get out of this place, okay?"

"Yes," I said. "Let's go home."

24

KAITLYN

We were driven to the airport, the same one we'd once arrived at by helicopter. It felt like so long ago. A small private jet awaited us there, the windows blacked out for the Ebonguard who were escorting us.

I stepped out of the car without a single backward glance at the dark valley of vampires. I was done with it, and I never wanted to see the place again, not even in my dreams, although I was sure it would haunt me.

My spirits were flying at full mast. Home. We were going home. Back to Los Angeles. Sunny and warm days, lemony yellow sunlight. Palm trees and ocean breezes, and wide boulevards with houses that were shiny new. Movie stars, and swimming pools, and life.

Owen said his goodbyes to Lance as I stared up at the spatter of stars in the sky high above, breathing my freedom in deep.

Lance leaned in to kiss my cheek goodbye. Owen turned and stalked away, up the steps of the small jet. As our perceived owner, he explained he didn't always have to be near us. He would say he'd sent us away without him on some errand. Claimed humans were often used by vampires for tasks in the human world. And he would come to visit us often, to maintain the illusion of his claim on us. The Synedrion didn't seem to really care, as long as the Ebonguard escort was always with us.

Lance gave me a small smile. "Look after yourself. I know you think you love him, but be wary of a relationship built around so much trauma. It makes it hard to see how little you really know each other."

I took a deep breath. I did love Owen, with all of my soul, but Lance's words echoed the exact same fears and worries I'd had myself, before I had so much more to fear. There was a lot I didn't know. But finding out was what would come next. Owen and me, living together, getting to know each other, loving each other, being alive together. Growing our relationship and our love. And I was looking forward to it.

"See you soon, Lance."

His black eyes glistened under silver eyebrows.

"Just look after yourself. Until we meet again."

I left without another word.

I met Owen at the top of the stairs, and we turned our back on the world of night behind us. The Ebonguard were somewhere on the plane, but they made themselves scarce, giving us our privacy.

I almost laughed in surprise when a human attendant, the same who'd flown with us to Owen's castle originally, came out with a smile. What were the odds? "Hello again, you two. This is my first time to this airport. Did you have a good getaway?"

Owen burst into laughter. I managed to stop giggling long enough to say, "I think we're making a perfect getaway now."

"We'll be off in a few moments," she said. Still smiling, she nodded and headed back behind the curtain.

Owen and I took our seats. Our luggage was there, and our phones were too. I grabbed at mine, the reality of life beyond the estate and the dungeon settling into me in a way it hadn't until then. That feeling of connectedness, of normality that came as I turned the phone on, couldn't be overestimated. My eyes swept across the screen to see hundreds of missed calls, emails, and text messages.

Many were from my agent, and I opened an email then gasped, my hand going out to clutch at Owen's sleeve.

"What is it?"

"My agent's been trying to reach me. I have a new part waiting for me when we get back. The one I really wanted." My eyes went wide, reading over the details. It was on another big-budget film, a supporting part, but a big one. A good one. The actress they had for the role had to bow out, and filming started very soon.

Owen wrapped an arm around me as the plane headed toward the sky. "I'm proud of you, Strawberry, and I love you."

"I love you too," I said. My voice was small and distracted.

The plane lifted higher, then smoothed out and we winged our way west, out of Europe and toward home.

My stomach rolled. I tried to breathe through the wave of anxiety that hit me. Back at the lab, Lin had confirmed my suspicions. There was a reason my blood had been different since returning from the Starved.

I wasn't becoming a vampire, as I'd worried at first. Shirina had confirmed that. Luckily, I hadn't lost enough of my own blood for the Starved blood that had made it into my system to take hold. It was something else, that had happened since then.

I didn't know what my future held. I didn't know if I could take the new movie role. I didn't know if I could continue to be an actress at all, or a normal human in any respect. The one life dream that had given me so much determination in the past now felt out of reach again in a way it never had before. After everything that had happened, and could happen, and would happen next, could I still follow those dreams?

Maybe I should, in spite of it all.

At least for as long as I could before my life changed forever.

The plane hummed and sang. I hit the screen fast and sent a brief message to accept the part before I changed my mind.

A wave of dizziness swamped me.

Owen watched me closely. He ran a finger down my clammy cheek. "Strawberry, are you all right?"

My eyes filled with tears.

My lips, numb and stiff, barely moved. "I'm pregnant."

Deathless

HeartsBlood

BOOK THREE

1

OWEN

I could only stare at Kaitlyn as the jet engines roared in my ears, merging with the sound of my racing heartbeat.

A million images flashed through my head. A million possibilities. A million feelings.

Kaitlyn's pregnant.

One horrible possibility hit me so hard it knocked the breath from my body. My mind spun back to the nightmare we just lived through—the Scarl trying to rape the woman I loved, *my Strawberry.*

I couldn't breathe through that thought, couldn't speak around it.

Kaitlyn whispered, "Owen, say something."

Her fingers reached for mine and I felt her trembling, shivering like a bird caught in a trap.

I gulped in thin air and muttered, "The Scarl. He … is it …?"

"No." She shot out that single, terse word. Her fingers clamped down tightly on mine. A red flush rushed up her neck and over her cheeks, and her eyes blazed. "He never … It's ours, Owen, from the night after we escaped. It's yours."

Mine. I was knocked speechless all over again. I'd never considered being a father.

Vampires didn't reproduce. Couldn't reproduce. Not counting siring, which is entirely different. It had never occurred to me that I'd have a *child.* Kaitlyn was always the one having to remind me about protection and contraception since I became human again. And that night after we escaped the Starved, so desperate for the comfort of each other's touch, we had both forgotten.

And now … there was a new life growing inside Kaitlyn. Life we'd created. I couldn't even grasp that monumental concept. Being human again was still so new to me, I hadn't yet spent time considering creating *more* humans. Whether it was something I wanted. Whether it was something I deserved to do.

I looked past Kaitlyn to the window behind her, blacked out for the non-humans on board. I glanced over my shoulder, seeing no one, but knowing we weren't really alone. The Ebonguard assigned to us were nearby, making themselves unseen and unobtrusive, but there, watching, listening. I scowled. Our invisible bodyguards were eavesdropping on our private conversation. But this was *happening. Now.*

Taking slow breaths, I tried to process the immensity of it. I tried to calm myself. But I couldn't shake the memory of Kaitlyn on that sacrificial altar. It slammed into my head like a steel mallet. What if she was wrong? If she was lying, or had blocked out the trauma? What if the child growing within her wasn't mine, or human at all, but the offspring of a dark ritual?

My heart rocked back and forth in my chest. I wanted to kill the monster who assaulted her. I wanted to fight, to scream. But the enemy was dead already, and right now, it was just Kaitlyn, staring at me with eyes full of vulnerability, fire, and hope, waiting for me to respond.

The longer I said nothing, the more I saw her eyes grow dull.

Say something. "This is ..." I didn't know what this was. My body was processing too many emotions to know up from down. A small ball of happiness and excitement had sparked deep within me, but its warmth was smothered beneath too many doubts. I wanted to tell her it was good, it was wonderful, but our lives were still too complicated for good or wonderful to exist in.

Everything shifted and stretched outward into a future I had never thought to want, and wasn't sure Kaitlyn wanted either. She'd said she wasn't ready for children. Her contraceptive implant the Scarl removed was meant to last for *years*. She'd just earned her big acting break. She'd finally gotten the career she'd always dreamed of. Was there any room in there for a baby?

Was there any room in her life now for me, after what had happened to us? Had it tainted our relationship too darkly? I swallowed back the anger that swelled within me. Anger I could barely contain. I was still relearning my own human life, these overwhelming emotions. How could *I* raise a brand-new human?

As if she'd been reading my mind, she said, "It's still really early, only days. Normally too soon to know for sure, but what with my weird situation, and all the tests ... Still, it's not too late for the pill."

How could birth-control pills work now? She was already pregnant. Not that I understood much about modern contraception. "Not too late? I'm sorry. I'm not following you."

Kaitlyn's throat worked, visibly swallowing. She pulled her hands free of mine and they went to her blouse, smoothing away imaginary wrinkles in the emerald green fabric. "I mean I can get an abortion pill."

"Abortion?" The word roared from my mouth before I even thought through what she'd said. My blood grew hot as my emotions firmed themselves in my mind. *I could be a father. I want to be a father. I want this child.* "No."

"I know it sounds harsh, but we have to think about this logically." Her face contorted, eyes shimmering with unshed tears. She drew a long breath. "Beyond normal human worries about being ready for this, we have that prophecy dogging us, vampires who may or may not be our enemies, and … I have a whole lot of mixed feelings. I don't know if I want to terminate this pregnancy. I just know I have to consider it. We both do."

I heard all her words but the one that buzzed the loudest in my brain was terminate. It was so final. "I will not consider that."

A hard, vertical slash appeared between her brows. "Because you were *so excited* about having a child a few moments ago. Either we want this, or we don't."

I gaped. Was she right? Did I only want this now because of the threat of it being taken away? Maybe we should be thinking about all our options. Maybe the fact I wasn't instantly excited by the idea meant I wasn't ready. But the news had shocked all logical thought from me, and my head still reeled from it, unable to lock down a solid thought or emotion, except one. "You can't do *that* to my child."

Her eyebrows tilted upward. "*Your* child? It's *my* body, and the *child* is barely a tiny cluster of cells right now." She shifted away from me in her chair, folding her arms. "I should have known you'd be this way! Ugh, you're so … I'm going up against the mindset of a person who's over four hundred years old. You vampires may have sorted out some of your sexist ways, but you're still way behind on dealing with who owns a woman's reproductive organs!"

This was going so far off the rails. I didn't understand what she wanted; I didn't understand the scope or consequences of our options. I was only starting to feel what I wanted.

I took a long, slow breath, and asked the question I should have from the start. "Do you want this?"

Kaitlyn's mouth froze in an open position, and then trembled. The light of hope, vulnerability, and something deeper and indistinguishable shone in her eyes again. The slightest turn of a smile formed on her lips as she began to speak.

Before she could, she was interrupted by the flight attendant approaching with a rattling food cart. A clean, crisp white cloth covered it nearly to the floor, and she stopped it just in front of my seat. "Let me arrange the table for you."

Her short blond hair was tidy and pinned back, but she still brushed it with her hand, almost nervously. I wondered how much of our conversation she'd managed to hear. I almost sent her away again. But an interruption was good to let my thoughts catch

up. Kaitlyn pursed her lips and gave a small shrug.

We hadn't ordered anything, so I assumed this was a parting gift arranged by Lance. The flight attendant deftly spread china plates and then silverware onto our small table. She reached to a lower shelf of her trolley and revealed a platter of fresh fruit, cheeses, delicate crisps of toasted bread, and thinly sliced, very rare beef. Then she brought up a slender bottle the same color as Kaitlyn's blouse. I shuffled about in the seat, uncomfortable in the silence, my gaze going back to Kaitlyn. I wanted the flight attendant to go away, but I also didn't want to keep fighting. The attendant being there was simply staving off the inevitable, but I took it because I needed a moment. I needed more than a moment.

The attendant set two small, ruby-red aperitif glasses on the table. The green bottle chinked softly against one glass and the sound, the sight of that bottle and those particular glasses, caught my attention. The flight attendant continued placing things on the table, and I was struck by the oddness that this same flight attendant from our previous flight was with us again.

A sense of something worrying grew inside me. Something *wrong*. But what? I knew there were puzzle pieces right in front of me, but I couldn't put them together. My gaze went from the bottle, to the glasses, to the silver tongs sitting in a small bowl filled with

delicate little cubes of sugar. But I was still bogged down by my argument with Kaitlyn. Still trying to absorb the concept that Kaitlyn was pregnant. I couldn't seem to grasp the current situation or what was wrong with it.

What am I missing?

In a soft and strained voice, Kaitlyn said, "None for me, thank you. Not a fan of absinthe."

Absinthe?

Was this Lance trying to be funny?

The wormwood in it burns vampires, and I might not be a vampire anymore, but I was still getting used to being human, and not particularly willing to drink things that may or may not be deadly to me.

The flight attendant poured one glass, straining the absinthe over a sugar cube. "And you, sir?" she asked, in a voice that should have sounded perfectly polite and correct but had a rim of tension running below it.

I was going to refuse but she'd already lifted the aperitif glass toward me. It glowed like a jewel, filled to the rim, and a waft of the herbal, anise scent reached my nose. Then her hand turned, just slightly. Not by much. A mere eighth of a rotation of her wrist. If I hadn't been staring at the glass so intently, I would never have noticed that slight spin. How intentional it looked.

The glass tilted. The liquid hovered in the air.

Everything felt like it had stuttered down into slow motion. The green drops fell, then landed with a splash on the back of my hand.

I caught my breath, held it for a moment, but only felt the coolness of the alcohol evaporating off my skin.

The flight attendant seemed to hold her breath too.

Kaitlyn grabbed one of the folded linen napkins from the table and dabbed at my hand, and where a few drops of absinthe tinted the white shirt at my wrist. She seemed concerned only by staining, oblivious to anything else.

The flight attendant acted flustered, but eyed me carefully. "I'm so sorry. Are you all right, sir?"

I bolted up out of my seat, snatching for the flight attendant's collar. She shifted quickly, keeping her high-buttoned shirt and neatly tied neck-scarf out of my reach. Her eyes narrowed.

Kaitlyn gasped. "Owen! It was just a spill!"

I yelled out into the cabin, "Ebonguard!"

Two vampires in all black appeared as though from thin air. Kaitlyn squeaked in surprise. Even though I knew what to expect, I was still shocked at how well their compulsion powers had hidden them from our human eyes.

"Grab her," I commanded the Ebonguard. I knew one was Joss. The other was Val. At the moment they were impossible to distinguish.

One of them lunged for the attendant. She tried to dodge, but wasn't fast enough, managing only to bash up against the trolley as she was caught.

"What's going on?" Kaitlyn got to her feet.

The Ebonguard held the attendant tight around the shoulders as I reached over and yanked her neck-scarf off and pulled open the top of her shirt.

Right below her collarbone was a green-black mark of a knife surrounded by a ring of fire. A tattoo I knew too well.

My suspicions were confirmed. She was one of Alam's Blades. The absinthe spill had been a test.

Kaitlyn stammered, "Who ... what ... Owen!"

"Vampire hunter."

"*What*?" Kaitlyn seemed more insulted than any-thing. "But we're not vampires!" she yelled at the Blade.

But the attendant must have known I was a vampire once. How long had she been tracking me? And she'd followed me to Umbravallis, discovered I was now human ... That was all dangerous information for the followers of Alam to have. She couldn't be allowed to escape.

The Ebonguard must have realized this as well. The one holding her shifted quickly as though to snap the woman's neck.

With her cover blown, the flight attendant didn't hold back. Blades were still human, but she moved with almost inhuman speed and flexibility. She slipped through the Ebonguard's neck-crushing fingers. Something clicked inside her sleeve, shooting a slim canister into her hand. She twisted it and a cloud of mist burst into the cabin.

I couldn't avoid getting a mouthful of the gas, and quickly identified the unique, rotting scent. Nemexia.

I shot the Ebonguard a fearful look. If the corpse-flower knocked them out, Kaitlyn and I would have no chance of stopping the Blade.

The Ebonguard swayed, unsteady. They each grasped at their fabric head-coverings, and pulled an additional layer of fine, filtering material across their already covered faces. They stumbled but stayed upright.

The Blade scowled, her pretty face twisted with ruthless anger. She reached beneath the covered food trolley. When her hands came back into view, they held a chunky black weapon the size of a sawn-off shotgun. It hummed to life like a camera flash recharging.

My arms swept out for Kaitlyn, trying to get her behind my body, to somewhere safe.

Both Ebonguard rushed the Blade, but they were slowed by the Nemexia, moving at a more human speed.

The Blade took aim. A streak of brilliant blue laser-sharp light shot from the end of the gun.

One Ebonguard jumped to the side. The other took the full brunt of the burst.

The Ebonguard loosed a high-pitched, female scream. The blast burned straight through her clothing, scorching away the fabric across her shoulder, taking most of the shoulder with it. Flakes of grayed skin peeled away.

Waves of false sunlight radiated through the cabin. The Ebonguard's scorched flesh smoldered then caught, flames and light exploding through the vampire's body.

Then she was gone, leaving only ashes drifting through the air.

"Joss!" Kaitlyn screamed.

"I'm here," the remaining Ebonguard called back.

Kaitlyn clutched me tight, and I felt the same relief. And the same fear as the gun hummed again. Joss was good—for now—but the other Ebonguard had been no match for that sunlight weapon. *What the hell is that thing?* It had been a long time since I'd encountered a Blade. Their tech had clearly advanced.

Joss was moving faster again, still not at her normal speed, but enough to get herself behind the woman. She planted a high kick into her back and sent her flying a few feet across the space. The Blade crashed into the wall. She was on her feet again in seconds.

Deathless

My arms remained around Kaitlyn, desperate to protect her. What would Alarn's Blades do if they found out about Umbravallis? About a vampire becoming human again? About the unborn child at the center of a vampire prophecy? I had to help Joss stop this woman from escaping.

I shoved Kaitlyn down behind a seat. "Stay here," I panted, then I ran, hands up and balled into fists.

My knuckles crashed into the Blade's jaw just as she was preparing to fire another blast from her weapon. The beam missed Joss by a hairsbreadth and shot a hole straight through the cockpit door.

The plane shifted, tilted. Then went into a violent spin.

I grabbed onto a seat and was pressed into it by centrifugal force. I couldn't get to Kaitlyn, who was clinging to a seat as well. She screamed. Her body twisted and spun, her hair flying up from her head.

Through the hole into the cockpit, I made out the pilots spraying fire extinguishers onto their control panel.

The plane banked again, and we went tumbling around like toys thrown carelessly from a child's hand. I lost track of the Blade, and Joss, as tablecloths and fruit smashed into the wall beside me. The plane whipped us right to left. Gray filled my vision. Ashes in the air. *Val.* I tasted her ashes in my mouth, breathed them into my nose and throat, unable to do a damn thing about it. My head struck the edge of an overhead locker.

I couldn't see Kaitlyn anymore. I screamed her name just as the plane finally, mercifully, leveled out then flew straight and true for a few precious seconds.

Joss and Kaitlyn re-appeared from behind a pair of seats, Kaitlyn with a cut cheek, blood dripping off her jaw. She gave Joss a nod of appreciation, then Joss scanned the cabin.

The Blade was down the other end, strapping something to her back. A parachute? She leveled her weapon again, but it wasn't aimed at any of us. She pointed it straight at the wall of the cabin.

No, we'll all die!

I ran toward the vampire hunter.

I'm too slow.

The gun went off. The blowback lifted me off my feet. I crashed into the opposite wall. An enormous hole had opened in the side of the plane and the Blade went out of it.

Wind tore through the cabin, sucking everything toward the hole and the sure death that lay beyond. Kaitlyn screamed. Her hands were wrapped around a seat, but the explosive decompression had snapped it off its base. Her and the seat flew out the gaping hole.

"Kaitlyn!" My scream was lost in the whip of the wind and the sound of the plane tearing itself apart.

The last thing I saw of her was one of her hands wrapped desperately around the side of the hole, then even those fingers were gone.

She can't be ... can't be gone.

The suction from the initial burst eased, but I ran toward the hole, as though I was flying out of it as well.

I was snatched back by Joss. "Stop. The pilots are regaining control of the plane. They can make a safe landing."

"Kaitlin can't!" I snarled, fighting her grasp.

I lunged again for the hole. The sun was just setting and clouds swirled by, and Kaitlyn was *out there.* Falling. Every second took her closer to the ground. She had, what? Maybe sixty seconds of freefall before she needed to open a chute? A chute she didn't have. I had been counting the seconds since she disappeared. *Nine, ten ...*

Joss threw me back across the cabin. I moved to fight her again then blinked, noticing that she'd strapped her tactical backpack onto her chest and a parachute on her back.

"I only have one chute. I have to take out the Blade. She's my priority. She's a threat to Umbravallis. But ... I'll see what I can do for Kaitlyn." Without waiting for a reply, she launched herself out the hole as fast as a bullet.

That wasn't good enough. *Fourteen, fifteen ...*

Joss thought I'd stay in the cabin. She was dead wrong. The only thing I knew for sure was I had to get to Kaitlyn. The woman I loved was falling, and there was no way I wasn't going after her.

I moved to the edge of the hole. The rushing wind blurred my vision, but I could just make out the three falling bodies below me. The Blade, in flight attendant white and gray. Joss all in black. Kaitlyn, in green. *Kaitlyn.*

I had to get to her. Fast, and before it was too late. *Seventeen, eighteen.*

I jumped, aiming my body for the woman I loved with no other plan than to be with her.

If she died, I died.

2

KAITLYN

I'm outside the airplane. I'M OUTSIDE THE AIRPLANE. It was every bad dream I'd ever had. It was a nightmare come to life. I could hardly believe it was reality, despite the sparkle of sunset in my eyes and the air roaring past me and the cold whipping through my clothes. I was falling, and I couldn't stop.

Maybe I didn't want to stop.

Falling wasn't the lethal part. The landing—that was what would kill me.

I stopped screaming, only because I couldn't draw in enough breath. My heart seemed to have expanded to five times its normal size, pummeling my insides, pushing all the air from my lungs.

Breathe. Think. My ability to reason had taken just as large a leap as my body had. I tried to focus.

I tumbled toward Earth. *How fast am I falling? How long do I have until I hit the ground?* I had no idea how high the plane was before I got sucked out of it. The little part of my brain that was still alert, and trying to think of a plan, insisted that the plane had to have dropped quite a lot, because if it hadn't, I'd already be dead. If I'd fallen from our cruising altitude, I'd be dead, frozen, or suffocated, or something, right?

Yeah, okay. So the plane had dropped a lot. That just meant the ground was coming at me sooner rather than later. I wanted to brace for that. Or should I stay loose and flexible and roll with it, so I could absorb the impact? Hadn't that worked for someone, once? I couldn't remember what was real, what was a one-in-a-million chance I could cling to, and what was foolish hope. I just wanted to think of a plan to help me stay alive.

And to help that tiny spark of future life inside me stay alive too.

I wanted it. Despite everything, despite logic telling me to consider all options, I wanted to have this child.

I found enough breath to scream again, a scream born of sheer rage at the injustice of it all. My hands clawed at empty air in the hope of finding some kind of handhold, some kind of braking system I knew didn't exist.

I couldn't tell which way was up, and I spun

uncontrollably, my hair catching in my mouth and eyes. I had to level out, stretch out, catch the air like a gliding squirrel. I giggle-sobbed hysterically. *As if that will save me.* I didn't know how long I'd been out there, *outside the plane*, seconds that felt like forever.

I stretched out my arms and legs, star-like. I flipped again, wobbled, then steadied horizontally on my back, staring up at the darkening sky above me. *Better than looking down, I guess.*

Shadows, blurry against the dusky sky, hurtled down after me.

They zoomed closer, taking shape. Two lean figures, rocketing headfirst, streamlined and fast. One headed off to my right, all black. The other came straight for me. I saw a white shirt, dark hair. *Owen? Joss? No.* Sorrow swept into me, threatening to upend whatever was left of my mind. They must have been sucked out of the plane too.

Joss shifted angles suddenly, heading to Owen. She was bulkier than usual, and she caught Owen quickly. They flew together for bare seconds, while she strapped something to Owen. Hope burned unbearably in my chest, along with confusion and grief. They hadn't fallen. They'd jumped. That was a chute she just strapped to Owen. But if she'd had the chute, did that mean she'd needed one and now didn't have one?

Joss grabbed Owen, spun him around in an orbit of her body, building speed, then threw him straight at me. His body shot toward mine, faster than before. The air wobbled me and I almost flipped into a spin again. I had to stay level, so Owen could reach me in time to open the parachute and save us both. If we still had enough time. I didn't dare look down to see. I could barely stand the intense fire of hope and fear waging war inside me.

A beam of light zigzagged across the sky, and I turned my head. The flight attendant. No, the vampire hunter, Owen had called her. Right before everything went crazy. She had her weapon out, firing up at Joss who had changed direction to go after her.

Joss crashed into the hunter, sending them both into a spin, a hurricane of limbs and ripping fabric and beams of light.

The hunter's chute flew out, catching the air, and it seemed as though they froze in place while I dropped out from beneath them with frightening speed.

A body slammed into me, grabbed me tight, and we tumbled together. Ropes and red fabric zipped and whizzed free, and a sharp jerk jolted my neck painfully.

Our tumble stopped. The ripping wind stopped. The fall became gentle.

Owen's body was as familiar as my own. He had caught me, and he shouted at me to hold on. *No kidding.* I held onto him tighter than I knew I could, and he returned that embrace.

"I've got you," he said.

Deathless

The hunter's heavy gun swished through the air beside us, and I craned my neck to try to see Joss. They were above us, slightly to the right, still a brawling mess. The hunter's parachute was ripped, and Joss tore it completely free, off them both. She tried to reach for the ropes—too slow. It fluttered away above us all, like a blood-stained kite. Joss kicked the clawing hunter off her. The hunter screamed. Joss and the hunter fell fast, one after the other, too far away for Owen and me to do anything to help. The hunter's cry curdled in my chest. She'd caused all this, she'd tried to kill us all, but I knew the very same fear just moments ago that she was feeling now. And nobody, nothing, could save her. Tears stung my windburned eyes.

And Joss ... could she survive this? I had no idea.

The ground was so close. Dusk hid most of the earth, but I could make out the tops of trees that would either break our fall or break every one of our bones. Or be hundreds of potential wooden stakes for a vampire traveling at terminal velocity. This wasn't going to be a smooth landing, even with a chute. Horror stretched its arms up and enfolded me in its cold embrace.

The hunter hit the tree line first. Her screaming stopped. She disappeared without even a thump.

Joss hit next. She smashed through the forest like a meteor, thundering and cracking trees in her path. *Joss … don't die.*

Then it was our turn.

"Hold on, just hold on!" Owen yelled.

I wanted to laugh at him being Captain Obvious again but holding on was all I could do as leaves brushed our feet.

Branches snagged and grabbed at our clothes. We pinballed from trunk to trunk. The ground rose fast, and we crashed down. We skidded out of each other's embrace. A rock slammed my hip and dirt flew up into my nose and mouth. I tumbled to a grazing stop. Owen fell beside me, and the shredded red silk of the parachute collapsed over us.

I waited a full ten seconds, counting, breathing, too scared to see if my body was in one piece, if I had really survived. Owen turned his eyes to mine; blue, alert, and swimming with relief.

Tears ran down my cheeks, salty and warm. I wiped them with my hands and saw that some of the warm wetness was blood, and could have been from my torn palms or my stinging face.

Warily, testing our bodies, we pushed away the remains of the parachute and got to our feet. We were battered, torn, but we could stand.

We were alive.

Owen dragged me immediately into his embrace. I pressed my mouth to his.

My high-pitched laughter of relief escaped between

our lips, and I looked up at Owen. "You saved me. You are, completely sincerely, my fucking superhero."

He was also out of his mind. But I kept that to myself. He'd jumped from the plane, after me, and he hadn't even had a parachute until Joss gave him hers. He jumped—and he did it to save me. And it could have all easily ended far worse than it did. My knees went weak, and I staggered closer into his body.

We held each other for a long moment, and I enjoyed each precious breath.

I whispered the worry on my mind. "Do you think Joss made it?"

"I did."

I jumped right out of Owen's arms and my own skin. "Damn it, ninja-woman!" I clutched my chest and turned around to see Joss. She stood behind us, leaning heavily against the thick trunk of a pine tree. Her backpack was resting at her feet.

She was wrecked. The loose silk layer of her ninja-like Ebonguard uniform had been torn almost completely off her, but there was another layer underneath, something high-tech and skin-tight, like a bullet-proof thermal. The metal armor that normally protected her neck and top of her chest was gone— who knew how or where or when. Her cowl was lost as well. Luckily the sun had completely dropped, so barely any light remained under the canopy of evergreens around us. Joss's party-pink hair glowed against her dark skin and dead-serious expression. Her face was a mess of cuts and scratches that didn't bleed, her hair tangled full of pine needles. One cheek had a black singe mark straight from jaw to hairline.

In her left shoulder, terrifyingly close to where her heart might be, a branch the size of a police baton was impaled right through her.

I pushed my wobbling legs over to stand beside her. Owen followed me.

My eyes filled again with tears.

Joss noticed. "The Nemexia is still slowing me down, slowing my healing, but I'll be fine." She looked down at the branch. "Could do with some help getting this out though."

The blood drained from my face and I probably turned green. But I nodded.

Joss turned around to face a tree, gripping it with her arms. Owen and I grabbed onto the stick protruding from her back.

"On three," Joss said.

"Oh god," I said.

"One, two ..."

Joss pressed her shoulder forward into the tree trunk, pushing the stick through from the front as Owen and I pulled. The stick slowly, stickily, slid free.

I squealed the entire time. Joss didn't make a sound.

We dropped the stick on the ground.

"Are you, do you need—?"

"Have you seen the Blade?" Joss went straight to digging through her pack. She pulled a black scarf out and wrapped it around her head and face, leaving only her eyes visible.

"Blade?" I asked.

"The vampire hunter," Owen explained. "They are called Alam's Blades."

"They are *theys*?" Not just one vampire hunter, but a group of them? It might have been good to know there were vampire hunters out in the world, if *they* considered Owen and me included in their list of enemies.

Owen told Joss, "We saw her hit the trees, not even sure which direction anymore. Haven't seen her since."

"You yanked off her chute. She has to be dead. Right?" I said.

"Here." Joss pulled some bundles from her bag and threw them near our feet. "I have to go confirm the kill, clear up her remains. I can't let her, or anything she may have recorded, make it back. Not with the information she could have."

"Y-you're leaving us?"

She zipped up the rest of her kit, put it on, and strode away, disappearing quickly into the growing gloom without another word.

3

KAITLYN

I stared around at the woods, fright sending long shivers through my body. The temperature had plummeted and we were out in the middle of the mountains of Who-Knew-Whereania.

Owen knelt down, going over the bundles Joss had left behind. He picked up and clicked on a torch. The light should have made me feel better, but it only made us seem smaller, a tiny glow in an endless black forest.

"It's okay," Owen comforted me. "Joss has us covered. Look. There's a tent."

"How nice. Is there a hotel room in there? Maybe an espresso machine? Some chocolate or a bag of chips?"

He straightened and shone the torch at me.

I held my hands up. "Don't you dare judge me

right now. We almost died. AGAIN. I want a bed, a soft one, and all the comfort food in the world. You know I'm a nervous eater."

Owen chuckled. "I know. I'm sorry, but I don't think a hotel is in the kit. Or an espresso machine. There is …" He picked up a silver-wrapped package and squinted at it, "some sort of dehydrated stew."

I grouched out, "Yum. What is Joss even doing with that stuff? She can't eat it."

"She's looking after humans. She's got to have human-care supplies, I suppose."

"Sure. Obviously she was prepared for the event of a crazy flight attendant vampire hunter blowing a hole in our plane and stranding us in the middle of the wilderness." I was so upset that I actually kicked a rock. And because everything wasn't screwed up enough already, I also happened to be wearing darling little open toe sandals. "Ow."

"Did that make you feel better?"

"Yes." I pouted. My petulant voice cracked and tears started flowing again.

Owen gathered all the bundles of gear into his arms and stood up. "Kaitlyn, we can survive this. We can survive anything when we're together. I need you now."

My breakdown halted in its tracks. I was still shaking all over from the massive dose of adrenaline and the temperature that was dropping as fast as I just had. I managed to find a breath and take it. He needed me. I needed him. We were out here in the woods, and we needed to survive, together.

"Okay. Okay, I'm good. What do we do now?"

"Find some water, and somewhere to set up this tent and build a fire. It's getting cold fast, and there's not much else to do in the dark until Joss or someone else comes for us."

I limped over to where he stood and gathered up the smaller supplies as he pointed the torch for me.

Owen tilted his head, quiet for a moment. "I think I hear running water. Might be a stream that way."

I followed his lead, and it only took a few minutes of careful stumbling through the forest to reach an open, grassy area leading down to a slow-running, rocky creek. Owen shone the light around, and it looked almost pretty. Lush green grass with flowerheads, closed for the night, bobbing softly above. The stream giggled and burbled as the water made its way around the weather-smooth stones. I would have loved to have picnicked there in different circumstances.

The trees stood back from the stream, giving us a window to a sky of brilliantly bright stars, and allowing the half-moon to cast its glow on our campsite.

Owen stomped an area of grass flat, and we put all our supplies down and took stock. A compact emergency tent. A thin, plasticky, two-person survival sleeping bag. A small first-aid kit. An empty canteen and water-purification tablets. The bag of dehydrated stew, a metal bowl, and a spork. It was already chillingly cold, so we gathered small branches from the edges of the clearing. Owen stacked them on a large flat outcrop of rock, in the shape of a neat nest, with a bundle of fine dry fiber in the middle. Just one strike of the waterproof matches from the kit and we had a nice little campfire going.

"Ooh." I stared at the warm licks of flame. "Girl like man who make fire."

Owen chuckled. "Some of my old skills from being a soldier way back when are still with me."

By the firelight, we washed our hands and faces in the stream, and applied some basic first-aid to our cuts and grazes. We filled the empty metal flask with water, put a purifying tablet in and gave it a good shake, then left it to sit to do its thing. We were lucky everything was labelled and had instructions. Owen had the tent—a low dome barely wide enough for two—popped up in just moments. All we had to do to make the stew was pour water into an opening in the bag, reseal it, and lay it near the fire to warm up. We sat there, waiting for our dinner, watching the flames leap high and golden.

Owen poured some of the stew, which smelled and looked just as appetizing as dehydrated and then rehydrated stew sounds, into the bowl. He gave it a

stir, then lifted a sporkful to my mouth.

It tasted almost like real food, except for that weird aftertaste that all highly processed and packaged-for-long-shelf-life foods have. The pieces of meat, small and few, had a spongy consistency.

I managed to swallow it. "Too bad that cheese from the plane didn't fall out with me."

Owen's pale blue eyes twinkled as he spooned a bit of the slimy concoction into his mouth. "Surely you could have pocketed some while you were being sucked out of the aircraft."

I smiled back at him and we shared the stew, mouthful by mouthful, snuggling close together. Between the fire, the hot food, and Owen's body, I finally warmed up enough to stop shaking.

Hoots and growls and cracking noises came from the woods, and I scooted even closer to Owen. His living heat seeped into my skin, reassuring me. An unwanted image of him as an ice-cold vampire came to me, and I shivered. *He is my real, human, living Owen,* I told myself. *He'll never be that monster again.*

He cleared his throat softly. "I'm sorry I reacted so badly before, about the pregnancy. I just … I never imagined I'd be a father. It took me by surprise, and I couldn't sort through my feelings fast enough."

"I'm sorry I sprung it on you like that. I guess I was hoping you'd know what to do and say, because I'm honestly terrified."

Owen squeezed me softly. "It can't be worse than what we've already faced, right?"

The flames leapt and danced, painting shadows on his handsome face, and my heart hurt so much I looked down to make sure I hadn't gotten a tree branch to the chest like Joss. Tears started up, and I couldn't stop them. "That's just the thing. We've faced so much. Too much. We've been kidnapped, tortured, fed on, enthralled, chained up, and starved nearly to death in that horrifying cavern. Dragged into dark rituals and creepy prophecies, had our fates decided by an inhuman court. Oh, and then we were attacked by a vampire hunter and sucked out of a plane. We've seen so many horrors, and I feel like we're far from guaranteed we won't be tormented with even more. I don't know how to deal with all of this. I don't. And adding a baby to the mix?" My voice faltered and my hands shook.

Owen tossed a piece of wood onto the fire. The flames made a roaring, sucking sound. His voice was rough with emotion. "I thought I'd lost you when you were sucked out of the plane."

"Yup. Well, if I wasn't suffering PTSD from everything already, tonight probably tipped me over the edge there. I am for sure seeing a shrink when we get home."

Owen started to talk, but I wasn't done. A rant had come upon me and I had to let it out. "As if it

wasn't enough to be worried about vampires wanting my super-tasty blood, or to treat me as a science experiment or prophecy mommy, now I have to worry about vampire hunters too? I mean, you're not even a vampire anymore. I was never a vampire! We're, at the most, vampire adjacent. Like, in the same neighborhood but we don't invite them over for barbeques."

His chest moved. A rumble of laughter came from his mouth.

I elbowed him. "It's not funny."

His hands wrapped around mine, warming my fingers. "I know. You have to trust me, Kaitlyn. I will always protect you."

I wanted to believe him. And I did believe he'd always try—he'd jumped out of a damn plane to save me. But he couldn't promise he'd always succeed. I reached over and gently touched his chest. I felt so protective of him. I wanted to always save him too, but how could I? I felt so weak, so powerless, so useless against what was out there.

I didn't know how I could keep myself and Owen safe from everything threatening us. How could I protect a defenseless child? Even now, so early along, I felt a desperate, fiery yearning to keep that tiny life safe. *I will keep us all safe. Somehow.*

As though on the same mental page, Owen said, "I'll protect both of you." And he put his hand on my tummy.

My breath caught, and my eyes stung with tears. The forest seemed to hold its breath for a moment as well, silent around us.

I blurted out, "I know we've just been through a lot and emotions are high and we should, really, think about this all properly while it's still early. And it's still so, so early that things can easily go wrong naturally, but …"

"You want to have a child," Owen finished my thought for me.

"Mm-hmm."

"With me."

"Uh-huh."

"And be a family together for as long as our ever-after lasts?"

"Yeah."

Owen wrapped his arms around me, pulling me right up into his lap. "Me too."

Our arms went around each other, tears ran down our faces, and smiles spread on our lips. His two words had filled me with relief greater than I'd felt from landing alive after our fall. Love filled me even more.

A wave of pure desire rushed through me. A yearning, clinging, revelry of this love and life and *Owen*. My mouth met his. He returned my kiss with the same desperate passion and our tongues met too. For breathless moments, that was all I needed: the crush of our lips against each other, consuming each other, warming us more than our fire ever could. And then I needed more.

Owen lifted me from his lap, across onto the grass. I lay back into it, the feather-soft blades brushing up around my neck, crinkling under the thin silk of my shirt. My vision was haloed by a fringe of green as Owen bent over me, his mouth pressing against my neck.

Once upon a time that would have filled me with horror. But he was my Owen now. His touch sent shockwaves of longing through my system, crashing down all my doubts and fears.

His hands caressed my body, and mine relieved him of his shirt then moved down to his pants. Owen carefully removed my clothes, and the grass prickled softly under my bare skin, teasing and tickling. I pushed his pants all the way down and he kicked them off.

Our bodies met again, moving slowly together. His hands tangled into my hair, and he lifted my mouth to his in a kiss so deep that I couldn't breathe through it.

Our love was as slow-burning and intense as the stars that shone down upon us. Primal and deep as the woods around us. Hot and wild as the fire beside us. His every move sent me closer and closer to an edge I wanted to topple over. But I clung on, fiercely, to him and our pleasure and every beautiful moment we had, until ecstasy exploded through me. It felt like sparks flew from my body and my head filled with blinding light.

We curled up around each other. The fire roared beside us, touching our naked bodies with its heat, and we lay together in the glow of it and our love. For the moment, all I felt was grateful that we were alive, that we were together.

We drifted away to sleep in that little bubble of happiness. Just the two of us, and the baby who hadn't yet come to be. And I knew, beyond anything else, that I needed to find a way to protect us all. From any threat to our lives and our happiness. Nothing was more important.

I will do whatever it takes to make sure Owen and our baby are safe.

The rest of it, my career and the films I might have to say no to because of the pregnancy—that didn't matter as much anymore.

Our very lives felt so tenuous and fragile in the face of unknown horrors. How could I keep pursuing my dream of acting when our lives were still at risk?

There would be time for that dream to be dreamed.

After these nightmares were defeated for good.

4

OWEN

Light penetrated the thin walls of our tent, awakening me. We had shuffled in there during the night as the fire died down and we grew cold. The space-blanket sleeping bag crinkled as I propped myself up on my elbows, yawning.

Kaitlyn murmured something and rolled over. The plasticky cover was pulled taut over her body, outlining every curve. She was so beautiful it took my breath away. Long, wavy black hair, and a face like those carved into statues of angels and long fallen goddesses. The slim curve of her pale neck awoke a deep, dark hunger, stoking its way into life inside of me.

My bloodlust had been replaced by simple lust, human lust, but sometimes it felt too similar. I had to look away. Kaitlyn needed more rest, and I needed space to think. I slipped out of the sleeping bag and stood up out of the tent.

A pearly light spread across the sky and treetops. When I was a vampire I'd lived for this moment—that time right before dawn when it looked like morning had come but it hadn't truly. The sun had not yet broken the horizon, but still spread a sheer wash of light over the sky that could be seen by eyes that couldn't handle true sunlight.

It was a moment that had anchored me to my forgotten humanity. To brave that light and force myself to remember had felt like strength.

Now I was human, and it felt like nothing but weakness. Sunlight and a stake to the heart were real dangers back in my vampire days, but now *everything* was a danger.

My scraped knuckles from the fall ached again as if to prove that point. As a vampire these trivial cuts would have already healed. I wouldn't even have had to think about whether I might get an infection that could kill me. Those things were serious now.

My eyes stung, and my body ached. I was dehydrated, hungry, and exhausted from stress and a night of rough sleep. That was the human condition, these pains and needs. I felt frail and very aware that I aged more every day.

I hadn't chosen this. Kaitlyn's blood had changed

me before I knew what was happening. I wondered, sometimes, if I'd have chosen this outcome otherwise. Now it was upon me, and came hand in hand with the gift of Kaitlyn's love, I accepted it. I treasured it.

But with all we'd faced, and could still face, could I continue to value Kaitlyn's love above her very life? Above the life of our child she grew inside her? Because as a human, I was powerless.

It wouldn't be hard to take back my vampire form. I had friends in Umbravallis who would take this mortality from me and return me to their kind. I remembered the pain of the change, of dying and being reborn in undeath. I would do it all to keep Kaitlyn safe.

But if I turned again, could I keep her safe from me? That blood of hers was intoxicating. Once I turned, I couldn't guarantee I would be able to control my thirst. I couldn't say I would treat her as more than just food, that I wouldn't enslave her again, for her own safety and the preservation of my delicious food source. Would keeping her alive be worth that?

I asked myself those questions like I'd already made up my mind to be bitten again. That was the only way I could be strong enough to save her, but it might also be the thing that got Kaitlyn killed. The only thing I knew for sure was it would mean sacrificing our love. I knew Kaitlyn only loved the

human me, and I would be killing him.

My thoughts had fragmented into warring camps when I saw a familiar figure coming into the clearing. It was Joss, moving at top speed, trying to outrun the dawn. The sky grew pink and the tops of the trees wore a slim haze of gold, chasing her.

Without even a greeting, Joss went past me and flicked the tent flap open.

Kaitlyn groaned. "Turn out the lights."

I chuckled. Joss didn't. Turning out the lights was exactly what she needed. She ducked inside the tent, dumped her pack, and began digging through it.

Kaitlyn sat up. Her face had a crease on the right cheek and her eyes held a sleepy look but they cleared quickly. "Joss!"

Joss nodded and yanked on a coat and hood made of shimmery, thin material, specially treated to repel sunlight.

"Cutting it close?" I said.

Joss flicked a shady look at me. "Had lots to do. Decisions to be made." She pulled out protective goggles and put them on, then stepped back out of the small tent. Every part of her skin was now covered, but I felt anxious for her anyway. A vampire out in broad daylight was like a human stepping out into the vacuum of space—one chink in the protective suit could have dire consequences.

Some device in her pack made a static sound and

beep. She checked it, then threw a protein bar to each of us. "Time to move. Refill your water; it's a long hike to the pick-up spot. You can eat on the hoof."

"Pick-up spot?" Kaitlyn sounded hopeful, yet guarded. She scooted deeper under the sleeping bag cover. "Sure, just give me a moment to *get dressed.*"

Kaitlyn leveled a look at me and I peered down at my own body. *And I'm standing here naked.* I retreated into the tent, and Kaitlyn and I dressed quickly. Joss covered the remains of our fire with dirt, then cleared up every sign of our campsite while we refilled and purified another canteen of water. Kaitlyn put her dainty sandals on with a pointed sigh. I gave her my socks to wear with them, but it was nowhere close to the hiking boots she'd need. I could tell my patent leather shoes were going to give me blisters in no time.

Joss adjusted her suit and the sun goggles. They darkened as the sun got higher in the sky, black like a welding mask. I knew they rendered her almost blind, but you could barely tell. Ebonguard were trained for conditions like this, trained to rely on their other senses so they were almost as effective without their vision as they were with it. She took the lead, moving us at a brisk pace.

We went into the thick reach of the trees. The sunlight fell in dapples, coin-shaped bits of light that moved and wavered and broke apart into patterns that looked like a glowing path. Kaitlyn moved straight through that spill of light, seemingly without even a moment's thought, because she had never had to think about it.

She caught up to Joss, and asked in a small voice, "What happened to the flight attendant?"

"The Blade's dead. I confirmed it. But we need to get clear of here because there's no telling how much intel got sent or who might be coming."

The sun weapon—that was some serious technology, and it was worrying what else the hunter might have had. I shook my head angrily. "She could have live-streamed the whole thing to anywhere in the world." *Shit.* I thought back to what info she may have gotten. "She deliberately checked to see if I was a vampire. She poured that absinthe on me on purpose to see if it would burn me. Either she suspected I was a vampire and was looking for proof, or she knew I had been a vampire, and was trying to work out if I was really human again ..."

That was the more worrying option. If that test was caught on video and sent out, if Blades knew I had changed, I was going to become their target. They'd want me to study me, and through studying and interrogating me they would find Kaitlyn. I was the weakest link. As an untrained human, I wasn't any match for the Blades. My hands clenched into fists, as though to spite my weaknesses. What else could I do? I already knew I would be getting Tiamat's ring back in my possession the first chance I got. That would be something. But I doubted it would be enough.

"Maybe you'll be lucky. She might not have even known you were a vampire in the past, and this was a simple hunt, confirm, and kill job, no recording necessary," Joss mused. She looked like some futuristic alien, and even under her protective covering she seemed itchy from the sun and pained by it. Every movement she made was tense. "But if they heard, somehow, that you were cured and they know now that you are, you have a massive problem."

Kaitlyn's lips had grown thin. "What are you saying?"

Joss hesitated. "I'm sorry. I have no clue whether the Blade got intel out of the plane. Her pack was ... gone. I searched for hours in all directions, but there's not a trace of it to check what tech she had, to check delivery of data. Without being able to confirm nothing was sent, we have to assume the worst. We have to assume you and Owen are targets of the Blades. Which means you will be returned to Umbravallis."

Kaitlyn inhaled loudly through her nose. "You have got to be fucking kidding me."

Joss didn't reply. I knew Joss wasn't kidding. It made perfect, horrible sense.

"How many of these Blades are out there? Are they really such a big issue?" Kaitlyn huffed.

"The Blades of Alam have hunted vampires for almost as long as there have been vampires. Alam was one of the original seven. After they turned, he found he didn't much care for the violence and thirst that overtook him and the other originals. He decided they made a mistake, that they had no right to even exist. He left and trained humans to hunt his kin." I glanced around, paranoid at the very thought of the hunters. "Tiamat, the first original to die was at the hands of his hunters. It has been war ever since, and the cult of hunters grew only stronger and more devout after Alam's death. Hunters live only to destroy vampires; even their children are trained from birth to hunt and kill."

Kaitlyn's hands went to her belly, and I regretted mentioning children. She had to be thinking of ours and the dangers the child would face. It was exactly what I was thinking too. I took her hand, trying to offer some comfort.

Kaitlyn said, "And having a cure for vampirism, that would be another way to destroy vampires, wouldn't it? If they could weaponize it, force it on as many vamps as they could. It's exactly what the Synedrion was worried about. They won't ever let us go now, will they?"

I wondered for a guilty moment if the Blades

having the cure would be so terrible. The end of vampires, the end of immortality and bloodlust, could be a good thing, but I had a lingering sense of loyalty to the culture I'd been part of for so long. And to be captured by the Blades would only be trading one warden for another.

"We'll work something out," I promised Kaitlyn.

She nodded sharply, determination tightening her features.

Joss stopped and pointed to a low peak ahead. "There. We need to head past those thinner trees to where the tracker can send out a strong signal."

My chest ached and burned, and Kaitlyn's face was flushed red by the time we reached our pick-up point. Joss sent out the signal and we stood there, waiting, wary at being out in the open. Kaitlyn gave me a helpless look and I smiled at her, hoping to reassure her. But judging from the stiff angle of her shoulders, I didn't think it worked.

It only took moments for the helicopter to arrive. Wind buffeted the dirt, and Ebonguard in full sun-protection rappelled down around us, then scooped us up into the aircraft as swiftly as children scooping up the knucklebones in a game of jacks. We were buckled in and on our way.

I leaned back, watching as the forest dissolved away below us. My heartbeat picked up, a sign of weakness I couldn't fight and hated myself for.

We were being rescued from the wilderness only to be delivered right back into captivity. Back to Umbravallis, a place we'd only just escaped. It was brutally unfair. I had to find a way for us to have a life, a real life, outside all of the darkness and blood and sorrow.

But I might have to become one with the darkness and blood and sorrow to do it.

5

KAITLYN

I had to wonder who was piloting the helicopter, as we flew through the midday sunshine back to the valley of shadows. A human thrall? An Ebonguard flying blind? I wasn't sure which of those ideas I preferred, or if maybe I would rather crash and burn than return to where they were taking us. Maybe they had roped an entirely normal, non-enthralled human pilot into the rescue mission. They'd had some time to arrange things between when the jet apparently made a successful emergency landing back in Umbravallis, and when they picked us up. Maybe it was one of the jet pilots. Could they pilot helicopters too? Would they fly again so soon after all that madness? Maybe the helicopter was autonomous, like the vampires' cars.

The news that the jet had returned safely was all the Ebonguard onboard felt like sharing with us. But it was something. If we were returning to that hellhole, at least I'd have some of my belongings with me, those that hadn't been sucked out of the cabin. I tried to be pragmatic about it all, but we were going to the last place I wanted to be.

The helicopter swooped down low and the sunlight vanished, blocked by the high mountains on either side. Landing at that small airport again, deep in the shadows of Umbravallis, triggered too many memories I'd been ready to leave behind. My lips and nose wrinkled with the effort to fight off nausea, panic, and deep, flaming anger.

The dust settled onto the tarmac, revealing Lance waiting beside a car, looking like he stepped out of an anime. His hair, with its sheer silver sheen that glinted even in the dimmest light, fluttered in the remaining updraft. His chest formed a perfect V-shape, and his legs and arms looked too long for his body. He was powerful despite seeming waiflike, and I knew to think otherwise was stupid and potentially fatal.

He'd been a friend to Owen when they were both vampires, and a friend to us briefly after he'd drunk from me, and my blood had given him a kick of empathy for a short time. But I worried that time was gone. Now, he was the vampire who, under vampire law, owned us. Just what would he do with his belongings when no empathy remained?

I knew that a long time ago, he'd made the choice to be a good man, or a good vampire. He'd even helped Owen make that same choice. But that was before something changed. Owen had told me it was when Lance's choice to spare a human went wrong, and his great-granddaughters were burned at the stake in broad daylight, and all he could do was watch from the shelter of a shadowy corner as they died.

I think, after something like that, his utter lack of give a damn was understandable.

We stepped out of the helicopter, flanked by Ebonguards. Joss remained close to us, and stood out amongst the rest in her makeshift and emergency uniform, rather than the official full sun protection the others wore. Down in the shadows of the vampires' home they'd removed their goggles, but still nothing but their eyes showed.

Lance gave us a cool nod and wry smile. None of us had been expecting to see each other again so soon, and his expression made it clear we'd just dumped unwanted trouble in his lap again.

"Just couldn't keep away, could you?" he asked.

"You know me," I replied. "Walking magnet for misfortune."

He inhaled deeply, and his fangs became visible. "In the brief time you were gone, I'd forgotten how delicious you are. Even knowing the cost to drink, the temptation is almost irresistible." His tone was flirty but his eyes sparkled darkly.

I bristled. My mind screamed that I wasn't food, that he had no right to my body. But my mouth stayed still, fearful.

Joss changed her path from beside me to in front of me, blocking Lance's view of me like a dare. *Just try and get through her.*

Past her shoulder, I could see him taking in her appearance. "Run-in with a Blade? Thought an Ebonguard would have come out of that less scathed than this cat-dragged-in look you have going on right now."

Joss didn't reply, but kept her pace right up until she was nose to nose with Lance. She matched his height and glared silently until Lance cleared his throat and squirmed out of her way.

"Right, then, let's get going." He opened the car door, mumbled something about not being hungry anyway, and let Joss in first. I followed right after, making no effort to hide the smirk on my face.

Owen and Lance got in too, and the driverless car set off down the road.

A sick feeling burbled in my stomach. I didn't know if it was due to pregnancy, terror, the rough night, or some combination of all three. I knew where the car was taking us. There was no other choice I could make with vamps all around us. A *no* could end in our deaths.

The heavy scent of leather filled the car, along with a heavy silence.

Shadows clung thickly to the face of the rocks and the sides of the cliffs that rose up either side of the valley. Little pinpricks of golden light shone from along the smaller side roads, houses and mansions filled with the dead and their slaves.

I closed my eyes to it all. I felt so useless I could barely breathe.

I've survived so much. I'll find a way. I silently chanted the words, but as the car pulled around in front of the palace of the Synedrion, I admitted I was just trying to keep my spirits up.

Wits and sheer luck had gotten me this far, but I couldn't keep relying on them. The only way to be sure to survive was to massively change the balance of power.

I needed to be the powerful one. Somehow.

We were marched without any hesitation or announcement straight into the Synedrion chambers. The leaders of this vampire society waited for us there, up on their thrones of bone-colored limestone. The rest of the assembly hall was empty. No spectators today. Small mercies.

I eyed the seven. Milton, all golden glow and false smile that did nothing to give him the appearance of being friendly or warm. Toren, wrinkled and wizardly.

Bertha, pixie-like and professional in her boyishly slim teenage body. Shirina, clothed in jeweled colors with ebony hair falling and pooling around her ankles. Viatrix, doing her part statue, part ghost impression. Lin, pant-suited, mousy, and practical.

Then the new guy, Dante de Silva. From the moment he threatened us when we first arrived last time, everything about him screamed danger for Owen and me. He was twitchy with barely concealed rage, the kind of rage I'd seen in men who were used to getting their way.

He'd replaced Delphine, who'd died so recently I could still too vividly picture the way her head had parted from her neck. He seemed to me an odd choice for a political ruler, although even in the human world elected leaders frequently confused me. But his installment and position as one of the Synedrion felt like a personal threat directed at Owen and me.

It wasn't just him with the mad face. It was very clear that none of them were happy with us. I was pretty damned unhappy too. I was the one who'd gotten sucked out of a plane, after all. They had lost one of their Ebonguard, but they were there to protect us. Vampires fighting vampire hunters seemed like the natural order that I, a human, had no part in. But here I was, being dragged to the principals' office to take the blame.

Lin spoke first, "Kaitlyn, Owen, I'm afraid we are

going to have to ask you to be our guests for a little while longer.”

“Guests my ass,” I grunted.

Owen, Lance, and Joss, all by my side, gave me the same look of warning.

“No. You know what? I am sick of you … you … people … vampires. Whatever! Say what you mean. Just say we’re your prisoners again.”

Dante grinned. “I’ll say it. You’re our prisoners. You should never have been allowed to leave, not given the new circumstances.” He directed the last remark straight at Lin and Shirina. “We should all have been informed of the pregnancy right away.”

Oh no.

I’d assumed if Lin and Shirina knew about the pregnancy, then all of the Synedrion did. That we’d been free to go anyway. I should have known better. The respect I found then for Lin and Shirina was overcome by fear of what the others would do with this new knowledge. I dragged in an audible breath, and my hand slid over my stomach reflexively. The way Dante’s grin twisted at the sight made me realize it was a mistake to let him know I cared.

Shirina, calm and composed, said, “I’m of the firm opinion that a human woman’s body and what happens in it are her own business. I stand by our decision not to share the information.”

“Maybe normally, but the prophecy can’t be ignored.

This isn't just some human statistic. It could have real, dire implications to our society." Trust Milton to have Dante's back.

Lin took over their defense. "Visions from the chalice are notoriously open to interpretation, and it's clear the pregnancy alone made changes to Kaitlyn's blood that have brought an interpretation of its outcome to pass. It was only after she became pregnant that her blood showed the potential for developing synthetic blood, the solution to our hunger while maintaining our immortality—the promise of the prophecy." She waved a hand. "The offspring itself is unimportant."

Unimportant. The word punched like a bullet into my chest. So much for newfound respect.

"According to you," Dante spat, as elegantly as a child. "But it was not your decision alone to make. I still move that Lin and Shirina be struck from the Synedrion for keeping that information from us."

Bertha's eye-roll was epic. "And nobody has seconded your motion, Dante, so move along yourself and get over it. The pregnancy and prophecy are something we could have monitored from a distance, as I believe Lin and Shirina intended to do anyhow. But the involvement of Alam's Blades has changed things. The implications there are ones we cannot ignore."

Shirina sighed. "Agreed. We can't risk Owen, or especially Kaitlyn, being captured by the Blades. Which is why they are here."

Deathless

"We could stop their risk of capture by simply terminating them now, if you could all make the right decision," Dante announced.

My muscles went rigid.

"But the prophecy," Bertha mocked in exaggerated worry. "I thought it was important to see that through?"

Dante growled, "More important to see justice."

I watched them arguing for and against us, with little regard for us even being in the room. Even with those arguing for us, it was all semantics over our importance or an understanding of moral guidelines that had no empathy backing it up. All politics and power plays, and no care for our lives.

"I can't." My voice was small but firm. "I can't be prisoner here again. I won't."

"You won't have to," Lance interjected then, stepping forward. "These two are my property. If the Synedrion have decided they must remain in Umbravallis, so be it. But I will keep them, as is my right."

There was silence for a moment, but nods spread across most of the members of the Synedrion—those that moved anyway, Viatrix excluded. Dante and Milton also remained still, but it had clearly been decided.

"You may keep them in your stable," Toren agreed. "Under ongoing Ebonguard watch, of course."

"Stable?" I hissed. "Like animals?"

"He means human stable, with his other thralls and property," Lin clarified, as though that made it better.

I knew, boy did I know, that for most vamps, humans weren't even a step above domesticated livestock.

Dante slunk back in his chair and snarled. "This is ridiculous. Normal rights don't apply here."

Lance's voice was equally cold. "I have claimed them. They're my property now, and I won't take someone trying to steal my property from me with any degree of lightness. Unless you intend to alter claiming rights for all vampirekind, we are done here."

Lance placed one hand on my shoulder and one on Owen's, directing us away. "Let's go."

The council stood, but didn't object. They left their thrones, moving past us, disapproval radiating from each face. As Dante passed, he paused for a moment, smirked at Owen, and said in a voice so soft it was barely audible, "I hope your accommodations are pleasant, and that you will be happy to see some old friends during your stay here."

Owen frowned. I doubted he was in the mood to be catching up with old friends right now, and Dante's pleasant words dripped with malice. The idea of chumming around with vampires made my hairs stand on end. *Owen's not one of you anymore,* I wanted to argue, but Dante's taunt made me question whether maybe Owen wanted to be. Whether he missed his old powers, his old friends, his immortality.

Lance stepped around Dante, ushering us away through a different door. "We really do need to go."

Deathless

We left the palace, and once we were outside again in the crisp and cold air, I grabbed large breaths, trying to cleanse away the anger. I could see blue sky, far above, but no direct sunlight touched anywhere in sight except for the Sun Shrine, a place I didn't want to look. My feet dragged as we followed Lance, and it was only the feel of Owen's hand in mine that kept me steady. I was way past exhausted. I didn't even know if there was a word for how tired I felt. I was so worn out that even my hair hurt.

I'd been sucked out of a plane, had a hard landing, spent the night in a tent, then walked a very long way before being whisked off to this particular corner of hell—and I was starting to feel it. I knew Owen must be too but was scared to mention it because it would just remind him of his mortality.

A slight grin lifted my lips when I recalled the first time he'd caught a cold. He was the worst patient, so dramatic, so pathetic. Like he'd thought he was dying from a rare mutation of the black death every time he'd sneezed. He was wholly offended by the coughing as well, before I assured him it was all normal. Although that memory was cute, the fact that he could be so angry at himself and his body, all the while surrounded by vampires who could give him back his old strength and healing abilities, was not at all cute.

It was flat-out terrifying.

6

KAITLYN

The building Lance lived in would have fit in nicely at the Hamptons. It was a sprawling, three-story mansion, with ornamental gables and large but heavily tinted windows, at least on the first two floors. The third floor appeared to have normal glass, and we were high enough up the slopes of Umbravallis that the mid-afternoon sun just touched those highest windows. The grounds spread out around us, gently rolling hills of lawn which grew patchily from the low light levels and apparent lack of care.

We were met on the wide front porch by the jarring cry of a huge bird, flapping wildly against the insides of its cage.

"Why don't you just let it go?" I said, and for a

moment I didn't know if I was asking about the bird, or about us.

Lance glanced into the cage, at the fierce predatory eyes glaring back, and the curved beak pulling at the bars. The hawk screamed in frantic protest.

"He was found with a broken wing. It's healed now, but he will never again fly well enough to catch his own food. He knows this, and is aware that if we released him, he would die. But, like all things that could once fly and feed, he misses the feel of wind under his wings and blood in his mouth."

Cold fingers of dread stroked downward into my belly and touched along the base of my spine. My gaze went to Owen. His skin was pale, from exhaustion and stress no doubt, but for a heart-shattering second, he looked so much like the vampire he once was that I couldn't breathe, couldn't think. I grabbed for his hand to feel the warmth of his skin. Only his fingers were chilled from the cold air, and my paranoid dread turned to real fear.

"It just wants to be free," I muttered, as we passed the bird and went inside.

"You know they aren't about to let the two of you go anytime soon. So you might as well settle in." Lance led us through the grand entryway and down a hall, which passed rooms full of books and comfortable spaces, high-tech media and an indulgent indoor pool, and a surprising amount of dust. No kitchens or toilets were to be seen. And I was looking. For both.

Lance seemed to read into my eager peering. "The top floor is set up for humans."

Owen scoffed. "And how many humans do you keep, currently?"

"Just the one, and she's not so much kept, as, well, you'll see."

"Last I knew you had dozens, thralls for every mundane task, and more for food."

Lance's lips grew thin. He turned his back on us and led us toward a tucked away staircase near the corner of the first floor. "I did. After my brush with Kaitlyn's blood, I freed them all. One smack of empathy and now my lawn has gone wild and my house is all dusty."

"You're welcome." I grinned pleasantly.

"Lance? You want me?" a woman called from up ahead.

"I said *dusty*," Lance replied. "But yes. Draw the blinds."

A beep and a swishing sound followed. We rounded the landing on the third floor and stepped straight into an open-plan kitchen and living area, thick curtains blocking out all external light. A woman stood by the counter, remote in one hand, steaming mug in the other, her back to us.

"There you are. It's so late! Thought you'd be hungry."

"I am, but we have guests who must be fed first."

She turned around fast. Her eyes, wide and alert, locked onto us.

Her hair hung long around her, a shade of red so deep it tinted toward purple, neatly brushed, but tattered and uncut at its lengths. Her skin knew sunlight, still pale but not deathly so, with a slim dusting of freckles across her narrow, upturned nose. My eyes went right to her neck. To the hashed mess of scars and fresh bites there. It was the only thing I could see once I looked at them.

She's his strawberry. The words rolled through my head, and sickness quivered up my throat. I wanted to run away from the ravaged skin of her neck. But I also wanted to take her with me. Free her. Save her.

"Oh, hi." She looked caught off guard, and then I saw she was wearing only a T-shirt and panties. My heart galloped. I looked for shackles on her wrists or ankles. *Nothing.* I looked for enthrallment in her eyes. Or fear, desperation. *Nothing.*

"This is Dusky," Lance said. "Dusky, this is Kaitlyn and Owen, they'll be staying here for a while. And Joss, who'll be around as well, keeping an eye on things."

She smiled and waved bashfully while tugging her T-shirt down. "Nice to meet you guys. Uh, if you give me a sec to get dressed, I can cook up something."

"I'd like to cook," Owen said, his expression blank.

"If you don't mind."

"Sure, go ahead. I've already eaten, so just help yourselves. Lance keeps the place stocked with plenty of amazing goodies lately."

Of course he does. He needed Dusky to stay strong, producing fresh blood on demand, so he could feed, and feed, and feed from her. The fanciest of foods for his pet. The sickness came up again, but this time it wasn't in my belly—it was in my heart. But she seemed so … happy? Normal. Not a captive.

"Sort some food out for yourselves then," Lance said. He pointed beyond the simple but comfy lounge area designed to fit a party's worth of people, to a hallway with lots of doorways. "One of the bedrooms is Dusky's, but the rest are empty so take your pick. Bathrooms are at the end. I allow some sunlight in here when it's just humans, but with your Ebonguard on duty, best you keep everything closed up."

"I was getting used to it being just you and me." Dusky seemed put out, pouting and fluttering her eyelashes at Lance.

I eyed the remote in Dusky's hand, wondering if I could grab it, but neither I nor the automated curtains would be faster than an Ebonguard. And I didn't *really* want to do that to Joss.

Maybe Lance though, especially when he said, "Dusky, come with me."

She perked up and trotted after him, a happy

puppy. They went downstairs into Lance's rooms.

When they were gone, I asked through a clenched throat, "He's going to drink from her, isn't he?"

"I imagine so." Owen had begun ransacking the cabinets and the fridge, placing selected ingredients on the counter. "It's hard to see, isn't it?"

"You mean the poor girl being used as a giant slurpee?"

He smiled without a single hint of humor. "It is for me too, all things considered. But he has to feed or die."

My voice held all my bitterness. "Maybe they should all die."

I regretted it immediately, casting a quick "sorry" over to Joss. Despite knowing she was just doing her job, she'd grown on me.

Joss tilted her head. "Would you care if she were a side of beef?"

"She's not a side of beef!"

"No, but cows are living creatures and you eat them. And they aren't even consenting, like Dusky is. Humans eat living creatures, just as much or more than vampires do. And you have other options."

I squirmed, unsure of my own ethical boundaries in the face of monsters. "I keep meaning to go vegan. But bacon."

Joss's eyes squinted slightly. Was there a smile under there? "Some vampires revel in the taking of lives, but many vampires would prefer not to be dependent on humans. You and your blood might be the way."

"Does my blood, you know, smell special to you?" I asked. "I mean, are you ever tempted?"

Joss stared me straight in the eye. "Always."

I gulped, and went to the closest window, poking the curtain with just a finger to peek out the gap. Joss stationed herself by the exit doorway, standing as still as a member of the Queen's Guard. I saw her eyes on me, but she didn't react to my curiosity or the tiny beam of sunlight it let in.

We were almost the highest building on the hill, but up a bit higher, along a ceremonial path of shining stone, stood the Sun Shrine. The tortured screams of the Starved that had once echoed from there throughout the valley had stopped, but still echoed in my mind. "Why does he even have so many windows?"

"He doesn't like pasty people," Owen answered.

I blinked a few times. "What?"

He looked up from the pan he was heating on the eight-burner gas range. "He used to say he wanted to give his thralls some quality of life, even as he kept more and more thralls and fewer of his moral guidelines. I'm pretty sure the truth was he just doesn't like pasty-faced servants."

"He should have sent his thralls to get spray tans with Milton, then."

Owen chuckled, tears in his eyes as he chopped onion. "And he thinks people don't know it's fake."

He poured some fragrant olive oil into the pan, then in went the onion with a sizzle, and suddenly, I was starving. I took the first real, deep breath I had for a long time, inhaling the appetizing aroma.

Owen cooked like he was born to do it, and the idea of eating something he made, of sitting down with him to a meal he'd cooked, soothed me.

The kitchen area seemed new and very modern with stainless-steel appliances, dark granite island and countertops, deep farm sinks, and wrought-iron barrel stools pulled up to one bench.

I made my way to his side, where he trimmed bacon and sliced mushrooms. Beside his chopping board was a container of fresh cream, a bottle of white wine, stock, and a brown paper bag rolled down to reveal rustic, handmade pasta. My stomach grumbled in anticipation. "Need some help?"

"Could you find a saucepan and start heating some water?"

I grinned as I searched the cabinets. "You want me to see if there's any tinned tuna?"

His lips peeled off his teeth in an expression of sheer disgust. A flurry of laughter escaped mine, despite everything. That time he'd been sick, I'd tried to make him some comfort food. I'd mixed a tin of tuna into packet mac-n-cheese. It was a go-to back in my poor, struggling actress days. To say he didn't like it was a huge understatement.

"That shall never happen again. I wasn't sure if you were trying to help, or trying to kill me faster. That flu was awful." A vertical slash appeared between his eyebrows, worrying, wondering, then cleared.

"It was barely a sniffle." I elbowed him gently, trying to make light of it, but I worried too. Dante's words floated back to me, seeming like both an offer and a threat.

I found a good-sized saucepan, filled it with hot water, threw in a big pinch of salt, and put it on the stove, then rested my hip against the counter. "Are you looking forward to seeing your old friends? Like Dante said?"

Owen's smoothly stirring hand paused above the frying pan for a moment, then continued. "I'm sure he was just having a go at me. I have no friends here anymore, not since I became human again."

Except maybe Lance. And that Niamh lady who'd met and chaperoned us briefly last time. He could try to deny it but that was at least two friends, or acquaintances.

Maybe I was worried over nothing though. Maybe it was Dante trying to get into our heads.

I tipped the Orecchiette into the boiling water.

"He *did* say it in a creepy voice … I half expected to hear dramatic organ music playing."

"As he sweeps his cape up over his face, bursts into bats, then flies away over the full moon?" Owen's eyes twinkled.

"You're the one who ran the campy vampire role-playing nights at your club."

He pouted. "I'd thought I was being ironic."

The pasta water overflowed, fizzing on the stovetop. It startled me and I jumped away from it, gasping. Being here, cooking with Owen, felt so normal, so nice, I'd almost forgotten the height of my trauma levels. All it took was a bubbling pot to make me burst into tears.

Owen turned the heat down on both burners and gathered me into his arms. I nestled close and closed my eyes, trying to stop the tears.

"I'm scared," I croaked.

He whispered, "I know. But I'm right here, and no matter what, I'm going to protect you."

What I couldn't say was that I was also scared of the *no matter what*. "No. It's not all on you. I can't let it all be you. It's going to take both of us to save our lives."

I held my breath after I spoke. Owen's pride was as strong as his love for me. I knew how much he wanted—*needed*—to protect me. But he had to know I was right.

He said nothing for a long moment, but the barely perceptible shake of his head was all I needed to see to know he refused to let me share that weight.

That he intended to take it all on.

Owen looked deep into my eyes, brushing the hair away from my forehead. "You should go lie down. You're exhausted."

I pulled out of his embrace, frustrated he couldn't agree with me. "The hell if I'm not eating some of this food before I go and sleep."

"Well, I've eaten, so I'm off to bed," Lance announced from the top of the staircase. "Just came back to check everything was sorted before I go."

Eaten. Ugh. A shiver tickled my whole body, and fear for Dusky drove panic into my heart until a moment later, Dusky appeared behind Lance. Her neck was blushed red around fresh puncture marks, and her face wore a dazed, drawn look that I recognized as once being on my own face. It made too many memories hit my brain and heart. I had to distance myself, and fast, from the beginning of my time with Owen. From the time when he wasn't Owen, but Vampire. Out in the human world, I'd learned to set those memories aside, but here, with Dusky's bloody neck in my sight, they pressed in on me, stirring up old pain and resentment. Old trauma that could still break us apart.

"I thought you said you freed all your thralls," I muttered with dripping hatred.

Lance shrugged. "I did free all my thralls, but Dusky ... decided she wanted to hang around."

Dusky smiled in a drunken way at Lance as she slipped by him, her hand circling his waist briefly as she brushed past. He didn't even seem to notice.

Oh … oh no. My brain finally caught on. Dusky chose to be there. Like I had sought out Owen after he'd freed me. She really was like his Strawberry.

Only Lance didn't love her back. He hadn't become human. He *couldn't* love her back.

"It is super late, guys. See you at nightfall," Dusky mumbled. I didn't know the exact hour—sometime in the mid-afternoon. But she was living on vampire time. She staggered off to what I presumed was her bedroom, with one last puppy-eyed look at Lance before closing the door.

"It is late," Lance agreed. He looked at Joss. "How long have you been on duty without a break?"

"I'm fine." Joss cricked her neck, and stretched one shoulder. The side the branch had gone through.

"Do Ebonguard even take breaks?" I asked, genuinely curious since Joss had become an almost permanent fixture beside me.

"Not usually. But sometimes they do to recover from, say, a dose of Nemexia, branch through the chest, and march through broad daylight," Owen said pointedly while plating up our food.

Lance raised his eyebrows.

"And taking on a vampire hunter with a laser-cannon," I chimed in. "Not to mention that fall

without a parachute. Joss probably saved our lives a half-dozen times. You should have seen how badass she was."

Lance frowned for a moment, taking another look at Joss. "You must need a break. Or some sustenance. I can ask Dusky out again?"

I could have smacked him.

Joss still wore her makeshift mix of daylight coat over the torn-up, skin-tight underlayer of her uniform, and her scarf wrapped around head, but under it all her expression was clear. "I'm perfectly capable of performing my duty. Kaitlyn's safety is my mission. I don't need anything from you."

Lance held his hands up defensively. "Just wanted to be sure you're at your best. You're guarding my property, after all."

"And the get-the-fuck-out award this evening goes to …" I patted the counter in a tiny drumroll while I waited for Lance to take the point.

"All right. I will go then." Lance started leaving but paused to ask again, "You sure? If you want to take an hour or two rest downstairs, I can stay with them."

Joss ignored him, still and at attention. Lance left.

I took the plate Owen handed me and started shoveling food into my mouth. I was sure it was delicious, but I couldn't taste a single thing except for the salt that lay in the back of my throat.

Another Ebonguard came to relieve Joss. He didn't bother introducing himself, but I heard Joss call him Heim. He was brusque, even compared to her. He seemed to speak down to her. I already didn't like him. Apparently, he was now in charge of our safety—mine, particularly. He brought with him thralled servants who delivered our remaining luggage from the plane. Joss left.

Owen's fingers brushed mine, and I looked up from a plate I didn't remember emptying. His face wore lines of fatigue and his hair was rumpled. "Bed?"

I slumped onto the counter, staring blankly at the litter of our dinner. I didn't want to sleep. I wanted to fight and prepare and plan.

But everything hurt, and I couldn't stop yawning. "Bed."

We picked a room at random. They were all equally bland, clean, and sparse, like budget hotel rooms. But the bed was an actual bed, rather than a foil-thin sleeping bag on the ground. Curling up together in any bed would have felt wonderful, and my whole body sighed.

Owen snuggled up against me. "You okay?"

I wanted to be strong and profess my okay-ness but for real, I was not okay. Really not okay. "Nope. You?"

"No."

I closed my eyes, my head swimming with sleep. "What are we going to do?"

"Try to escape."

"Of course," I replied. "Because it will be so easy."

Even if we lost our bodyguards and got clear of Umbravallis somehow, we would be hunted, and no place was safe or far enough away from these vampires. "We could use a backup plan."

Owen hummed, a thinking sound, and it tickled against my ear. "Try to cooperate, gain some leverage, and see if we can somehow lessen their influence on our lives?"

"Totally doable."

7

KAITLYN

I snapped from the blank nothingness of total exhaustion to alert panic some hours later. My body needed more rest, but my brain was in overdrive. Owen lay beside me, deep in sleep, and I envied how peaceful he looked. After futilely lying still for twenty minutes, I got up and peered out a curtain. Nighttime. The moon was sliced down the middle, half light, half dark, and insects chirped away in the long grass. I peeked out our bedroom door. The lights were all on, there were voices in the living area, and Heim stood on guard right beside my snooping face.

He followed me and my bundle of clothes and toiletries down the hall to the bathroom, but thankfully stayed outside. A shower, fresh clothes, and toothpaste returned some of my humanity. In my luggage, I also found the small history book Lance had given me before we left. Maybe I could learn some more about vampires from it. *Leverage.* That was what I needed in this world of power plays. And that started with knowledge. I pocketed it and went out to the stable's common area, Heim remaining a few paces behind all the way.

I heard the clash of steel on steel, and my heart skipped a few beats. My first thought was that we were under attack again, like the night with the Starved. Maybe it would be the Overfed this time. I saw Lance circling an Ebonguard on the largest rug of the room, sword drawn. It was Joss. I knew her by her eyes now. She'd returned, uniform clean and intact.

"What'd you do to piss her off this time?" I asked Lance.

Lance gave me a swash-bucklingly handsome smile. "I wanted to see just how good an Ebonguard was, up close. Joss agreed to show me some of her tricks."

I took a seat on the gray modular lounge next to Dusky to watch. The curtains were all drawn open, showing the starry night through the large windows, the perfect backdrop for the show.

Joss's movements were formal and lightning-fast. She struck at Lance, lethal blows she pulled back on at the very last moment. He tried to dodge or block her with an antique sword he'd probably pulled

from a wall downstairs. He only saved his own life one in every four strikes with the sound of ringing metal. He seemed more thrilled than frustrated at his defeats. His silver hair swished around his growing smile.

Dusky sighed deeply. "I swear he's so hot I just want to die. Don't you think so?"

"Yeah, I s'pose." She'd been fed from, and recently. I looked away, trying not to see the raw and red wounds on her flesh. I did think she wanted to die. The evidence to back up that belief was carved into her flesh.

"It must be so amazing to be one of them."

"A vampire?"

"You never wanted Owen to make you into one? Before you changed him?" There was a level of distaste to those last words.

Shudders ran all along my skin. Of course, immortality was alluring, but the price, in my mind, was always too high. Sure, some vampires could pass as human casually, and maybe calling them all evil was taking it too far. But I'd seen evil right up close. I'd heard it speak through lips stitched shut and looked into its dried and dead eyes.

"No. I never wanted that."

Dusky gushed, "I want to be one *so bad*, but Lance won't make me into one no matter how much I beg, and neither will any of the others, because they don't want to piss him off."

"I wonder if they have some kind of quota. Like they are only allowed to turn a certain number of humans to vampires each. Like a single-child policy. Otherwise, you'd think they'd quickly turn the whole world to vamps and end up with nothing left to eat." It wasn't necessarily comforting to Dusky, but I couldn't help thinking out loud.

Dusky shook her head. Her tone broke my heart. "He just doesn't like me. I know it. But it's because I'm human. If he'd just turn me, if I could just be like him, I could be his equal, and then maybe he could look at me the right way."

I wanted to reassure her, but I didn't know what I could say and sound sincere. I watched Lance and Joss go at it, and uneasiness sparked into my being. There was tension between the two of them, and it wasn't homicidal—it was all sexual. I looked over at Dusky. Her lips were pursed and her eyes narrowed. Her voice was high and thin. "I don't know why he wants to spend so much time with her. I swear she's just like … I mean, she's just …"

Joss was strong, confident, loyal, and smart. All of that added up to her being sexy as hell, even when you could only see her eyes. Eyes Lance couldn't look away from.

They were locked in a tense embrace. Despite holding weapons, it looked more like foreplay than

warfare. I bet it looked the very same way to Dusky, and I bet it hurt.

I sympathized. I fell in love with Owen, even though he fed from me. I told myself I grew to love the human who slowly emerged, all the while hating the vampire who fed from me and kept me prisoner, but could I truly completely separate those two entities?

Even when I loved him, I still wanted to flee, because I knew I wasn't safe. Dusky had to know that at some point Lance could drink too much and kill her. Whether by accident or design, it wouldn't matter. The result would be the same.

"If you're free to leave, you should go. This isn't the place for humans," I said.

"I kno-ow," she sang. "That's why I've got to become a vampire to be with him."

If you become a vampire, he won't need you anymore. I wanted to say it, make her realize the truth, and run far away. But it felt too cruel.

She seemed to read my silence and expression as equally cruel. "I'll find a way." Her eyes narrowed, and she huffed off.

Lance paused, watching Dusky go. He said something to Joss, and they broke apart. He came over to me, skin matte and fresh, not a broken sweat or labored breath to indicate he'd just been fighting.

"I need to do something with her." He grimaced, like Dusky was an unwanted pet he'd dumped out

in the woods that kept bringing itself home.

"You could try not drinking her blood," I snapped.

He shrugged. "She offers."

"Of course she does! She's a vampire groupie in general, and a Lance groupie in particular. You must know she's in love with you, and she thinks you care for her because you keep feeding from her." There it was again, a truth uncomfortably close to my past slapping me in the face at every turn. "She's going to keep sticking around because you keep feeding from her and giving her the hope that one day, you're going to turn her and declare your undead undying love."

"I have to feed from someone. Why shouldn't it be someone free and willing?"

"Because infatuation can be just as much of a prison as enthrallment. It'd be hard to re-integrate into society after what you've put her through. If you cared at all about her, you would stop taking her blood and give her some walking papers. Maybe a nice memory wipe while you're at it. Set her up in some sweet little apartment and give her compensation income until she gets it together."

Lance stared at me blankly for a long moment. "I've forgotten how to care. Centuries of letting myself make no effort in moral regards have made it hard to make correct decisions anymore. Maybe you're right. But maybe you aren't. Humans have so many feelings about everything, and you could just be projecting your own feelings onto her. Dusky seems happy enough."

"For now," I muttered. I didn't even know why I cared. If Dusky wanted to fangirl the vamps, maybe that was her business. But it hurt to watch her give her blood so willingly. It made me sick, because it brought home what I might have become had my blood not changed Owen.

I walked away from Lance and the lounge and went over to Joss. She had continued to run through a series of martial arts stances on her own.

She paused when I stood in front of her.

"Can you train me to fight?"

A single strand of pink hair edged into the open eye area of Joss's head covering, shaken loose. She squinted at me. "You're pregnant."

"So you expect me to spend the next nine months lying in bed?"

Joss shrugged. "It's been a long time since I was around a pregnant human.

"Well, it's not like that these days. I still have a fully functioning body right now."

That squint again.

Lance announced from across the room, "I have to head down to the Synedrion estate. Been summoned for an update on the humans, no doubt. I'll be back shortly."

Joss and I both replied with a grunt.

I waited for Lance to walk out, leaving Joss and I alone, except for Heim stationed like a robot by the exit door.

"Come on," I pleaded. "I did some stunt training for my acting—fight choreography—so I already know the basics."

Joss laughed. She actually laughed out loud, in my face.

I was caught so off guard I asked, "Are you okay?" Between the laughter and her moving freely around the room, sparring with Lance and generally showing freewill, I'd become concerned.

"I'm off-duty. This is my recuperation break, not my train-the-civvies time."

"If you're off-duty, why are you here?"

Joss glanced across at Heim, then back to me. She shrugged. "I was returning to duty here in the morning anyway—"

"As second," Heim felt the need to interject.

Joss didn't continue her thought, just stared at Heim.

He stared back. "I am in charge of the female human's protection now. And there are plenty of Ebonguard stationed around the property. You aren't required here."

"But you are appreciated," I said. I liked Joss, as much as I could like a vampire. I would have much preferred she remain my bodyguard than the new guy.

With a sniff, Joss turned back to me. "You want to train to fight?"

"Sure do." I lifted my fists, ready to go.

Joss still wasn't sold. "Why?"

Why? I had so many reasons they rushed my mouth like a crowd stampeding a doorway, all getting stuck in there, none getting free. My hands patted my belly, trying to soothe the quivering. Just nerves, but part of my brain felt like the anxious flutter and lift in my gut was my child reacting to danger, asking for protection from it.

Joss answered for me. "You're afraid you'll be killed."

"Wouldn't you be if you were me?"

"No. I … *we* are here to guard you."

"And what happens when your orders change? If you are the one ordered to kill me?"

Her eyes held no expression. "Then you will die."

There it was. I couldn't expect Joss's loyalty to be given to me. She was loyal to her kind, her cause. She was here doing her duty, even off the clock, because she was proving herself to her superiors. I knew she'd already failed in the past, already hit two strikes on the Ebonguards' three-strike system. And I knew she'd follow any order to not be struck out.

But for now, she was ordered to protect me, and

I could use that. "Then while we're on the same side, I want you to train me, so I have some chance on my own."

"You know there's no way you could ever win against me in a real fight."

"You know if we ever got into a real fight, I'd do everything, anything, to survive."

"I do." Her head bowed in the slightest nod. "And I respect that. But you could change everything. Our entire world. For better or for worse. I don't intend to let you go. I'll help train you, but don't mistake that as my being weak."

"I'd never think you were weak. Not after what we've been through together." It felt like we were exchanging some strange wedding vows. "But I still want to be able to protect myself, and this baby. I have to. I can't let it grow up in a prison, captive, like this. We have to have our freedom."

Joss paused, sniffed, then tucked her errant strand of hair out of sight. "I can understand that." She moved back into one of her stances. "Okay. We'll start simple."

I copied her pose and managed a smile. "Simple's good."

But would it be good enough?

8

OWEN

I was a prisoner to my dream. Too tired to wake, too aware to ignore the horror. Fangs and blood, screams and pain. Suffering dealt out by my hands, my teeth, bloody gifts given to a woman by me. Not just any woman either.

Kaitlyn.

I sat up. My hands wiped my sweaty face as I tried to get my breathing under control. The very need to breathe, and how panic could overtake control of that and other functions, was so new to me.

Panic again set in when it hit me that she wasn't there. My eyes still blurred with sleep, and I patted at the sheets and mussed covers like I was going to find her huddled down within them, but all I felt was the cool mattress.

"Kaitlyn?"

No answer. The sheets tangled around my body as I swung my feet free of the bed and grabbed at the pants I'd left on the floor. Where was she? All I knew was she wasn't in here with me—she was out there. With Lance?

Jealousy zoomed into my being, and I couldn't shatter it any more than I could shake off the last terrible vestiges of that dream. Whatever Lance might feel for Kaitlyn, she didn't reciprocate that feeling. She loved me. Wanted nobody but me.

I still reeled with jealousy.

I pulled my pants up and buttoned them, then stopped to take a breath. Why? Why was I so upset when I knew how she felt about me?

Because he could protect her.

My heart raced, and my hands shook as I tried to work past the nightmare, to get it to loosen its hold, to let me think clearly.

I'd had that dream more than I'd like to admit—but it wasn't all dream. It was part memory. Part fear of *what if?* What if I had killed Kaitlyn when I held her captive, when I drank so greedily from her?

What if her blood had not turned me human and she still suffered?

What if I was no better as a human than I was as a vampire?

What if I became a vampire again?

Deathless

A sour taste grew in my mouth. I flung open the curtains. Still nighttime, but the barest hints of dawn had chased the stars away. I stepped out of our room and down the hallway.

The loungeroom was lit up, and Kaitlyn was there. Safe. Wearing pajamas and mirroring Joss's movements as they kickboxed their way across the rug. The sight of her calmed me, and I leaned on the wall, watching.

"You look like hell." Lance's voice turned me to him. He had just walked in, dressed in a full suit, making me feel awkward in my disheveled pants-only look.

"This place is hell, so I'm fitting in." I knew my words were rude. I couldn't bring myself to hold back.

"Hardly," Lance replied, whether to this place being hell or to me fitting in, I didn't know.

I regarded him carefully. We could use an ally, I just wasn't sold on the idea that our ally would be Lance. He'd told me Kaitlyn's blood had changed him, reminded him what it was to choose a moral path again. Him claiming us as his humans had saved us from being claimed by some other—probably worse—vampire. But any change from her blood was now gone. No true empathy remained. He was just as mired in the politics of this world as the rest of them, and if something didn't serve his agenda, it didn't matter. The real question was, what did he want from me? Or, really, what did he want from Kaitlyn? Drinking from her could turn him human. He didn't want that, but that didn't mean he didn't crave her blood. It was like a siren's call. I knew how hard it was to resist.

Kaitlyn glanced over then, noticing me. I saw her eyes look over my shirtless chest, and the small smile it brought her.

Lance elbowed me. "No need to worry about your style, we'll have you fitting in again soon. There's a masquerade ball next-night."

Kaitlyn joined us, patting at her sweaty forehead with the back of her hand. "A masquerade?"

I managed a taut smile. "Vampires do love their masquerades."

"You're to go, both of you." Lance drew two cards from his suit pocket. "Invitations direct from Dante de Silva."

"Gross," Kaitlyn said. "Another mandatory invitation, right?"

"Of course." Lance grinned.

"Of course," Kaitlyn echoed, deadpan.

"Kaitlyn has also been requested to see Lin and Shirina in the lab the morning after. So we will have an excuse to leave before the party gets too wild."

I took the invitations off Lance, frowning. I was more worried about our safety with Dante and his grudge against me than the threat of Alam's Blades.

Deathless

The careful calligraphy told me the party started tomorrow evening, and would no doubt go until the early hours. Getting used to vampire time was a pain, but even having just woken up, I was sure Kaitlyn and I could easily sleep through another day. I longed to be curled around her again. It was the only time I could pretend we were both safe, in a bubble together that nothing could burst.

I moved toward her and slid an arm around her waist. Her body was hot to touch, and her face flushed with a sheen of sweat. Concern swamped me. "Are you all right?"

"Might need another shower."

"I mean, is the exertion good for the baby?" I genuinely had no idea. I was sure the treatment of pregnancy had changed greatly since the last I'd cared to know anything about it. I was sure I remembered something about women needing to stay still so the baby wasn't shaken free of their bodies. I really needed to read some modern books.

She gave me a look. "I was being careful."

Of course she was. "I know. I just worry."

"I know." She popped up on her tiptoes and kissed me on the cheek.

Lance cleared his throat. "I'll have some outfits sent for you both. See you at nightfall."

"Good night," Kaitlyn said, not looking away from me. "Or good morning, whatever it is."

LENA FOX

My eyes didn't leave hers either as we made our way back to the room we'd claimed.

I knew she was out there training with Joss because she wanted to protect us, all of us. But no training in the world would save a human from a pack of pissed off vampires.

Alam's Blades were human. At least, most of them. But they had weapons like I'd never seen, and they knew what to do with them. Maybe I could align us with the hunters, but doing that would set us at serious odds with the vampires and might be the thing that got Kaitlyn and our child killed.

When we reached our room, a comfortable silence crept in. I pulled Kaitlyn tight to me, and the touch of her skin stirred up desire. I would always want her. Always. Her body was real and solid against mine. Warm and alive. Our lips met, and hers tasted like salt. Birds sung their morning chorus out on the windy hills around us. Through the open curtains, the sun hung cradled in the high mountains, gifting us with a single thin beam of light.

I didn't want to give this up. I didn't want to stand away from the sunlight, hidden in the shadows. I didn't want to reverse my life yet again and become a creature of darkness.

But this wasn't about what I wanted. It was about her. Everything was for her, and our baby.

KAITLYN

The masquerade was in full swing when we arrived at the Synedrion palace. Lance had ensured we arrived late—fashionably, but not enough to annoy our hosts.

The cave that housed the estate was lit up bright, floodlights making the stalactites translucent and milky, hanging above us like giant teeth. Revelers swarmed the grounds and palace entrance, and all eyes turned to us as we stepped out of our ride. More teeth were showing.

"A little help?" I said, halfway out the car door. I was stuck, my gown far too impractical for a car. I felt like I required an open-top horse-drawn carriage to float elegantly down from upon arrival. But horses shied away from vampires, so there was no carriage to be had.

Owen took my hand, trying to help me wiggle free without tearing the dress. The gown was impossibly pretty but built like a torture device. The corset was so tight I was going to spend the entire night hoping I didn't breathe so deeply my breasts popped out. The skirt was made from yards upon yards of rich red satin, twisted into rose shapes, and it was so heavy it had to be held out by a crinoline cage.

I could almost imagine the champagne cork sound effect as I popped free from the car. Owen caught me in his arms as the momentum toppled me forward.

"At least I can save you from costume malfunctions," Owen said wryly.

"You legit jumped out of a plane for me, so you're good in the hero books. But I wouldn't turn down trading outfits if you wanted to save me again." I eyed his puffy white shirt, brocade jacket, and skintight gray breeches. *Yeah, I could pull that off.*

"Red *is* my color," Owen mused. The smile reached his eyes, even behind his barn owl-themed mask.

"No outfit trading," Lance called from a few paces ahead. "We're already late." He could talk, in his far more modern suit in a subtle metallic silver. Dusky, standing a step behind his shoulder, also got away with a simple slimline evening gown in muted purple.

Joss and Heim, at our backs, still wore their usual black uniforms, but most of the other party-goers were wearing what seemed to be period costumes, ranging from Renaissance, to French Revolution, to Victorian. Like they were reliving their heydays.

I grumbled a sigh.

Owen shrugged and hooked my arm in his, leading us inside. "I never enjoyed wearing this stuff, even when it was modern and fashionable."

That thought made me cold. He *had been* alive when these clothes were in fashion. It was overwhelming, that he actually had memories of a time that seemed like fiction me. "At least your clothes are practical."

My heart hurt. I hated this. I hated being forced to go to a party with our captors. I hated being forced to relive a history I never knew and didn't really want to know either.

I hated that this all brought home just how wide the gulf between Owen and I really was.

We stepped into the main building, then through to the grand ballroom where the party was underway. Dancers were all over the floor, a confection of swirling fabric and glitter and masks. A chamber orchestra played something classical yet upbeat, but the musicians all wore blank, fixed expressions. Tables laden with the most decadent-looking cakes and tiered treat towers lined the edges of the space, untouched, while vampires fed on enthralled humans instead.

I wanted out, even though we'd just got there.

I reached a hand to my face, feeling the mask

of red feathers, velvet, and white pearls. Only my lips and chin were visible underneath it, and my eyes shadowed through small holes. The feathers splayed out wide and high over my hair piled on top of my head. That I was almost unrecognizable didn't matter. Every vampire there would be able to smell my blood.

And from the looks on their faces, they did.

I turned my back on the room and beelined for a food table. I wasn't hungry since we ate before we left, but the food table was always my go-to sanctuary at awkward social gatherings.

Owen crushed my hopes. "I wouldn't eat any of that. It's all decorative."

"No cake?" I poked a towering gateau and found under the heavy layer of gummy fondant it was nothing but polyfoam. "Kill me now."

"I could probably rustle you up a glass of water?" he offered.

"We should have BYOed. I could badly use a glass of wine. Just one. I'm sure it would be fine." Inner guilt shook its head at me. "Maybe half a glass. *Fine.* Water."

Owen began unlooping his arm from mine, and I clung onto him. "On second thought, just stay with me?"

He squeezed my hand, then let go. "You'll be fine. I'll be fine. I'll get you some water."

Deathless

As he stepped away, Joss split off and followed him too. Heim remained near me, always nearby. Even here I had to be protected. Maybe especially here.

The vampires knew I was out of bounds, but they watched me regardless, avidly. Given the chance, I was sure they'd take a bite of the forbidden fruit.

"Night's greetings to you all." Niamh swanned up to us, arms wide in a non-embrace as she leaned in to peck Lance on each cheek. She seemed ready to do the same to me, but thought better of it. "I heard you were back with us again, Miss French. Owen too?"

"Yeah. He's around." I looked up and down the great height of the blond beauty. One of Owen's *old friends*. I glanced around behind her, and also spotted Milton and Bertha, enjoying themselves among the dancers. Dante watched from the nearby corner. *No welcome from our inviter? What a shame.*

Lance and Niamh continued their small talk, and I turned away to find myself face to face with Dusky. Her eyes glittered through the holes carved into her satin mask. "Isn't this amazing?"

"The best." I admired her enthusiasm but couldn't control my sarcasm.

She missed my tone, apparently, because she beamed. "It's so magical! I've been to some masquerades before. I think. But not like this." Her gaze flicked over to a vampire feeding on a human nearby. "I don't

really remember. It's hard to remember everything from when I was enthralled. Either way, I couldn't really enjoy it like I can now. Thank you."

"Thank me?"

"Didn't you talk Lance into letting me come?"

Had I? If I had, he really didn't get the right message. Maybe he just invited her because he knew she'd be pissed if he took his new humans to the ball without her.

I shrugged, passing off my confusion as modesty. She bumped her shoulder against mine like a silent thank you, and my heart ached for her.

The music changed and a cheer rang out. The orchestra played like they were possessed, because they were. Sweat and exhaustion dripped from them, but they couldn't slow, couldn't stop. Resentment sizzled along my nervous system.

Dusky grabbed my arm and dragged me forward. "Let's dance. It will be fun!"

I wanted to say no, but in a way, this was Dusky's Cinderella night. Her time to be included. Her time to be seen and feel special after so much hardship. As the only other free-willed human woman there, I couldn't say no to her.

I managed a smile as Dusky hauled me out into the crowd of predators. Waves of perfume, cologne, and that ever-present coppery scent assaulted me. I checked back to see if my Ebonguard still had

eyes on me, comforted that he did. But the crowd swirled. Glittering jewels and sparkling fabrics spun and created a haze between us.

Dusky glowed with joy as she squeezed into her position in the women's row, and I giggled as I took a spot opposite her in the men's row. I laughed even harder when I realized I had no idea of any of the dance moves all the vampires followed, but it became clear that neither did Dusky, so we just did our best to copy along and ad lib when needed.

I was almost having fun, caught up in the rhythm of movement, until everybody shifted along, swirled about, and partners were swapped. The female vampire I came face to face with was caught as much by surprise as I was. I tried to step away and twirl myself back to Dusky, or off the dancefloor entirely.

I pinballed from one place to another. Laughter rose, and passing me from vampire to vampire seemed to become a game. Everywhere I looked there were diamonds and lace, pearls and taffeta. No escape. My heart pounded furiously as I swiveled right with the other dancers to face my next partner.

She wore a stunning gown of ice blue, cinched in tightly at the waist, her skin as pale as the gown. She seemed amused, probably because I was delivered to her instead of a male dancer.

"I was in the wrong line, sorry," I gasped, trying to back away.

Black eyes peered out from behind a mask covered in so many brilliant diamonds it was hard to look at. "I'm happy to lead, if you prefer."

Her smile was pleasant, and I sighed with relief as she switched places with me. One small humiliation dealt with. But as all the other men bowed to their partners, she caught me up in her hands, ignoring the choreography.

Her fingers, strong and so very cold, gripped mine, and she swept me deeper into the sea of dancers. My feet stumbled, and she caught me expertly. A bad feeling settled in. I felt like a mouse that almost got away. But *almost* never really counts.

I tried to keep pace, keep a smile on my face, and wait for the next partner change.

The music swelled, and we were moved by the bodies surrounding ours. The dance had become too fast, beyond human speed, and I couldn't keep up. I couldn't catch my breath. The gown, so heavy, and billowing out all around me, kept sending me off balance. The vampires all moved freely in their tight and heavy gowns. Weight and breath meant nothing to them. Their feet were fleeting, and their bodies moved in sharp and precise motions. Partners changed, but the icy woman didn't let me go.

I gave up the effort to smile, to be polite. I yanked hard, trying to get my hand out of her frozen grip. She pulled me close, chest to chest like we were lovers dancing. Her breath, smelling of tangy blood, washed over my face. She spoke, seductive and poisonous in my ear. "He lied to you."

"What? Who?"

Her smile was all fangs and blood-red lips. "Our precious Owen. He's lied to everyone about how I died."

I was lost. "How you became a vampire?"

She peered at me with fevered eyes. "He thought me gone forever. Destroyed. He was wrong. Now I can tell everyone how he killed me. With Tiamat's ring."

I shook my head, tried to shake my body free. "The cursed ring? It chooses its victims." And killed them. It killed Harvey. It killed …

"No!" I gasped.

"Oh, you do know me." Her laughter was a whisper of sheer malice. She ran her nose along my neck, inhaling my fear. "You do smell so delicious. It will be a delight to remove something so special from Owen's life. You tell him. Tell him I'm returned, and that I will destroy him, you, and all he holds dear."

Horror coiled inside me, and I unleashed a scream that shook the chandeliers above us. "JOSSSSS!"

It didn't matter that Heim was my protector now. Or that my heart was screaming for Owen. It was Joss my mouth cried out for. My hands clawed and punched at the woman but in the next moment I was freed, and she was swirling away in Dante's arms.

My scream had stopped the music, and the entire

crowd stared at me for the fraction of a second it took for half a dozen Ebonguard to circle around me.

I was scooped off my feet, taken off the dancefloor. The one carrying me asked, "What happened?" *Joss.*

My insides churned. My heart slammed into overdrive and my mouth went dry. "Something bad. Where's Owen?"

"I'll take you."

I had to talk to Owen before I talked to anyone else.

Because Owen's ex-girlfriend was back from the dead and out for revenge.

10

OWEN

I made my way back, a champagne flute of water in each hand, to find Lance chatting with Niamh, and Kaitlyn and Dusky gone. It had taken me some time to find the glasses, and I'd had to go all the way into the thralls' kitchens for drinking water. I'd hated leaving Kaitlyn for those long minutes, but I wanted to make a show that things were somehow *okay*. They really weren't, but the act of going to get my partner a drink at a party should have been okay. It was a small freedom I wanted for us.

I put the flutes down on a table and looked around for Kaitlyn. Heim remained at attention, watching the dancers, and Joss had my back, so I tried to calm the nerves that rose at finding Kaitlyn absent. If anything was wrong, they would be on it. Kaitlyn

was probably just—

Joss sprang into action, speeding off so fast she left only a black blur. Heim followed. My heart went with them because their action could only mean something was wrong with Kaitlyn.

I hadn't realized I was trying to run after the Ebonguard until the force of Lance's hands on my shoulders started to ache. He forced me into a corner of the room.

Then Ebonguard appeared all around us, a small army of black. One of them carried Kaitlyn in their arms, a mountain of rose-red fabric piled all around. She was placed back on her feet and stumbled straight into my arms. I felt her whole chest lift and sigh in relief.

Then she separated herself from me and shoved me with both hands. Her expression was wary, her skin as pale as death.

"What is happening?" I asked.

She glanced at the wall of Ebonguard surrounding us, Lance and Niamh and half the ballroom listening in. "Nothing. I'm fine. I just ... I was dancing and I panicked and can-we-go-some-where-private-like-right-now-okay?"

The words spilled from her shaking lips in a rapid tumble. I nodded, then led her through the nearest exit door. I knew the Ebonguard would be right behind us, but at least we'd be away from the gawking crowd.

The doors opened out into a small side chamber sitting room of dark wood, ancient books, and velvet lounges. A vampire was feeding on a human in the corner, but one look at us and our entourage had the two of them clearing out.

We went to the opposite corner, as far from the Ebonguard as they'd allow. Kaitlyn moved a tasseled floor lamp out of our way and placed it in front of us, as though we could have hidden behind it.

She yanked her mask off, and her eyes were wide and frightened. Her voice was a low hiss. "Adelle is alive. She's here. She danced with me, and she threatened to destroy you and everything you care about."

"Adelle? Adelle St Delaurents? That's who she said she was?"

"No, she didn't exactly introduce herself formally, but I know it was her." Kaitlyn's fingers grabbed at my sleeve, tearing away a slim strip of lace.

I took her hands, trying to calm her. "Adelle is dust. It must have been someone else. Someone trying to scare us."

"Oh." It was a long, drawn-out syllable of under-standing. "She was with Dante, left with Dante. Is that what he meant? Is this all him? No, this was definitely personal to her too. I could see it in her eyes."

I had no idea what she was talking about but could clearly see she was shaken. "Slow down. Tell me what happened."

Kaitlyn took a long breath. "I ended up dancing with this vampire. All icy blond bombshell. She seemed nice at first, but it got bad real fast."

"That certainly sounds like Adelle." But Adelle was undeniably dead. Her earlier words sank in. "Wait. What did you mean when you asked if this was what Dante meant?"

"Remember him being all ominous about meeting an old friend? Could this be him playing with us?"

"Maybe. That's why she went for you. If it was an imposter, I would have picked her straight away, but dropping a few clues with you would be enough to rattle us. What exactly did she say?"

Kaitlyn lowered her voice, so low I could barely hear her. "She said you killed her. With Tiamat's ring."

Tiamat's ring. I was punch-drunk, swaying on my feet as though those words had knocked me cold. This wasn't a trick or a set-up. This wasn't a mistake. Kaitlyn was right. It had to be Adelle. Only Adelle and I knew what had happened that night. Dante claimed to have seen, hiding in the room like the jealous lover he was, but even he didn't know what I'd retrieved from Adelle's ashes. Or did he? I'd thought only Adelle knew I gifted her the ring, only she had seen it right before it took its effect and had been able to identify it for what it was. The ring I was not supposed to have, and yet did and still do.

Deathless

"Owen?"

"Huh?"

"What does that mean? Did you—?"

I halted her words with a kiss. There was a chance she'd be overheard, if she hadn't been already. Vampires didn't have better hearing than normal humans, but these days, for all I knew, Kaitlyn and I were bugged. Dread rolled through me like a snowstorm. If it really was Adelle, and it seemed to be, I was as good as dead. Whether she claimed her revenge on me herself, or revealed the truth of my crime, it didn't matter. Adelle loved to destroy things, and loved to destroy me most of all.

Kaitlyn watched my face with growing horror. "It's true, isn't it? It is *her.* And you did—"

"I want to tell you everything, but I can't. Not here."

I had to tell Kaitlyn what really happened to Adelle. It was a secret I'd intended to take beyond the grave, but if Adelle was back, that changed everything. All my lies and stories, the fiction I'd created, was going to fall apart, and Kaitlyn deserved to hear the truth from me.

"Tell me now." She crossed her arms and her eyes flashed dangerously.

I scanned our surroundings, checking the Ebon-guard still across the room. They looked put out at the big fuss Kaitlyn had made, and that we now appeared to be either canoodling in a corner or

having a spat, or both. If they'd been listening in, I'd be done already.

I pressed my cheek to hers and whispered in her ear, "Don't let the Ebonguard know anything is wrong. I'll tell you everything."

I leaned into Kaitlyn and gathered her close. Her body was rigid and didn't fit against mine. "The ring, the cursed ring of silver with the tear-drop ruby—I lied about it. It doesn't choose its victims like I said, it must be gifted to the victim. It is an artifact with the power to cause untraceable death. The perfect murder weapon." Unless it turned out there was a hidden witness, like Dante. But even then, he could prove nothing. Until now.

"So you killed Adelle with it on purpose?" Her whisper was shaky.

I nodded. She already knew I had sought Adelle's death, but after that she believed a cursed ring chose Adelle to die. Now Kaitlyn knew how direct my part was in her death, she looked at me differently.

"Do you still have the ring?"

I nodded again.

She pouted. "You have a magic ring and you didn't tell me?"

"I didn't tell you because I didn't tell *anyone*. I can be killed just for having it. It's *Tiamat's* ring, a sacred object that belonged to one of the original seven. To possess it and not turn it over to the

Deathless

Synedrion—that alone is a crime punishable by death, no matter if you are a vampire or a human."

She sniffed a harsh breath. "And it's against the law for a vamp to kill another vamp. A crime you get bound to the sun for. And she knows you killed her. When you were both vampires. With that ring. That you shouldn't have."

I didn't even nod, just looked her in the eyes as it all settled on her.

"Oh man, we're screwed."

A wry smile quirked my lips. "I know. For now, the ring is hidden, but if I could get it back, if I could use it on her again before she told anyone—"

Kaitlyn's head shook as she laughed dryly. "I can't believe we're actually at the point of planning murder by magical ring. Is this really where our lives are right now?"

"What else can we do? She's a vampire. A dangerous one. And we're humans."

"I know. I just hate that this is what we've come to: forced into kill-or-be-killed situations. You're not a vampire anymore, Owen. Killing shouldn't be your go-to solution."

I wanted to say it wasn't, but every nerve inside me cried out for bloody carnage. Death had been part of my world for so long, it had become so normalized. But that didn't make it right.

Kaitlyn huffed. "I get the need for self-defense.

I get needing to do whatever we have to do to stay alive, but if only we could do that some other way. A deterrent, like the Nemexia.”

“If we could get our hands on some again, which isn't easy. Just having the ring alone isn't much of a deterrent. We can't let anyone know I have it, and it only works on one person at a time.”

Kaitlyn nodded, eyes searching my face as though in thought. Her hands fluttered to her mouth, hiding it for a moment, then dropped away again. Her whole body tensed, and she backed out of my arms. “Does the ring work on humans too? How many times did you use that thing?”

I frowned, worried by the way she looked at me. “I took many lives when I was a vampire, you know—”

“You weren't a vampire when Harvey died. Was that you?”

Harvey Hall. Her old agent. The man who'd sent her into a vampire LARP game, knowing the girls he sent there sometimes didn't come back. A man who I knew had sent girls off to far worse fates for the right price. I had decided his fate, and I couldn't look away from Kaitlyn's accusing stare, couldn't lie to her. I just nodded.

Her hand flew out and smacked into the wall beside us, but the expression on her face said it was me she wanted to slap. “I feel like I don't even know you.”

Deathless

The door opened and Lance, Bertha, and Niamh strode into the room. "Owen?"

Kaitlyn went silent, but she shot me a look that said our conversation wasn't over.

Bertha marched straight up to me, her gold and blue mask pushed up to her hairline, and her matching gown rustling with every step. "Adelle St Delaurents," she announced, startling Kaitlyn and me to attention. "You told the truth when you said she had died? That she could not have been hiding, or tricking you all this time, secretly alive? Or were you hiding her?"

I stuttered, unsure what to say that wasn't sealing my own fate, unsure what Bertha knew or where her line of questioning came from. "I am sure she was dead."

"She's not anymore. I saw her just now, undead and well."

And there was the proof. Bertha would recognize Adelle. She had known her, because she already ruled on the Synedrion during the short time Adelle and I lived in Umbravallis. Adelle and Bertha were even close, briefly, while Adelle tried to weasel her way into power before deciding the laws of the Synedrion didn't suit her darker tastes.

And now Bertha had seen Adelle. And I had to hope that was all she'd done.

"I saw her too," Kaitlyn said. "She threatened Owen and me."

"And you didn't tell anybody? If she's truly been restored from dust, that has implications. Big ones." Bertha tsked like a much older woman than she appeared to be. "Did you see Dante with her?"

Kaitlyn's eyes were wide. "Can you read minds?"

"No, I can just confirm suspicions. That fool-born varlot!" She muttered a few more unflattering words, then clicked her fingers at the nearby Ebonguard. She shot out orders, and two disappeared from the room. Joss and Heim moved to stand so close to Kaitlyn and me that their shoulders pressed against ours.

"What has Dante got to do with this?" Lance asked. "Not that I don't agree with your description of him, with respect to his position, of course."

Bertha lifted a hand and said nothing. The door swung open again and the rest of the Synedrion members flooded into the room. Even Viatrix. But not Dante.

"Is it true?" Milton demanded. "Has a vampire been raised from the dust?"

"Yes, and one who has a grudge against our humans here, to boot," Bertha confirmed.

The six powerful vampires glanced between themselves. Toren shook his head. "Dante's doing, no doubt."

Shirina swept her arm out, jingling the small bells sewn into her gown. "Why else would he not be here with us now? He also has a history with the risen vampire, Adelle St Delaurents."

"They must be found at once."

Bertha nodded. "I've already sent Ebonguard to rally more and hunt for them."

I was torn. If they were found, Adelle would surely tell the Synedrion what I did with Tiamat's ring. If they didn't find them, Kaitlyn and I would have two more very powerful enemies out there. I looked away, not willing to let any of them see the conflict in my expression.

Lin came toward Kaitlyn. "You two must be protected at all costs."

Does she mean me and Kaitlyn, or Kaitlyn and the child? I didn't know, but relief filled me. As long as they were intent on protecting Kaitlyn, that was all that mattered.

"The Remortalis development is so close," Lin added, frustration clear in her voice. "And we're dealing with grudges and spurned lovers! Why would Dante do something so foolish? He and Adelle must be captured and contained."

Bertha said, "He raised Adelle from the dust, against all orders, knowing he was condemning himself. He must have some sort of plan."

They gave each other grim looks. Shirina pointed to Lance. "Take your humans home. We will double their guard. I'm sure we'll have the criminals captured soon."

Lance nodded, and then we were on the move.

Kaitlyn and I jostled against each other, pressed in from each side by our bodyguards as we made our way out to a waiting car. Joss helped push Kaitlyn, and her pile of skirts and hoops, in through the door, and Bertha joined us on the trip.

As we sped through Umbravallis, she grilled me on everything related to Adelle. Where she might have gone. Any acquaintances they could seek shelter with. Why she and Dante had such a grudge against me.

As I hesitated over my answers, Kaitlyn spoke up, saving me, "Why is this even happening now? How could Dante bring her back?"

Bertha sighed, a motion of her chest which exhaled no air. "You returned Kissare's chalice to us."

"This is *my* fault now?" Kaitlyn's fury was palpable. "Oh, sorry I got kidnapped by an eating disorder cult for vampires who happened to have one of your precious vampire artifacts. My bad."

Bertha smacked her lips. "You done? Of course it's not your fault. It's a simple case that your misfortune was our good fortune. And fortune indeed, because that is the power of Kissare's chalice. I speak of the timing, that once the chalice returned to us, we were able to see in it the function of Ri's flute and Damkina's veil."

I whistled softly. That was big news. The veil and flute had been in the possession of the Synedrion for centuries, but never in our history had anyone discovered their powers. Some believed they had none and debated whether they were even true artifacts of the seven. This proved that they were. "They bring vampires back from true-death? How?"

"I obviously can't share that information with you."

"They have to be used together," Kaitlyn whispered.

"How could you know that?" Bertha snapped.

"Just from what you said, and what I read of vampire history in the book Lance got me. You said 'the function,' singular, of the *two* items. And Ri and Damkina, their love story, their tragic end, their vow to return to each other even after death? I mean, it's obvious."

Bertha's voice turned cold. "Only the members of the Synedrion possessed the knowledge that such a revival could even occur. We agreed, all of us, that it wasn't to be used, and was to be kept secret. Dante only agreed begrudgingly."

"This better not be a 'now you know we have to kill you' moment," Kaitlyn muttered.

"The important point to note is that in order to revive the dead vampire, you must have their remains. Dante must have kept some of Adelle's ashes all these years, and if he had her ashes, it may have been true after all that he was there when she died, or soon after." Bertha directed this all at me, her eyes narrowed. I couldn't say anything in return.

Kaitlyn saved me again. "Does that include your

gruesome statue collection? The ones turned to stone with What's-His-Name's dagger?"

"Potentially. But that is the danger of this knowledge and power. The potential."

We all grew silent then, dwelling on that potential. We already stood at the doorway to a whole new world, one where vampires could become human again, or wouldn't be reliant on human blood, and now there was the power to truly have vampires live forever, no matter what. It was clear from the silence that all of us thought that was too much power. But some would demand that power be used. Among those turned to stone by Alam's dagger were two of the original seven themselves.

We arrived at Lance's just as Bertha received the news that Dante and Adelle were nowhere to be found. Dawn was coming, and Bertha left us so she could oversee the continuing hunt.

Once back inside, the Ebonguard gave us some space again, and Kaitlyn and I headed straight for bed. She refused help getting out of her monstrosity of a gown and into her pajamas. When she lay down beside me, she was stiff as a board and silent.

I stared at her, unable to say all the things I wanted to say, only being able to mutter, "I need to make sure you are safe."

I rolled over to face her but she wouldn't look at me, just lay there staring up at the splashes of

early morning sunlight on the ceiling. "If I was a vampire ..."

She launched herself from the bed. Her lips curled back in disgust. "You'd kill me. Or feed from me. Also, the baby. Would you feed from this baby too?"

Her words, so cold I could feel the chill in the air between us, sent me toward her. But when I tried to get close to her, she backed away.

"I would never."

"No. No, you wouldn't, and do you know why? Because I won't ever be your captive again. Never. I won't stay with you if you become a vampire. You would never be able to protect me as a vampire because I would have nothing to do with you."

She stormed out the door and slammed it so hard behind her the room shook. I slumped onto the side of the bed, groaning with frustration. A few minutes passed. She didn't return.

And just being away from her, those moments when she was out of my sight and I missed her and feared for her and wanted her, told me everything I needed to know. That I couldn't protect her as a vampire. That all I could do, and what I *had* to do, was just be there for her. To love her, and be better for her as I was. As a human. Because that was who she loved.

I muttered a few swear words, then headed out the door.

Lance was in the hallway. Joss guarded one end and Heim guarded the other.

"Kaitlyn?" I asked him.

He pointed his chin at another room. "I wouldn't. It's locked."

"You heard all that?"

"I was just looking for Dusky. But you weren't exactly being quiet." He looked me up and down. "You looking to rejoin us?"

"Are you offering? You refused me before."

He shrugged. "I had a bad case of the feelings at the time. But you're like my brother, or once were. I owe you many times over. You ask a favor of me, I will help you."

Immortality. Strength. Power. All right there for the taking. And all it would cost me was Kaitlyn.

"No. I don't want that. Not anymore." I leaned heavily against the wall. Tears sprung into my eyes and hung there, the truth stinging my heart and making it grow full. "But there is something you can help me with. I have to go and get something from the castle in Slovakia."

Lance lifted an eyebrow. "You need it now? I said ask a favor, but that is pushing it, considering everything going on."

"Yes. I need it now. And it has to be in secret."

"What could be so important?"

"A ring. For Kaitlyn."

A huge grin grew on Lance's face. He touched a hand to his chest as though surprised. "How about that? I guess my case of the feelings is still hanging around after all."

11

KAITLYN

I sat cross-legged on the bed in one of the many unoccupied bedrooms. The only light came from the glow of my phone screen as I scrolled down through all the missed calls and messages. We'd been allowed to keep our phones this time, but something had been done to them so they only received incoming messages. Nothing outgoing, no internet.

Just enough so I could sit here and read all the angry messages from my agent and PR company, demanding to know where I was. Why wasn't I answering my phone? Why hadn't I made it to that entertainment magazine interview? Was I in rehab? Was I going to make it to that premiere? Tonight?

No. I didn't think I was going to make it. And I couldn't even let them know why.

I was so sick of my life not being *mine*. I'd been held captive for too long, trading one prison for another, one horror for another, and I was done with it.

Hot tears pricked my eyelids. All I'd ever wanted, since I was a child, was to be an actor. I'd gone to LA as a fresh-faced small-town girl determined to make it. I'd taken every crappy walk-on bit part I could. I'd studied my craft. I'd worked as a low-paid extra. I'd stood in cattle-call lines for sometimes twelve hours at a stretch just to be told that they'd already cast that part.

I'd been so desperate I'd agreed to play a victim to vampires in a LARP game that turned out to be way too real. And I was *still* playing victim to those vampires. They weren't drinking my blood, but they were still taking my life.

I kept thinking about a script I'd looked at last month. The heroine was a badass, fighting her way out of anything, with martial arts and perfect hair. I'd thought I could take on that role, had even started training for it, because I had faith that I was a good enough actress to do anything. I wished reality was like that—that I could just step into the role I needed to play and deliver the perfect one-liners as I kicked vampire butt and saved myself and those I loved.

I knew too well that that wasn't reality. I'd still fight, tooth and claw and matted hair. But I was just an actress and would never be strong enough

compared to a vampire.

Maybe Owen was right.

I whimpered. Right or wrong, he was trying to find a solution, and we were in this together. Sulking and shutting him out wouldn't get us anywhere.

I unlocked the door and stepped into the hallway. Heim stood at the end of the hall, guarding. Joss was gone, which could only mean Owen was gone too. Now she was on 'secondary' duty; she shadowed him just as Heim shadowed me.

I snarled as I walked past him into the living area. I wished he'd do that Ebonguard invisible-to-humans trick like they had on the plane, so I could stop seeing his dumb face, even what little I could see of it. Sure, he was doing his job, protecting me, but that protection came at the cost of my freedom. At that point, I'd rather be free.

Lance paced in the kitchen, running a hand along the granite counter, back and forth. "Night's greetings," he said, distracted.

"Owen's gone somewhere?"

Lance glanced at me and shrugged.

"Do you know where he is?"

"He'll be back soon." Under his breath he added, "Better be."

"So you do know where he is."

He paused in his pacing, grimacing as though caught out. "Maybe."

I walked over to the lounge and flopped onto it, too tired for vampire riddles. I patted the seat next to me.

Lance shook his head. "Shouldn't. I haven't eaten, and you're smelling remarkably delicious. Have you seen Dusky?"

Oh. Dusky. Shit. "I think we left her behind. At the ball. After all the commotion."

Lance grunted, his fangs showing, and came over to dump himself down in an armchair across from me. I tried to be subtle as I measured with my eyes the distance between him and me, and Heim and me, just in case an intervention was needed.

"She should still be back by now."

"Maybe she decided to stay and have fun for a bit longer, since we totally abandoned the poor human girl there." I leaned into the words, trying to get Lance to see what dicks we'd been.

Lance waved my tone away. "She'll be fine. Everyone knows she belongs to me."

I raised an eyebrow. "Will Owen be fine? Where is he?"

"Joss is with him."

"That wasn't an answer to my question. Why are you being so secretive?"

"Because he asked me to? Because you two aren't meant to be going anywhere? Because sorting out his little excursion to Slovakia could get us all in trouble?" Lance lifted his hands, clearly at a loss.

I tapped my fingers on the arm of the sofa. "Slovakia?"

Lance grimaced again. "This is unfair, interrogating me when I'm hungry and *distracted*." I didn't miss how his fangs sat over his lips and his eyes stared at my neckline.

But all that mattered at the moment was that Owen was gone. And he hadn't even said goodbye. He'd found a way to be gone, a way maybe we could have escaped, but he hadn't taken me. I took a long, calming breath. No, he could have only convinced Lance to help him get out if he'd promised to be right back. Just a quick trip. To get something. There could only be one thing he'd risk that for.

I lowered my voice, turning my head away from the watching Ebonguard. "Did he say he was going to get something? A ring, maybe?"

Lance looked shocked. "You already know?"

"Yeah. I'm surprised that you do."

"He just told me when he asked to go." Lance tutted. "It was meant to be a surprise."

I eyed him. He was taking the whole cursed-forbidden-ring thing very lightly.

Maybe I was the one overreacting. Maybe this was all everyday shenanigans in vampire world.

I sighed, slumping back into the lounge, trying to let it absorb me. "Maybe we do need a weapon after all."

Lance leaned forward, eyebrows raised. "Sorry,

what? How did we get to weapons?"

"Just, you know. We need a way to protect ourselves. We're no match for vampires as we are."

"I can't make the offer of change to you as well, sorry," Lance said. "The Synedrion want to keep their precious blood-sample human. Not to mention your condition." He pointed to my belly.

Part of me hated the idea of becoming a vampire, but part of me had become desperate. "It would mean losing the child, wouldn't it? Becoming a vampire."

Lance nodded. I wasn't that desperate.

"Maybe it wouldn't be so terrible if Owen was a vampire again. Maybe he could feed from me just enough to keep his human empathy, but not enough to be human. Maybe he could keep us safe. He would be able to fight other vampires if he was one." And maybe after everything was over, he could change into a human again.

But it might never be over. That might become our unhappily ever after, being fed on and protected by a being I would grow to despise.

Vampires had no empathy. They could have loving relationships, but not as we humans understood love. They didn't have the emotional toolkit for that complex stew of emotions. Their love was cold, unflinching, a power play of greed and want and lust, geared toward whatever suited them, and not the other person in the relationship.

I couldn't let him do that. He wouldn't be *Owen*. He wouldn't be the man I loved.

"I don't think it would be terrible. Mortality, that sounds terrible," Lance scoffed.

"But wait, you said make the offer to me *as well*? Did you offer to turn Owen?"

Lance shrugged as though it was nothing. "He turned me down."

"He did?" My heart jumped to a gallop.

"You seem surprised. Or is it disappointed?"

"No, not disappointed." Proud. Warmed through with love. Burning with the happiness of getting to keep Owen tinged with the fear of losing everything.

That was why he went to get the ring. He needed something, some way of offering protection that didn't come at the cost of losing *us*. A token to prove we did still have options.

Maybe there were other options we hadn't looked at enough. Like if only we could get away, we could switch sides and get help from the vampire hunters. With the tech they had, surely they had an R&D department that could weaponize the cure from my blood. Free the world from vampires forever.

But as long as even one vampire remained, they could turn more. And with the veil and flute trick they'd discovered now, even actual death wasn't permanent to them anymore. I had to accept vampires were a thing and they weren't going anywhere.

I grumbled, "Are there any magic wands out there that make people immune to vampires?"

"Sure," Lance said. "Check down the back of the couch. I think I lost one down there with some pocket change."

"Don't be crabby at me because you're hungry. I was serious. Kind of."

"No. Well, maybe. I mean, magical objects aren't exactly common. The only known items of power are those cursed with the spirits of the original seven. And of those, we know Alam's dagger, Kissare's chalice, Tiamat's ring, Ri's flute, and Damkina's veil. We have no idea what Dagan's item even is."

I counted off the names on my fingers. "That's six. What about the seventh? What was his name again? Mordak?"

"Marduk. He was the very last of the seven to die. He was the one who wrote many of our laws. Many of the cruelest laws as well, and also put them into practice. It was him who built the Sun Shrine. Those who knew him say he was benevolent at first, but insanity took over toward the end, and he took a bit too much joy in delivering punishments."

"So, a vampire who enjoyed burning other vampires alive for days? Okay, I can't wait to find out what his object does." I hid my interest under sarcasm.

"You and all of vampirekind. It is also unknown, undiscovered." Lance leaned forward, as though telling a spooky campfire story. "But there have always been rumors that it was something devastating to vampires, that it has remained hidden because no one desires to be near something so awful."

"A bit like me, huh?" A high-pitched voice broke the mood. Dusky had walked up behind Lance, looking frazzled with her red hair let out and high heels dangling from one hand.

I winced. "I'm sorry. We had a bit of a situation and had to leave in a hurry."

Dusky's voice raised an octave. "And you all just forgot about me?"

"Not at all," Lance said. "I've been wondering where you were."

"Why? 'Cause you're hungry?"

Lance's fangs were a dead giveaway.

She stamped a bare foot. "I had to walk home!"

She stormed off to her bedroom. Lance tried to follow her in, but the door slammed in his face.

I leveled a look at him. "You've got to end this, Lance."

Lance growled at me, and sped off so fast I could only see a blur.

12

KAITLYN

I wandered around Lance's dusty mansion for some time, waiting and anxious, before I found a small door leading to an even smaller balcony, one with a narrow, steep staircase that led right up onto the roof.

The pitched tiles shifted and crunched under my weight as I climbed up, and I tentatively shuffled over into the valley between two roofs, which made an almost comfortable place to sit.

I could just make out Heim's silhouette against the night sky, watching from a ridge on the lower wing, but I could pretend I was alone.

I sat there while the sky lightened, and swallows darted across the eggshell-blue expanse, chasing clouds of tiny gnats. A low wind made the long grass all around the house sway like ocean waves.

The sun appeared, the first thin beam shining straight, like a golden arrow, through the gap between cliffs, right into the Sun Shrine. From up here, the shape of the ancient temple stood out clearly. Megalithic stones met together in two curves, with two more circles of stones inside, almost like an eye. The inner circles were covered, and the whole thing was built down into a sort of amphitheater, carved out of the stony mountainside.

The rumble of a helicopter came from the distance, then a moment later, Joss appeared on the path leading up to the house, carrying Owen. Joss placed Owen back on his feet, then she looked directly up at me. I felt almost like I'd been caught out, but I wasn't the one doing something wrong. How did she spot me so fast? She probably smelled my blood.

It wasn't long before Owen came up and joined me on the roof.

"Night's greetings," he said. *The greeting of a vampire.*

"It's dawn."

He turned to look at the sky, as though verifying what I'd said. "You look tired."

"My days and nights are already getting mixed up." A tear crept down my face.

He moved forward, catching it with his finger.

"You have a nice trip?" I didn't mean to be catty,

but it slipped out.

He sighed and sat beside me. "It was meant to be a secret."

"I can't believe you managed to escape, even for a while, and you didn't take me."

"I didn't escape. Joss was with me the whole time." He thumb-pointed behind us where Joss had joined Heim on the other ridge, like two gargoyles, their eyes and faces completely masked from the rising sun.

"You know what I mean. How did you do it?"

"Lance can be persuasive. Joss was still technically fulfilling her duty, guarding me. She's the only one who knows how far away we actually went. And I promised to be back by morning." He sucked in a breath. "I'm sorry I went without you, but I had to—"

"I know why you went." And I understood. But a night of overthinking had left my emotions ragged. A sob squeaked out.

I wanted the freedom Owen had just had, even if only for a few hours. I wanted my life back. It was *mine* but it kept being stolen from me. First by Vampire Owen, then the Starved, and now the Synedrion. I wanted to be forever free of the vampires, to be free of this. I couldn't even think past the need to *go*, the need to have my own life again.

Owen tried to pull me close, but I resisted. I couldn't let him hold me, because if I did, I would forget how awful everything was, just how badly I needed to be free.

The sun had risen high enough to touch us with its light, and I yawned. I was tired of living a life flipped upside down. I should have been waking up, not ready for bed. I should have been on a beach or sitting at a table drinking coffee and reading scripts, or preparing for my premiere, or … or shopping for baby clothes and nursery furniture.

All the normal things people did.

Owen relaxed onto the tiles, lying on his back, and staring at the few puffs of cloud floating above us. "I'm sorry for using the ring on your agent. I'd created this whole story of a ring that sought out those who deserved it. And I *knew* Harvey deserved it. I think we both did."

I nodded, propped up on my elbows beside him, heart heavy.

"My thinking was messed up, but I just didn't want to leave you thinking that he *didn't* deserve it—that if such a thing existed out there, that could deliver righteous vengeance for us, I didn't want to leave you questioning why you had no vengeance for his crimes."

My tears dried up, and I sniffled away the remains of them. "But that's the thing. I never really wanted vengeance. Justice, maybe. Or knowing that he wasn't sending other girls to terrible fates—that

would be good too. But not *vengeance*. It's not a thing I generally seek out. That's what monsters do, what vampires do."

"And I'm sorry I made you think that was what I wanted to be again. I don't want that. Not anymore."

"I know. Lance told me you turned him down." I reached out and squeezed Owen's fingers.

"There's more though." Owen turned onto his side, staring into my eyes, his own the color of the sky around us. "I know now that just becoming human isn't enough. I have to actually work hard to be a *good* human. And I promise you I will. For you, for me, and for our child."

I turned onto my side as well, pressing my body to his, my forehead to his, nose to his. "I love you," I said, at the same time hushed and bursting with passion.

I smothered his reply, feeling the word love on his lips as I met them with mine. The kiss was long and lingering, countless smaller kisses flowing together into one.

A big yawn cracked my mouth open, and I stared at the full morning sunshine for a moment.

Owen nuzzled a kiss into my hairline. "You need sleep."

"I wish. I have to go be a good little lab rat for Shirina and Lin, remember?" My mouth folded downward.

"Tell them to wait. Tell them no."

"Ha," I barked it loud enough that the Ebonguard

turned their heads our way. "No, you know that isn't going to work. Besides, it sounds like they're also pulling all-dayers to try to get their cure finished. You can smell the obsession on the air."

The word obsession made Owen frown, and my first thought went to Adelle. A thought that felt too close to jealousy. I swatted it away, because Owen chose me. He chose me over becoming a vampire again. He'd always choose me. As long as we survived.

"Owen, if …" I drew closer to him. I put my mouth to his ear and dropped my voice. "If they find out what happened with Adelle, what will they do?"

His gaze went straight to the Sun Shrine. My heart sunk all the way to my stomach.

"Then we have to fight fire with fire. Or with whatever we can get." I nodded toward the shrine as well. "Lance was telling me about the guy who built that place, that his relic still hasn't been found, but is probably something powerful. *Devastating*, he said. If we could find it, if we could work it out, it could be like our nuclear deterrent."

"That's a lot of ifs," Owen said.

"I know. I know I'm basically daydreaming, but I need some hope to keep me going. That other thing you have, well, I know it's only good for one-at-a-time stuff, and I think it's probably best kept hidden to avoid trouble, yeah?" I gave Owen a pointed look, hoping he understood. "But something *devastating,* well, we could be flashy with that, because who would come after us if we had it?"

Owen smiled, his eyes thoughtful. "It's a good plan." He kissed me between my eyebrows. "Come on then, let's get off this roof. I'll stay up as well, so I'll be awake when you return."

I took his hand and he helped me to my feet. "It's okay. You can sleep."

He shook his head and kissed my nose. "I have something for you, for when you get back."

I tilted my head, curious. What could he mean? Owen loved treating me with gifts, but surprise presents seemed out of place with the situation we were in now. Maybe he was just trying to keep things feeling normal. Keep being the man I loved.

I wanted to pretend things were normal too. I couldn't believe I was suggesting we find a mysterious magical relic, one with devastating powers. Fighting and killing weren't what I wanted.

But as I followed Owen down off that rooftop, saying goodbye to the sunlight and stepping back into the shadows again, I knew I was going to have to fight to be free.

I had to stop thinking like a victim and start thinking like a predator.

13

OWEN

I meant every word I said to Kaitlyn. I wanted to be a good person, a better man for her. But I also still wanted to protect her.

Not as a vampire. Not anymore. But somehow.

What she mentioned about Marduk and the Sun Shrine got me thinking. It was true his relic had never been found, but there had been plenty of rumors about it over the centuries. It may have been an impossible hope, but I had managed to find one of the seven's possessions before. Maybe I could find one again.

In the past, I'd had the time, resources, and freedom of a wealthy vampire. Now, I'd just have to make do with what I had. And it *had* to be enough. This body, this life. It was enough.

Straight after I'd showered, I convinced Joss to take me to the Synedrion estate. After all, it should be one of the safer places in Umbravallis. With Kaitlyn off in the lab with Lin and Shirina, guarded by Heim, Joss seemed antsy herself. I would have preferred if Joss was still Kaitlyn's primary bodyguard too.

A car took us to the estate, and we entered a long, low building, off to the side of the main palace. I had no idea where to start looking, but Umbravallis's archives seemed like a good choice. Maybe I could see the old stories in a new light. Kaitlyn had so easily understood the use of the flute and veil based on Ri and Damkina's relationship. Maybe looking with human eyes, with that bit of extra emotion, could give me a clue that a vampire wouldn't see.

I walked up the smooth marble steps and pushed the heavy wooden door open. The floor was cold below my shoes—the chill drifted up through the soles and the thin protection of my dress socks, and I found myself longing for the ranch, for the sunshine, and smell of horses and orange trees blossoming. For hot wind blowing dry dust across the day. I knew Kaitlyn longed for that sunshine, that freedom, just as much as I did if not more.

We had to be on the offensive now. Not just to save our freedom, but to save our lives.

I knew the time that Kaitlyn's life was protected

was limited. As soon as they'd perfected their synthetic blood and vampirism cure from her actual blood, the Synedrion wouldn't need her anymore. What would happen to Kaitlyn when she was no longer necessary? When it wasn't worth protecting her, but the risk of letting her go was too great?

The archive entryway was lined with statues, just as the entryway into the Synedrion's chambers were. Not really statues, though. I stared at the face of the woman in front of me, her flesh turned to stone by Alam's dagger. I wondered what her crime had been, to deserve this punishment. Or if *any* crime deserved this punishment.

That the ones I once called friends were cruel enough to turn living, thinking beings to stone, and then display them in such a manner, wasn't something I had thought much about before. But now, standing here, I wondered if there was still a working mind inside that stone prison. If there was hunger and thirst. If there was pain and sorrow.

And if I might be the next statue in that terrible display.

An archivist nodded silently to me as I walked down the aisles. Tall shelving of carved dark wood and leather-bound tomes ran the length of each room, with gaps here and there filled with armchairs and study desks, each room joining another similar space. I breathed in the earthy smell of the books and headed for the section housing titles on the original seven. I'd only have access to the basic, public area, despite knowing that underground were floors and floors of archives, only accessible with permits. But I couldn't ask for one without a good reason.

A lot of the information in the archives had been digitized, but Kaitlyn and I weren't currently allowed online, and the digital collection of history texts were exclusively accessible by vampires, so my access had probably been revoked.

I would simply have to look and read the old-fashioned way to try to find a magical object that had remained unknown for more than a millennium.

I continued toward the back of the archives. Each room was colder than the last, and the aisles of books seemed to go on forever. The place was pin-drop quiet, and my footsteps echoed.

Through the final doorway at the very end of the building was a treasure trove of ancient books. Glass cases displayed the oldest documents, opened to whatever the archivists deemed the most interesting or visually beautiful page, and the whole room was temperature-controlled to preserve those books for as long as possible.

Joss walked in beside me, covered by the usual uniform and armor. Would that armor be much protection against whatever devastating effect Marduk's relic held? I shouldn't care. I had to keep reminding

myself she was the enemy.

Thankfully, once we reached the final room, she stationed herself at the door and let me be. The last thing I needed was for her to work out what I was looking for.

But even I wasn't sure exactly what I was seeking. I started with the shelved books, picking relevant titles and flicking through them until my eyes grew weary and blurred. I rubbed them, sighed, then turned my attention to the glass table-top cabinets. I leaned over the protective cases, peering down at the illuminated pages and ragged papyrus scrolls on display. The first showed an illustration of Tiamat burning at the stake, a medieval representation of an event that had occurred nearly three thousand years ago. Another had a portrait, executed in angular and stilted Babylonian-style brushwork, of Ri playing her flute, as Damkina sat with her jealous husband, Kissare. I skimmed along, looking for anything on Marduk, and finally found a selection of loose pages with silverpoint sketches, showing the Sun Shrine. The largest sketch depicted a carving from within the Sun Shrine of the face of Marduk. His single eye stared up at me.

"Owen?" Bertha's voice made me flinch.

"What are you doing up in daylight hours?" I turned around, trying to pretend I hadn't been caught off guard and wasn't interested in what I'd

just been looking at.

She made a face at my informal greeting, but seemed to shrug it off. "Wandering. Thinking. Waiting for news."

"And has there been any?"

"Nothing yet. No sign of Dante and Adelle." She walked over and peered down into the tabletop display I had been studying.

"How hard are you looking?" I asked.

"Hard enough. They took Ri's flute and Damkina's veil with them when they left. They must be recovered before any more damage is done."

"More damage?"

Bertha sighed. "A statue is missing."

I didn't know what to say to that. I stood silent, wondering why Bertha was being so free with information with us lately. As though our existence was already deemed so temporary it hardly mattered. "Which statue?"

Her lips pursed and she shook her head. Whether she was unwilling to admit it due to the gravity of the theft, or my knowing was not allowed after all, I wasn't sure.

She stared at the silverpoint sketches, then with a perfectly manicured red nail, tapped the glass directly over the image of Marduk, the carving of his face with only one eye.

"I'd forgotten about that carving; it's been so long

since I've seen it. It's been covered in ash for centuries."

I shuddered. The ash of all those who'd been bound to the sun. Their ashes were left where they burned, and since their bodies regenerated each night and burned each day, sometimes for weeks, a lot of ash had accumulated over the centuries. As the Sun Shrine and the rituals there were considered sacred, that ash was never cleared away.

She tsked. "One eye? That doesn't seem right."

I looked again, but couldn't see anything out of place. Marduk was famous for only having one eye. He'd lost one when he was still human. Trying to become whole again was part of the driving force for why he and the others became the first seven. But becoming a vampire, gaining immortality, hadn't helped him regrow that eye.

She leaned in closer, and I saw her squinting at the fine print scribbled below the sketch. "Of course, this was drawn a long time after the shrine was constructed and filled with ash. The artist probably drew it based on assumptions or false information. I feel though that I remember the carving in the temple showing Marduk with two eyes. The story was he commissioned it to show himself as he'd always wished to be."

No other depiction of Marduk showed him with two eyes. He was always shown with one, even when he'd commissioned the works. At least to my knowledge. And some distant memory told me the carving in the temple was only completed after Marduk's death.

I looked again with human eyes, imagining Marduk's longing to be whole. Many of the other cursed relics or their powers in some way symbolized a yearning of its owner. Kissare wished for visions to prove his wife's infidelity. Tiamat swore death and vengeance as she was burned. Ri and Damkina wished to save each other, in that life and forever afterwards. And Marduk and his eyes ...

This... this could be something.

But my memory and knowledge were nothing compared to Bertha's.

"You knew them, didn't you? Marduk and Damkina?"

Bertha turned away from the drawing, leaning her slim teenage figure against the case and folding her arms. "I only knew Damkina for a short time. I was one of the last of her many children. Marduk, I knew for longer, but I missed knowing him in his days of greatness. I only knew him when his insanity had taken hold."

To have known the original seven, to have walked the earth at the same time as two of them, was awe-inspiring. "I often forget how old you are."

Bertha's head dipped, and she looked tired. "Me too."

"You're sure it has two eyes? The carving in the shrine?" I tried not to sound too interested.

Bertha's expression had become distant and she wandered away. "No. I'm not sure. It was too many lifetimes ago."

She said her goodbye as she passed Joss at the doorway, a quiet, sad goodbye, and I waited a moment longer before taking my phone out to take a picture of the sketch. I found an empty office on the way out and ran off a copy of the photo. I folded the thin paper and pocketed it, still warm from the printer.

I stepped out of the archives and the cold air slapped against me, a fresh wind that awakened my spirit. I felt alive, and hopeful, and eager to share my discovery with Kaitlyn.

Joss and I returned to Lance's, and since Kaitlyn wasn't back yet, I went straight to find the ring box I had buried in a jar of rice in the kitchen. Joss watched from the corner, but it didn't matter if she saw it. She'd already seen me collect it when she took me to the castle in Slovakia.

I grabbed a pen and marked up the copy of the sketch, folded it small, tucked it inside the ring box, then placed them on the counter. And then I paced, waiting, eager, and excited.

Footsteps dashed up the stairs and I turned to them, only to be met by Dusky. Her face was twisted in fear.

"It's Kaitlyn! Quick. Kaitlyn's in trouble and needs help!"

Ice shot through my nerves, and I turned straight to Joss. She was already halfway out of the room, but paused, and looked back at me.

"No, go. Go fast. Don't worry about me—just get to Kaitlyn. I'll be right behind you."

Joss gave a single nod, then disappeared in a black blur.

Kaitlyn's in trouble. What trouble? It didn't matter. I only hoped Joss was fast enough. I knew I was slower, too slow, but I couldn't help anyway. I only had one thing powerful enough to even possibly help, and I had to get it.

I rushed into our bedroom, tearing off the covers and reaching my hand into the gash I'd cut in the side of the mattress. My fingers closed on the small book and pulled it out. Adelle's diary.

I opened the petite journal, and stared down at Tiamet's ring, nestled in the pages. I'd cut out large hunks of Adelle's handwritten words and placed the ring that killed her within them. It felt right and wrong all at the same time, but it worked as a hiding place for forbidden treasure.

I dashed back to the living area to find Dusky lounging there casually.

"She really has become obsessed with Kaitlyn, hasn't she?" she said.

"Who?" My first thought was Adelle. That Adelle had gone after Kaitlyn.

Dusky laughed. "Joss, silly. She didn't even stop to think of your safety, which, you know, is her job. She just ran to save precious Kaitlyn."

I stood there, Adelle's diary in my hand, staring at Dusky in horror as more footsteps pounded up the stairs. A dozen human thralls poured into the room.

Headed straight for me.

14

KAITLYN

The lab was crisply lit, and the smell of the alcohol wipe Lin pressed against my arm was extra strong.

"Everything seems to be progressing normally with your pregnancy," Lin told me. She'd run a few tests since I was there, including a quick ultrasound. I had a little printout of the scan in my hand, although it was barely more than a grainy gray background with a grainy gray dot. I also held a couple of printouts from the internet she'd found for me on early pregnancy care, since I hadn't had a chance to look into it myself. I knew the basic stuff, like no alcohol, but no soft cheeses? For nine months? Were they kidding me?

"Thank you," I said, and meant it. Lin was one of the few vampires who still treated me somewhat like a human. Shirina wasn't bad either, but she still looked at me more like a specimen than a sentient being. She had kept herself busy on the cure project, which she'd dubbed Remortalis, running some high-tech process on the blood sample I'd given when I first came in.

I was almost ready to leave when she requested just a bit more. She seemed excited, like she'd made some kind of breakthrough. "Two vials, please," she called from the back corner. "This is very promising. Very."

I looked away as Lin clicked the vacuum tubes on and off. I could never watch as they drew blood, or gave me injections, which seemed to come in equal measure for one reason or another. I pretended not to notice as she licked her lips. "Be sure to rehydrate. Next time, try to hydrate yourself more before having blood drawn too."

Next time. My inner voice was super petulant. It even blew a raspberry. I smiled politely as I applied pressure to the needle hole with a cotton ball.

Lin handed the vials to Heim, who was standing guard by my side, and shooed him off. He didn't appear to be happy being used to ferry my blood samples across the room to Shirina, but he did it anyway. Lin went to find a plaster for my arm.

The glass door banged against the wall, clattering as Joss appeared like a black flash in front of me.

"Kaitlyn! Are you—?" She broke off, looking at

me, then the room, assessing everything.

I gawked at her.

Heim returned, looking around as well. "Why are you here? Where is your human charge?"

Joss's eyes were wide. "Dusky just told us that you were in trouble. That I had to come and help."

"I'm fine. No trouble." Trepidation wormed itself into my belly. Prickles shot along the base of my spine and lodged into my hairline. "Wait. Why would Dusky tell you that?"

Joss's head shook, but she had no answer.

My voice came out thin and highly pitched. "Where's Owen?"

I didn't even wait for an answer. I took off at a dead run. Hands closed around my waist and I cried out, expecting to be pulled back. But the hands lifted me and I was being carried in Joss's arms, since she was able to run so much faster than I ever could.

The shadowed town passed by us in flashes, our path as straight as an arrow with no garden or wall or building standing as obstacle to Joss's momentum. She cradled me easily as she leaped and dashed through the quiet daytime streets, empty even though the sunlight didn't reach into the dark valley. Then we were on the road up the hill, through the long grass, and up the stairs into Lance's top-floor human habitat.

Sunlight flooded in and Joss dropped me, gasping

and shielding her uncovered eyes with her arm.

I was vaguely aware of her finding the remote and closing the curtains, but all I could see was the chaos before me. All I could hear was the scream echoing in my brain.

Owen!

"OWEN?" I called out into the space but knew there would be no answer.

The living area had been trashed. Rugs were kicked up and humped over in weird shapes. A side table had been smashed. The cushions from the lounge were all over the place, stuffing ripped and torn.

Joss bent down to sniff something. Blood.

When she slammed her fist into the floor so hard I felt the house shake, I knew whose blood it had to be.

No, he can't be gone. Horror flooded through me. He'd been taken, taken from me. And I was pretty sure who took him. And that Dusky, vamp fangirl extraordinaire, had helped them.

It didn't take a genius to figure that out. There was more blood near the kitchen and … I blinked at the tiny box on the counter. A ring box. *Oh no.*

I dashed over to grab it, hoping Joss didn't notice.

Dread coiled like a boa constrictor around my stomach. In this box was the cursed ring, Tiamat's ring. I didn't want to look at it, to see it. But I had to check that it was still in there.

The box snapped open on its spring, and the ring

inside was … gorgeous. Pale rose-gold filigree and a large, clear diamond that sparked rainbows in every facet. No blood drop-shaped ruby. No tarnished silver. I inhaled a shaky gasp.

Joss stood by me, looking at the ring as well.

"Was this the ring he went to get?" My heart pounded, sounding in my ears like a grieving bell.

"That's what he went to Slovakia for. A big risk when he could have proposed with something else," Joss said softly.

I felt tears spilling from my eyes. "He didn't get anything else?"

"Just that ring and a small book."

I touched the ring softly with one finger, wishing I could be touching Owen's cheek. I noticed a piece of folded paper wedged up into the top of the ring box.

Joss crumpled, dropping onto her knees. "I have failed."

Heim appeared, followed by two other Ebonguard he must have collected on the way. "Where is he?"

Joss was back at attention before I could blink through my tears to see clearly. I slipped the ring onto my finger and quickly pocketed the box.

"Gone," Joss reported.

His hand shot out, and Joss went flying across the room. Her back hit the wall and she crashed to the floor.

An indignant scream broke from my lips. "What

the fuck is wrong with you?”

He pushed me out of his way so easily I might as well have been made of the lightest straw. “Be quiet,” he ordered.

Joss got to her feet, composing herself again into a neat pose of attention. “I’m sorry. I should have known something was wrong. I acted in haste.”

“You acted against your commands. You should never have left your charge.” Heim’s voice was cold, but there was a dark revelry in his words. “You were always the fastest, the most talented, but you never were good with orders. You’ve just used your third strike.”

I tried to step between them. “Dusky tricked her; it’s not her fault.” I knew just how seriously Joss took her job. She’d jumped out of an airplane for it. “She was just trying to help me, and why are you just standing here being mad at Joss when Owen’s been kidnapped, and Dusky and whoever she’s working with could still be on the grounds? Go after them!” My voice rose and broke, nails on chalkboard in the quiet tension. But nobody moved.

Heim spoke to Joss in a low, grim voice, “You will be stripped of your rank, take your punishment, and be exiled forever.” He stepped forward, and ripped Joss’s cowl straight off her, leaving her face exposed. Her dark skin shone hot with fury and shame, lit up with an inside glow as pink as her hair. She

remained at attention, her whole body shaking. Her lips were set tight.

"No!" My voice rose in a wail. "I want her as my guard! I need—"

One of the other Ebonguard clapped a hand over my mouth. I bit at his fingers but he didn't even flinch. I sagged against his stone-like body, my thoughts swirling and flying uselessly.

Joss took one long, slow look at me, bared her teeth in a snarl, then pushed Heim out of her face with both hands. He crashed into the opposite wall hard enough to leave a crater.

And then she fled.

"Joss?" I whispered, but she was gone.

Heim picked himself up from the floor. He moved at odd angles and reset broken bones with a crunch until he could stand properly again. Then he glared at me.

"Guard her, and do not leave her side for even one second," he told the remaining Ebonguards.

Then he too was gone, and I was left there, weeping furiously, with my thoughts tangled and my heart breaking into a million shredded bits.

Joss was gone.

Dusky had betrayed us.

Owen had been taken.

And I was helpless to find him, or help Joss, or even help myself.

15

OWEN

My body ached all over, bruised and cut from trying to fight the thralls that had come for me. I'd fought my hardest, but there were just too many of them. I winced as they carried me, bumped and jostled in their zombie-like grasp, slung between them like I was being taken to a cannibal's feast.

They'd bound my wrists and ankles and thrown a bag over my head so I couldn't see where we went, but when they took the bag off, I knew exactly where we were. I'd never forget that place. Even though it had been changed.

They dumped me out onto a stone table, and sickness lurched through me. This was the place the Starved had taken us, the same table they'd bound Kaitlyn to, the place where they'd enthralled me and I'd almost harmed her in a way I could never forgive myself for.

I looked up at the grotesque statue, still covered in the Starved's blood, where they'd sacrificed themselves and let it run for their dark ritual.

There was dried blood on the stone near my cheek, and I wondered if it was Kaitlyn's.

The rest of the space came into focus, different to how I'd last known it. The dank cavern had been dressed in plush carpets and throw blankets, velvet curtains and soft bedding, all red and gold like a romantic boudoir. Nearly two-dozen thralls stood idle around the walls, awaiting orders from their master and their mistress.

Adelle.

"Hello, Owen. I must say, I'd forgotten how pathetic you were as a human."

And there she was, standing with Dante beside the stone slab, looking down on me with cruel black eyes that stood out starkly against her icy-white skin and crystalline hair.

It was really her, back from the dead. "Fuck you, Adelle."

Adelle raised her eyebrows and looked to Dante.

"It's an insult," he clarified.

She looked amused, but her red smile dripped with hatred. "Indeed? How much you've caused me to miss out on."

Deathless

She whistled, as though calling hounds, and some thralls approached. One had heavy chains in his hands, dragging them behind him.

"String him up," she commanded, pointing to the statue.

Dante turned his back on me as the thralls hoisted me off the slab and clamped the irons onto my wrists. He muttered, "We should kill him now, stop playing around. Then we can go after the woman. Her blood will destroy vampirekind, and we can't let that happen."

Adelle tapped a long nail against his chest. "You have no imagination at all, Dante, and you have no idea how disappointing that is."

Dante lifted his hands, as though at a loss. "We have the ring. Use it then, to kill him like he killed you, if you want to be creative about it."

My teeth clenched. I'd hoped the book and the ring it contained had been overlooked after the fight. Adelle and Dante having Tiamat's ring was all kinds of bad.

Like quiet worker ants, the thralls got the end of the chain up over the statue's neck then pulled, bringing me up by my wrists until my toes only just touched the ground.

Adelle kept her gaze locked on me, and smiled as the chain was secured.

"Oh no, he deserves worse than that. And I already

know just the thing." Adelle's fingers toyed down my chest, popping open all the buttons on my fight-torn shirt.

"Get your fingers off me, you filthy creature!"

Adelle gave me a practiced pout. She seemed amused by my insults, my useless thrashing, and just pressed her fingers closer to my bare skin. Her sharp nail cut the flesh of my sternum. The smell of my blood hit the air, and Adelle's tongue stroked across her full bottom lip.

Dante watched with a twitching jawline. "We don't have time for this. You act like you'd spare him out of love."

"Don't you *ever* mistake my actions as being those of love." Adelle whipped around to face him. Her feral expression softened instantly, becoming perfectly ladylike and demure. Her eyelids fluttered. "Dante, darling, you know I'm not interested in him like that. You are my one true love; you brought me back from the darkness, from dust."

She reached a hand behind his head and drew him into a long, deep kiss.

Then she turned her cheek to him, as though whispering in his ear, but speaking to me, "You will love what I have planned for Owen. It will destroy him over and over, and destroy that woman as well. First, I'm going to turn him. And then deny him the first feed vampires so desperately need. We will starve him to the point of insanity, and then we will set the woman he loves with the delicious blood in front of him."

Panic left me short of breath. My head shook.

Adelle's eyelids drooped, almost lustful. "And we will watch. We will watch him *tear her to shreds*."

A roar of sheer rage bellowed from my mouth.

My fingers curled and strained, and my body jerked, trying to snap my bonds. But they were solid iron. I was trapped. There was no way out.

"And when that woman's blood turns him human again, how you will *feel* her loss. I wonder just how much must be drunk from her to steal the gift of night from a vampire? Never mind, though, because when he changes, we will turn him again. After that, we will deliver him back to the Synedrion to be bound to the sun for his crimes. I'm sure when he's found with Tiamat's ring and Kaitlyn's blood all over him, they'll be more than happy to finish him off for us. As slowly as possible."

I prayed. I prayed for a miracle, for a savior, for the Ebonguard to burst into the room and deliver me from the terrible fate Adelle had planned. I prayed like I hadn't for centuries.

But it was too late.

Adelle's fangs punctured my neck, and all I could feel were pain and an icy sensation skidding underneath my flesh. I could feel my blood being drawn into her mouth, feel my veins collapsing. My heartbeat slowed and slowed again. She was taking me all the way to the brink of death.

I can't let this happen. I grasped onto that one wish, finding enough fight left in me to scream and thrash so wildly I broke free of Adelle's bite, tearing my neck wide open. Searing pain blinded me, and hard hands held me still—Dante, digging in his nails as Adelle returned her mouth to me, feeding in long, greedy gulps.

The sound of her contented sighs, washing through my ears and echoing down in my brain, were the last I knew as darkness took me.

Then it reversed.

I came back into a dim, gray awareness. Blood dripped into my mouth.

The darkness parted long enough for me to see Adelle's wrist, the long blue veins running along the shining white surface of her skin, the dark blood running into my mouth. I gagged and turned my head, but Dante's fingers gripped my temples and pushed me back.

I spat and flailed, trying to escape that rich, bloody flow coming from her arm. The thick drops splattered, landing hot and slick on my face. It coated my chin and cheeks, burning when it landed in my eyes.

I won't do this. I won't swallow it. I won't be turned.

Deathless

I want to live.

But I could already feel the undead, cursed blood moving in my system, changing me, bringing me back from the very edge of death. I tried to hold onto my humanity, everything that made me human, the man Kaitlyn loved.

I tried to hold onto the feeling of my beating heart as the beating stopped.

I tried to hold onto the warmth of my skin as my flesh turned cold.

I tried to hold onto my love for Kaitlyn, that feeling, that unique and incredible *feeling*. But everything within me spiraled away. Even my shock and anguish felt as distant as the moon.

There was only pain, and death, and a hunger that built and burned in my veins, and a longing, lingering desire for …

Strawberry.

16

KAITLYN

I'd been summoned to the Synedrion council for an update on what had happened, then interrogated, as though I was the one who'd done something wrong.

The door to their chambers closed, hitting me on my ass on the way out. Literally.

The six remaining council members didn't care one bit that Owen was gone. They'd tested his blood. There was nothing in it that could be reverse engineered. Owen might have blabbed about the cure, but as long as I was still here, safe, with Heim on one side and some new Ebonguard on the other, never to be free again, they didn't care.

They didn't care when I pleaded for Joss's punishment to be revoked, that she didn't deserve it. They didn't care when I told them I was sure Adelle had taken Owen, that she was sure to torture him. They didn't even care that Dante and Adelle had stolen Lance's "belonging." They were already criminals now, and that crime ranked way down on their list, under stealing relics of the original seven and using them to bring a vampire back from the dead.

Lance had stayed with me through the entire audience, after having found me weeping on the floor with Owen, Joss, and Dusky all gone. His eyes flashed with anger, and something more, when I told him about Joss hitting her three strikes and fleeing. Now, they wore the most haunted look I'd ever seen.

"This is my fault. I should have sent Dusky away. Before she turned on us."

"You'll have plenty of time to blame yourself later," I hissed. "How about you stow it and go get Owen back instead, since nobody else seems interested in doing it?"

"They are still looking for Adelle and Dante. If Owen is with them, like you believe, then he'll be recovered."

It didn't seem like they were doing enough. There had been no sign of hunting parties out searching, no alarms going off. It wasn't *enough*. I had to do something. I had to save him.

My words came from the very center of my aching heart. "You have to help me. You owe me for what you let happen, for letting Owen pay for your mistake.

You had to know that Dusky would do anything to be a vampire, to be with you, and you let her stay on because it was convenient for you to feed. You flirted with Joss in front of her—"

Lance raised his eyebrows.

"Don't pretend you didn't. You trampled all over Dusky's feelings. You used her, and never once thought about her."

The night of the ball, when Dusky was forgotten and left behind, was that when she met Adelle? I imagined it was, and I could also easily imagine what Adelle had promised Dusky in return for helping capture Owen. She would have promised Dusky the one thing Lance kept refusing her.

I laughed wryly. "I can't wait to see your face when Dusky comes back as a vampire, and comes after you."

Lance grabbed my arm and yanked me close to him, his mouth next to my ear. "Watch yourself, Kaitlyn. I can understand your hatred right now, but I'm not your enemy. Unless you want me to be."

His fingers were like hard steel bands on my flesh. His warning was the ringing of a bell.

"Release the human!" Heim barked.

Lance let go, holding up his hands in a peaceful gesture and taking a step back.

He was right. I hated them at that moment, even him. All of them. I hated them because the man I loved was gone and nobody cared. But I sure didn't need any more enemies.

"I'm sorry," I said.

"Me too. You know, I do care about Owen as well." Lance looked down. "He gave you the ring?"

I blinked at him, confused. *Tiamat's ring?* No. He meant the beautiful diamond ring I wore on the ring finger of my right hand. Lance mustn't have known about Tiamat's ring after all. "No. I found it. After … everything."

"Oh. He was so determined to go and get it for you."

My skin prickled all over. Owen should have been here. He should have been able to give the ring to me himself. I shook my head and slid down to the floor with my back against the door. "I thought he went for something else."

I lifted the diamond ringed finger close to my face and stared at it. I knew now he went to get this ring, that maybe he was going to … It was too painful to think about.

But maybe he got Tiamat's ring as well. Maybe he had it with him right now. Would it help him, if he did? I had no way of knowing. I didn't even know if he was still alive.

The diamond glinted, and I remembered the box it came in, and the small piece of paper inside it, both still in my pocket. I pulled the ring box out and unfolded the sheet, hoping for a handwritten note, a final love letter, a proposal, a magic spell to save and free us.

I frowned at the image in front of me. Just a printout of a badly taken photo of a sketch of a strange one-eyed face. A second eye had been drawn on in red pen over the top. What on earth did it mean?

"What is it?" Lance asked, crouching in front of me to look.

"I have no idea." My words were a harsh sob.

The door behind me suddenly opened, and I fell flat on my back. I just lay there, feeling useless and hopeless and exhausted, and stared up at Bertha's quizzical expression.

"What are you doing on the floor?"

I crumpled the paper in my hands, hoping she didn't see it, whatever it meant. I dabbed my eyes with it as though it were a tissue, then shoved it back in my pocket.

Bertha ignored my antics. "Listen, I've convinced the rest of the council that we should allow you to take a vision from Kissare's chalice. Dante and Adelle must be brought in, and it could help us. And it could help you if Owen is indeed with them."

"Really? Do you think it could show me where he is?" The chalice which showed visions of the future, like telling the Starved I was some kind of mythical baby-momma. I was intrigued, but skeptical. They'd said before, its visions were wildly open to

interpretation. And the whole thing just stank of evil.

"Maybe. I think it's worth a chance. I think it's worth seeing what the chalice shows you."

Me with my stupid special blood. Me with all my *implications* for vampirekind. Of course she was interested in what the chalice would show me.

But if it could help me find Owen, I was in. I nodded sharply.

Lance extended a hand for me and helped me to my feet.

"Come on then," Bertha said, moving off at a brisk trot.

I felt out of place walking the halls of the Synedrion palace with Bertha in the lead, wearing what had to be a custom-sewn dress that made her look like a film star from the '40s, Lance in a suit, Ebonguard in their armor, and me in the jeans and hoodie I'd been in since leaving Owen that morning. Maybe vampires could always dress up because their general toughness meant they never got uncomfortable.

We went down stairs, and down more, through hallways lit with electric candles, where the décor wasn't as modern as it was in the plush and renovated main areas of the palace. We went deep into the oldest parts of the building, with the smell of damp limestone and aging tapestries hung from walls.

"Should I be knowing the way to where you keep this thing?" I asked. "You're not going to memory-wipe

me after this?"

"The location of the reliquary is fairly common knowledge," she said. "But only Synedrion members can get inside, so generally it's safe."

"Generally, until one of your own turns on you. How did someone like Dante get onto the council in the first place?"

"Sheer bloody luck," Lance replied.

"Maybe not," Bertha grumbled. "What with the mix of immortality and corruption, our government for many centuries has run on a sortition process. Any vampire who meets certain requirements can go into the draw when a seat becomes vacant. But I suspect the draw which appointed Dante was rigged. I have no idea how he did it, but I'm not the only one who suspects. That's why we haven't appointed a replacement for him yet, although we will have to soon."

The hallway opened out into a formal entryway, with a very serious vault door guarded by equally serious Ebonguard. Bertha greeted them, and they cleared the way for her to approach a high-tech interface.

"This feels like the part in a spy movie before everything goes wrong," I said, as Bertha had her fingerprint, retina, and voice scanned before a little light turned green and the door made chunky, sliding, mechanical sounds.

The inside of the vault was roomy, lined with

streaky white marble. The lights were dimmed, and the air was cool and dry. Four pedestals stood in a line. On one, Alam's dagger lay on a red velvet pillow. Two were empty. On the fourth was Kissare's chalice, looking just as it had the first time I saw it in the Scarl's monstrous hands.

All of the vampires with me paused, heads bowed, as though in a moment's silence. I twiddled my thumbs, awkwardly, waiting while trying to fight down the anxiety that was rising. I wasn't sure I even wanted to do this. Knowing the future always seemed alluring, but I was pretty sure it fell into the "be careful what you wish for" category. What if I saw the time and means of my own death? Not really something I wanted to know. But if there was a chance it could help me find Owen, I was in.

Bertha went to a side table where she picked up a silver jug. Lance looked at the empty pedestals.

"Thank the night Dante didn't take the chalice and dagger as well," he said.

Bertha returned, and poured some water into the ornate silver cup, inlaid with blood agate. "We think they only took the flute and veil because they didn't have time to put them back after using them. They've made themselves much greater criminals by taking our sacred relics."

I wondered again about Marduk's relic, what it was, and whether possessing it would be worth the risk of being hunted as a criminal for having it.

"Your hand, please." Bertha waited, her own hand outstretched for mine.

I reached out tentatively with my left. She gripped it hard, and swiftly punctured the tip of my finger with a sharp nail. I gasped, but she held tight, and squeezed a few drops of blood into the water in the goblet. *Drip, drip, drip.*

Red light shone out of the liquid, flickering and swirling.

My breath fluttered with fear.

Bertha took the chalice in her hands and held it before me. "Look into it," she instructed.

I gazed down. The few drops of blood had changed the water, thickening it to a dark red, viscous, rippling surface, lit from below. My belly rolled. I squeezed my eyes shut for a moment, breathed, found my courage, and looked again.

Think of Owen. Find Owen. I didn't know how this all worked, whether it could be directed, but I tried to focus my thoughts on him. I pictured his thick hair, and the little lines that had formed at the corners of his cornflower-blue eyes.

My heartbeat slowed, and my head swam. A strange languor filled me. The blood swirled against the sides of the cup, a whirlpool, parting to reveal the light below.

Images flashed straight into my mind, monochrome,

like a black-and-white film but all the black was red.

There was Owen. His face came into focus and so did mine. I could see us locked in an embrace, bodies moving together in passion, writhing. No ... thrashing, panicked, fighting. No pleasure—only fear. Owen's teeth were in me, his fangs deep in my neck, my chest, blood dripped all around me, increasing the red of the already scarlet world.

All I could see was blood. My voice, filled with agony, unleashed screams of sheer pain and torment as Owen fed in feral, ravenous, shredding bites. A face watched over it all, large and strangely shaped, a carving with only one eye smiling in sick enjoyment. Then it winked another eye at me, light flashed, and a coin chinked and clattered, and twinkled as it hit the ground then disappeared under a pool of blood.

I scrambled backward. My legs went out from under me.

I was on the floor again, looking up at Bertha.

She knelt beside me. "What did you see?"

My head was shaking, trying to deny my words. "They're going to turn him. And he's going to kill me."

Lance's hand shook my shoulder so hard that my head lolled on my neck. "Where is he? Where, Kaitlyn?"

"All I saw was the two of us." And that face. The same face as the one on the paper Owen had left. It might be a clue to where he was, or to something more. That coin. I had to find it, but didn't want Bertha or the Ebonguard to know about it.

I struggled to my feet.

The vision still echoed in my head, snippets of trauma on replay. Lance put his arm around my waist and I sagged into him, drained and afraid that I couldn't escape the fate I'd just seen. It ate at me all the way back to his house, with no way of knowing if the cursed chalice had shown me a certain future, or just a vision of my deepest fears. But it had shown me that carved face, and it had shown me a coin. And that had to mean something. I kept that hope held tight and secret, because I knew no matter what, Owen and I didn't have much time left. Lin and Shirina had the Remortalis formula almost at testing stage. When it worked, they wouldn't need me anymore, and I knew, deep down, that they never intended to let me go.

Perhaps Owen killing me was just the solution all the vampires needed.

17

KAITLYN

Sunset tinged the mountains around us with a pink-orange glow, and I stared out the window at the eye-shaped Sun Shrine. The carved face, the winking eye, the note from Owen, all haunted me. It must mean something, and that shrine that Marduk himself built was involved. I knew it, and I knew I had to get there. I was going crazy with the need to act, but with Heim and another Ebonguard attached to each of my elbows, I could do nothing but go insane. They weren't even letting me go to the bathroom alone anymore.

I watched until the night turned blue and stars twinkled. My eyes ached in their sockets, but I couldn't sleep. In the kitchen across the living space, Lance brewed some coffee for me. He was trying extra hard to be helpful, and I wondered what else he could do, whether I could trust him with the knowledge of the face and the coin. If he would help me find it. But I couldn't even broach the subject with the Ebonguard here. So I stood and stared at the sky, as the fear of all being lost ate me from the inside. *Even if I can get away, how can I do this alone? How can I save Owen, myself, and our future?*

Everywhere I looked, all I saw was Owen's absence. His phone on the side table, and a shirt draped over a chair in our bedroom. The ring box and note in my pocket. The ring on my finger. My body kept swaying, like I expected to turn right into his arms.

But when I turned around, it was Joss who stood at the door. She had a black military pack over one shoulder, and her standard Ebonguard cowl was gone, replaced by a wicked expression.

"You came back," I gasped. I didn't know why she'd returned, but I was happy to see her.

Heim seemed weirdly happy too, in a much creepier way. "Didn't run away like a coward after all? Come back to receive your deserved punishment?"

"Fuck you, Heim," she said.

Heim and the other Ebonguard both bristled, but before they did anything, Joss sped over to Lance and threw him to the wall behind her.

Then she shot something straight at me.

I gasped, waiting for pain to strike, wondering why Joss had turned on me.

Deathless

I did get her in this trouble, after all, a cold voice spoke in my head as a tiny canister exploded in the air.

Joss snatched a thick scarf up and over her nose and mouth, and the cloying, rotten scent of carrion filled the air, like she'd shot us with roadkill.

I choked on it, spat the disgusting fragrance from my mouth, but was otherwise unharmed. Heim and the other ebonguard hit the floor, deadweights as the corpse flower extract took its paralyzing effect.

My brain caught up with the situation, then my body a moment later, pushing the window behind me open to clear the gas from the air so any remaining scent didn't get to Lance and Joss across the room.

Joss nodded approvingly, then ran a kitchen towel under water and threw it to me. I moved across to the other side of the room and wiped myself as clean as I could from the spray of misted scent, but still kept my distance from Lance and Joss while my clothes aired out, as much as I could kiss Joss for relieving me of my bodyguards.

"Thank you. I've been trying to work out how to get rid of those guys. But why? How?"

"I wanted to help you." Joss slapped the pack on her back. "I never ran. I went to recover this. The vampire hunter's belongings."

"You said you couldn't find them," I said.

"I lied. I hid them so they wouldn't be confiscated. Thought I might need them." She hesitated. "I also went to find Dusky."

"Where is she? You didn't …" I gulped, unsure what fate I wished on her.

"She's dead, but I didn't kill her. Adelle and Dante do have Owen, thanks to Dusky's help. They promised to turn her in return for it." She glanced over at Lance, and he dropped his gaze to the floor. "But they used her, drank from her, and dumped her on a hilltop, near death. That's how I found her. She told me everything before she died."

No, I didn't wish that fate on her. She was just young and dumb, and going after something she desperately wanted. I could relate to that. My nose scrunched up, and my eyes stung with angry tears. The poor girl. Even after what she did, she didn't deserve that. But I was starting to feel that Adelle and Dante deserved far worse.

I sat on the couch for a moment, pulling myself together. Lance joined Joss by the kitchen counter. "Glad to have you back," he said.

Joss's smile was too small to reach her eyes, but came quick and easy. Just how often had she smiled under her cowl, nobody but her aware?

My fingers clawed into the arm of the couch. "And Owen? Did you find out where they're holding him? If he's still alive?"

"I know where they were taking him. But I can't promise they will still be there when we get there."

"We?"

"We." Joss nodded. "If you want to go with me, that is."

"Damn straight I'm going."

"We're all in then," Lance agreed.

Joss touched his shoulder briefly. "You can still remain innocent, outside of this."

"And miss out on all the fun? I doubt it." He smiled roguishly.

Hope swelled inside me. This was my chance. *Our* chance. Owen wasn't dead. The chalice had shown him turned, feeding on me. If it was true, then at least he could be saved. And maybe I could change the future, with help.

Could I trust them? They were putting themselves in danger now, stepping outside the laws of their kind, for me and Owen and what they thought was right. Joss could have run and never come back, but she hadn't. *I think I can trust them.*

"There are some things we're going to need." I stood and walked toward them, but Joss held up her hands and I checked myself, staying where I was. I took the paper from my pocket, uncrumpled it, and held it out. "Owen left me this, and I think it has something to do with Marduk's relic. I also saw it in the chalice vision."

At Joss's questioning look, I filled her in on my trip to the vault with Bertha. "I saw this face, and a coin. Do you know where this sculpture is?"

Joss squinted at it. "It's in the Sun Shrine."

"I knew it."

Lance frowned at the crumpled printout. "You really think that's what it is, where it is? Marduk's relic?"

"I'm sure. And I'm sure we need it."

"A coin? It doesn't exactly sound dangerous, or useful. We have no idea what it does."

I raised my palms, exasperated. "A flute and a veil bring vampires back from the dead. If those chalice visions mean anything, we have to try."

"Agreed," said Joss. "I can go to look for it now, but we have to get moving. The Nemexia will keep those two knocked out for a while, but they are supposed to report in regularly, and as soon as they don't, we'll be in trouble."

Joss could probably zip in and out mostly unseen, thanks to her ninja-like abilities. She was fast and sly, and no doubt capable of a covert operation. But that was why I needed her to do something else.

"No. Lance and I will try to get the coin. I have another mission for you. If you choose to accept it."

I went over my plan with Joss.

If Owen was already turned, I had to be able to cure him. And I couldn't trust it to happen from drinking my blood again, not without him killing me. Lance had explained how ravenous vampires were right after being turned.

Deathless

The cure was still untested. It might not even work. But it might save me from Owen's hunger. Or, if all else failed, I could jab Acelle or Dante with it to even the playing field. Either way, we needed it. And only Joss could get it.

She looked thoughtful for a moment, hesitant, then nodded. "I can do that." She hoisted her pack of vampire-hunter toys back on and left.

Lance folded his arms, regarding me. "Ready to go treasure hunting?"

I put on my game face. "Always."

"You know this mightn't work. The cure, the relic—any of it. It's all a pretty slim chance at this stage."

"I know. I'm willing to risk it." A hand went to my stomach automatically. "I have to believe it will work. For all of us. Because what future do we have otherwise?"

Lance nodded slowly, staring wistfully toward the door Joss had just left by.

"What future indeed," he muttered.

I had to wonder too, what would happen to Joss after this? Whether she'd survive her mission I'd sent her on, and where she would go when this was over. If her kind would ever accept her back without punishment.

She'd chosen to help me. She had given me the chance I needed.

I only hoped it wasn't too late.

18

OWEN

I was empty, hollow. Claws of hunger scraped at the insides of the husk of my mind.

The pain of it twisted my limbs. My face contorted, my stomach clenched, my veins ached.

So hungry.

I tried to hold on to awareness. I tried to remember being human, feeling love. Tried to retain the lessons I'd learned as a human. *Be better. Humans aren't just food. Choose to do the right thing.*

But all I could feel was hunger, and thirst, and the overwhelming desire to sate myself. I couldn't reason anymore. Everything kept fading away into visions of blood, of feast, of the end to cravings. Of crimson flowing from a smooth column of neck, spilling thick across my fangs and parched tongue.

My body was strong again. I reveled in that strength. Why had I ever decided to stay human? Only some feeling made me think I wanted that, a feeling I'd forgotten. I could almost thank Adelle for changing me back, except I knew her reasons why.

"Damn it, Adelle. Free me!" I shook my arms in the chains that still held me, not strong enough to break free. "I must feed."

She floated into view and patted me like a child. "My, my, you seem hungry enough already."

I growled a response. I didn't even care anymore that she'd turned me. I kept telling myself I should, that I didn't want the result that she was hoping to achieve, but I'd lost the ability to care.

I'd heard and smelled Adelle feeding earlier. I'd screamed in rage and misery as the coppery scent of blood had filled the air, at the contented sounds Adelle made as she sucked at the human she had under her thrall. I was starving.

Adelle's laughter was low and taunting. "Don't worry. We'll feed you before you shrivel up like a Starved. We'll feed your love to you on a silver platter, unborn child and all. Can't you already taste her?"

My fangs were sharp against my bottom lip. I wanted Kaitlyn. But it was a dangerous sort of wanting. When I thought of her, and I thought of her constantly, all I could imagine was the deliciously sweet taste of her blood. Of how her blood, so rich and

Deathless

filled with life, reminded me of the ripe strawberries that grew wild under the bright sun.

That blood.

I wanted it.

I'd kill for it.

Adelle whispered cold breath into my ear, "We'll bring her to you soon, dear heart. Then you shall feed until you are full, and she is dead. I will see you destroy her, and yourself in the process. I long to see her blood turn you human again. How you will suffer then."

She walked away, over to a low table surrounded by plush cushions and blood-drained thralls. She picked up a flute, Ri's flute, and twirled the ancient carved wood in her fingers. "But you must be a vampire to be bound to the sun. Isn't it lucky we have so many options now? I can punish you as human and as vampire, drive you insane with emotions, then burn you in the sun, over and over. Then I can even return you from true death. We could do this forever, my love."

"I killed you once, Adelle. I can kill you again."

Her shrill laughter echoed through the stony cavern.

Dante walked out from somewhere behind me and the huge statue I was chained to. He snarled. "Are you sure this is only for revenge, *my love*? He will have to die; you know that. You should want that."

Jealous fool. "She always did like me best." I managed a hunger-weak grin.

Dante took my throat in his hand, as though he would rip my head off. I clung to one final straw of reason that told me that would be for the best. Then I wouldn't be driven to kill Strawberry.

No. Her name is Kaitlyn, she's an actress, she loves food, she loves me, and I love her. I recited the lines to myself to try to remember, but they were only words.

"Let him go, fool. You have nothing to fear from him. He's only still alive for our entertainment. Only until we can bring that woman here for him to feed upon."

"If she can even be found."

Adelle chuckled. "She will be. She will come to him, one way or another."

Dante sniffed, as though he hardly cared, and released my throat. My dry, aching throat.

So hungry ...

Memories of my first turning toppled through my thoughts, reminding me of hunts and blood, and times and people long dead. I groaned and thrashed. A fever, an animal bloodlust rode through me, making my head spin and my hands clench into fists. My nails tore at my palms, but released no pain, no blood. Adelle bled me nearly dry and gave me just enough blood to turn me but not enough

Deathless

to sustain me.

I'd be mindless soon.

I had to remember. I had to remember that her name was Kaitlyn and that I loved her. That she was carrying our child and our future within her.

My body shriveled against my shrinking heart.

Her name is …

Strawberry. She was a ripe and delicious strawberry, begging to be consumed. And I could think of no reason why I shouldn't. I couldn't think at all.

19

KAITLYN

Long dewy grass wet my ankles as Lance and I dashed to his car. It would have been faster and more inconspicuous for him to carry me, since the shrine was just up the hill from his estate, but he worried my hair or clothes were still wafting with Nemexia. I couldn't smell it anymore myself, but it wasn't a risk we could take right now.

Lance took the driver's seat and I jumped in the back, carrying a clean sweater and jeans I'd snatched on the way out. Lance grabbed the wheel, turned off all automated safety restrictions on the touchscreen, then sped along the curving mountain road.

I did my best not to crash about as I got changed while taking hairpin bends at a breakneck speed. Lance opened the front windows to keep fresh air streaming through.

"What do I need to know about this place? Is it guarded? Boobytrapped? Full of snakes?" I asked, wriggling my hips into the tight denim.

Lance kept his eyes on the road, and the amphitheater that surrounded the Sun Shrine came into view. "Might be guarded. There are monks dedicated to the shrine's rituals and protection who may be around. We'll have to work out a way to get past them."

"On it," I said. I tugged the sweater over my head and realized I'd grabbed one of Owen's instead of mine. It swam against my skin, and I hugged it there.

"I'm not really sure what to expect. I've avoided attending the ceremonies, including the most recent one for the Starved," Lance said. "It's not the sort of place vampires are dying to break into though."

I wondered how many break-ins the lethal injection rooms of human prisons had to deal with. But they weren't hiding ancient powerful artifacts.

Lance reached for something in a bag he'd brought with him, then handed it back to me. A wooden stake, made of wickedly sharp, pointed hardwood. "Here. I'm not going to use it. I don't want to risk spending the rest of my life in the Sun Shrine for killing other vampires. But you should have it." Then he muttered, "Not that what we're doing tonight isn't treasonous enough."

"Thanks," I said, and meant it. He was risking a

lot to help me, and in return I'd try to keep as many crimes directly off him as I could.

I shoved the stake into my back pocket. I felt like a character in some movie I hadn't acted in yet, and I embraced the role. Courageous Kaitlyn. Adventurous Kaitlyn. Bulletproof Kaitlyn. I was a good actor. I could be those things tonight. I could save Owen. Why did I ever think me and my acting were weak? I could do anything, be anything I needed to be. And tonight, I'd be the kick-ass treasure hunter who would find the magical artefact and tear any enemy that stood in my way to the ground.

We drove in through open gates to a small parking lot.

Outside, we could see down into the amphitheater, and make out a single golden-robed figure standing near the entrance to the ancient central temple.

"Wait for my signal. I have a plan," I said, hopping out of the car.

I wandered down the weather-smoothed stone steps toward the shrine's guardian. He watched me all the way, but didn't move. He kept his back to the massive stone slabs and dark opening behind him.

I hugged the bundle in my arms.

"Night's greetings," I said cheerfully. As I grew close, I saw that the bottom hem of his gown was a dull gray.

"And to you." He looked me up and down, and

inhaled through his nose. "Apologies, but the Sun Shrine is not open to visitors at this time."

I looked as disappointed as I could until I was right in front of him, within reach, then I shoved my bundle of dirty clothes in his face. He seemed simply insulted at first, and I hoped there was enough Nemexia left on them to knock the guy out.

He struggled, pushing the clothes away. Lance sped down to us and took hold of the monk's arms from behind, and we both fought for a long moment to keep the scent-laced clothing against his mouth. Finally, I felt the golden-clad monk weakening. He drooped, slowly, slowly, like a woozy drunk, until we could lay him onto the stone at our feet. We left the clothes there with him, close to his face so he wouldn't wake up again and surprise us during our search.

"Let's hope he was the only one," I said, and we stepped in through the largest gap between the megaliths that formed the outer curved walls of the shrine.

Up close, they were more like a series of linked dolmens than a solid wall, giving lots of spaces for sunlight to flow in that lined up again to more small vertical holes cut into the solid inner wall of the circular center. The limestone was pockmarked from the weather, the moonlight making it look silver and cratered like the moon itself.

We had to duck low to go through the entrance

into the main chamber. Inside was dim and musty, with not enough light to see by. Lance pulled a flashlight from his bag and handed it to me. I clicked it on and shone it around the space.

Before us was a mountain of ashes.

I gagged. "I thought you said those monks maintained this place. When was the last time they cleaned?"

"I said protected, and that includes the ashes. When a vampire is bound to the sun, their ashes are never cleaned away."

The ash filled the room, curving in swathes up the walls. Paths had been tracked in it here and there, leading to manacles which were barely visible on the walls under more ash. I took a tentative step forward, and my shoe sunk into the ash like it was the softest of snow. I pulled the neck of Owen's sweater up over my nose and mouth, trying to block the burnt smell.

I turned a circle in the space. Just this single, round room. The wall was made up of massive stones, and the roof had a secondary raised dome in the center, but there wasn't much else to see. "Where is the face? Marduk's face?"

Lance tipped his head toward the largest of the megaliths directly across the room from the entrance, through the deepest stretches of ash. "Should be right over there."

"Ugh, I think I would have preferred snakes." I stepped forward, and by midway across the room

I was wading through ash up to my thighs. My clothing turned gray and stiff, and my skin dried at the touch of it.

Lance stalked along behind me, silently, placing his footsteps in the holes I had made.

Something clamped onto my ankle. I clenched my teeth, swallowing my scream. I stumbled backward into Lance, and he grabbed onto me, pulling me back. My foot was still trapped, dragging the ashes and whatever was beneath along with it. Through the shifting dust, a skeletal hand wrapped around me. I kicked at it with my other foot.

More ash cleared, revealing the hand of one of the Starved. It was so emaciated it must have fallen free of its shackles and become lost, too weak to move, in the sea of vampire remains.

Its body twitched beneath a tattered robe. Its sewn-together lips ground against each other, dry as dirt. I wondered just which one it was, whether it was one of the ones who had captured me, or pinned me down on the sacrificial altar, or danced and chanted awaiting the terrible things they wished for me and my body.

I managed to shake my ankle free of its grasp, and it just lay there on the floor. It was as close to death as an immortal creature could be, and suffering more than anything deserved to suffer.

Lance's voice was hushed. "Just ignore him. He's

no threat."

It was true. He didn't even have the strength to drag himself across the floor to attempt anything.

I said in a sibilant whisper, "No, I'll deal with this."

Lance didn't question me as I drew the stake from my back pocket, didn't ask if I was sure. He knew I was.

I stood over the Starved, the stake held firm in both hands.

The Starved lifted a quivering finger, and his dirty nail split the stitches that held his lips shut. A single word wheezed from his mouth, *"Please."*

"Yes," I said as gently as possible. I lifted the stake high, then drove it downward in one long, smooth stroke that split his chest open and found what remained of his decayed heart. He curled up around the stake, like some alien caterpillar, then ash flaked off, drifting away to join the rest around us. The robe collapsed onto a pile of shrunken, bleached bones that disintegrated into nothing with a soft whooshing sound.

I stared for a moment longer, then blinking the ash from my eyes, I retrieved the stake.

Lance cleared his throat and put a hand over his chest. "I'm not entirely sure anymore if giving you the stake was a good idea."

"Maybe Joss and I can both join the vampire hunters after all this is done."

Lance looked even more conflicted.

"You don't want her to go, do you?" I asked.

"No. But I can't ask her to stay, either. Not with the punishment awaiting her."

"What's it like, to care about someone when you're a vampire?" I was genuinely curious.

"We don't. Not really. Not the way humans do. We *want* things. But we don't often care what damage our wants cause, as long as we get what we want." Lance grinned roguishly. "Which is why it's understandable that Owen gets jealous of me. If I wanted you, not much would get in my way."

"Yeah, I'd be getting in your way, for starters," I countered, pointing my stake at him.

"I don't want you though. Not like that. What I've wanted is the love you show. I've been jealous of you and Owen, seeing you together, what your love has been capable of. I want that. And I find myself wanting Joss. But I'm not sure where that leaves me, since I also want to remain a vampire."

"Conflicting wants? That actually sounds pretty human to me." I turned the stake around, holding the blunt end outwards. I placed my hand on Lance's shoulder. "What I want right now is to find this damned coin. Thank you for being here, and helping me."

"As long as I live unpunished to tell the tale, you're welcome. Otherwise, we'll have words."

Taking the stake as a bat to the ash in front of me,

Deathless

I moved through with long strides, clearing the way until I reached the wall. The ash was thicker against the stone, almost as though the cinders had fused against it, but I used the stake and my hands to scrub it clear, and soon found the rough shape of Marduk's head, carved underneath. The face was as tall as I was, and even though worn and misshapen with dusty residue, its expression was twisted in evil pleasure.

Lance shook his head at it. "Still watching the victims of the torture he designed after all these years."

It looked at me with two eyes, but the sketch of it Owen gave me only had one. I checked the copy again, and Owen had drawn a second eye on the right side in red pen. I dug and scratched all around that eye, but couldn't see anything other than stone.

I grunted in frustration.

"Let me have a go," Lance said. He stepped forward, made a fist, and jabbed swiftly at that right eye. "I never liked that guy."

The stone cracked, crumbling away.

A small chamber sat behind it, and within, the glint of gold.

"All yours," he said. "Not a chance I'm touching that thing."

All my bravado faded away at the sight of the coin within that small stone hollow. All my courage crumbled in the face of this ancient item that could make or break my future.

For all I knew, I was the one who would burn to a crisp upon touching it. I had to hope it did something that only affected vampires, not humans. I had to trust I was shown this coin in the chalice vision for a reason.

I don't have to act the part. I am *brave.*

I took a deep, steadying breath, and reached my hand in, wrapping my fingers around the cool gold.

I closed my eyes, counted to ten, and found myself still whole.

The coin was small in my palm, unevenly round, stamped with a stylized eye.

I blew out a whistling breath. "Okay, we found it. Now what?"

20

KAITLYN

We left Lance's car up a quiet back road, under the cover of an ancient pine tree. After a sniff of my hair to confirm he wasn't going to pass out, he scooped me up and ran us to the meeting point we'd arranged with Joss.

The small cabin sat on a rocky slope. The moon illuminated untended fields edged with toppled stone walls. Lance told me this was where he'd taken Owen when he'd rescued him from where the Starved kept us before. An old, abandoned farmhouse, within walking distance of where Adelle had Owen—the very same place.

No way did I ever want to go back there, into that dark cave system where we were nearly destroyed by the Starved. But I would. I was going to march right in there to save Owen. As soon as I could make this damn coin do something.

I sat in the musty cabin alone, trying all sorts of things to get the coin to work. Lance waited outside, unwilling to be around for whatever was about to happen. The danger level didn't seem high though. It felt like hours had passed, and I had nothing.

I tried pointing the coin like a gun, throwing it at things, holding it against my head and thinking really hard. I reopened the scab from the chalice vision and bled on it. I searched the coin under torchlight for symbols or clues. I held it against my eyes. I whispered wishes and magic words, abracadabra alakazam, worketh-you-fuckingeth-thingeth.

The rickety chair I sat on wobbled as I stomped my feet. "Come on!"

I needed more ideas. *Why didn't this thing come with instructions?*

Maybe it only worked in combination with some-thing else, like the flute and veil. Maybe it only worked when actually targeted at a vampire, but I wasn't going to test it on Lance.

Maybe it didn't work at all.

I thumped my forehead on the wooden table. Dust puffed up around me.

Voices came from outside. Lance was talking to someone, and then the door opened just a little. I pointed my torch and squinted.

"Joss? You made it!"

"All clear?"

"Yeah, just me and a useless chunk of gold. I swear I'm going to pawn this thing when I get back to the human world."

The door creaked as Joss came through. She was wearing her full Ebonguard uniform including the cowl, looking covert and kickass.

"Lance, you can come in too if you want. This coin isn't doing anything."

"I'm good out here, thanks," he called back.

Joss held up a clear sample bag with a couple of syringes in it. "Got it."

The Remortalis. "At least your mission was a success."

"Partially. These samples were ready for testing, but haven't yet been trialed."

"So we've got a useless coin, and some scientific concoction with unknown results? We are so winning right now."

Joss came closer and peered down at the coin on the table. "Marduk's coin. You really found it. Amazing." She reached for it, then seemed to think better and stepped back.

"It would be amazing if it did something," I grumbled. "Sorry for being a grump. Thank you for getting the cure."

She shrugged, as though it was no big deal. But

I knew it was. She'd put her whole existence on the line for me.

"And I'm glad you made it back safe. That you came back to help us at all—it means so much, and I know you've sacrificed a lot because of me."

Only Joss's eyes were visible, making it hard to judge her expression. She walked around to the other side of the table but didn't sit down. "I think I realized early on that I was becoming more loyal to you than I was to my orders. That was why I hid the hunter's gear. I knew I needed options, being so close to three strikes and knowing an order might have come that I couldn't or wouldn't follow."

"Like when you said you'd kill me if ordered to?" I smirked.

Joss chuckled. "Like that. I feel like you've changed me. Maybe just being close to you for extended periods, just the scent of your blood, is enough to produce sensations of empathy."

Lance called in through the open door, "There might be something to that. It's been so long since I fed from you, but I still feel ... different."

"And I have never fed from you," Joss pointed out, as though it were a contest.

"Did you vampires ever think it could be nothing to do with blood?" I sighed. "There are human studies that show simply being treated kindly, or witnessing empathy, makes people more empathetic. Could it

be that I'm not magically changing you, but just changing your minds? I mean, I know scientifically my blood does something. But ideas are powerful too."

"That they are," Joss agreed.

And here I had been feeling useless and weak for being human. But it was the parts of me that were human, my ideals and morals, and ability to feel love and empathy, that had brought Joss and Lance to my side as allies. Maybe even friends.

I lifted the coin from the table and balanced it in the palm of my hand. "Although, ideas aren't exactly going to help much when the Synedrion catches up to us, having escaped and stolen their precious relic. And they aren't going to help get Owen back from Adelle and Dante."

Joss leaned against the edge of the table. "We might have to give up on that coin, make a plan around using the Remortalis. I can try to get Owen out of there, and if he's turned, bring him back here for the cure."

"It would be three vamps plus who-knows-what-else against one," I said. "I can't let you go and do that alone."

"Neither can I," Lance agreed from outside.

"And if Owen's turned, will he be willing to go with you?" *Will he be at all the man I remember? Will he be the cold, calculating creature who imprisoned*

me? Or will he be something else?

Concern flashed over Joss's eyes. "Hard to say."

"And the Remortalis might not work. It might take too long, and Adelle and Dante or the Synedrion could find us at any moment. This is only going to work if we can take out Adelle and Dante, and I can't ask you guys to stack that onto your list of crimes for helping me."

"We could go to the Synedrion for help," Lance called in.

I snorted. "Us criminals? They haven't helped us at the best of times, and if Owen has been turned, I might lose my only chance to turn him back." I eyed the pack that had belonged to the Blade of Alam. "Got any Nemexia left?"

"Nope, used the last of it getting out of the lab."

And the sunlight gun had disappeared into the forest after the fall and was probably smashed to bits. "Absinthe Molotov cocktails? Anything?"

Joss shook her head.

"Then we sneak in, you guys jab Adelle and Dante with the Remortalis, and I let Owen feed on me until he changes back to human. Then we get our asses out of there."

"No," Joss said firmly. "I could only get two doses. And I'm keeping one of them."

"What?"

Joss straightened up and walked over to the other

side of the room, her back turned. "I don't know what's going to happen after this. I want to help you get Owen back, but after that, I have to go my own way. I cared for you too much, and I've lost my whole identity for it. Being an Ebonguard was my life. And I can't be that anymore. I might not even be able to be a vampire anymore. So I'm keeping one of the doses. I don't know if it works, or if I'll have to use it, but at least I can use it as leverage, a bargaining chip, if I need to."

I didn't want to admit she was right, that it was only fair, that I knew she couldn't easily get her hands on more, that the Remortalis was as valuable to her future as it was to mine. I had to do something. I didn't know for certain if Owen had been turned or not, but either way they'd be torturing him. Every moment we wasted here, he suffered.

I was so frustrated I said, "I tell you what. We'll flip for it. Heads, you win and keep one of the doses. Tails and let me have it, and we do my plan and work out the rest later."

Joss turned around and glared at me. "This isn't up for—"

Before she could finish her sentence, I flipped the coin into the air.

The coin flew up, flipping over and over in the dim light, hovering and spinning.

Gaining speed. Not falling back into my waiting hand.

A brilliant blast of light erupted from the coin. Everything stood out in sharp, stark relief, bright light and black shadows, before even that was lost and there was only burning white.

Joss was screaming. Outside, Lance was screaming.

My skin grew hot, and my eyes watered, eyelids screwed shut but still stinging from the blast. I tried to duck but there was no escape. It was like a nuclear weapon had gone off, or a new sun had been born within that room.

The coin landed on the floor with a bell-like tinkle, but I still couldn't see. The light dimmed, slowly, and my vision swam with burned-in spots. I smelled smoke.

"Joss!" I screamed.

21

KAITLYN

"Joss!" I cried out again when there was no answer. "Lance?" I yelled, needing his help, and hoping he was there to give it. No reply.

I blinked, trying to get my vision to clear. There was no need for the torch, as a low level of light still lingered and reflected around the room, as though re-absorbing into the coin.

When I spotted the smoking mound of Ebonguard uniform, my first instinct was to turn back the other way and run as fast as I could. The stench of burning was unbearable.

But then she shifted, moaning. The sound of her agony split my eardrums. *What have I done?*

I ran to Joss and landed on my knees beside her. Then I heard Lance shouting from outside, cursing.

"Don't come in, there's still light, and Joss is ...

He appeared at the door, slouching and singed, smoke drifting from his clothes. He held his arm up over his face, and even the low light in the room made his skin bubble and blister. Then he was kneeling beside us, scooping his arms under Joss.

"Get back outside," I cried.

He stumbled, his face riddled with agony. He lagged, burning more with each step. Even my human skin felt hot all over, red and raw, like I had a bad sunburn. I put my shoulder against Lance and helped push the two of them outside into the cool night air.

The three of us landed in the grass. I coughed and choked, the terrible, charred, fatty smell of burned flesh filling my lungs.

It was a nightmare. Joss had stopped screaming. She just twitched beneath the armor that should have protected her. That *had* protected her from normal daylight. It was the only reason she was still here at all.

Lance wheezed out, "What just happened?"

"I finally figured out how the coin works. And I wish I hadn't."

Lance's face was red-raw, peeling like a bad sunburn, but flaking ash instead of flesh.

"Are you going to ..." I didn't know a polite way to ask if someone was about to spontaneously combust.

Deathless

"I'll heal. It's just the surface. Not sure about Joss though."

He leaned over close to her, pulling away her cowl in a flurry of gray flakes. He covered his mouth, as though he might vomit. "Her eyes. They're gone."

"Gone?" I squeaked. I couldn't even bring myself to look.

"Burnt right out. Fuck. She needs blood, and now, if she has any chance of regenerating."

My mouth hung open as all the implications of Lance's words flew through my mind. Because I was the only human there. "You know what my blood might do to her."

"She's past the point of regenerating on her own. She needs blood now, or she'll keep turning to ash. She just needs a little, to regenerate enough to stop the burning."

If I did this, then maybe I could fix it. "A small amount shouldn't be enough change her," I reasoned, talking myself into it. "Okay. Okay. I'll do it." My voice shook and broke. The idea I was going to willingly offer myself up to her fangs knocked my heart into high gear.

"I'll stop her when she's had enough."

"You better," I warned. It wasn't just me at risk; it was the baby too. I doubted Lance would be able to pull Joss off me if she were at her full strength. But right now, she barely seemed alive.

Lance took my wrist and placed it against Joss's mouth, or what remained of it. I still couldn't look. But I could feel crumbling ash over sharp fangs.

Nothing happened. Lance forced my wrist against Joss's teeth, puncturing them with his pressure, and I stifled a cry.

Then my blood flowed. Slowly at first, and then a strong suction built through my veins. The pain was intense, and dizziness swirled through me.

The remains of her lips around my wrist began to change, shifting and regrowing, and she let out a feral growl.

Her hands came up, still in black gloves, and joined Lance's grip on my arm. I panicked, trying to struggle away. "Enough. Stop!"

Lance let go of me and pried Joss's hands away, then pulled my wrist from her mouth.

She reeled, trying to claw her way back to me, wanting more. I finally looked at her face, a sickeningly twisted mix of ash and regrowing flesh and flecks of blood. I still couldn't see her eyes under it all.

Lance dragged her up off the grass, taking her back into the cabin where the light had completely subsided. He fought to pull her through the main room into the bedroom, the only other room in the small building. He shut the door behind them. Thrashing and crashing and fighting sounds burst through the walls.

Deathless

I sat on the damp ground, put pressure on my ravaged wrist, and tried not to weep.

Time passed, and the sounds from the room stopped. The night felt like it had gone on forever, and I wanted to lay down in the dewy grass and sleep, but I couldn't. Not now I had the coin, and the cure, and at least one of them worked.

I staggered inside, then fell back to my knees again in the cabin, crawling around to recover the coin. It had landed just under the seat I'd been sitting on before, and I picked it up delicately then squeezed it into my palm, pressing it there, as though making it a permanent part of myself.

I went to the bag Lance had brought and rummaged through it, almost weeping again to see he'd thrown some food in there for me. Just a handful of individually wrapped cake treats, but they were like sugary cloudy bliss to eat, and replenished some energy. I scoffed them all down in an instant.

I was still unsteady on my feet, but I couldn't wait any longer. It was time to go after Owen.

I lifted my hand to knock at the door when I heard a voice coming through.

"I'm sorry. I could have let you drink more, but I didn't want ..."

I held my breath, waiting, and hoping for a reply.

"I understand. You didn't want me to change, but I am changed."

Joss. She was alive, conscious, talking. But changed? Surely, she didn't drink enough to turn her human.

"It might not be permanent," Lance offered.

The first drink shouldn't be. It hadn't been with Lance. But what if my blood had gotten stronger? No one had drunk from me since I became pregnant.

"What color are they?" Joss asked. "My eyes?"

I couldn't bear it, and pushed through into the room to see for myself.

Joss sat on the edge of the bed and turned to the sound of me coming in, but didn't look directly at me. Her normally black vampire eyes were the gray of an overcast summer.

"Kaitlyn?" she asked, as though confused.

"Yeah, yeah, it's me."

She blinked. Her eyes shifted again to find my voice, and it hit me.

She's not human. She's blind. Her eyes, her skin, had all regrown, but not fully recovered. Her hair was still pink around the back, but the front was all a dark brown, grown back in its natural color.

"I'm so sorry," I said.

Her expression held a vulnerability I'd never seen before. But I was still getting used to seeing her face.

"I'm fine. Really. Ebonguard are trained to be just as efficient without our eyesight." She flinched a little on the word Ebonguard. We all knew she wasn't that anymore.

"You might still regenerate fully, in time," Lance said softly. He was mostly healed too, but there were still some raw spots on his hands and face that I had to look away from.

The question of what would happen if her eyesight didn't regenerate dropped us all awkwardly into silence.

Joss's lips grew tight. "Stop looking at me like that."

"Like what?"

"I don't know, but I can tell you're looking. I will be fine. You two go, go and use that damned coin on someone who deserves it."

"I'm staying," Lance said.

"I don't need your help," she argued.

"I'm sure you don't. But maybe you need some company. Just until your eyesight comes back." Lance glanced over at me, and I nodded. Someone should stay with her. This wasn't the time to be alone, even for someone like Joss. He smiled at me. "Also, I have no intention of ever being around you and that coin, if you are going to use it again."

"Same," said Joss.

"Fair enough," I agreed. "You two have helped so much already. I've got this now."

I hesitated for a moment, then stepped forward and hugged Lance, and then Joss, squeezing her extra tight. Lance walked me to the door and pointed the way, and in the far distance I could just make out the little mud-brick cottage that I recognized, and that held the entrance to a world of terror beneath.

The temperature had dropped, a strong northerly wind blowing frost through the air, and I shivered. Lance gave me his jacket. "Good luck."

"Thanks. See you soon … I hope."

I picked up one of the Remortalis syringes, and the coin, and put the stake in my back pocket, then took to the road. I slushed through the long grass and along worn goat tracks. There was a brush of color on one rim of the horizon, a rosy-pink glow of hope, and promise of future days.

And now, I carried my own sun in the palm of my hand. I only hoped I wouldn't have to use it on Owen to protect myself and our baby. Some of the scenes the chalice showed me have proven to be true. I helped make them become reality, but could I keep shaping the future? There might be no escape from the other horrors shown in that blood-red vision.

22

KAITLYN

As I walked, I plucked some stitches free in an inside hem of Lance's jacket and placed the syringe and coin into the inner lining. I was about to hand myself over to a den of evil, and I didn't want my only chances of survival taken from me. I just had to get in as far as I could, use the cure on Owen, then flip the coin. *Sure. Easy.*

The coat was too big for me, and it hung loosely from my narrow shoulders. I drew it closer as I reached the tumbledown cottage. Dead vines clustered around the walls, and the smell of something old and dirty rose from the tunnel inside. The wind smelled sour and bitter, like even nature knew there was something awful here, something evil.

The lair of the Starved.

A thrall stood at the entrance, guarding with glazed eyes. His sun-worn skin and strong hands were those of someone who had farmed his whole life. When I moved near him, he grabbed my wrist and started shambling down into the tunnel.

"You can let go. I'm going that way anyway," I said. But I knew he could hear no one but his masters, nothing but their orders. I was an intruder, and I would be taken to them.

At least I wouldn't have to wander the torch-lit tunnels aimlessly on my own.

We went past the dungeon, the cells Owen and I had once been kept in, and the tunnel led from there in a direction I knew. The way to the main chamber, with the hideous, massive statue, and the stone altar. I tried to prepare myself for what I would find there, for even being in that space again.

And then we were there.

"Isn't this cozy," I muttered.

Adelle and Dante lounged together on a low make-shift bed, amongst piles of plush cushions in reds and golds. My approach ended their game, which had been flicking drops of what looked like blood out of a bowl toward the howling, feral, nightmare version of the man I loved. Their attention shot my way as the thrall dragged me toward them.

Fangs bared, Owen turned his attention to me as well. He inhaled a long, deep breath, then went wild, jarring at the chains that held him in place, dangling from the same statue I'd once been bound to.

That was it. He was turned. He was a vampire. A taunted, tortured, and starved vampire. His cheeks were sunken in, his eyes were dark, and I could see the hunger all over him. And here I was, walking in as the most delicious thing he had known in four hundred years.

Owen ... I hope this works.

"What do we have here?" Adelle looked honestly surprised.

"Didn't mean to interrupt. Actually, no, I did. That's why I came." I shook my wrist free of the thrall, who seemed happy to let me go now I'd been noticed by his masters. His job complete, he wandered away.

Dante got to his feet and growled. "How did you find us?"

"She's a sly one." Adelle slowly raised herself, looking me over. "But it saves us having to go and bring you in. Isn't that nice? We were going to wait until Owen was even hungrier, but I think he's probably hungry enough."

I nodded, already knowing what she alluded to. "You turned him, starved him, and were going to make him feed on me. Get your petty revenge. And then what? Be on the run for the rest of your immortal lives? Until Adelle turns on you too, Dante, of course."

Adelle snapped her fingers and the thrall came back. "She's awfully cocky. Search her for weapons."

The thrall patted me down awkwardly, and found the stake that was jutting from the back pocket of my pants. He yanked it out and tossed it away into the corner of the room. Good. I'd left it there as a decoy. I didn't need it anyway.

Adelle seemed amused by my pointy stick. She wandered over to a table and leaned on it, picking up a very old-looking black veil and toying with it. "Come on then. Let's begin the show, shall we?"

She made a little shooing noise with her mouth, and gestured with her eyes.

I did as she wanted. I forced myself to walk forward, bringing myself closer and closer to the being of only fangs and bloodlust in front of me. Owen. But not Owen. A monster in the body of the man I loved. My body shook violently as I looked upon everything I had been afraid of.

Dante walked over to Adelle and wrapped an arm around her waist, lust in his eyes. "Smell that warm, ripe human flesh, Owen. So easily torn, so easily parted with your teeth to reveal the sweet nectar inside. Doesn't it just drive you insane?"

Adelle loosed a high-pitched giggle as Dante mimicked feeding on her neck.

I ignored them, edging carefully toward my goal.

"Owen?" My voice cracked, shattered. I tried to

hold it together. "You in there at all?"

His only reply was gnawing, frothing, bestial rage.

"Do you remember me? Or this?" I held up the ring I wore, that he'd left for me. "Or this?" I placed that hand over my belly.

Nothing in his expression changed. His shirt was gone, and every muscle was tensed to the extreme. The chains groaned as he strained toward me. With a metallic screech, one chain broke free. He swiped his newly freed hand at me, clawing the air an inch in front of my nose.

Adelle cheered and Dante applauded.

I flinched, but held my ground. There was no reaching him now. The coin was my secret weapon, but I couldn't use it yet or he would burn. I wouldn't do that to him. The man I loved was still there, somewhere, under the vampire curse and the hunger.

I reached into the inner lining of the jacket, took the syringe in one hand, and the coin in the other.

"Owen? I love you." I stabbed the syringe into his chest and pushed the plunger. He roared, and broke his final chain.

He stood there, staring down at the thing sticking out of his torso.

Adelle yelled, furious, "What is that? What are you doing?"

Owen brushed the syringe away, shook his head, locked eyes with me, and growled.

Then he lunged at me.

Nothing. I did nothing. It didn't work.

I staggered backward, trying to get away, but Owen pounced upon me like a jungle cat, and I hit the mountain of cushions behind me. Adelle's laughter echoed throughout the huge chamber. Owen took his first tearing bite of my neck, plunging his teeth in deeper than I'd ever known.

I screamed.

"No, Owen, no!" I tried to push him off. Tried to fight. He pinned me to the floor, gulping so fast my whole body convulsed.

Adelle came closer. The image of her seemed to swim, wavy between the dark patches that overtook my vision. "Yes, oh yes, this is beautiful." She twirled the veil in her hands, placed it on her head, and skipped around, as the man I loved tried to drink every last drop of my life.

Tears flowed faster than my blood and I knew what I had to do. I had to live. And that meant every vampire in this room had to die.

Including Owen.

My arm was outstretched on the floor, stuck under Owen's body. The coin within my palm was hard and warm from my skin. I just hoped I had the strength to flick my wrist …

I wailed in pain, in grief, as the coin flew from my fingers, up into the air above Owen as he fed. Lying on my back under him, as the world faded away, I saw it hover, spinning, faster and faster. And then all the world was light.

And pain.

And fire.

Above me, Owen burned. He reeled back and off me, curling into a ball, turning gray, flaking away.

Bright and harsh like the outlines of distant suns, Adelle and Dante went up in flames, crumbling into ash.

The light filled every space, but darkness had entered me, filled me whole, and I faded. Light and dark competed to steal my existence. The last thing I saw was the coin landing in a pool of my own blood.

23

OWEN

Everything hurt. I folded in on myself. Flesh on fire. Hunger burning away, from all-consuming to consumed by agony. I could only think one thought …

This is … finally … the end of me.

And then the smallest flutter. A lurching pressure in my chest.

Bu-bump.

Bu-bump.

I tried to draw in air, desperate for it, needing oxygen like I hadn't a moment before. I choked on a thick layer of dust. My body had seized up, hands like rigid claws, spine rolled up in a fetal ball. My feet cramped, and my eyes were crusted closed. Everything felt hot and dry. I was encased in ash. It floated into my nose and throat, tasting of blood and bitter regrets. I had wanted Kaitlyn's blood. Adelle had turned me, starved me to the point of madness, and made me feed. I'd fed on Kaitlyn.

And I'd burned, but I'd survived. *Because I was human again.*

My memory flowed around patchy images of torture and madness.

It delivered me memories from what felt like so long ago. Kaitlyn, swimming in the pool of the house where I held her captive. Kaitlyn, eating, her tongue licking crumbs from one corner of her mouth. Kaitlyn's eyes crinkling, and her head tilting back to expose the slim arch of her neck—not for feeding on, but in laughter. Kaitlyn, looking wistfully at the waves, and telling me she'd never be happy unless she was free. Kaitlyn, staring into my eyes and telling me she was pregnant.

I broke away from the agony that imprisoned me, soaring on memories of her and me together, of the love and blood that made me human. Of the woman who'd made me whole and happy for the first time in my long and too-lonely life.

I dared to move, pushing free of the of ash around me, emerging from my chrysalis. I worried for a moment that when I stood up, I'd crumble into nothingness. But I didn't. My skin burned and tingled but was whole and unblemished. My body ached all over, yet my heart pounded in my chest, throbbing away with life, real life.

Thanks to Kaitlyn.

Kaitlyn.

I turned and saw her on the floor beside me, motionless and covered in blood. She'd saved me. Injected me with something? Or was it her blood that had changed me? Or both? Then she'd flipped a coin that had filled the room with sunlight. *Did that really happen?*

It had, and it was *devastating.* Marduk's relic? She must have found it.

And I'd almost killed her.

I tried to kick my brain into gear. I had to act fast if I was going to save her. Her lips had turned blue from blood loss, and her neck had been savaged. *By me.*

I choked that thought away. That was Adelle's doing. I couldn't, and wouldn't, be responsible for it. I was not that monster anymore and never would be again.

I scanned the area around us. Piles of ash on the floor were all that remained of Adelle and Dante. A few thralls stood stunned around the room, slowly coming back to themselves. I hoped they would come to their senses quickly and free themselves of this house of horrors.

Beside Kaitlyn, a glint of gold caught my eye. The coin she'd flipped.

I snatched it up, and then cradled her into my arms. She was clammy and still, her pulse slow and weak. I couldn't stay there any longer, not for the thralls or for anything. I had to get Kaitlyn to safety, wherever that was for us now.

I carried her out through the tunnels, squinting as sunlight came into view.

Parked right outside the entrance was a long black car. I tensed.

A solidly tinted window rolled down just a fraction, and I heard Bertha's voice.

"Quick, bring her in here."

I hesitated, but I had few other options. I had no clear plan in mind, but would do anything to save Kaitlyn, even go back to the Synedrion.

The door opened as I dashed toward it, then it quickly slammed once I was inside.

I laid Kaitlyn as gently as I could along the seat, leaning her against my body.

Bertha sat on the long seat facing ours. Ewan, the Synedrion's doctor for humans, was beside her.

"Had quite the adventure, I see?" She tapped her fingers on crossed arms.

"Are you going to help Kaitlyn?" I snarled.

"Of course," she said, and the doctor got to work. He hung a couple of IV bags up by the car's coat hangers and then hooked Kaitlyn up before seeing to the wound on her neck. I noticed another bite

mark on her wrist, and wondered if it was from my fangs as well.

Everything had all happened so fast, and I had no idea what state things were at with the Synedrion, or where we now stood. I looked between Kaitlyn and Bertha, unsure. "How? Why?"

"Lance tipped me off. He was awfully cryptic about trying to warn me not to involve the rest of the Synedrion, and how I'd be sorry if I treated you two badly. He seemed conflicted about it, but it looks like he made the right decision."

Bertha pointed at the liquids running into Kaitlyn's veins. "Something Shirina cooked up, since Kaitlyn is so prone to blood loss. A special replenishment formula just for her. I thought it might come in handy."

I could only nod, confused, trying to catch up. "Where is Lance?" And more importantly, why hadn't he come for us himself?

"Gone, somewhere. He can come back, as we have no proof of him being directly involved in the kidnapping of Kaitlyn, theft from the lab, and destruction of parts of the Sun Shrine. It looks more like Joss was involved in all of that."

I raised both eyebrows. They had been busy, and there must have been more to the story. I hoped Kaitlyn could tell me soon, but she was still unconscious and deathly cold.

I rubbed her fingers, hoping to warm them with

mine. The doctor shooed me away, needing her hands to clip heart monitors onto, to slide cannulas in. I let him, and waited impatiently, a lump in my throat.

"You're human?" Bertha stared at my mouth, and I wiped at it, discovering it was wet with Kaitlyn's blood. I took an offered wet-wipe and cleaned myself up as best I could.

I quickly explained what Adelle and Dante had done, how they'd made me feed on Kaitlyn. I glossed over how Kaitlyn had managed to defeat them both, muttering something about stakes and being too out of it to see for sure what had happened as Kaitlyn's blood changed me.

Bertha tapped a few controls on the touch screen beside her, and the automated car began moving away. "I've already called in some Ebonguard to check the place over. To see what can be recovered. But for now, let's get you two home."

"That place isn't my home." Kaitlyn's voice was a raspy whisper, her eyes still closed and her body still.

I brushed my hand down her cheek, cleaning away drying blood and ash. "Shush," I chided, despite loving the sound of her voice, loving that she had awakened. "Rest."

"Can't rest. Need to kill Lance for snitching on us. Would have been a clean getaway," she grumbled.

"You can't even open your eyes," I replied, my smile growing.

"Can too." Her eyelids twitched, and her nose wrinkled, but her eyes didn't open. "Maybe later." Her forehead wrinkled. "I thought I'd killed you." She turned her cheek into my open palm. "You feel warm. The Remortalis worked."

Bertha's eyebrows both shot way up.

Kaitlyn gasped. "The ... the *thing*. The THING. Owen, did you *get the thing*? We need the thing."

"The thing?"

She struggled, as though trying to get up from the seat and go back to where we came from. She whispered, "My lucky coin."

I squeezed her softly in my arms, made my voice soothing. "I got the thing."

She relaxed, right away. "Thank fuck. That thing is our ticket."

"Is she okay? She seems to be having a strange reaction to the medication," the doctor inquired, leaning across to take Kaitlyn's pulse.

"You're a strange reaction," she retorted. Her eyes finally opened, clear and green, looking up at me.

"I think she's fine. I think she's going to be more than fine." I kissed her on the forehead. My brave, resilient, amazing Kaitlyn.

"What about"—her voice caught, and her eyes turned glossy—"what about the pregnancy?"

"Have you had any bleeding? Abdominal discomfort?" the doctor asked.

"Only bleeding from the neck, which I know isn't the kind of bleeding you were being vague about, but it was a lot." She looked back at me. "Not your fault."

"I know."

The doctor shrugged. "Too early to say. We can keep you monitored and do some tests when we're in a better medical facility than the back of a car on a bumpy dirt road."

Kaitlyn nodded, then wrapped her hands around mine. I felt the brush of metal and saw a glint of diamond.

"You're wearing the ring. You found it," I said.

She held her right hand out, looking at it herself. "Yeah. I hope you don't mind."

"Well, actually ..." I delicately plucked the ring from her finger. "This is a family heirloom. I was supposed to give it to the woman I wanted to spend my entire life with, but then I waited centuries without finding a true love. I didn't think I'd ever use it."

"Oh." Her hands closed up, and drew away, but I took her left hand back into mine.

It was over. I knew it, and she did too. This nightmare was coming to a close. The cure had seemed to work, and they had no more reason to hold us prisoner. There was the chance Alam's hunters might come for us, or the Synedrion would want to dispose of us, but now we had our *ticket*. Kaitlyn had acquired for us something that no vampire would stand against. We were not going to be hidden away anymore, kept from our lives out of fear of anyone or anything. We were done living in twilight and darkness. We were done with vampires.

We were ready to move on with our lives. Free. Together.

We jostled against each other in the back of the car, and her drip tubes tangled between us. We were both covered in ash and blood and sweat and tears.

"Kaitlyn French, will you marry me?"

"Is this real?" Tears and laughter streamed from Kaitlyn. "Are you really asking me to marry you?"

"I am." I held the ring in front of her. She still leaned against me, almost in my lap, so I couldn't kneel. But I also couldn't wait a moment longer. "I have waited so many lifetimes to find a love like ours. You have made me human, and made me want to be a better person. You've saved my life and my heart over and over, and now they belong to you, entirely. I want to spend every moment of my existence with you. You are my future."

Kaitlyn's eyes fluttered closed, and for a moment I feared she'd fallen unconscious again. But a smile spread, brightening her whole face, and she looked up at me. "Ask me again."

"Will you marry me?"

"Yes!" she shouted.

I slid the ring onto her correct finger.

Bertha and Ewan clapped politely.

I bent down and placed a tender kiss onto Kaitlyn's lips. The kiss grounded me, filled me with a joy of life that felt like it could shine out of my skin. Even here, even now, in this terrible place, in the midst of so much awfulness, there was light and love and laughter, and I could feel all those things thanks to her. My heart swelled, fuller with every breath.

"Ouch," Kaitlyn mumbled between our lips.

I supported her head and lowered her into my lap, letting her rest.

She smiled, and that smile grew cheeky. "I do want to marry you, Owen. But ..."

"But?"

"The only way to stop people from thinking I was in rehab is to tell them the truth."

Bertha frowned. "You can't—"

"I'm going to have to tell them I fell in love with an incredible man and ran off to Europe to be with him. That means you can't hide anymore. You have to start going out with me in public."

My lips spread in a wide smile. "I'm looking forward to it."

Kaitlyn turned to address Bertha. "And I can do whatever I want now. I'm not going to be your prisoner anymore. I'm going to make my own rules. We will be walking away from this shadow world,

the Synedrion, all of this." She turned back to me, smiled, then closed her eyes. "As soon as I can walk again. And no one will dare to stop us."

Epilogue

KAITLYN

The castle—*my* castle, I could still barely believe— was alive with the sounds of laughter and music. They flowed into the ballroom from out on the grounds where the guests were gathering, and my body swayed in time with the slow tempo playing. Flowers covered every surface, red roses and white wisteria emerging out of beds of wild strawberries, their lush green leaves spotted with ruby red fruit. Their fragrance filled in the air and I breathed the aroma in with a large smile on my face. Under that scent was just the faint hint of the perfume both Owen and I wore every day now; a custom blend on a base of unscented Nemexia essence.

Caterers were setting up the tables, decking them with white linens and fine china, antique silverware

and delicate wine glasses. The floors, solid white marble, were gleaming and ready to be danced upon. I was meant to be doing final checks and getting ready, but I just stood there, taking in all the fairy tale gloriousness.

"Aren't you supposed to be dressed by now?"

The familiar voice swung me around. "Bertha? But it's, uh ..."

I glanced from the huge windows through which bright daylight streamed in, back to her.

She chuckled. "Don't worry. I'm not going to blow up and ruin your nuptials. I took the cure. It's still in early stages. Lin and Shirina want to observe some of the first cured for a long period before it's widely available, but I talked them into letting me be part of their trial."

I snatched in a breath and looked her over. She seemed nearly the same as before, pale skin and pixie-cut, her teenage body in a perfectly fitted red gown suited to a femme fatale. And her eyes were green and brown? Heterochromatic, one of each color.

"Wow. You look amazing. Although, you're going to have to learn to dress your age. I suppose. Eh, screw it, what is age really, anyway?"

"Something I'm looking forward to experiencing, that's what." Her smile held a soft and wonderful emotion. "You have no idea how much it sucks to have people consider you immature just because your body stopped aging at sixteen."

I barked a laugh. "I know people who would kill for that."

"Yes, but would they be killed for it?"

"You've clearly not met the guests from Hollywood yet."

She snorted. "It is good to see you again, Kaitlyn, and you look well." Her gaze went to my belly. "You must be happy that it's ..."

She paused. I knew what she meant without her having to finish that sentence.

I was showing now, just a little. The baby was growing normally, and the relief over that was so sweet and pure that I often hugged that feeling to myself, glowing just to remember that this child was ours. Not mine and a vampire's. Ours, mine and Owen's. Two human beings having a nice, normal human baby.

"Very happy. Now, I know I didn't send any invites to vampires for our wedding, you know, given the time of day."

Bertha shrugged, and unabashedly picked a strawberry from one of my floral displays and popped it in her mouth. She made a face. "Oh, they are so tart!"

"The wild ones are," I said. "Why are you here?"

She held something up for me to see. "I noticed this out on the gifts table. Thought I should bring it to your attention sooner rather than later."

A black envelope with a silver stamp showing a blade surrounded by a ring of fire.

Dread flickered over me. "From the Blades of Alam?" There it was, proof they knew of us, and knew where to find us. But also proof they hadn't done anything with that knowledge, yet.

"Should I open it?" I asked.

"Well yes. That is why I brought it in for you."

"Is it safe?"

Bertha managed a perfect teenaged eye-roll. "I doubt it's going to explode poison all over you."

"For all we know, it might. If this ruins my wedding day, I am going to be very upset." I took the envelope gingerly and slit the side open with a finger. My eyes darted back and forth over the letter, and then a smile appeared.

"It's from … an old friend!" *Joss! She's okay!*

It was a short message, details terse and minimal, in true Joss fashion.

"You have friends in the Blades?" Bertha asked with raised eyebrows.

I bit my lip at my slip up. "No, of course not. I was being sarcastic, you know? Like, oh, my old buddies that tossed me out an airplane that time!"

Yep, I was still relying heavily on my acting skills to keep me out of trouble. I looked over the letter again. Joss didn't explicitly say she was part of the Blades of Alam now, or whether she was still a vampire, or whether she was still blind. I swallowed my remaining guilt over that. I wondered whether Lance was still keeping her company.

"It's an invitation to us, Owen and me, letting us know that we would be welcome to join the Blades."

Bertha asked softly, as though without any judgement, "Would you be interested in that? Becoming an official vampire hunter?"

I cackled out a hard laugh. "No way! I don't want anything to do with any of that ever again."

She considered me for a moment and nodded. "Apart from coming across the letter, the reason I'm here today, is that now I'm cured, I've become a sort of human liaison to the Synedrion. For a while at least. I wanted to let you know that there are some new laws in place."

"We're not bound to vampire law," I pointed out, but Bertha continued.

"It has been made illegal to give a vampire the cure without their consent, by vampire or human. Luckily, the law came into effect after you did so to Owen—yes, we found the syringe—so we are letting that one slide. They're also forming new laws around the treatment of humans in general."

I smacked her hand away as she reached for another strawberry. "Smart, since some of you are becoming human."

I didn't bother mentioning that the ethical treatment

of animals hadn't exactly been a deterrent to humans when it came to food, and vampires are way more ruthless than even we are when hungry. "How will all this affect us? Me, Owen, our child?"

"You're all protected under our new laws. Any who follow Synedrion law will not harm you."

I nodded in a sharp, damn-straight kind of way. But that still left those who didn't follow Synedrion law. My spine straightened. So be it. I had the coin, and I had survived it all even before that. If anyone, or anything, came for me or Owen or our child, I was ready. We were free from vampire claims and rules. We could protect ourselves now and didn't need bodyguards anymore, no Ebonguard hiding in the shadows.

We'd only spent a single day with the Synedrion after dealing with Adelle and Dante. Just enough time for me to get the strength back to be able to walk away from there forever. After explaining the power of the coin, no one came after us, despite grumbles of us stealing a precious relic. I knew that Ri's flute and, much to the Synedrion's surprise, Tiamat's ring had been recovered from the lair. They believed Dante must have had it all along, and didn't connect it to Owen. Damkina's veil burnt up when Adelle did. At least that meant no more vampires returning from the dead.

"The lab is close to cracking artificial blood as well, it's already in trials too. Seems the pregnancy was all that was needed to fulfill that prophecy after all," Bertha said.

"I hope so. I don't want anyone coming after my child," I replied. I had so many hopes for this child, and its future. Hope it would be healthy, and safe. But maybe I could only hope for those things as much as any parent could hope that for their child. Even the mundane world and life had risks and challenges. And I was ready to be there for it all.

"I don't think they'd dare." Bertha reached out and brushed a finger over the coin that I wore around my neck. Owen had it set into a circle of gold, one that allowed the coin to spin freely at a moment's notice, if it was needed. It wobbled, and Bertha stilled it under her fingertip.

I cleared my throat. "I actually do need to go and get dressed."

Bertha nodded, and took a few steps away. "I'll be in the audience, cheering you guys on."

I watched her go, watched her touching the flowers, smelling them, stealing another strawberry, and turning her face to the sunlight.

Then I went back to the dressing room set aside for me. It was quiet, and I stood there for a little while, just breathing.

Soon, everyone was there with me, my family and bridesmaids, helping me to dress. It was noisy and joyful, and I laughed and cried as the artist tried

to get my makeup done, scolding me happily as she re-did my eye-liner.

I was enveloped in hugs and giggles, and all the nightmares of the past fell away in the folds of antique lace and silk. Before I knew it, I was dressed and ready. My dark hair was pulled up high and piled onto the top of my head in curling tendrils bejeweled with silver leaves. The dress was long, flowing, with an Empire waistline to help hide my growing baby bump. It swished and swayed around me like the most delicate bell ever created, and I longed to dance in it. The veil, long and sheer, trailed down to my ankles and mingled its folds into those of my glorious dress.

I took a deep and very shaky breath. I'd never imagined myself married, not really. I'd been too busy imagining myself as an actor. I'd also never believed in true love until I fell in love with Owen. Tears misted my vision. It was so perfect, all of it. The stuff of dreams and fantasy, but real and mine.

A sweet, simple joy hit me hard, right in the chest. Joy that I could go be here, getting married to the man I loved, and that he could be present in my public life and not have to be a hidden figure just moving through the background of it all.

That was a true and immense pleasure. He didn't have to hide from vampires who would kill him for being cured, or me for creating the cure. With the first vampires already choosing to become human again, soon there would be many like Owen. The world had changed so much, so fast. I was still constantly scared for our child to be, but also in awe of all they would experience in their life. I supposed those feelings were a core part of becoming a parent.

I clutched at my trailing bouquet and then the door opened. I stepped out of the dressing room and into a short hallway with my eyes still watery, my breath coming hard and fast, and my heart ticking along at a happy and hectic pace.

The music started and I stepped down the aisle, where Owen was at the end waiting for me. The man I loved so very much. His hair was freshly barbered, and his dark suit and crisp white shirt and cuffs caught my eye. He was so handsome, so solid and real, and he stood in a long bar of sunlight that fell in through a window, haloing him. The glow outlined his every feature, and he took my breath away. I forgot all about the carefully rehearsed steps that were supposed to lead me to him in time to the music and broke into a run.

"I dooooo!" I hollered the words as I bolted down the aisle, and because I just couldn't stop myself, I hurled my body at his and kissed him deeply.

All the guests howled with laughter and applauded. The woman who was marrying us looked nonplussed as I broke away from Owen and our kiss. I grinned at her, totally unashamed of my antics.

Owen chuckled. "Um, maybe we should start the ceremony first?"

Laughter swelled all around us, and that was how we were married, in a long column of golden sunshine with laughter spilling from our mouths, with our hands joined and hearts entwined.

We were there, with so many of our dreams having come true, and still more to first dream up and then create. We were in love, happy, and healthy, and the sun would come up in the morning, and we would watch it shine its light down on us, together.

It was hard to believe anymore that he was once a vampire. That he once stole me and held me captive so he could feed from me. His Strawberry. That he was once a creature of the darkness, of dark feelings and dark actions.

Now, my every feeling was for them. For Owen and our unborn child. I would do anything to protect this love, these feelings, this family.

Because without them, my entire sunlit life would just go dark.

When we'd danced all we could dance, and ate all we could eat, and enjoyed as much of our guests' company as we could, I stole away up into the tower bedroom of the castle, *my* castle, with Owen, *my* Owen, for my perfect, fairy tale, happy ending.

The End

ABOUT THE AUTHOR

Lena Fox is a pen name of Selina Fenech. Professional daydreamer, Selina Fenech writes "adorably dark" Epic and Urban Fantasy for teens and adults. Filled with sweet and quirky characters, laugh out loud moments, and breath-taking adventures, her unique worlds are perfect for readers who love thrilling twists paired with happily ever afters.

Artist, mother, and cancer survivor, Selina is determined to live life to the fullest, and loves escape rooms, gardening, and all forms of food and geekery.

Selina also applies her distinctive take on magical realms as a world-renown fantasy artist and has published many illustrated books, oracle decks, and colouring books.

FIND OUT MORE
ABOUT SELINA

Official Website www.selinafenech.com

NEED MORE TO READ?

Discover more urban fantasy, paranormal romance, contemporary romance, young adult, epic fantasy, fairy tale retellings and more from Lena Fox and Selina Fenech.

Visit www.selinafenech.com
to sign up for a free sampler library!